THICKER THAN WATER

THICKER THAN WATER

Anthea Fraser

This first world edition published 2009
in Great Britain and in the USA by
SEVERN HOUSE PUBLISHERS LTD of
9–15 High Street, Sutton, Surrey, England, SM1 1DF.
Trade paperback edition published
in Great Britain and the USA 2009 by
SEVERN HOUSE PUBLISHERS LTD

British Library Cataloguing in Publication Data

Fraser, Anthea
  Thicker than water
  1. Family secrets - Fiction 2. Detective and mystery
  stories
  I. Title
  823.9'14[F]

ISBN-13: 978-0-7278-6752-0   (cased)
ISBN-13: 978-1-84751-118-8   (trade paper)

Typeset by Palimpsest Book Production Ltd.,
Grangemouth, Stirlingshire, Scotland.
Printed and bound in Great Britain by
MPG Books Ltd., Bodmin, Cornwall.

PART I – ABIGAIL

One

It was the timing that was so damnable, James thought, as he took a corner rather too fast. Sylvie was bound to be hurt, and he regretted that, but the truth was that though they'd known each other since schooldays, he'd never imagined himself in love with her. Basically, she was his sister's friend, an attractive, intelligent girl whose company he enjoyed, and who was useful for making up foursomes.

Not quite fair, he conceded, negotiating another bend; it had been more than that. He'd known for years that she was in love with him, and on more than one occasion had taken advantage of the fact; but when friends began to link their names seriously, he'd panicked and taken a two-year assignment in the States. Over there, there'd been girls aplenty, God knew, but none that had lit sparks inside him, and by the time he returned, he'd decided to settle for Sylvie. He was in his mid-thirties, most of his friends were married, and he wanted a home and family of his own – a home and family like Tina's.

Not everyone, he'd told himself, was lucky enough to experience the kind of love vaunted in fiction, and he knew of friends who, having married in the heat of passion, lived to regret it. Affection and companionship weren't a bad base to build on, and who knew, in time love might grow. In the meanwhile, he and Sylvie had several shared interests – jazz, travel, the theatre, and – importantly – were good together in bed. He knew, without vanity, that he could make her happy.

So three months ago, shortly after his return from the States, they had become engaged, to the delight of both families. No date had been set for the wedding, though when he tentatively suggested the spring, he'd sensed her disappointment. Admittedly there was no reason to delay, since they'd be living in his flat, which he'd no intention of leaving. It overlooked the square of a small Cotswold town, and he enjoyed being at the centre of things, with the weekly market only steps from his door. It was also equi-distant from his parents' home and that of his sister and her family, both of which he visited on a regular basis. He was, in fact, on his way to Tina's now, and, for the first time, with mixed feelings.

Because, after all his philosophizing, his concluding that *le grand amour* was not for him, it had sprung upon him out of nowhere, devastating, annihilating, all-consuming, rendering him helpless under its onslaught.

And he'd have to tell them. There was no way he could keep this life-changing news to himself, though he knew with sinking heart that their reaction – Tina's and Ben's – would not be the one he hoped for. How, in the circumstances, could he expect it to be?

Ben Rivers walked into the large, steamy kitchen and kissed the back of his wife's neck.

'Something smells good.'

'James is coming to supper.'

'Ah. So he's back from his stint in London.'

'He rang at lunchtime, asking if he could scrounge a meal. After five days away, his larder is bare.'

'I'm surprised he didn't phone Sylvie.'

Tina shrugged. 'He'll be exhausted after the course, and only fit for slobbing out with us.'

'I'd hardly call boeuf bourguignon slobbing,' Ben said mildly.

'You know what I mean. He enjoys his weekly visits, bedding down with the family and hearing all the gossip.'

'He'll be staying the night, then?'

'I was speaking figuratively, but it'll depend on how much he drinks. He knows there's always a bed for him.'

She stirred the pan and lifted the spoon to her lips. 'I'm just glad his engagement hasn't put a stop to his visits,' she added, reaching for the salt.

'His marriage will.'

'They can both come.'

Ben poured two glasses of wine and placed one on the counter beside the cooker. 'Where are the kids?'

'Charlie's at football practice and Lily's supposed to be revising, though she's probably mooning about listening to her i-pod.'

Ben leant against the table, sipping his wine. 'I saw Freddie Hargreaves at lunch. He suggested a game of golf on Sunday.'

'We're lunching with the parents. Had you forgotten?'

'Damn it, I had, yes. Perhaps he could make tomorrow instead.'

The back door swung back on its hinges as their son burst into the room.

'What's for supper?' he demanded, sniffing appreciatively.

'Good evening, Mama and Papa. I hope I find you well.'

Ben's wife and son ignored him. 'Burgundy beef,' Tina replied. 'Did you put your bike away?'

'It's in the porch.'

'Then put it in the shed, please. James is coming for supper, and I don't want him breaking a leg over it.' As they lived in a converted farmhouse, the back door was the accepted means of family access.

Charlie paused by the table to help himself to a slice of French bread, and chewed it reflectively. 'Old Smithers says I might make the team next term.'

'Excellent. Now, bike!'

Grumblingly, he went out again, and through the open back door came the sound of tyres on gravel. James had arrived.

The meal was over, the children had gone to bed, but the three adults remained comfortably round the table, the second bottle of wine open in front of them.

Tina refilled her brother's glass. 'You're very quiet, Jimbo. Was the course pretty gruelling?'

He stirred, raising his eyes from the spoon he'd been turning in his fingers.

'No more than usual.'

James worked for an international IT firm who, a few years ago, had followed the trend to decentralize, and, to his delight, relocated to Cheltenham, a mere ten miles from home. It was then he'd bought his flat, and rejoiced in the drive to work along country roads instead of the traffic-jammed capital.

'Something on your mind, then?' Ben suggested.

'You could say that.'

Tina put a hand on her brother's. 'We're listening.'

He'd been planning this speech all day, but now the carefully chosen words deserted him, and he said simply, 'I've fallen in love.'

Tina and Ben stared at him for a minute, then Tina gave an uncertain laugh. 'Well, we know that! You're engaged, for heaven's sake!'

'Not Sylvie. I've met someone else.'

Tina frowned and withdrew her hand. 'You can't have! You've only been away five days!'

James forced a smile. '"Twenty-four hours from Tulsa,"' he said.

Ben leaned forward. 'You're not serious, surely?'

'Never more so.'

'But – who is she? And what about Sylvie?'

'We met my first night away, and it was like being hit with a sledge-hammer. I *knew* – I just *knew*, immediately. *Coup de foudre*, don't they call it? I've never believed in it.'

Tina's frown deepened. 'And Sylvie?'

James looked at her wretchedly. 'I know; why couldn't this have happened before we got engaged? But Tina, I've never been *in love* with her. You must know that. I'm fond of her and always have been – but it doesn't come within a thousand miles of how I feel about Abigail.'

'And that's some kind of excuse?'

He didn't reply, and Ben said coolly, 'So who is this Abigail? How did you meet her?'

'She was staying at the same hotel, attending an interior design course. God, Ben, she's fantastic! Gorgeous looking – almost as tall as I am, with the most amazing green eyes.'

Tina said brutally, 'And you fell in lust with her.'

James passed a hand over his face. 'I can't explain it. I hoped you'd try to understand.'

'How *can* I, when you leave home a happily engaged man, and come back five days later, raving about another woman? God, James, you don't *know* her! How can you, in less than a week, the best part of which you spent on your respective courses?'

'I can't explain,' he repeated helplessly.

'So apart from looking like Julia Roberts, what do you actually know about her?'

'Well, she's a couple of years younger than me, and, as I said, an interior designer. She has a flat in Pimlico.'

'But what's her background?' Tina broke in. 'Parents? Brothers and sisters?'

'She didn't mention them.'

Tina looked at him despairingly. 'Been married before? Children?'

'No, no, nothing like that.'

'As far as you know,' she qualified darkly, 'which doesn't seem to be much. So you meet this mysterious woman, and in the space of a few days convince yourself you love her, and are prepared to jettison Sylvie, who's loved you for years? Get real, James! You're back home now.'

He said stolidly, 'She's coming for the weekend. I'd like you to meet her.'

Tina pushed her chair back and stood up abruptly. 'Well, I've not the slightest intention of doing so. *You* might be ready to betray Sylvie, but I'm not.'

And as her eyes filled with angry tears, she hurried from the room. The two men looked at each other.

'Ben?'

'I have to say I'm with Tina on this. Sorry, James.'

All he had wanted was to slink home, tail between his legs, and lick his wounds in private. He knew that for the moment he wasn't welcome, but he'd had too much wine to risk the twisting country lanes. He'd make damn sure, though, that he left before anyone was up.

As was to be expected, he didn't sleep well. The dinner table conversation revolved endlessly in his head, and he cursed himself for not having expressed himself better. Yet how could they understand, when they'd never had so much as a hitch in their own relationship? Ben and Tina had married straight from university; Lily was born within a year, Charlie twenty months later, and all four of them had lived happily ever after. Well, he thought resentfully, they should be bloody grateful.

Lying in the familiar bed, with the moving curtains allowing intermittent shafts of moonlight, he accepted that the next day would be no less fraught. Hopefully, Tina would tell the parents, thereby sparing him their initial shock, but he owed it to Sylvie to break the news in person, a prospect he was dreading. After which, he must clean the flat and buy-in supplies for Abigail's visit. And as her name flooded his mind, he turned with a groan and buried his face in his pillow. Yes, it would be a rough ride with Sylvie and the family, but he could face anything, so long as he had Abigail.

There was a perfunctory tap on the door and Sylvie came in, closed it behind her and leaned against it. Tina turned from the sink, and across the suddenly still room the two women looked at each other. Sylvie's face was white, seeming to make her eyes larger and darker.

'Tell me this hasn't happened,' she said.

Tina made an instinctive move, but halted as Sylvie held up a warning hand. 'I'll put the coffee on,' she said, realizing that overt sympathy would undermine her friend's control.

Sylvie seated herself at the kitchen table. 'When did you hear?' she asked, almost conversationally.

'Last night. He came for supper. Sylvie—'

'I was in the bath,' Sylvie broke in. 'Grace answered the door, and called to me that James was in the living room. It was an enormous relief; he hadn't picked up on his mobile all week. I just grabbed a bathrobe and ran through, leaving wet footprints on the carpet.'

'He must have gone to you straight from here,' Tina said, spooning coffee into the cafetière. 'He'd left by the time we came down, and there was a note on the table saying simply "Sorry".'

'What exactly did he tell you?'

'That he'd met this woman his first night in London, and apparently been bowled over. Sylvie, I just can't believe it. It's an obsession – it has to be. He'll get over it.'

'The question is, when? And though *we* might not believe it, James certainly does, which is what counts. Perhaps I should have seen this coming. He's all I've ever wanted – you know that – ever since he took me to my first dance, with you and Ben. But I was the one who made the running, and eventually he fled to the States to escape me.'

'That's nonsense!' Tina said sharply, though she knew it to be true.

'When he came back and asked me to marry him, I thought he'd realized it was me he wanted after all.' She gave a bitter laugh. 'I should have known it was too good to be true.' She brushed back a strand of hair, and Tina saw, with a lurch of the heart, that she was no longer wearing her ring. Would James be insensitive enough to give it to Abigail?

'Don't do yourself down,' she said fiercely. 'You've had plenty of other chances; Steve Barker, for one, has been after you for years. You're an attractive woman, don't you forget it, and just because my idiot brother is messing you about doesn't alter the fact.'

'What did he tell you – about her?'

Tina pressed down the plunger with more force than was warranted. 'Very little. He doesn't seem to know much himself, other than that she's beautiful and no doubt sexy. She was attending an interior design course, but her background sounds very vague and she never mentioned her family.' Tina hesitated. 'She's coming over this weekend. James wants us to meet her.'

Sylvie looked up sharply. 'And will you?'

'Not on your life.' Tina put two mugs on the table and brought over the cafetière. 'I phoned Ma earlier. I thought I ought to warn them, but there was no reply, and it wasn't news I could leave on the answerphone. They'll hit the roof when they hear about it.'

'I haven't told my parents yet. Only Grace knows, since she happened to be there. I keep hoping it's all a mistake, that he'll phone any minute and say it's not true. God, Tina, it was only a week ago that we went to the cinema, and I spent the night at his flat. I was bracing myself for *five days* without him, not realizing it would be for ever.'

And, her voice breaking at last, she covered her face with both hands and began to cry.

Abigail turned on to the M40 and forced herself to concentrate on her driving – a difficult feat when her mind was in turmoil and the life she'd constructed so carefully was about to be turned upside down. Having learned from a young age that love led to loss and heartbreak, she'd resolved never to lay herself open to it, and until now, she'd succeeded.

There'd been relationships, of course, some lasting a year or two, but her emotions hadn't been engaged, and as soon as marriage was proposed – as it invariably was – she'd ended the affair. Nor did she accept guilt; having made her position clear from the outset, she couldn't be blamed if her partners believed they could change her mind.

But in James Markham she'd met her Waterloo, and over the last week had been drawn helplessly into a maelstrom of the very emotions she'd sworn to avoid. A part of her still had difficulty accepting this, yet the very fact that she was driving along this unfamiliar road to meet him, was proof enough.

It had started so innocuously, too; eye contact down the length of the hotel bar, his strolling over to enquire if by any chance she was enrolled on his course. Nothing momentous; such conversations were taking place all over the hotel, as attendees sought out others on the same syllabus, scheduled to start the next day.

From the first, though, there had been danger signals which she'd ignored at her peril, certain she'd remain in control as she always had. Not this time. They'd dined together at a corner table, over which they talked about their jobs, their interests, their views on current affairs. She learned that he worked in IT, lived in the Cotswolds, and had recently spent two years in the States. What he didn't tell her until later that night, after they'd made love, was that he was engaged to be married. And by then it was already too late; lying beside him on the rumpled bed, she had known beyond doubt that, engagement or not, there was no way she could give him up.

On the second night, he had asked her to marry him.

And the irony, she thought now, was that she'd not intended to stay in the hotel. Living in London, she could have attended daily, but the course organizer had persuaded her otherwise, pointing out that she'd meld better with the group than if she returned home each evening. Incredible to think that if she hadn't acquiesced, the odds were that she'd never have met James.

She glanced at the clock on the dashboard. A quarter to three. They'd agreed she should postpone her arrival until the afternoon, giving him time to break the news to his fiancée. Abigail felt a passing wave of sympathy for the girl, whoever she was. James had said little about her, and she'd not asked, thankful that at least they weren't living together.

The road stretched ahead of her, with little to hold her interest, and her thoughts began to wander. It was a blessing, she reflected, that, working from home, she could do so as easily in Inchampton as in Pimlico. James had told her that though his flat wasn't large, the loft had been converted at some stage, and while he used it only for storage, it could easily be made into a comfortable work room, the additional windows offering plenty of light. The possibility of moving to somewhere larger didn't appear to be an option.

The CD ended and she inserted another, though she must be nearly there. Excitement began to build in her, anticipation at seeing James, and the prospect of their being alone together for twenty-four hours. Her turn-off was signalled, and as she left the motorway, she fumbled for the directions he'd given her and spread them out on the steering wheel. Then, as instructed, she switched on her hands-free mobile.

He picked up immediately. 'Abigail?'

'Hi. Just to let you know I've left the motorway.'

'Great. You should be here in fifteen minutes. Pull into the pub car park I told you about – the White Bull. I'll meet you there.'

Abigail followed the signs along quieter, narrower roads, lined by farms and cottages built of the local honey-coloured stone, with fields stretching on either side where cows and sheep grazed. She'd known Inchampton was a market town, but she'd not expected its surround-ings to be quite so bucolic. A culture shock indeed, after the frenetic life she was used to.

And here, on her right, was the White Bull public house. She turned into the gateway, following directions to the car park behind the building. And there, leaning against the wall, James awaited her. She switched off the engine, and as their eyes met through the windscreen, was aware of a sudden awkward shyness. Then he was opening the door, helping her out, and enfolding her in his arms.

'I wasn't entirely sure you'd come,' he said against her hair.

'Why was that?'

'Once back home, it all seemed like a dream.'

'I know; I felt the same.' She searched his face. 'You haven't changed your mind?'

'Do you have to ask?'

'And your fiancée? How did she take it?'

His face sobered. 'I think stunned is the word, but I didn't hang around. Still –' he straightened his shoulders – 'the job's done, so let's forget it. Now, I'll get in the car with you, and show you where to leave it. There's no parking on the square, but we have an access road behind, with parking bays. They're supposed to be for delivery vehicles, but a blind eye is turned for residents.'

'I'm not a resident – yet.'

He leaned over and kissed her cheek. 'You soon will be.'

Under his direction, she drove out of the pub car park and turned right to continue into town. It was more built-up now, houses, a filling station and a parade of shops lining the road. Then, ahead of her, it widened into a square, and just before they reached it, James indicated a turning to the right, and she obediently slipped into it. The access road was narrow and cobbled, but as he'd said, parking bays lined it on both sides, most of them empty this Saturday afternoon.

'Go in this one,' James instructed, 'next to my car. It's almost directly behind the flat, but there's no rear access, so we have to go round the front.'

He took her case from the boot, and they walked together in the warm autumn sunshine round the corner and into the market square. It was an attractive setting, with a small open-sided building in the centre, topped with a clock. Scattered around it, market stallholders were engaged in packing up and reloading their vans, while a few last-minute shoppers poked among the remaining wares. A selection of interesting-looking buildings surrounded the square; several accommodated shops, one was a pub, and a tall, gabled building looked like the Town Hall.

'This is the oldest part,' James said, with proprietary pride. 'As you can see, there's a T-junction at the far side. The right-hand leg leads to the new shopping centre, cinema, supermarket, and so on, and the left to the church, railway and bus stations. The town's expanded a lot in the last few years, but thankfully the planners tried to harmonize with the original buildings.'

He stopped in front of a smartly painted door with a brass knocker, sandwiched between what looked like an office, closed for the weekend, and a bakery-cum-café, from which enticing aromas emanated.

James, turning the key in the lock, saw her appreciative sniff, and grinned. 'That's where my breakfast comes from – croissants, hot rolls, warm bread, even Danish if you can stomach it.'

'My breakfast consists of yogurt and black coffee,' Abigail told him.

'What's the betting I'll convert you? Now, welcome to Markham Towers.'

He flung open the door, which gave on to a flight of linoleumed stairs, and stood back for her to enter. She went slowly up them, and, emerging from the stairwell, found herself on a small landing. The door to her left stood open, displaying a wide room flooded with sunshine, through the windows of which lay a panorama of the square they'd just left.

James deposited her case on the landing and took her elbow. 'In you go.'

Abigail, allowing herself to be led forward, looked about her with pleasure. The floor was polished wood, adorned with a couple of vibrantly coloured rugs, the walls pale and for the most part bare, but a striking abstract over the fireplace echoed the rugs' vivid shades. Sofa and armchairs were in soft, honey leather, and on a low table was a tray bearing two champagne flutes. The general ambience was of comfort and welcome.

James was watching her anxiously. 'What do you think?'

'It's – great. Just great.'

He breathed a sigh of relief. 'Really? I've been wondering how my humble abode would appeal to an interior designer.'

She laughed. 'Now you know. And what a fabulous view.'

She walked to the window, noting that beyond the busy little town lay encircling hills, gilded now by the late afternoon sun.

James followed her, slipping an arm round her waist. 'It's wonderful, isn't it? I often stand here, just people-watching. I love being the centre of things – a residue, perhaps, of two years in New York.' His arm tightened. 'Oh, Abigail, it's so wonderful to have you here.'

She turned her head to him, surrendering to his searching kiss before giving a little laugh. 'We're right in front of the window, remember! You might not be the only one who people-watches!'

'True! Come on, I'll show the rest of my domain. It's just two large rooms, this and the bedroom, and what estate agents call "the usual offices" – a minute galley-kitchen, which I confess I use as little as possible, and an en suite off the bedroom.'

'You mentioned a loft conversion?' Abigail said tentatively.

'That's right.' He gestured at a trap door in the hall ceiling. 'We'll have to organize some sort of ladder if you want to use it; I just stand on a chair and haul myself up.'

The bedroom décor was similarly understated, and Abigail, noting the large and comfortable-looking bed, felt a shaft of jealousy as she pictured James there with his fiancée. This, too, was a new emotion, and not one she relished.

'There's champagne in the fridge,' he said. 'It's a little early, perhaps, but this is a special occasion.'

'Never too early for champagne!'

He retrieved the bottle en route to the living room. Yes, she thought; once that loft ladder is in place, I could happily live here. There was a satisfying pop as the cork was removed, and James poured the foaming liquid into the flutes.

'Here's to us, my darling,' he said, handing her one. 'For ever and ever, amen!'

'Amen!' she echoed, and, holding each other's eyes, they drank.

And in the same minute a buzzer sounded in the hall, making them both jump.

James swore. 'Who the devil can that be?' He left the room and Abigail, the glass still in her hand, felt a frisson of unease. Could the jilted fiancée, recovering from being 'stunned', have arrived to make a scene?

'Yes?' James said abruptly into the entry phone.

'Oh good, darling, you *are* back,' came his mother's voice. 'Could I come up for a minute? I've something rather exciting to tell you.'

Abigail, watching him, saw him stiffen, and her apprehension increased. He glanced back at her and said carefully into the phone, 'It's not – terribly convenient just at the moment.'

'I shan't keep you, if you're on your way out. Admittedly it could wait till tomorrow, but you mightn't want everyone to know.'

'Tomorrow?' he repeated blankly.

'Oh, darling, you're coming to lunch, with Tina, Ben and the children. Don't say you'd forgotten? Look, can you buzz me? My shopping basket's getting heavier by the minute.'

'Of course,' he said dully. 'Sorry.'

He pressed the entry button, and turned to Abigail. 'I'm very sorry about this,' he said rapidly. 'It's my mother, and I haven't had a chance to tell her.'

'Your mother?' Abigail gazed at him in horror. 'She lives nearby?'

'The whole family does. Didn't you realize?'

Panic fluttered in her throat, all her old doubts and fears resurfacing. She'd not even known he *had* a mother! she thought hysterically; she'd pictured them living just for each other, cocooned from the world. There was his fiancée, of course, but she was now past tense and, despite Abigail's initial fear, unlikely to put in an appearance. But a complete family, comprising God knew how many—

A voice reached them from the stairs. 'It was pure chance that I bumped into Chloë Bainbridge in Waitrose. She was telling me—'

Rosemary Markham, having rounded the stairhead, broke off, her eyes going past James to Abigail's motionless figure, champagne flute in hand.

James, moistening his lips, said carefully, 'Ma, this is Abigail. We met in London. Abigail, my mother.'

His mother – not safely buried in some country churchyard, as she'd subconsciously assumed, but very much alive, and, still more unbelievably, *here*: slim, attractive, and staring at her in growing bewilderment.

'How do you do?' Abigail said numbly.

The older woman nodded acknowledgment. She glanced at the champagne bottle on the table. 'You're celebrating something?'

James looked helplessly from one blank face to the other. He cleared his throat.

'Ma, I'd meant to give you some warning – in fact, I thought Tina – but you've – taken us by surprise.'

'So it seems.'

'In which case,' James continued miserably, 'I'd better come straight out with it. Abigail and I are going to be married.'

Two

Andrew Markham was sitting in a canvas chair on his front veranda, a glass of beer at his side. From here, he had a grandstand view of the cricket match, nearing its close on the green opposite. The village team had earlier declared for two hundred, and the visitors were now on a hundred and seventy-five, with their last man in.

Impinging on the shout of the umpire came the sound of a car rapidly approaching, followed by a crunch of gravel as it turned into the drive. His wife had returned home. Across the road, the batsman began an ill-considered run, reaching the safety of the crease a breath ahead of the incoming ball. The car door slammed, but instead of garaging it, as she invariably did, Rosemary came hurrying round the corner of the house towards him.

'Andrew! You won't believe what's happened!'

'Then you'd better tell me,' he answered mildly, his eyes still on the match.

She ran up the veranda steps, her face flushed and her voice breathless. 'It's James. He's dumped Sylvie and become engaged to someone else!'

A loud shout went up from the green as the batsman was caught out, and Andrew, retuning his attention to his wife, belatedly took in what she had said. He stared at her as she dropped into the vacant chair beside him.

'He's *what?*'

'We've not received any phone messages, have we? Apparently Tina knows, and I can't believe she wouldn't have told us.'

'I didn't get in till gone three, and came straight out here.'

'Without checking the answerphone?' It didn't surprise her; Andrew never checked, believing that if the message was important, the caller would ring back.

'Anyway,' he continued, 'never mind Tina, what's this about James? Has he taken leave of his senses?'

'I think he must have, and it was pure chance I found out. After the exhibition and lunch, I popped into Waitrose, and Chloë Bainbridge was there. She was asking if we'd fixed a date for the wedding, then she very kindly said they'd be welcome to have her villa in the Maldives for their honeymoon. So I thought I'd tell James straight away. He was most reluctant to let me in, and I soon discovered why: there was this girl, standing in the middle of the living room with a glass of champagne in her hand, and the pair of them looking as guilty as sin.

'James introduced her, said they'd met in London, and were going to be married!'

'Met when?' Andrew interrupted. 'He's never mentioned her before, has he?'

'Met *last week*, would you believe, while he was on the course. That's the point! They can't know each other at all! I can't imagine what he's thinking of!'

'What did you say?'

'When I got my breath back, I asked what he proposed to do about Sylvie. It was most embarrassing, I can tell you, with the girl standing there. And he calmly told me he'd already been to see her, and broken off their engagement.'

'Ye gods.' Andrew reached for his glass and drank. 'Sounds as though he's serious, then.'

'Oh, he's serious all right. For now. But Andrew, it's infatuation! It has to be! One day he'll wake up and realize what he's done. He can't just switch his affections like that, in the batting of an eye!'

Andrew rotated his glass in his fingers. 'In my opinion,' he said slowly, 'they were never very heavily engaged with Sylvie.'

Rosemary stared at him. 'But they've always been together! We always thought—'

'And that's just the point: everyone expected them to get married. He held off as long as he could, didn't he? If he'd loved her, he wouldn't have gone off to the States for two years, and risk losing her to someone else. Oh, I don't doubt he's fond of her, and they'd probably have been happy enough, if he'd not suddenly come face to face with the real thing. If, of course, it *is* the real thing with this girl. What's her name, by the way?'

'Abigail something.'

'What's she like?'

'Lovely to look at: almost as tall as James, with flawless skin, green eyes, dark hair. As to personality, I've no idea. I don't think I actually spoke to her, or she to me, except for the initial introduction.' She paused, gazing across the road to where the cricketers were drawing stumps and collecting their belongings. 'He wanted to bring her to lunch tomorrow.'

Andrew stiffened. 'You didn't agree?'

'No, I did not. We need time to assimilate this, make sure it really is going ahead. Anyway, it would seem like a betrayal of Sylvie. The only reason *she's* not coming is because it's her sister's birthday.' She put a hand to her head. 'Oh God, Andrew, what are we going to do?'

'There's not much we *can* do,' he said with a sigh. 'I agree we're not ready to socialize with this girl, but I think we should see James. How long is she here for?'

'I didn't ask, but she'll probably need to be back by Monday.'

Behind them in the sitting room, the phone started ringing. Rosemary went to answer it, and her daughter's voice immediately exclaimed, 'At last! Why do you never have your mobile switched on?'

'Because it's the height of bad manners to receive calls when being shown round an exhibition and attending a formal lunch. I presume this is about James?'

'Ah.' An exhalation of breath. 'You've heard, then.'

'More than heard. I walked in on them.'

'God, Ma, what happened?'

'Embarrassment all round.'

'What's she like?'

'Beautiful. That's all I know. When did you hear about it?'

'He came for supper last night, and sprang it on us at the end of the meal. By the time we'd finished talking it was too late to phone, and when I tried this morning, you'd already left.' She paused. 'Sylvie came round.'

Rosemary caught her breath. 'How is she?'

'Shattered. It was – awful. God, he's my brother, but I could willingly strangle him! He's no right to hurt her like that. She'll have to face all our friends – and for that matter, so will we. Everyone will be on her side, and who can blame them?'

'Who indeed?' said Rosemary dully.

James returned from showing his mother out to find Abigail tense and white-faced.

He hurried to put his arms round her. 'Oh, darling, I'm so sorry. What a way to meet your future mother-in-law!'

Her fingers gripped his lapels, and he felt her trembling. 'It's not only that,' she said shakily, 'it's the whole family thing. James, I don't *do* families! I thought there'd be just us, not a whole host of relatives clustering round and dropping in on us all the time!'

He stroked her hair soothingly. 'That was a bad first impression, I know, but normally we get along fine. We're really a very close family—'

He broke off as she shook her head violently. 'I don't *want* a close family – I want you to myself!'

He frowned in bewilderment. 'What about your own people? You must—'

She straightened, moving away from him. 'Both my parents are dead. I suppose that's why I assumed yours were.'

'You must have someone, though?'

'No one who counts.'

'But – they'll come to the wedding, surely?'

'I shouldn't think so; I've not seen them for years.'

He said gently, 'That sounds a very lonely existence.'

'I've had my work, and my friends.'

'Well, I'll make sure my lot don't crowd us, at least in the early days, though I hope you'll soon think of Tina and Ben as friends, too.'

'But you told me – Sylvie, is it? – is your sister's friend. She's not likely to welcome me, is she?'

'Nonsense; Tina's never one to hold a grudge. Still, it's a pity you can't meet them all tomorrow, and – get it over with.'

He remembered his mother's cool reply when he'd suggested just that: 'I don't think so, do you?'

'In a week or two,' he added resolutely, 'we'll be wondering what all the fuss was about. In the meantime, we mustn't let this cast a blight over your visit. I've booked a table at a super little restaurant, and since it's within walking distance, we needn't worry about drinking. OK?' He looked anxiously into her face.

She nodded, summoning up a smile. 'OK. Sorry if I overreacted. Of course it was a shock for your mother, especially when she'd no fore-warning.'

'They'll soon come round, just you see.'

He reached for her hand and drew her to him. The length of her was still a novelty, thighs, breast and mouth almost on a level with his own, in marked contrast to petite Sylvie, kissing whom had frequently resulted in a crick in the neck.

But this was no time to think of Sylvie. Abigail's caresses were becoming more insistent, and dinner was a while off. Still clinging to each other, they moved towards the bedroom.

Monday morning, and James's mobile sounded as he was running up the stairs to his office.

'James Markham.'

'Good morning, James.' A voice he didn't immediately recognize. 'Robert Warren here.'

Sylvie's father! James came to a sudden halt, moving to one side as people continued to clatter past him up the stairs. 'Good morning, Robert.'

'I'm wondering if you'd be good enough to meet me for a drink after work?'

James groaned inwardly. Shotguns to the fore! 'Well, I—'

'The bar at the Queen's Hotel, about six?'

His mind fumbled for excuses – previous engagements, dental appointments – but could come up with none that sounded plausible. 'I'll be there,' he said.

The prospect of the meeting clouded his entire day, even diluting memories of his weekend with Abigail. After she left, late yesterday afternoon, he'd succumbed to a welter of conflicting emotions, miserable and elated in turn, and quite unable to settle. Meeting his friends was not an option, since he couldn't face telling them his news; and Tina and Ben, his usual port in a storm, were for the moment barred to him. He was persona non grata at his parents', and now, to cap it all, he'd have to account for himself to the father of his ex-fiancée.

While he was not looking forward to the prospect, it was only as he was eating a snatched lunch in a sandwich bar that a truly awful possibility occurred to him: *suppose Sylvie was pregnant?* Vague memories of breach of promise suits blundered round his head. Were they still in effect? He thought not but couldn't be sure, and the uncertainty added to his apprehension. He wished, passionately and uselessly, that he and Abigail could fly away to some tropic isle, and let the rest of them go hang.

Robert Warren was there before him, seated at a table against the wall. Mentally crossing his fingers, James walked across to join him. Warren rose to shake his hand. Good sign, or bad?

'What are you drinking?' he asked.

'Oh, let me—'

'Not at all; you're here at my request.'

'Then a pint of best, please.'

He watched his host go up to the bar. Warren was of medium height, broad-shouldered and balding. James had always considered him fairly laid-back, but then, he'd never jilted his daughter before.

He returned with two brimming glasses, set them down on the table, and seated himself. Each of his actions seemed to James unduly protracted. Get on with it! his nerves were screaming.

Warren raised his glass and James responded, though no toast was given. Then he wiped a hand across his face and said, 'This is a bit of a turn-up, isn't it?'

'I know. I'm – sorry.'

'What happened, exactly?'

'I was on a course in London, and I met this girl.' How lame it sounded.

'It does happen,' Warren said drily. 'However, you happened to be engaged to my daughter.'

'I know. I've no excuse, and I can't explain it. All I can say is I'd be no use to Sylvie, having met Abigail. The kindest thing seemed to be to end it straight away.'

'Kindest for whom?' Sylvie's father took a long draught of beer. 'I might as well admit that meeting you was my wife's idea. She wanted me to see you immediately, before, as she put it, things had gone too far. By which I think she meant before too many people heard about it, and while the situation might still be salvaged.'

'I'm sorry,' James said quietly.

'There's no chance of that?'

'No.'

The two men were silent for a while. Then Warren sighed. 'It's not easy, you know, seeing your daughter breaking her heart. And that's no exaggeration; she really loves you, James. Always has done, though she'd kill me if she knew I was meeting you like this.'

'I'm very fond of her,' James said wretchedly. 'The last thing I'd have wanted was to hurt her.'

'Yet you didn't think twice about doing so. Look, I know how these things happen. You can be strongly attracted to someone; but there's always a point at which you can pull back, put a stop to it. You must seize it at once, though, because the longer you leave it, the harder it'll become. You admit the truth of that?'

'Perhaps.' If he hadn't walked down the length of the bar to speak to Abigail, hadn't then suggested dinner, would he have been able to put her out of his mind? He doubted it. He'd not been granted even that split-second in which to pull back. And why hadn't he? The answer was clear: because he'd not loved Sylvie enough.

He looked up to find Warren's eyes searchingly on him.

'I'm so very sorry,' he said.

At least there'd been no mention of pregnancy, he thought, as he made his miserable way to his car. But his relief was short-lived; incredible as it now seemed, it was less than ten days since he and Sylvie had last made love, on the eve of his trip to London. There was still time.

They were in an Italian restaurant in Soho, where they'd been meeting one Tuesday a month for at least two years; even sitting at their usual table. Everything was as it had always been, and yet was totally different.

Abigail looked about her as though seeing her surroundings for the first time – the counter dividing the kitchen from the diners, behind which a group of dark men in white coats performed miracles with tuna, veal and pasta; the waiters in their tight black trousers and short jackets; the saucer of olive oil on the table between them, in which Sarah was dipping her ciabatta. She even reached out to touch the straw-covered Chianti bottle, in a kind of caress. Because, for her at least, this was the last of their monthly Tuesdays.

'I've something to tell you,' she said, breaking into the general chatter. The three of them turned questioning faces towards her, and she studied them with the same sense of distance: Sarah, who worked in television and looked like a soap star herself, with her springing chestnut hair; Eleanor, grey eyes huge behind outsize glasses, an up and coming lawyer; and Millie, a platinum blonde who appeared not to have a thought in her head, but ran her own catering business.

Abigail drew a deep breath. 'I'm getting married,' she said.

Her friends stared at her blankly. Then Sarah, the first to find her voice, said, 'You're joking, right?'

Abigail smiled. 'No joke. I'm really getting married.'

They all started to speak at once: 'But you swore you never would!' 'Not Theo, surely?' 'Why didn't you say something?'

'To answer you each in turn: I know that's what I said, but I've changed my mind; it's a woman's prerogative, isn't it? No, it's not Theo, and the reason I didn't tell you before is because I only met him last week.'

This time their reactions were identical, and voiced as one. '*Last week?*'

Abigail smiled. 'Love at first sight,' she said.

'Now I really don't believe you!' Millie. 'There must be some other reason. Is he a millionaire, or something?'

Abigail laughed and shook her head.

'So the Ice Maiden melts at last.' That was Eleanor. 'Who'd have thought it?' she added rhetorically.

Sarah moved impatiently. 'Enough surmising. Start at the beginning, and tell us exactly how it happened.'

So Abigail related her meeting with James, their immediate attraction, and his almost immediate proposal. She skated over the fact that he was engaged – because it was no longer relevant – and made light of her meeting with his mother.

'The thing is, though,' she finished, 'he lives in a small town in the Cotswolds.'

'You're never going to bury yourself in the country?' Eleanor demanded incredulously. 'Not you, Abigail?'

'I can work there just as easily as in Pimlico,' she said.

'But work's only part of it!' Millie put in. 'What about restaurants and theatres and concerts and shopping? Not to mention us! What about us?' she repeated on a rising note.

'I'll miss you all, of course, but we can email and text, and I'll have to come to London every so often anyway. It's not the other side of the world.'

'Does Theo know?' Sarah asked suddenly.

Theo Hardy had been – probably thought he still was – Abigail's latest partner, presently away on a business trip to China.

'I've not had the chance to tell him. It didn't seem fair to email.'

'So where is this James now?' asked Millie. 'When are we going to meet him?'

'After a week away from the office, he can't take time off at the moment. I'm driving up again at the weekend.'

'So when will this Wedding of the Year take place?'

'It won't be that, Sarah,' Abigail said seriously. 'In fact, it'll be a very quiet affair in a register office, but of course you're all invited. As to when, probably one day next month.'

Again, they all stared at her in astonishment. Abigail, who had been the most resolutely anti-marriage of them all; who swore she'd never been, and would never allow herself to be, in love; who weighed all possibilities before reaching a decision – this same Abigail, marrying a man she'd have known less than four weeks – and for love, at that!

Who said the age of miracles was past?

The family's meeting with Abigail couldn't, of course, be postponed indefinitely, and his parents' first move was to invite James to supper, when a long and searching discussion took place. No punches were pulled, and he was left in no doubt that they considered he'd behaved shabbily. But once they'd seen he was adamant, they'd no option but to make the best of it and extend some sort of welcome, however restrained, to their proposed daughter-in-law. It was either that, or risk estrangement from their son.

So an invitation was extended, via James, that she join them and the rest of the family for lunch the following Saturday. The change of day was significant; Sunday lunch was a family institution. Saturday would be less formal, and as it happened, suited himself and Abigail better, since the prospect would not be hanging over them all weekend. Also, she wouldn't have to set off for London again immediately afterwards.

James delivered the invitation when he phoned on the Wednesday evening.

'Tina, Ben and the kids will be there, too. Can you face it?'

'Better to jump in the deep end,' Abigail answered philosophically. 'As you said last week, there's a lot to be said for getting everything over at once.'

'Don't worry about it, sweetheart; I'm the one they're annoyed with, not you. I'm sure it will all be very civilized.' He paused. 'We've not really discussed this, but it might help if we can give them a definite date. Have you thought about it?'

'Sometime next month?'

'Perfect. I'll just about last that long! A Saturday?'

'It would be easier for my friends; they're all working girls.'

James waited, and when she didn't enlarge on that, prompted, 'And your family?'

Her tone of voice changed. 'I told you, there's no one I want to be there. We're completely out of touch.'

He was aware of disappointment and a vague feeling of unease. He'd have liked their families to meet; it would have somehow rooted her more securely, made it a more normal affair.

Relinquishing the prospect, he asked, 'So who *would* you like to be there?'

'Just my three closest friends, your parents, and Ben and Tina, if they'll come.' She paused. 'Is that all right from your angle?'

'Well, I'd have liked to show you off to the world, but there'll be time for that later. We can all have lunch afterwards – I'll book a private room somewhere. So – name the day, my darling.'

'How about Saturday the eighteenth, in three weeks' time? Will that give you long enough to sort things out?'

'All I have to do is fix a loft ladder!'

She laughed. 'I'll have to consider what to do with the flat. Since there's no room at your place, I think I'll let it furnished, and just bring personal things with me. Which, of course, includes my easel and work materials.'

'But there must be some things of sentimental value? I'm sure we could find room.'

'I don't do sentiment, James.'

'You mean, you didn't!'

He heard the smile in her voice. 'Even now, only in very prescribed circumstances. No, really. I bought the furniture when I moved into the flat; now I'm moving out, I've no further use for it.'

'OK, you know best. Admittedly we'd be rather strapped for space. I must go, sweetie; I'm off to make my peace with Tina and Ben. I'll phone tomorrow, and you'll be here on Friday, won't you?'

'Yes, as soon as I can get away.'

'I'll have an extra key cut, then you won't be dependent on my getting home before you. Speak to you tomorrow, then. Love you.'

'Love you, too. Good luck with Tina and Ben.'

After a cool and cloudy week, Friday ushered in an Indian summer. The forecast was for continuing high temperatures, and Abigail was thankful to leave the humid, air-starved city and head west for the country. She drove with the windows open, relishing the wind of passage that lifted her hair and, though warm, provided the illusion of freshness.

On this occasion, she drove straight to the alleyway and parked, as before, next to James's black Peugeot. Rounding the corner into the square, she found the front door of the flat standing open, and a bouquet of roses on the bottom stair.

'James?' she called, and he came running down to greet her.

'I've never known such a long week,' he declared, pulling her close. 'But only another three to go, and we'll be together all the time.'

'I see I have an admirer,' Abigail commented, eyeing the bouquet.

'A very devoted one.'

'It's gorgeous. Thank you.' She stooped to retrieve it, and they went together up the stairs. Already, the sunny room with its pale walls and colourful rugs felt like home. Abigail drew a long, tremulous breath.

'It's lovely to be back,' she said.

Three

By the Saturday, it would be hard to say which of the three couples meeting for lunch was the most apprehensive. Though James had been told twelve thirty, Rosemary asked her daughter to arrive at twelve, 'to provide moral support'.

Tina's family had not been cooperative. 'But we went there last weekend,' Charlie grumbled. 'Archie's parents have invited me to go swimming.'

'Well, I'm sorry, but this is a special occasion. Aren't you interested in meeting Uncle James's new fiancée?'

'No!' he said flatly.

'Surely you are, Lily?'

Her daughter shrugged. 'How long will this one last? He was going to marry Sylvie till last week.'

'That's enough!' Ben said sharply.

'Anyway, Saturday isn't grandparents' day, and Debs and I are booked to go riding.'

'You can't always do as you want,' Tina retorted, her patience wearing thin. She wasn't looking forward to the day herself, and could do without aggravation from her family.

As the children sulkily left the breakfast table, Ben put an arm round her. 'It'll be all right,' he said.

'I thought we'd eat in the garden,' Rosemary announced. 'It's less formal, and it seems a shame to waste the good weather. It'll be autumn soon enough.'

'Won't it be too hot?'

'Not under the chestnut; there'll be plenty of shade. Be a love, and move the table and chairs, would you? There'll be eight of us.'

Andrew surveyed the selection of food laid out under protective netting – curried eggs, bite-sized home-made pizza, savoury tartlets. There were several salads in the fridge, together with a bowl of couscous and a selection of cheeses and desserts. This meal, he reflected, ranked as what Tina had dubbed Ma's Harvest Home – a scaled-down version of the fare she presided over on the church catering committee.

'You're doing her proud, love,' he said.

* * *

Abigail was dismayed to find James's parents lived a mere fifteen-minute drive away, in one of the hamlets that fringed the town. The house was approached along one side of a village green, where a group of boys were kicking a ball about. Across its expanse she could see several other houses, a church, and an old-fashioned pub, whose customers were sitting or standing outside in the sunshine. A gale of laughter reached them on the still air.

'Very rural,' she remarked, and felt James look at her, unsure if approval or censure was implied. Then they were turning into a wide, gravelled drive alongside a stone-built house with a veranda running along the front of it.

'Dad's grandstand for cricket matches,' James commented, seeing her glance at it. They drew to a halt next to another car, and he switched off the engine.

'Well, here goes,' he said.

As he held the door for her, Abigail heard voices coming through the open side gate.

'They'll all be in the garden,' he added, and, taking her arm, led her to meet his family.

Everyone turned as they appeared, and Rosemary, conscious of their last unsatisfactory meeting, came quickly forward.

'We got off to a bad start, my dear,' she said, 'but I hope we can be friends.' And, bending forward, she kissed Abigail's cheek.

'Thank you,' Abigail stammered, and saw to her embarrassment that the rest of them were lining up to meet her. James's father was tall and straight, with plentiful grey hair and shrewd blue eyes. His handclasp was firm as he subjected her to a long, assessing gaze.

'Welcome,' he said briefly, and she smiled and nodded, turning as Tina approached. She had James's colouring, though she was considerably shorter, and her shoulder-length hair was a tumble of curls. She smiled her welcome, but her brown eyes were guarded.

As each in turn was introduced, Abigail searched their faces for a possible ally. Not Tina, she thought regretfully – at least, not immediately; nor was she convinced Rosemary's overture was genuine, after her previous hostility. Andrew would clearly need winning over, and Ben, who'd smiled at her kindly and was her best bet, was, as Tina's husband, sadly out of bounds.

The children, pushed forward by their parents, she initially discounted, being unsure how to deal with them. Charlie had stared at her with frank curiosity, but there was a flicker of admiration in the eyes of fourteen-year-old Lily, and Abigail breathed an inward sigh of relief. Here, then, might lie her chance of infiltration.

Ben appeared with a tray of Pimm's, and Abigail, released from being the centre of attention, was able to look about her. The garden was large and secluded, with several old trees and a lush, central lawn. Down near the end wall, she caught sight of an old swing, and memory knifed into her, making her catch her breath. Instantly, James was at her side.

'All right?' he asked anxiously.

It was an effort to smile. 'Someone walking over my grave.' *Or someone else's.* She added quickly, 'It looks an interesting house; what period is it?'

'Early Victorian. It's called The Old Rectory, and used to be owned by the church. Would you like to see over it?'

Abigail, always interested in interiors, brightened. 'Would anyone mind?'

'Of course not.'

They entered the house through the open doors of a conservatory to find themselves in the family sitting room. The large fireplace was obviously original, as were the cornice and ceiling rose, and the deep cream walls and turkey-red carpet were in keeping with its age. In room after room, Abigail found much to admire. The Markhams had achieved an elegant blend of old and new, even the bathrooms, with all their modern accoutrements, seeming appropriate to the style of the house. Two of its six bedrooms had been transformed into en suites and the old scullery was now an up-to-date utility room. The house had been built, Abigail reflected, when the clergy had large families, but she doubted if any man of the cloth could afford to live here now.

They reached the kitchen, a large, cool room where a tempting array of food was laid out, as everyone was coming in from the garden to collect their lunch. Plates and cutlery were at one end of a central table, and they slowly circled it, selecting their meal from the various dishes.

Back outside, Abigail was careful to seat herself next to Lily, who greeted her with a shy smile.

'Thank you for giving up your Saturday,' she said. 'I bet you'd rather be doing something else!'

The girl flushed. 'Not really,' she muttered.

Her brother, across the table, wouldn't let that pass. 'She wanted to go riding,' he said, and received a savage kick for his pains.

Another jolt from the past. Though Abigail's throat constricted, some comment seemed called for, and she made herself ask, 'So you're into horses?'

Lily nodded, her embarrassment fading at the show of interest. 'I love them,' she said.

Oh God, what could she say now? 'So did I, at your age.'

Lily turned to her interestedly. 'Did you have your own?'

Abigail's hands clenched. 'I did, yes.' *Why was she pursuing this? Lily's potential friendship was costing her dear.*

'I'm getting one for my birthday. I can hardly wait!'

'We've stipulated she'll have to look after it herself,' Ben put in, 'but we have a fair bit of land round about, so it shouldn't be a problem.'

Tina, feeling that since her family was fraternizing, she should do the same, cleared her throat. 'James says you're an interior designer. What exactly does that involve?'

An olive branch, and, even better, a change of subject.

'It's a wide spectrum,' Abigail replied. 'Sometimes people send me a diagram of their room, detailing its size, aspect and any fixtures, and ask me to suggest a new colour scheme, complete with curtains and soft furnishings. Or I might be approached by a building firm to furnish a show house, or by businesses, for ideas on modernizing their foyers or board rooms.'

'It sounds fascinating.'

'I was pretty nervous about her seeing the flat,' James put in, 'but it seems to have passed muster.'

He was relieved the conversation had moved to a subject she seemed comfortable with; he'd not missed her reaction when riding was mentioned, and it was brought home to him yet again how little he knew of her past. Was it the thought of riding itself that distressed her, or simply the reminder of her childhood? And in either case, why?

Helped by more general conversation, Abigail relaxed and consciously set herself to charm them with amusing comments and questions about their interests, gratified that the atmosphere had noticeably thawed.

Among other snippets, she learned that Rosemary, as well as being a pillar of the church, had been a magistrate for some years, and was thankful she wouldn't have to appear before her; she didn't doubt her hostess would penetrate with ease the fragile web she'd so carefully woven about her.

As the meal came to an end, James rose to his feet. 'Ladies and gentlemen, I'd like to take this opportunity to invite you to a wedding in London on the eighteenth of next month. Formal invitations will follow, but this is advance notice so you can note the date in your diaries.'

There was an outbreak of exclamations.

'So soon?' Tina, thinking of Sylvie, who'd been told to wait for a spring wedding.

'But that's only – what? – three weeks away!' Rosemary.

'Three weeks today,' James confirmed. 'Time enough to buy a new hat, Ma!'

'But – aren't there things to arrange?'

'Nothing major. Obviously, we'll be living in my flat, and Abigail will lease hers. She'll use the converted loft as her studio.'

'Is there any heat up there?' Andrew, ever practical, enquired.

'I'll get one of those portable radiators; it won't be a problem.'

Soon afterwards the party broke up, and having helped carry dishes inside and had their offers of further assistance declined, the guests made their various ways home.

'What did you think of her?' Andrew asked, as he helped stack the dishwasher.

Rosemary straightened, rubbing her aching back. 'I'm not sure. She's intelligent and charming, and, of course, stunning to look at, but – I don't know. There's something I can't put my finger on that makes me slightly uneasy.'

'She seems to adore James.'

'So I should hope, after causing this upset.'

'And he her, of course.'

Rosemary sighed. 'Poor Sylvie,' she said. 'I'd be much happier if it was she who was joining the family.'

'What did you think of her?' Charlie enquired of his sister, as they lay in the long grass of the meadow.

'She's all right,' Lily replied, guarded as always in her brother's company, since she never knew when her comments might be repeated. In truth, she was torn, being fond of Sylvie, whom she'd known all her life. But Abigail was glamorous and sophisticated, and her clothes and shoes were to die for. What was more, she liked horses, a sure way to Lily's heart. All in all, she was just the role model she'd been looking for.

'Actually,' she added more honestly, 'I rather liked her.'

'What did you think of her?'

With no meal to prepare, Tina had joined her husband in their sitting room.

'She seemed very edgy to begin with. Not that you can blame her.'

'And?'

He was quiet for a moment. Then he said slowly, 'I know it sounds ridiculous, when she and James are so obviously in love, but I got the impression that she's deeply unhappy.'

'Belated conscience, perhaps, for ousting Sylvie.'

'I doubt if that worries her. No, this goes much deeper; an old unhappiness that she's spent years fighting.'

Conscious of his wife's stare, he gave an embarrassed grin. 'Sorry to go all psychic on you, but you did ask. It was something in her eyes.'

'Oh, so you've been gazing into her eyes, have you?'

He laughed. 'You must admit they're worth gazing into. Seriously, though, did you notice how she reacted when Charlie mentioned riding?'

'Can't say I did.'

'She actually swayed in her chair. I thought she was going to pass out, but she quickly recovered herself.'

'Oh, come on! You're imagining things!'

He shrugged. 'Possibly. All the same, I think there's more to our Abigail than meets the eye.'

'No wonder poor Sylvie couldn't compete,' Tina said.

'Where shall we go on our honeymoon?' Abigail asked idly, as they lay in bed on the Sunday morning. The sound of bells drifted in from several of the town's churches, mingling and chiming in repetitive relay, and she felt a passing regret that they wouldn't ring for her wedding.

James smiled. 'That's supposed to be a secret!'

'I hate secrets!' She propped herself on one elbow and looked down at him, her hair falling forward. 'Tell me.'

'Well, if you insist; I've booked us in at a very luxurious hotel over-looking Lake Garda. Everything laid on – gym, sauna—'

He broke off as he felt her stiffen, and her face took on the same haunted look that had alarmed him the day before. He reached up, gripping her bare shoulder.

'Darling, what is it?'

She shook her head distractedly, hair swinging across her face. 'I'm sorry – I can't—'

'Can't what?'

She moistened her lips. 'Go there. Oh James, I'm so sorry!'

'But – why? I don't understand. Don't you like Italy?'

'I love it, but couldn't we find somewhere in the mountains instead?'

'What have you got against lakes?' he asked gently. 'You can tell me, darling. You just said you hate secrets.' Though he knew instinctively she'd meant other people's.

She flashed him a quick glance, then lay down again, staring up at the ceiling. James waited, his heart unaccountably thumping, and after a minute she said in a low voice, 'My father drowned in one.'

He was at once contrite and relieved: nothing untoward, then; she was simply avoiding unhappy memories. 'You should have warned me, sweet-heart. Of course we'll go to the mountains.'

And as he bent over to kiss her, her arms came round his neck and she clung to him fiercely. He could feel her trembling, and struggled to think of the right thing to say. But before he could, she released him, giving him a shaky smile.

'Sorry to be such a goose!' she said.

*   *   *

The wedding passed off better than they could have hoped. Though the earlier heat had abated, the day was warm and sunny, the sky cloudlessly blue. Abigail wore a cream silk suit, a fascinator on her dark hair, and carried a bouquet of pink roses. She looked stunning, Tina thought a little sourly, noting the admiring glances she was attracting.

James, handsome in pale grey, impressed his bride's friends, and everyone seemed determined to put reservations aside. The service was simple but moving, the following lunch excellent, and even Rosemary acknowledged it had all gone admirably.

When the newly-weds had left, Tina and Ben set off for home, needing to collect their children from a friend's house. Rosemary and Andrew, however, had elected to stay on to see a show, and were spending the night at the hotel where they'd lunched.

When they finally reached their room, tired after the day's crowded happenings, Rosemary stood for a moment, looking down at the bright lights and moving throngs of the unsleeping city.

'They will be happy, won't they, Andrew?' she asked pensively.

He joined her at the window and put an arm round her. 'I hope so, my dear,' he said.

The replacement hotel offered all the amenities of the original, and was surrounded by majestic mountains, the higher ones already snow-capped.

Abigail had said nothing further on the change of venue or the reason for it. That her father had drowned was still all James knew about her family or, indeed, her life before they met, but he was confident that in time she'd confide in him more fully, and by talking through her worries, they'd be able to eliminate them.

They walked on the mountains, swam in the hotel pool, soaked up the sunshine and luxuriated in the excellent food and wine on the menu. And the other guests, indulgently smiling at the honeymoon couple, could have had no inkling they were virtually strangers to each other.

One afternoon, as they sat high above the town, their picnic lunch in a hamper beside them, Abigail reached for James's hand.

'Oh, darling, I wish we could stay here for ever!'

He laughed. 'I bet all honeymooners say that.'

'But I'm serious. We're together, just the two of us, away from everyone and everything.' Her grip tightened, and he felt her shiver. 'I'm frightened, James.'

He frowned. 'What on earth of?'

'Of being so happy. I've no right to be, and I'm terrified it will all come crashing down.'

'Everyone has a right to be happy,' he said gently, 'and I'd say you more than most.'

She gave another little shiver, then the tension went out of her. 'The pursuit of happiness,' she said reflectively. 'Isn't that part of the Declaration of Independence? But pursuing it doesn't mean you'll find it, does it?'

And he could think of no reply.

So the two weeks passed, and Mr and Mrs James Markham returned, however reluctantly, to the flat in Inchampton.

In their absence, autumn had arrived. A couple of storms had stripped most of the trees, the clocks had been put back, and daylight was fading soon after four o'clock.

It took their combined efforts to manoeuvre the larger items up the new ladder, and Abigail spent some time that first week running up and down as she set out her equipment. James had promised to put up some shelves, but in the meantime her books and files were stacked neatly against the wall.

The loft, though well lit, was dependent on skylights, denying her a bird's eye view of the square; yet despite its limitations, she was pleased with her eyrie and happily embarked on her work. With James back at the office, they settled comfortably into a new routine, and the family, watching from a discreet distance, allowed themselves a tentative sigh of relief.

It was a week or two later that the first incident occurred. It was a Saturday morning, and they were at breakfast when they heard the clatter of the letter box and the thud of mail landing on the mat. James ran downstairs to retrieve it, and flicked through it as he came back into the room.

'There's a postcard for you, darling,' he remarked, 'but they've forgotten to write the message! Hope we didn't do that with any of ours.'

He dropped it, picture side up, in front of her, glancing over her shoulder at the view displayed.

'Looks a nice place. Where is it?'

When she didn't reply, he glanced at her and saw she'd frozen, staring at the card as though it were a poisonous snake while the colour leached from her face.

'Abigail? Whatever's the matter, love?'

Very slowly, still with her eyes on the card, she pushed her chair back from the table. Then, with startling suddenness, she sprang to her feet, brushed him aside and ran from the room. Seconds later, James heard her vomiting in the bathroom.

He hurried after her, staring helplessly at the locked door. When the retching finally stopped, he tapped on it gently.

'Darling, come and lie down and let me get you something.'

Silence.

'Abigail? Are you all right?'

Still no reply, and he knocked more loudly. 'Darling, please let me in. I'm worried about you.'

He heard her voice then, faint and hoarse. 'I'm all right. Please leave me alone.'

He waited a moment longer, rattling the handle in his frustration. Then, defeated, he slowly returned to the living room. The card lay where he'd so casually dropped it, and he picked it up and studied it.

It showed a lake, surrounded by hills, and though his first thought was that it was in Italy, the caption identified it as the English Lake District. It must have been the lake that upset her, he reasoned, but surely that in itself couldn't account for such a traumatic reaction? Thank God her father wasn't run over by a bus! he thought, with gallows humour.

Turning the card over, he saw it was addressed to Mrs A Markham, at this address, and had been posted in Manchester the previous day. Who did she know in Manchester? he wondered. She couldn't have recognized the handwriting, because she'd not even seen it. Was it some link with her mysterious past?

He pulled himself up. Mysterious? An odd word to use about his wife, but it was again borne in on him how little he knew about her. He went determinedly back through the bedroom and knocked on the bathroom door.

'Darling, if you don't come out now, I'm going to call the doctor,' he said.

For a moment longer there was silence inside. Then, with a huge sigh of relief, he heard the bolt slide back and the door opened. Abigail stood there, her face white and her eyes staring at him with an expression he couldn't read.

Gently he took her arm and led her back to the living room. Her eyes went straight to the card on the table, and he felt a tremor go through her.

'I know it's of a lake, love, but there's nothing unusual about that, and you must have seen others since your father died. Is it the lack of message that spooked you? It's easily done, you know. I used to buy a stack of cards on holiday, and address and stamp them while I had my address list to hand. Then, rather than sit down and write them all at once – boring in the extreme – I sent them off in batches. It's quite easy for one with no message to get mixed up with those waiting to be posted.'

He knew he was gabbling, but hoped his everyday words would calm her, restore her balance. She still didn't speak, and he realized with a faint shock that apart from asking him to go away, she hadn't done so since the card arrived.

'Abby?' he said softly, and she spun to face him, her face contorted as she shook him off.

'Don't call me that!' she cried, a note of hysteria in her voice. 'Don't *ever* call me that!'

'Darling, I'm sorry – I'm sorry. Look, you're really worrying me now. What's wrong? Please tell me. You can tell me anything, Abigail, you know that. I won't judge you, whatever it is. I *love* you!'

Her eyes had a wild look in them, and she gave a sudden laugh. 'You wouldn't judge me?' she said. 'I wonder. I just wonder.'

Tentatively he put his arms round her, and after resisting briefly, she leaned against him.

'I love you,' he said again. 'For ever and ever, amen – remember?'

He felt her nod. 'Then what's wrong, sweetheart? Tell me. I'm sure we can sort it out.'

A ripple shook her. Then she gently disengaged herself. Her face was still white, but some of the wildness had left her. She cupped his face in her hands and stared into his eyes.

'And I love you,' she said. 'More than you'll ever know.'

He gave an uncertain smile. 'That's all right, then. So—'

Her hands dropped and she turned away. 'I'll go and have my shower, or the morning will have gone without getting anything done.'

'Abigail—'

She started to walk purposefully from the room. 'Don't worry about me, James,' she said over her shoulder. 'I overreact. You know that. It was probably the curry last night, but I'm fine now.'

Slowly, James picked up the offending card and put it in the top drawer of his desk. Out of sight, he hoped, out of mind.

For the rest of that day, the postcard and its effect continued to prey on his mind. Abigail appeared to have reverted to normal, and he didn't dare bring the subject up again. However, the next day he made one last attempt to get to the bottom of it.

'Darling, about that postcard . . .'

'What postcard?' she said.

Four

Afterwards, James looked back on the incident of the postcard as the first portent of what was to come. It was as though a gauze curtain had descended between them, keeping him at a distance, and try as he might, he couldn't penetrate it.

Nor could he share his unease with his family, since they'd been against the marriage in the first place. Though Tina would never say, *I told you so* in as many words, he'd see it in her eyes, and that would be enough. There was a saying: *Marry in haste and repent at leisure*, but he wasn't repenting; on the contrary, he longed for them to be close again, as they'd been on their honeymoon. What was it Abigail had said then? That she was afraid it would all come crashing down? But surely one innocuous postcard couldn't be the catalyst?

Yet, when he tried to analyse the change, it was hard to pinpoint. She seemed glad to see him when he came home each evening, they continued to make love – though possibly with not quite the abandon of before – they'd even been to Tina and Ben's for supper, and to his parents for a Sunday lunch. James was aware, though, of her continuing dislike of family occasions, and he'd declined several invitations rather than overexpose her to them.

But there were little things – things that in themselves were trifling, but which taken together added to his concern. Several times she'd not replenished household supplies, claiming she'd been too busy or had a deadline to work to, and suggesting they go together on a Saturday morning. Nor, even when alone in the flat, did she retrieve the post. He would find it lying on the mat in the hall, when she'd been in all day. It was the same with the telephone, which she never answered, maintaining it wouldn't be for her. He became used to arriving home each evening to see the red button flashing. Once or twice, the messages had indeed been for Abigail, from her London friends.

'Why not answer it, darling?' he asked lightly one evening. 'It won't bite, and there might be something urgent from a client.'

But she shook her head. 'They email me,' she said.

It was towards the end of November that James came out of his office one lunchtime to find his sister in the foyer.

'You're taking me to lunch,' she announced. 'I need to talk to you.'

'That sounds ominous!' he joked.

'I'm hoping not.'

At the Montpellier Wine Bar, Tina waited till they had their drinks and their food was ordered before putting her elbows on the table and surveying her brother.

'I'm worried about you,' she said.

'Me?' He tried a laugh, not too successfully.

'You and Abigail. Things don't seem to be – right.'

'They're fine,' he said evasively, not meeting her eyes.

'James, this is me you're talking to. Before the wedding, you were walking on air. It was because you were so deliriously happy that I tried to ignore my – misgivings.'

'If you're referring to Sylvie—' he began defiantly.

'I'm referring to Abigail. Have you found out anything more about her? Her family, where she used to live, who her friends are, apart from those three at the wedding?'

He was silent.

'Well, have you?' She waited a moment, and when he still didn't speak, went on, 'I also want to know why you hardly ever come to see us. The children keep asking for you, but even when you did come, you spent the whole time watching Abigail, waiting for her reactions.' She paused again. 'Has something happened?'

He shook his head.

'James?'

He looked up unwillingly. 'Abigail's my wife, Tina, and I love her. I'd feel disloyal discussing her, even with you.'

She laid an impulsive hand on his. 'Jimbo, I'm not trying to criticize her! I only want to help you – both.'

The temptation to confide in her was building. Though his unease remained nebulous, it was none the less real, and the one concrete fact – Abigail's reaction to the postcard – preyed continuously on his mind. Before he could stop himself, James found himself recounting what had happened.

Tina frowned. 'And it was of somewhere in the Lake District?'

'Yes; I know lakes bring back her father's death, but that could hardly cause vomiting, for God's sake!'

'There was nothing else on it that might have upset her?'

'Not a thing. I scrutinized it inch by inch. The only odd thing was that there was no message, but that could have been an oversight.'

Tina frowned thoughtfully. 'Postcards are usually of the place where you are – "Wish you were here" kind of thing. But you say this one had a Manchester postmark?'

'Yes. Anyway, since then, she won't answer the phone or pick up the mail or even, as far as I can see, go out by herself. It's as though – it seems ludicrous, but as though she's afraid of something. As to visiting you, she said right from the start that she doesn't "do" families. It's probably because she hasn't one herself that she doesn't know what to make of ours.'

'She actually said she hasn't one?'

'No parents, anyway. She told me that early on, and she's heard nothing of the others for years.'

'So you don't know who they are?'

He shook his head, and they were both silent as their food was laid before them.

'Don't you think it's – odd?' Tina asked, as the waiter moved away.

James shrugged. 'Unusual, certainly. But just because we're a close family doesn't mean everyone else is. You often hear of families being split and people losing touch.'

'But always with a reason.' Tina picked up her fork. 'What about Christmas?'

Since James had moved to Inchampton, it had become the custom for him to spend the three days of the holiday at Brambles, though Christmas lunch was, as always, at the Old Rectory. He'd even flown home from the States to spend it with them all.

'You will come to us, as usual?' Tina added.

He hesitated. 'It's sweet of you, sis, but if you remember, it started because you said I shouldn't be alone in the flat over Christmas. Obviously, I won't be alone, and of course we'll go to the parents for lunch as usual, but—'

'Three days with the Rivers would be too much for Abigail's sensibilities,' finished Tina tartly.

'I think for our first Christmas together,' James said peaceably, 'it might be nice to be at home, that's all.'

She made a little face. 'Sorry,' she said.

Unaware that her relations were discussing her, Abigail descended from the loft and went to prepare her lunch, surprised to discover she was hungry. Since the arrival of the postcard two weeks ago, she'd had to force herself to eat, and had frequently skipped lunch altogether. But though, sick with fear, she'd waited daily for developments, none had been forthcoming and she was beginning to breathe more easily. Then, lying awake last night, what now seemed an obvious solution had occurred to her. The sender must be a family member, who, having somehow learned of her marriage, was repaying her for not being invited to the wedding. She should have known that was the logical answer, since who else could it possibly be? She'd not seen the handwriting – James had removed the card – but if she had, she was now sure she'd have recognized it.

She laughed aloud in sheer relief. So after all that needless worry, she could put it behind her and resume normal life. To prove it, she ran downstairs to collect the mail, no longer fearing it might contain enigmatic warnings, and, having set it out on the table, replayed the answer phone to retrieve three innocent messages. One was from the library, informing her that a book she'd ordered was awaiting her, and she decided to collect it that afternoon. It would be good to be able to walk into town again without looking over her shoulder.

When James returned that evening, staring in amazement at the neatly sorted mail and quiescent phone, he cursed himself for having confided in Tina. If he'd waited just one more day it would all have blown over, and the hitch in the smooth running of their lives been known only to themselves.

Later, Abigail further surprised him by suggesting they invite Tina and Ben to supper. 'We've been to them,' she said. 'We ought to ask them back.'

And James, with happiness welling up inside him, caught her round the waist and swung her round. 'I love you, Mrs Markham!' he said.

Since her broken engagement, there'd been an awkwardness between Sylvie and Tina that, despite their efforts, they'd been unable to dispel. The intervening weeks had been hard, having to bear the condolences of family and friends while aware she was the source of gossip among them; but what had upset her most after the loss of James was the apparent loss of his sister also. As November slid into December, she determined that the hiatus had gone on long enough, and one evening, taking her courage in both hands, she phoned Brambles.

It was Ben who answered, and she was warmed by his spontaneous, 'Sylvie! How good to hear from you!'

In the background, she heard Tina's exclamation, and the next instant she had seized the phone from her husband and her voice came over the line.

'Sylvie, how are you? You must be telepathic! I was just about to phone you.'

'I'm fine,' Sylvie said steadily. 'I was wondering if you're up for our Christmas shopping trip?' Since they were schoolgirls, it had been the custom for the two of them to shop together for their Christmas presents.

'Just what I was going to suggest!'

'I've a couple of days' holiday due, so I could fit in with you. One day next week?'

'Perfect. How about Tuesday? Both the children have after-school activities, so we shouldn't have to rush back. Could you stay for supper, as usual?'

'Oh, Tina, I'd love to!'

'It's a date, then. I'll pick you up when I've done the school run.'

Tina put down the phone and stood for a moment, her hand resting on it. When she finally turned, her eyes were moist, and she and Ben exchanged a smile.

'Well done,' he said quietly.

'I'm so thankful, Ben. I was afraid this business with James might have done for us.'

'You've both too much sense for that. It was bound to be awkward for a while, but it looks as though you've weathered it.'

'The next hurdle will be when the two of them meet, as they're bound to.'

'Well, unless it happens here, which is highly unlikely, it's not your worry. In the meantime *sufficient unto the day . . .*'

'Amen to that,' she said.

The following Tuesday dawned sunny and crisp with frost, perfect weather for Christmas shopping.

Having dropped the children at school, Tina drove to the flat Sylvie shared with a work colleague, and, parking at the kerb, tooted on the horn. She appeared at once, a red scarf knotted at her throat and clutching a capacious shopping bag. Tina reached over to open the passenger door, and they gave each other a quick, slightly embarrassed, hug.

'Ready for the fray?' Tina asked.

'Absolutely. I have a list, but I'm not sure that's a good thing; if you've too definite an idea of what you want, you never find it.'

'Well, let's think positive. We usually do well together, sparking off ideas.'

As they drove through the rime-encrusted countryside, conversation was at first rather stilted, but by the time they'd circled several car parks, finally securing a space in a multi-storey, their reserve had completely disappeared.

'Right,' Tina said, locking the door and shivering in the blast of cold air. 'Let battle commence!'

The Promenade was already crowded with shoppers, the shops festooned with decorations and miniature Christmas trees, windows piled high with tempting goods – jewellery, cocktail dresses, exotic foods. They shopped

solidly for two hours, with varying degrees of success, and had just decided
on a coffee break when Tina suddenly seized Sylvie's arm and pulled her
behind a rack of dresses.

Sylvie looked at her in surprise. 'What's the matter?'

Tina nodded towards someone approaching down a near aisle. 'Abigail,'
she said.

Sylvie gave a little gasp. She'd never seen the woman who'd stolen James
from her, and her eyes fastened avidly on the slender figure, taking in the
careless elegance of the sheepskin jacket and tightly fitting trousers, the
high boots, the dark hair shining under the shop lights. Then she was past,
and Sylvie let out her unconsciously held breath.

'My God, she's gorgeous, isn't she? No wonder James fell for her.'

Tina squeezed her arm. 'Let's have that coffee.'

Minutes later, they were seated at a table, two cappuccinos in front of
them. But an unspoken pact had been unavoidably broken, and almost at
once Sylvie returned to the subject uppermost in their thoughts.

'How *is* James?' she enquired carefully, not looking at her friend.

'He's fine,' Tina said shortly.

James had, in fact, phoned her the day after their lunch together, asking
her to forget what he'd said and reporting that all was now well. To
emphasize the point, he'd passed on an invitation to supper, which was
to take place the coming Friday. Until she saw them together, Tina
was reserving judgement, but she could not tell Sylvie that.

'Funny to think,' Sylvie was continuing, spooning the froth from her
coffee, 'that on our shopping trip last year, he was in America, and I'd given
up all thought of our ever being together. Pity I can't just wave a wand
and delete the past year – or at least, the past six months. Then I'd be no
worse off than I was then.'

'I'm so sorry,' Tina said in a low voice.

Sylvie squared her shoulders. 'Don't be – I don't mean it. *'Tis better to have
loved and lost*, and all that. I wouldn't want *not* to have had that time with
James. And at least I didn't lose him to a mousy little creature with halitosis!'

Tina laughed. 'I suppose there's some comfort in that,' she agreed.

The dinner party at the flat was an outstanding success. Abigail had metamorphosed back from the tense, edgy person who'd come to their house
into the charming and amusing one they'd met at the Old Rectory.
Furthermore, she revealed herself as a talented cook, and the meal was
delicious. James, too, was his old self, deftly playing his part as host, and
the general atmosphere was happy and relaxed. So much so, that Tina felt
able to reissue her invitation for them to stay over at Brambles.

James and Abigail exchanged glances, as though the subject had already been discussed between them.

'How about, for this year at least, we compromise?' James suggested. 'We'd love to come to you for Christmas Eve dinner, if we may, but we'll come back here afterwards, and see you again at the parents' the next day.'

'That would be fine,' Ben said quickly. 'An admirable solution.'

'And we'll bring the mistletoe as usual,' James added. He turned to Abigail. 'It's my contribution to the decorations. We'll forage for some the weekend before Christmas.'

'Will it involve climbing trees?' Abigail asked guardedly.

James smiled. 'Not really; I usually go to a derelict orchard, halfway between here and Brambles. The trees are mainly apple, and pretty stunted.'

'We're lucky,' Ben put in. 'This is one of the few areas in the country where mistletoe grows. And did you know it's the only native British plant with white berries?'

'I can't say I did,' Abigail admitted, 'but I confess I've never given it much thought except at Christmas – and then only to kiss under!'

'Actually, it's a fascinating plant – a parasite, of course, and as I said, quite particular about where it grows and what trees it chooses. There are legends and traditions about it dating back to Ancient Greece and Rome, not to mention the Druids.'

'I can see my education has been sadly neglected!' Abigail said ruefully.

Tina phoned her mother the next day.

'I know you've been worried about James and Abigail,' she said, 'so I thought I'd let you know that we went to the flat for supper last night, and everything was fine. I don't know what's been troubling her, but whatever it was seems to have passed and she's back to normal. James seems much happier, too.'

'Well, thank goodness for that,' Rosemary Markham replied. 'Your father and I were beginning to wonder if the marriage had been a mistake.'

'I think we all were. She's still a very private girl, and I suspect there are areas in her life that are no-go, but as long as she makes James happy, who are we to complain?'

'Who, indeed?'

'And incidentally, I saw Sylvie earlier in the week. We had our usual Christmas shopping marathon.'

'How is she?'

'Coming to terms. She'll be fine, given time.'

'I'm still embarrassed when I meet mutual friends. The whole business was most unfortunate, but if you say Abigail has settled down, perhaps all will yet be well.'

The final weeks before Christmas passed in a rush. Abigail spent a night in London with Millie, and the four friends had their usual celebratory meal. She and James went shopping for family presents, and attended a couple of drinks parties. On the work front, she landed a lucrative contract with a London hotel that was undertaking extensive refurbishment. All of which added to her euphoria, and she was actually looking forward to her first family Christmas since childhood.

On the weekend before, however, it rained unremittingly, and they were unable to make their pilgrimage to the orchard.

'I don't see when I'll get the chance to go now,' James said worriedly, staring through the streaming windows at the deserted square. 'It's dark long before I get home these days.'

'I can go,' Abigail offered, 'if you give me directions how to find it.'

'Would you, sweetie? It's no use trying the shops, because although they're stacked high with holly, mistletoe's always in short supply, even here, and it'll all have gone by now.'

He took out an ordnance survey map, and they spread it on the table while he traced the route to the orchard.

'There used to be a house there years ago, and there's still a wall round it, so it looks like private land. Perhaps that's why not many people know about it.'

'It isn't private, though, is it?'

'I don't see how it can be. No one's been near it for years. Look.' They bent over the map again. 'You turn off the road down this narrow track – you'll have to watch out for it, it's easily missed. It's on your left, just after the second bend past the Fox and Grapes. Then, a few hundred yards along the track, there's a gap in the wall where a gate used to be. OK?'

Abigail nodded. 'As long as you're sure I shan't be arrested,' she said, 'I'll go tomorrow.'

But the rain continued over the next two days, and by breakfast on Christmas Eve, they were still without mistletoe. However, as they stood together looking anxiously out of the window, a watery sun broke through, and the prospect looked suddenly more hopeful.

Abigail handed James his briefcase. 'Don't worry, Father Christmas,' she said. 'I'll go and get some this morning.'

'Thanks, love. It's the office lunch today and I'll come home straight after, so I should be back by three thirty. Then we can wrap the last presents to take to Brambles this evening. They'll need to be placed under the tree.'

It was later than she'd intended when Abigail set off, and the sky was darkening with the threat of more rain. She armed herself with a pair of strong secateurs, slipped on a waterproof jacket, and, having let herself out of the flat, walked quickly round to the alleyway to collect her car.

There were several vans parked in the other spaces, some of them being unloaded by harassed shopkeepers trying to cope with a last-minute rush on their stock. The man from the bakery was among them, and gave Abigail a cheery wave.

'Hope you're all right for mince pies!' he called. 'We're down to the last couple of dozen.'

'Thanks, but I make my own,' she called back, and he pulled a face.

'Lucky there aren't too many of your sort around!'

She was smiling as she eased the car over the cobblestones and turned on to the main road. The square was thronged with shoppers, and it took her some time to thread her way through the congestion and turn left at the T-junction towards the station and, beyond it, the road to Brambles. The ordnance map, folded to show her route, lay beside her on the passenger seat, but provided she didn't miss the turning, she shouldn't need to refer to it.

The country road was slippery with the past days' rain, and mist lay low over the hedgerows. Abigail gave a little shiver and turned the heater up a notch. This, she thought ironically, was what was known as a green Christmas; grey would be nearer the mark. Because of the winding road, she was driving at a steady thirty miles an hour, and one or two cars passed her when opportunity arose. As one overtook her too near a bend, she wondered if he'd already been celebrating, and hoped James wouldn't encounter dangerous driving on his way home.

And here, on her right, was the Fox and Grapes public house. She slowed down still further, aware of an impatient driver behind her, but fearful of missing her turning. One bend, two – and there it was, on her left as James had said. She indicated, earning an irritated toot from the driver behind, and as she turned on to the track, saw the stone wall bordering it.

Behind her, cars whooshed past on the road, but here all was quiet and still, the only sound that of her windscreen wipers rhythmically clearing it of the persistent drizzle. Abigail drove slowly, watching out for the gap in the wall that would be her means of entry. And there it was. Though the pitted road, with weeds growing in the centre of it, indicated that little traffic passed this way, she drew in close to the wall, and switched off the engine.

Silence swooped down on her, not even the comforting caress of the wipers to break it. Suddenly, Abigail wished James was with her. She gave herself an impatient shake, pulled up the hood of her jacket against the strengthening rain, and let herself out of the car, secateurs in hand. Ten minutes, fifteen at most, she promised herself, and she'd be back here, laden with her booty and able to make tracks for home.

The gateway, such as it was, was filled with knee-high brambles, and she was glad of her boots. Ahead of her stretched row after row of stunted trees, bent and misshapen like little old men huddling in the mist. But, as James had said, among their bare, twisted branches hung gleaming green balls of the elusive mistletoe.

How much should she get? It was a point they hadn't discussed. Not much, she guessed; just enough to hang in doorways and under a few light fittings. She ventured further in among the trees, looking for the balls that bore the most berries. Odd, that theirs alone in this country were white. She remembered Ben's comments about myths and legends, and wasn't there a mournful ballad called 'The Mistletoe Bough'?

She shivered. There was no point wasting time in searching for the perfect specimen; she'd collect the most easily accessible, and get home as quickly as possible. She was already cold and hungry, and the rain was beginning in earnest, pattering on the leaf-strewn ground like ghostly foot-steps. Balancing on tip-toe, she reached up and pulled down a branch to reach the glistening green globe nestling on it. Then, loud in the silence, a twig snapped, and instinctively she stiffened. But before she could turn to see the cause of it – a rabbit? A squirrel? – a voice behind her said softly:

'Hello, Abby.'

James turned into his usual parking place, and frowned. Abigail's space was empty. He glanced at his watch. A quarter to four, and, because of the rain, almost dark already. Where could she be?

He climbed out of the car and looked about him. Possibly her space had been occupied when she returned with the mistletoe, and she'd had to park elsewhere. It had happened before. But there was no sign of her car in the alley. Perhaps she'd remembered something they needed, and driven into town? Though she usually walked, it was understandable to take the car in such weather.

As he stood for a moment, undecided what to do, Stan emerged from the back gate of the bakery.

'Merry Christmas, squire, if I don't see you again.'

'And to you, Stan. I suppose you haven't seen my wife, have you?'

'I have, as it goes. She went out while I was unloading – about twelve, it must have been. Told her I'd only a few mince pies left, but she said she makes her own.'

James smiled absentmindedly. 'That's right, she does.'

So Abigail had gone out at midday, no doubt to collect the mistletoe. She should have been back long since. Could the car have broken down somewhere?

Stan was saying something else, but James had started at a run for the flat. As he'd feared, it was in darkness.

'Abigail?' he called. 'Are you there, darling?'

He went up the stairs two at a time, hurrying from room to room switching on lights. Her shoes lay half under the bed, no doubt where she'd kicked them off to put on her boots. On the table in the living room was a small pile of presents still waiting to be wrapped.

James went to the phone and dialled her mobile. After a few rings, it switched to voice mail. Trying to keep incipient panic from his voice, he said, 'Where are you, darling? It's four o'clock and almost dark. Please ring me, I'm worried about you.'

Suppose, he thought suddenly, she'd had an accident in the orchard? Tried to climb one of the trees and fallen, for instance?

She'd have used her mobile, said the other half of his brain.

But suppose she hit her head and was knocked unconscious? Or the phone might have slipped from her pocket and be out of reach?

He snatched up the pad by the phone and scrawled a note.

4pm. Worried you might have had an accident in the orchard. Am going to look. If you get back before me, please phone my mobile at once. Love you. J.

Then, collecting a torch from the kitchen cupboard, he hurried back to his car.

Tina loved this time of year. The living room, lit only by firelight and the fairy lights on the tree, had taken on its once-a-year magic, compounded of the scent of pine needles, the strings of Christmas cards, the holly behind the picture-frames. All that was missing was the mistletoe that would arrive with James and Abigail.

She'd not yet drawn the curtains, and the cosy, firelit room was reflected in the dark glass of the rain-lashed windows. Ben had finished work for the holiday, and tomorrow the whole family would gather at the Old Rectory, to exchange presents and partake of Christmas lunch. With a contented sigh, she reached again into the decorations box and extracted a length of tinsel.

'What time is Uncle James coming?' Lily asked, hanging a chocolate soldier on the tree.

'About seven, I should think.'

'It's a pity he's not staying. It's more fun when he's here for the stocking-opening. Have you done one for him?'

In the Rivers family, it was tradition for the adults also to have stockings.

'Of course not. You have to be here at seven on Christmas morning to qualify.'

Lily laughed. 'Perhaps Abigail will give him one.'

Tina's eyes met her husband's, both of them doubting the possibility.

'What time's dinner?' Charlie asked.

'Not for another couple of hours. You can have an apple or tangerine if you're hungry.'

'Can I have a biscuit?'

'No, only fruit.'

Grumblingly, Charlie went in search of some.

Ben looked up suddenly. 'Was that a car?'

Tina frowned. 'Surely they're not here already?'

They both went quickly into the hall, reaching the kitchen as the back door was flung violently back on its hinges, letting in a gust of wind and rain as James, hair wild and white-faced, burst into the room.

Tina's hand felt instinctively for her husband's as they both stared at him. Then, his face suddenly contorted, he burst out, 'It's Abigail! Oh God, it's Abigail! Somebody's killed her!'

PART II – CALLUM

Five

Mindful of her floury hands, Judy Firbank pushed a strand of hair off her face with her forearm. Her friend Elaine, seated at the kitchen table, watched her with resignation.

'Lord knows why you don't *buy* the things from Waitrose or M & S, like the rest of us,' she said.

'I enjoy doing it myself,' Judy replied. 'Anyway, it's not all that often – only for the children's parties.'

Elaine glanced at the elaborate birthday cake on the side, a fairy castle covered in pink icing, with six candles distributed among the turrets and ramparts.

'You make me feel totally inadequate,' she complained humorously. 'My kids get whatever's on the supermarket shelves. Come to that, Bob's tarred with the same brush, sitting back while Callum coaches Josh with his maths.'

Judy, her hair screening her face, frowned fleetingly. 'He enjoys it,' she said lightly as she rolled the pastry. 'Being a father of daughters, he looks on Josh as a surrogate son.'

'And it doesn't stop at the coaching,' Elaine continued. 'If you ask me, Bob gets off altogether too lightly, lounging around or playing golf while Callum takes his son to football matches.'

'Well, it's not easy for Bob to plan his free time, is it?'

Bob Nelson was a doctor at the local hospital. He and his family lived next door to the Firbanks, and over the years they'd become close friends, often holidaying together.

'I'm simply saying you're a paragon pair. Don't argue – just accept the compliment!'

'But let's face it, Elaine, apart from my voluntary work, it's all I do. I have all the time in the world to bake fancy cakes and make my own patés and things – and enjoy doing it. You not only have to run your household, but hold down a responsible job as well.'

'Will you settle for domestic goddess then?'

Judy smiled. 'If you insist. Anyway, you're both doing your bit tomorrow, taking Luisa to the cinema. It's beneath her dignity to spend an afternoon surrounded by six-year-olds.'

'No problem, she'll be company for Phoebe. Send her round about one thirty – the film starts at two – and we'll feed her afterwards.' She put down her coffee cup. 'I must go; I've some things to collect from the drycleaners before meeting the kids. Thanks for the coffee, and good luck with the party.'

After she'd gone, Judy, continuing with her baking, mentally replayed her friend's comments. Though Elaine hadn't realized it, she'd touched on a sore point, for over the last year or so, Judy had become increasingly resentful of the time her husband devoted to their neighbours' son. Many was the weekend he'd taken Josh to some sporting event, instead of helping her entertain their daughters.

Once, Luisa, not remotely interested in football, had begged to go with them – simply, Judy knew with a tug of the heart, in order to be with her father.

But Callum had said lightly, 'Not your scene at all, poppet. This is boys' stuff.' And he and Josh had set off, leaving the forlorn little figure gazing after them.

Judy had tackled Callum about it afterwards. 'Anyone would think you loved Josh more than your own children!' she'd accused, close to tears. He'd been genuinely surprised.

'Sweetheart, you know I worship you and the kids. You're my whole world. How can you say that?'

'You spend more time with him than you do with them.'

He'd pulled her gently into his arms. 'I can see you're upset, but that really is nonsense, you know. It's just that I feel sorry for the boy. Bob's so tied up in his own affairs, he never seems to take him out, and lads that age need quality time with a father figure.'

'Not a father *figure*, a father,' she had said.

But she'd not been entirely fair; Callum *was* a good father. He had played with his children, read them bedtime stories, taken them to the zoo and for walks along the river. It was only over the last year that he'd spent noticeably more time with Josh.

Damn it, Judy thought now, with a spurt of anger, the Nelsons weren't short of a bob or two. If the boy needed extra coaching, they could afford to pay for it, instead of taking advantage of Callum's good nature.

She caught herself on the thought, shaking her head. It was no use blaming Bob and Elaine; Callum had volunteered for the duty – been quite pressing, as she remembered. They might have felt he'd be offended if they made other arrangements.

Judy spaced the sausage rolls on the baking tray, slipped it into the oven, and set the timer. Then, out of the blue, a memory, long forgotten, came back to her, and with it, a sense of unease.

It had been the weekend after their engagement, when she took Callum to meet the family. It was a fairly large gathering: her parents, grandparents, her brother, his wife, and their three children. And suddenly, amid all the laughing and talking, she'd realized Callum wasn't in the room – that, in fact, it had been some time since she'd seen him.

Alarmed that he might have been taken ill, she'd gone in search of him, finally running him to ground in the den, engrossed in a video game with her thirteen-year-old nephew.

He'd been teased mercilessly at the time – preferring the company of a young boy to his new fiancée, and so on, and though Judy had joined in the general laughter, she'd been hurt. Odd, she thought now, that Giles had been exactly the same age then as Josh was now. Did Callum secretly long for a son? He'd shown no sign of it when the children were younger, professing himself delighted with his 'two princesses'. Perhaps it was only when a boy was old enough to share his interests that the lack had been felt.

She shook herself free of her musings, glancing at the clock on the wall. The children would be home soon – it was Elaine's turn to do the school run – and she'd not completed as much as she'd hoped. Now, her preparations would be slowed down still further, with Flora insisting on measuring, stirring and tasting. It was part of the build-up to the party, Judy thought with a fond smile, but Callum would have to settle for a takeaway tonight.

'I had lunch with Callum,' Bob Nelson said, pouring out a measure of whisky. He gave a brief laugh. 'Would you believe, he actually offered to take the kids to the cinema tomorrow, so we could, as he put it, "do our own thing".'

'What did you say?' Elaine asked.

'That he'd be drummed out of hearth and home if he didn't attend his daughter's birthday party.'

'Quite right, too. Anyway, it's not that often our two have the benefit of your company.'

She looked up from the potatoes she was peeling. 'Sometimes,' she said reflectively, 'I almost get the impression he'd like to adopt Josh. He certainly puts you to shame, the amount of time he spends with him.'

'Well, good luck to him,' Bob said good-naturedly. 'I did enough maths in my youth to last me for life, and as you know, football's never been my thing.'

'Fair enough, but surely you could find something you both enjoy. Josh is growing up, Bob; he needs your input. Judy said Callum thinks of him as a surrogate son; if you're not careful, Josh will think of *him* as a surrogate father, and when you *are* ready to spend more time with him, it might be too late.'

'Hey!' Bob protested, hitching himself on to a corner of the table. 'I'm not an absentee parent. I'm here, aren't I? Josh knows if he has any problems, he can always come to me.'

'My point,' said Elaine, 'is that you should sometimes go to him.'

Callum, driving slowly home in rush-hour traffic, contemplated the weekend ahead with little enthusiasm. To be honest, he'd have much preferred to see the latest Harry Potter with Josh and the others, than face a horde of excited little girls who needed entertaining every minute of the two hours they'd spend at the house.

Judy had shown him the list of games she'd drawn up the previous evening. He'd be called into service to halt the music for Pass the Parcel, adjudicate the winner of Pin the Tail on the Donkey, and help distribute the food at teatime, no doubt mopping up spilt apple juice as he did so.

He frowned, his thoughts returning to Josh. Something was worrying the boy, he felt sure. The last couple of weeks he'd seemed abstracted, though he insisted nothing was wrong. Callum had considered mentioning it to Bob over lunch, but decided against it. He was chary of suggesting he knew more about the boy than his own father – even though that might be true.

All the same, he felt uneasy. Thirteen was a critical age; what happened at that stage of a boy's development could have a lasting effect on his life, as he knew only too well. It was essential to keep the lines of communication open, try to protect Josh from himself, steer him in the right direction, but to his frustration, Bob didn't seem to realize this. Thank God he had daughters! he thought wryly, as he turned into his gateway.

Josh Nelson sat at the desk in his room, staring down at his maths home-work. He wished passionately that this was one of his coaching evenings, not only so that Callum could suggest methods of working out the sums, but so that he'd have to concentrate on what he was doing, and his mind wouldn't keep going back to the incident at the school gates.

He'd been flattered at first when Dave Harris, a prefect, had compli-mented him after he and some other sixth-formers had stopped to watch his football training after school. Dave was a hero to the younger kids, excelling as he did at all sports, and according to Susie Tennant, who sat next to Josh in class, he was good-looking as well, with his mop of fair hair and easy grin.

But over the last week or two, Dave's attentions had become an embarrassment, and Josh wished he'd just leave him alone. Several times he'd watched from the sidelines when Josh was playing and come up to him afterwards. Then today, as he was leaving school, he'd been waiting for him, and asked if he'd like to go for a coke.

Luckily, it was just as Mum drove up and he had the perfect excuse, hurrying, scarlet-faced, to the car with Phoebe and the others. Next week was half-term so he had a break, but he wasn't looking forward to going back to school. He wondered how Dave would react when he ran out of excuses.

Once a month, the Firbanks and the Nelsons went out for dinner to a Cambridge restaurant, taking a taxi both ways so they could all enjoy wine with their meal.

That February evening, in the middle of half-term, Callum was still undecided about whether to mention his worries about Josh. The more he considered it, the more intrusive it seemed, and he'd spent the day trying to balance Bob and Elaine's probable annoyance against his concern for the boy's welfare.

But soon after they'd placed their order, Bob made a comment that banished Josh from his mind.

'Someone was asking about you today, Callum,' he remarked, holding up his wine glass to check the colour.

'Oh? Who was that?' No alarm bells so far.

'Didn't catch his name – approached me as I was leaving the hospital. Said he'd been trying to trace you, and someone had told him we were neighbours.'

'He could have found me in the phone book, if he knew my name.'

'Actually, he didn't – or at least, not all of it. He asked me your surname, and whether you'd ever lived up north.'

Callum went still, his heart setting up a heavy thumping in his chest.

Judy glanced at him, surprised by his silence. 'Well,' she said lightly, 'the answer to that is no. You were brought up in Surrey, weren't you, darling?'

Callum nodded, moistening his lips. 'What else did he say?' His voice sounded strained to his ears, but the others didn't seem to notice.

'Nothing, really. I was in a hurry, so I didn't prolong the conversation.'

Callum made a supreme effort to appear casual. 'What did he look like, this chap?'

'Pretty unremarkable. Medium height, sandy hair, about our age. Ring any bells?'

'No. You didn't give him my address?'

Bob shook his head. 'He didn't ask for it, but I wouldn't have anyway. It's not something I hand out to passing strangers.'

The waiter materialized with their first course, and they sat in silence as he placed the dishes in front of them. Callum was desperately trying to think how he could learn more about this stranger without appearing overcurious, but as the waiter moved away, Elaine said, 'I meant to tell you, Jude, I saw Miranda yesterday, and she's all right for Tuesday.'

And, as the conversation switched, his chance was lost. He stared down at the whitebait in front of him, wondering now he could force it past his closed throat. God, this couldn't really be happening, could it? Not after all this time?

'Remember that chap I told Callum about?' Bob said, coming into the kitchen a couple of days later. 'The one who was asking after him?'

Elaine paused in her ironing. 'Can't say I do.'

'He asked if I knew him, and what his surname was. Actually –' he frowned – 'when I told him, he said, "So that's what he's calling himself now." Odd, don't you think? I forgot to mention that.'

Elaine picked up her daughter's skirt and shook out the pleats. 'So – what about him?'

'Well, I thought I caught sight of him just now, in the park across the road. When I drove past, he ducked behind the gate, as if he didn't want me to see him. Ironically, that's what drew my attention.' Bob paused. 'Do you think I should mention it?'

'It's not important, surely? If it *is* the same man, he's probably waiting for Callum, and if it isn't, you'd have alerted him unnecessarily. Either way, it could look like interfering.'

Bob shrugged. 'I suppose you're right,' he said, 'though I still can't fathom how he knew I was a friend of his.'

As the days passed, Callum's panic began to recede. After bracing himself to be approached by every stranger he saw, and jumping each time the phone rang, he gradually regained a semblance of calm. He'd overreacted. Guilty conscience, he thought grimly. The stranger could be any number of past acquaintances – someone they'd met on holiday, a fellow attendee on a business course. It was only the query about the north that couldn't easily be dismissed, and he convinced himself there'd be an explanation for that, too.

Judy, however, had noticed his jumpiness, and it worried her. He was a complex man, her husband, and over the years of their marriage there had, on occasion, been things that puzzled her, in particular his evasiveness when she asked about his childhood.

Then there was the way he'd reacted when she'd had a bump in the car. She'd broken the news over supper, nervous that he would blame her for the damage caused. What she'd been unprepared for was for him to lose colour, jump up from his chair and pull her feverishly into his arms, holding her so tightly she could scarcely breathe. It had taken her the rest of the evening to calm him down.

Sometimes, uncomfortably, she wondered if he loved her too much, wearying as she did of being asked repeatedly if she still cared for him. Continual reassurances were even required of the children. 'Do you love Daddy?' he'd say. 'How much?'

And, laughing, they'd hold their little arms wide apart to show how much. Even now, with what she was beginning to think of as his obsession with Josh, that bedtime testimony was asked for, and willingly given. His childhood must have been very unhappy, she thought sadly, to leave him so insecure.

Yet, oddly, this apparent vulnerability was confined to his personal life; where business was concerned, he was confident, successful and well respected, attributes that, reflected in his generous salary, allowed them to live in one of Cambridge's most affluent suburbs, enjoying an extremely comfortable lifestyle. If the past held demons for him, Judy reflected, they must have been of a very specific nature.

It was the first Saturday in March, and Callum had still not managed to fathom what was bothering Josh. They were leaving the football ground, his hand casually on the boy's shoulder to pilot him through the crowds, when a voice made them turn.

'Enjoy the game, Firbank?'

It was one of his business rivals, a man he privately disliked.

'I'd have enjoyed it more if we'd won,' he answered levelly.

Benson's eyes went to the boy at Callum's side. 'I didn't realize you had a son.'

'He's not mine,' Callum replied, his hand dropping from Josh's shoulder. 'His parents are friends of ours.'

'Really?' There was a wealth of innuendo in Benson's voice, and to his fury, Callum felt himself flush.

'Yes, really,' he answered shortly. 'Come on, Josh, they'll be expecting us.' And he steered the boy swiftly away. Filthy-minded bastard, he raged to himself; if Josh hadn't been present, he'd not have got away with it. But if Josh hadn't been there, the question wouldn't have arisen. It was a sad world if you couldn't take a friend's child out without being suspected of perversion.

He was still bruised by the encounter that evening, which accounted for his sharp response when Judy broached the subject.

'Darling, don't take this the wrong way,' she began, 'but I think it would be wise if you cut down on your time with Josh.'

'Why?' he snapped. 'Are people talking?'

Her train of thought disrupted, she stared at him blankly. 'I don't follow you.'

He bit his lip, not looking at her. 'We bumped into Benson as we were leaving the stadium, and he insinuated I had designs on Josh.'

'Oh, Callum, surely not!' There was horror on her face.

'Well, that was the way I took it. Just because I had my hand on the lad's shoulder.'

The lad, her brain repeated, before she could stop it. A northern turn of phrase, surely, yet one he frequently used. It hadn't registered before.

She said quickly. 'I'm sure he meant no such thing.'

'I think he did, but I shouldn't have let him rile me.'

'Josh didn't – notice, did he?'

'No, I'm sure not. It would never have occurred to him.'

She nodded, partly mollified. 'But to come back to what I was saying, the way things are, you're in danger of usurping Bob's place.'

Callum lifted his shoulders. 'He seems happy enough to let me.'

'That's not the point. He's Josh's father, after all, and you're showing him up.' She smiled wryly. 'Elaine described us as "paragons" – I, apparently, because I make my own cakes, you in what you do for Josh.'

'There's nothing noble about it,' Callum said slowly. 'I enjoy taking him to football, pointing out the finer parts of the game. And as to the coaching, he's a quick learner, and it's rewarding to see him begin to grasp the principles. Numbers have always intrigued me, and if I can pass that interest on, it'll stand him in good stead.'

'But it's not up to you to do it,' Judy said gently. 'Can't you turn your attention to your daughters, who love you and who at the moment are being sidelined?'

She saw that had gone home. 'You don't really think that?'

'Yes, I do.' Her fists clenched. 'I'm sorry I didn't provide you with a son, but—'

'Judy!' It was a cry of pain. He crossed to her quickly and seized her hands. 'Don't ever, ever think that! You know my three girls mean more to me than anything, and I wouldn't change them for the world.'

She smiled shakily, trying to lessen the tension. 'Then just ease off, will you? Obviously, I'm not saying you should stop seeing Josh — it wouldn't be possible anyway — just tone things down a bit.'

'But — how do I go about it?'

Judy shrugged. 'Simple enough. Tell Bob you've been happy to coach during the winter, but the guest room's still waiting to be decorated and with spring round the corner, there's a list of other things that need doing. He'll understand, and I'm sure Josh will. It was never supposed to be a permanent arrangement.'

Callum nodded. 'All right, but I'm committed for next Saturday; I promised to take him to the motorbike rally in Fenby.'

Judy looked surprised. 'I didn't know Fenby went in for that kind of thing.'

'They're trying to widen the appeal of their Spring Fair, offering a programme of stunts, followed by five-minute pillion rides. There'll be the usual things as well — refreshments, side-shows, dodgems — you name it. It'll be packed and very noisy, but Josh is keen to go, and Bob's on call next weekend. As it turns out, it'll make a grand finale, and then we can reinstate family days. Don't know quite how they fell by the board.'

'That'll be lovely,' Judy said contentedly.

She was weeding one of the borders the next morning, when Elaine put her head over the fence.

'We're having an impromptu barbecue, and yes, we're quite mad! We'll be eating inside, obviously, but the kids have been asking for ages, and we thought, well, why not? It'll taste the same, but we can sit in comfort round the kitchen table. Bob will do the necessary, of course, and I'm sure he'd welcome Callum's help, if you'd like to join us?'

Judy sat back on her heels. 'Our two will jump at it. I was about to put the meat in the oven, but it'll keep. Thanks, Elaine. Anything I can bring?'

'You could do the baked potatoes, if you wouldn't mind. And some of your special dressing. As you know, mine comes out of a bottle!'

Judy laughed. 'I'll bring it on condition you don't refer to me as a paragon!'

'Done! See you about twelve, then.'

*   *   *

When they walked round, Josh was in the back garden with his father, and Callum and the girls went straight out to join them.

Bob turned from lighting the barbecue and ruffled Luisa's hair. 'Hi there, Luisa-without-an-o,' he said. That had been her standard answer when asked her name as a small child, and it was how he'd always greeted her. She supposed resignedly that he always would, at least until she was old – eighteen, or something. 'Phoebe's in her room, and she's got something to show you both.'

The girls ran back into the house.

'Don't forget to wipe your feet!' Callum called after them.

Bob passed Callum an apron. 'Josh here tells me you've offered to take him to the rally next weekend?'

'That's right. He assures me he has your permission to ride pillion.'

Bob nodded. 'Obviously they'll have helmets and all the necessary safety gear. It's very good of you to take him.'

'I'll enjoy it.' Callum paused, then seized his chance. 'Actually, though, I'll have to back down for a while after that, and if you don't mind we'll call a halt to the coaching, too. The evenings will soon be getting longer, and there's a list of things I should be seeing to.'

'Of course. You've been more than generous with your time, and I'm confident we now have a mathematical genius on our hands.'

He lifted an eyebrow at Josh, who grinned self-consciously.

'And all for the price of a few bottles of whisky!' Bob added. 'Seriously, we're very grateful, aren't we, Josh?'

'Yes, thanks a lot, Callum.'

'You're very welcome,' Callum replied, and breathed a sigh of relief. It had been surprisingly easy.

It was a happy and boisterous meal. Judy loved the Nelsons' kitchen, with its Welsh dresser displaying a collection of blue and white pottery, the comforting bulk of the cream-coloured Aga. The pine table was a riot of colour with glasses of red wine and fruit juice, bowls of salad and glinting, foil-wrapped potatoes, and the patio doors stood open to the garden. Beyond them, the men were turning the meat, while Josh, proud to be one of them, made repeated forays back and forth with chops, sausages and burgers.

She sighed contentedly, and her eyes moved round the table – to Luisa and Phoebe with their heads together, to little Flora determinedly sawing her potato skin, to Elaine who, catching her eye, exchanged a smile. The tableau they made, with the men framed by the window laughing at a shared joke, seemed almost preternaturally vivid, as though it were painted on the canvas of her brain. How lucky she was, she thought, to have such a family and such friends.

It was as well she didn't realize that image of them all would have to last her a lifetime.

Monday morning, and the school run. Elaine, harassed as always at this time of day, was shepherding the Firbank girls into the back with Phoebe, while Josh, as the eldest, took his place in the passenger seat, a heaviness in his stomach as the prospect of Dave loomed large.

His mother slid in beside him, and the car moved away from the kerb. Flora was engrossed in her Nintendo game, and the older girls, as always, were whispering together.

'Mum,' Josh began tentatively.

'Um?' Elaine switched on the radio, waiting for the travel news. There'd been heavy rain overnight, and she hoped the route she had to take after dropping the children wouldn't be flooded.

'Mum?' Josh said again.

'Yes, darling? What?' She must remember to collect that parcel from the sorting office, too, and it closed at midday.

'Suppose someone likes you,' he began hesitantly. 'Someone older, I mean, but you don't want to be with them. What can you do?'

'I'm sure you can find some excuse,' Elaine said absently. 'You will remember to bring your games kit home, won't you? Judy will be picking you up, so I shan't be there to remind you.'

Josh sighed. 'I'll remember,' he said.

Six

Having stopped to fill up with petrol, it was shortly after nine when Callum reached his desk.

'You just missed a call,' his secretary told him.

'Typical,' he replied, dropping his briefcase to the floor. 'When did anyone last phone before nine fifteen? But the one time I'm late . . . Who was it?' He reached for his phone, but her voice stopped him.

'I didn't get the number, I'm afraid. It was personal, and he didn't leave a name.'

Slowly, Callum let his hand fall. 'What did he say?'

'Just what I told you. That—'

'*Exactly?*'

Phyllis Jones flushed. '"Callum Firbank, please." I told him you were due any minute, could I take a message, and he said, "No, it's a personal call." So I started to ask if you could ring back, but he cut in saying it didn't matter, and rang off before I'd a chance to ask his name. I'm sorry,' she finished, eying his taut face. 'I even tried 1471, but the number was withheld.'

'Typical,' Callum said again. He frowned, looking up at her. 'How did he sound?'

'A bit abrupt, I thought.'

'Any accent?'

'Hard to tell; he only said a couple of words, but it was a – flat voice.'

Callum sighed and ran a hand through his hair. 'All right, Phyllis; you can bring the post in,' he said.

The call lodged at the back of his mind all morning. Each time the phone rang, he snatched it up, hoping to identify its originator, but each time he was disappointed. He'd always loathed uncertainties, needing immediate answers to anything puzzling him, and now there were two outstanding – this morning's caller, and the stranger who'd approached Bob ten days ago. Were they one and the same? If so, who the hell was this guy, and why was he trying to contact him?

A flat voice. Try as he might, Callum could think of no one to whom that description might apply. *Why*, he asked himself repeatedly, had he not waited to fill up on the way home?

At twelve o'clock he switched off his computer, giving up all pretence of work. He needed some fresh air; a brisk walk, followed by lunch, should clear his head. And if the stranger rang while he was out, to hell with him.

He took a bus to the botanic gardens and walked solidly for an hour, taking in very little of what he saw. There was no point working himself up over this; whoever this man – or these men – might be, could have no link with the past. He'd taken great care to ensure that was well and truly buried, and there was no way it could be resurrected at this late stage. If either or both were subsequently identified, so much the better. If not, he'd simply expunge their existence from his memory.

By the time he returned to the office after lunch, his equanimity was restored, and he did not even enquire if there'd been any calls.

During the rest of that week, the weather steadily deteriorated, dominated by cloudy skies and biting winds. One morning, they woke to find a blanket of snow, but it melted almost at once in the weak March sun.

There'd been no further personal calls, and Callum had for the most part succeeded in putting the incident out of his mind. During the day, that is. Unfortunately, and possibly as a direct result, he was suffering one of his rare periods of insomnia, and in the long night watches he'd considerably less control over where his mind led him.

Wary of waking Judy, he first tried reading by torchlight, but the strain on his eyes rapidly led to headaches. So he took to prowling round the house, glancing in at his daughters, asleep and untroubled in their beds, wandering downstairs to pour himself a whisky, sitting in the shadowed family room watching overfamiliar DVDs. Eventually he would doze off, his head at an awkward angle, so that he'd wake an hour or two later with a stiff neck, which as often as not lasted throughout the day.

Once or twice Judy, waking to find an empty space beside her, came down in search of him, sliding cushions under his head if he was asleep, bringing him hot milk if awake. He hadn't the heart to tell her that he loathed it, that drinking it almost made him gag, and that it had unwelcome connotations with his childhood.

'Perhaps you should try some sleeping pills,' she suggested towards the end of the week. 'Just a short course, to break the cycle.' She paused, stroking the hair back from his damp forehead. 'There's nothing worrying you, is there, darling?'

He'd forced a smile, reaching up to pat her cheek. 'What could possibly worry me?'

'I don't know – problems at work?'

But he smilingly shook his head. At least there could be no financial difficulties, she assured herself; in addition to his substantial salary, Callum had a sizeable amount of family money – inherited, she assumed, from his parents, though he'd never said.

When, after fitful snatches of sleep, he woke on the Saturday morning, Callum had both a stiff neck and a raging headache, and all he wanted was to crawl back to bed and pull the covers over his head. Instead, a horrendous schedule lay ahead of him: a half-hour's drive to Fenby, the stress of finding somewhere to park in an already overcrowded village, and, to top it all, the constant soundtrack of exhausts and revving engines for the rest of the day.

Even the weather was against him, he reflected gloomily; whereas the previous days' cloud would at least have been kind on the eyes, this morning the sun was back, glinting blindingly on the frosty grass.

Judy surveyed him over the breakfast table. 'You don't look well,' she said worriedly. 'Ring up and cancel it, darling. They'll understand.'

He shook his head. 'I can't, love. Josh has been looking forward to this for weeks, added to which it's our last outing together, at least for a while. I can't let him down.'

'Couldn't you go in later, then? Make it half a day instead of a full one?'

'Can't do that, either. The parade starts at eleven.' He gave her a crooked smile. 'Don't worry, I'll survive. Just have a large drink ready when I get back – medicinal, of course!'

'It's the least I can do,' she said.

When he backed the car out of the drive, Josh was waiting for him at the gate, flushed and bright-eyed.

'Are you OK, Callum?' Elaine asked, as she steered her son on to the passenger seat and handed him his seat belt. 'You look rather pale.'

'Bit of a headache, that's all,' he said. 'The fresh air should clear it.'

'What time do we expect you back?'

'Things usually start to wind down about three o'clock. We should be back by four, or soon after.'

She nodded. 'Have a good time, then. And you, young man, behave yourself, and do everything Callum tells you.'

'Yes, Mum,' Josh drawled in bored tones.

She lifted her hand in a wave as Callum pulled away, and as he turned the corner, he could see her in the rear-view mirror, hand still raised.

'Will the pillion rides be before or after the parade?' Josh asked eagerly.

'After. According to the programme, the fair itself opens at ten, with stalls, hot dogs, coconut shies, et cetera. Then at eleven the motorbikes ride in convoy through the village and into one of the fields, where they'll give a display of some fancy riding and stunts.'

'And *then* we can have a go?'

Callum smiled. 'You can. Count me out of that.'

'I asked Dad how soon I could have a motorbike, and he said never!'

'Well, you might be able to talk him round when you're eighteen. On the other hand, by then you could be more interested in cars. A lot safer, I'd say.'

'Safer!' Josh repeated with derision.

As they drew nearer to Fenby, the narrow country road became more congested, until they were driving bumper to bumper in a stream of traffic converging on the village. The sun was warm through the glass and glinted blindingly on the rear window of the car in front, scarcely dulled by his sunglasses. Callum's head set up a steady thrumming. It was going to be a long day.

As they reached the front of the queue of traffic, a steward waved them into a field that was providing a temporary car park, and another guided them into the requisite slot. Looking about him, Callum was unsurprised to note that the crowd streaming towards the village was almost exclusively male – fathers, sons and grandsons, most of them attired, like themselves, in jeans, trainers and padded jackets, eagerly anticipating a day spent admiring what Judy referred to as 'boys' toys'.

Even from this distance, blaring music reached them, amplified by loud-speakers positioned around the village. Every now and then it ceased mid-tune, to give way to a raucous voice reminding everyone of the timing of main events, and extolling the goods on offer at the stalls. There was also a tombola, they were informed, and a raffle with 'stupendous prizes'.

Josh had already set off towards the gate, and Callum hurried to catch up with him, joining the moving throng streaming towards the village.

'Keep close to me,' Callum advised the boy as they entered the main street. 'It's easy to get separated in this crowd.'

Josh nodded, but his eyes were everywhere, scouring the stalls and amusements lining the road.

'Can I have a hot dog?' he asked eagerly, as the scent of frying onions wafted malodorously over them.

Callum held down a wave of nausea. 'You've only just finished breakfast!'

'That was ages ago!'

'All right.' He felt in his pocket for cash, but Josh shook his head.

'Dad gave me some money. I'll use that.'

He joined the queue by the kiosk and Callum stood waiting, marvelling at the digestive systems of young boys, and wondering how soon he could top up the painkillers he'd taken before leaving home. The music continued to blare overhead, and he was jostled continuously as the crowds surged past, each push seeming to send a hot poker through his head.

The next forty-five minutes were a rarefied form of torture. Josh moved from stall to stall, his pocket money dwindling. Among a selection of other bric-a-brac, he bought something claiming to be a whale's tooth, a miniature ship in a bottle, some candy floss and a couple of CDs selling for fifty pence each.

Not wishing to be thought a wet blanket, Callum allowed himself to be coerced into having a go at hoop-la and the coconut shy, managing to acquit himself reasonably well. But he drew the line at the dodgems, which had been set up on the school playground, and contented himself with standing on the perimeter watching the endless bumping and manoeuvring.

Josh had just climbed reluctantly out of his car when the loudspeaker announced it was time for people to make their way to the main street for the arrival of the motorbike cavalcade, and there was more pushing and shoving as everyone jostled for a good view.

The roar of the approaching bikes, loud in the expectant silence, preceded their arrival by some minutes, then, suddenly, they were there, a flashing rainbow of red, blue, black, silver and green, chrome gleaming, paintwork shining, as they sped through the street, did a sweeping turn at the end of the village, and roared back again, horns blaring as the crowd cheered wildly. Callum reckoned there must be about twenty in all. Beside him, Josh was jumping up and down with excitement, and even he, in his weakened state, was stirred by the spectacle.

The bikes wheeled again to ride down the street a third time, and when they reached the far end, turned into the field designated for the display. Immediately, the crowd began to stream in their wake, while the loudspeaker informed them there would be a fifteen-minute interval to allow the spectators to take their places.

'Didn't they look wicked?' Josh demanded, as they were swept along.

'They did indeed, Josh.'

'Thanks ever so much for bringing me, Callum. It's really cool!'

'Glad you're enjoying it. Have your ticket ready – we'll need to show them as we go in.'

The field was large and rectangular, and plastic barriers had been set up to separate the audience from the performers. Callum noted that some of the older spectators had had the foresight to bring shooting sticks and folding chairs, and envied them. The only other option was the grass, which the melting frost had left damp and unwelcoming. He should have thought to bring a rug, he chastised himself.

Once everyone was in place, the display began. Only twelve of the original twenty riders took part, and the next half-hour was a breathtaking performance of stunts, the mere names of which – Circles, No-handed Wheelies, Hyper Spin, Standing Burn-Out, High Chair Stoppies – were enough to quicken the blood. The reactions of the crowd echoed Callum's own response – silence, followed by gasps, and then wild cheering as each of the riders in turn seemed to take his life in his hands.

Prolonged cheers greeted the end of the display and the riders lined up to take a bow by bringing up their front wheels and lowering them again. The performers then rode out of the arena, leaving only the eight bikes that had not taken part, and that would be providing the promised pillion rides.

Another interval was announced, this one a lunch break of thirty minutes. Some families had brought picnics, but a barbecue was set up at one end of the field, and a fish and chip van at the other. After their recent barbecue, Callum and Josh settled for fish and chips, eating them, sprinkled with salt and vinegar, out of the paper bag, washed down with cans of coke. Callum had wondered if he could face food, but soon realized he was hungry, and as he ate, swallowing more pills with his coke, his headache at last began to lift.

By the time they'd finished, the queue for pillion rides was stretching down one side of the field, and they went to join it. Josh started chatting to the boy in front of him, and Callum exchanged a word or two with his father.

'Quite a display, wasn't it?' the man commented.

'Amazing,' Callum agreed. 'I hadn't known what to expect, but they certainly gave value for money. I wouldn't have thought half those tricks were possible.'

'Gravity-defying, certainly,' nodded the man. 'Used to ride a bike myself once, when I was young. Makes me hanker for it again.'

Inch by inch, they moved forward. Only two bikes went out at a time, presumably for safety reasons, and from what Callum could make out, the ride consisted of six circuits of the field. He was reassured to see a St John Ambulance vehicle by the gate.

'Prepared for all eventualities,' said his companion with a smile, seeing the direction of his glance.

'Hope it won't be necessary.'

At last Josh and the other boy reached the front of the queue, and were fitted with their helmets. Callum felt a flicker of nervousness as Josh climbed

on the machine and put his arms round the rider's waist as instructed, glad
he had Bob's permission for this ride to take place. Josh's rider waited till
the bike in front had reached the far end of the field, then they too were
off, flying round the perimeter with dizzying speed, leaning into the corners
at what seemed to Callum acutely dangerous angles, straightening again to
roar down the long side of the field. The noise was deafening, and he feared
for his recovering head.

Then it was over, and a hyper Josh was being divested of his helmet.
'That was awesome!' he enthused. 'Can I have another go?'

Callum nodded to the length of the queue behind them. 'It'd be the best
part of an hour before you worked your way to the front again. Sorry,
Josh, enough is enough. We'll head back to the village, and you can have
another go on the dodgems if you like.'

Josh pulled a face. 'They'll seem tame after the bikes.'

But he fell in beside Callum cheerfully enough, jingling his remaining
money in his pocket. The wind was stronger now, and the sun had
disappeared, giving way to heavy clouds.

'Looks as though we might be in for some rain.' Callum remarked.

Josh barely heard him. 'I can't wait to tell Dad about it,' he exclaimed.
'It felt *great* going round the corners – I could almost have touched the
grass.'

'I'm glad you didn't,' Callum said feelingly.

When they reached the centre of the village, they found several of
the stalls had already closed, having presumably disposed of their stock. The
strengthening wind was blowing bits of paper and plastic bags along
the road, and quite a number of people were making their way back
to their cars, the excitement of the day behind them. Callum glanced at
his watch. Two thirty. He hadn't been far out in his estimate; by the time
the last of the pillion riders returned, the fair itself would be virtually over.

As promised, they made their way to the playground and the dodgem
cars, where Josh, despite his reservations, spent a happy quarter of an hour
zooming round crashing into everything in sight.

The ride over, they walked back to the main street, finding it still crowded
as people continued to pour back from the display field.

'Nothing else you want to do?' Callum asked. By this time he was longing
for the warmth and comfort of his car; his back was aching after all the
standing, and the first tendrils of pain warned of a return of his headache.

'I'd love another coke,' Josh said.

Callum sighed. 'The stalls are closing down now. I doubt if—'

'We passed one just before we turned off for the playground,' Josh told
him eagerly.

Callum looked back the way they had come. It would mean forging their way against the crowd for a hundred yards or so, and his heart sank. 'Can't you wait till you get home?'

'I'm thirsty,' Josh said simply. 'Look, you wait here if you like. I'll only be a tick.'

'I don't think—'

'Really, it's fine.' And with that he was off, vanishing as the oncoming crowd parted to let him through. Callum edged back against the wall of the adjacent building and briefly closed his eyes. Well, their last expedition had been a resounding success. He was sad that it must be the last, but Judy had a point: without realizing it, he'd been neglecting his own kids, and that was unforgivable.

Somewhere to his right, a clock began to chime the hour. Callum opened his eyes with a start, and looked up the road. There was no sign of Josh. He should have been back by now – Callum wasn't sure of the exact time he'd set off, but it must be getting on for ten minutes ago. Perhaps there was a queue for the coke.

He turned up his coat collar as the wind came whistling down the street, his eyes scouring the faces coming towards him. He shouldn't have let the boy go by himself, he thought. But after all, he wasn't a young kid; he was surely capable of going a hundred yards by himself along a crowded street. All the same, anxiety began to needle him, and, pushing himself away from the wall, he began to walk towards the coke stall, scanning everyone he passed in case he inadvertently missed the boy. The turning to the school and playground led off to his left and he glanced down it as he passed. Several fathers and sons were leaving the dodgem track and making for the main street. Callum went on, and a few yards further along, came to the stall that had sold coke. There was no queue, and the stallholder was packing up.

Callum's stomach contracted. 'Did you serve a lad some coke a few minutes ago?'

The man didn't look up. 'Been serving 'em all day, mate.'

'But just now? A boy of thirteen, wearing jeans and a blue jacket?'

The man shook his head. 'Sold out some ten minutes since.'

Callum's heart started thumping. 'Then did he at least come and ask for one?'

'No, I've not turned anyone away.'

'Who bought the last one?' Callum persisted.

The man frowned. 'A geezer getting one for his kid. Haven't seen a boy the age you're after for a half-hour or more.'

'Oh God,' Callum said. 'Right, well I must have missed him along the way.'

The man nodded and returned to his dismantling, and Callum, now distinctly worried, started to walk quickly back the way he'd come. Had Josh a mobile? He'd not thought to ask. God, *why* hadn't he? Because, he answered himself, he'd never anticipated them being separated, and Josh's decision to go back had been so quick, he'd had neither the time nor the thought to ask.

Somehow, despite his care, they must have passed each other on the crowded pavement. Josh wasn't very tall – he could easily have been obscured. When Callum reached the place they'd parted, he was sure to be waiting.

But he was not. Above the pounding of his heart and the corresponding thump of his head, Callum tried to think what the boy would do when he realized they'd missed each other. Wait here for Callum's return, or make his way to the car? God, what should he do?

In an agony of indecision, he decided to stay where he was for another five minutes, and if Josh didn't reappear, he'd go to the car. But that was almost ten minutes' walk away, and if Josh weren't there, twenty minutes would have been lost. Useless to ask passers-by if they'd seen a boy in jeans and trainers; every boy who passed him was similarly attired.

Most fairs these days had a lost child centre, but the loudspeaker had made no mention of one, perhaps because no very young children were expected. Then, as though in answer to his prayer, he caught sight of a policeman – a good, old-fashioned village bobby, passing the time of day with a man on a bike.

Callum approached him, breaking into their conversation without ceremony.

'Excuse me, officer, I wonder if you can help me?'

'I'll do my best, sir.'

'I seem to have lost a boy of thirteen. I wonder if he's been trying to find me?'

'Your son, is it, sir?'

'No, the son of friends. We were on our way to the car, when he said he was thirsty and ran back to buy some coke. I – haven't seen him since.'

'How long ago was this, sir?'

Trying to respond to the officer's calmness, Callum glanced at his watch. 'About twenty minutes.'

'Did you arrange where to meet?'

'Well, no. It all happened very quickly. He suggested I wait where I was while he ran back, and then he was gone. I waited, and he didn't come back. So I went to the coke stall, and the man said he'd sold out some time before and hadn't seen him.'

'Could you have passed each other in the crowd?'

'That's what I thought, but when I got back to where we'd parted, he wasn't there, either.'

The policeman frowned. 'Well, sir, I reckon it's a bit too soon to start panicking. Not as if he's a young kid. Got a tongue in his head, hasn't he?'

'Yes, he's – a sensible boy, but I just – don't know what to do. He could have gone back to the car, I suppose. I was about to go and look, when I saw you.'

'Well, why don't you do that, sir? In the meantime, I'll make a few enquiries. If you find him, well and good. If not, come back here. I'll be at the church gateway, just over there, at –' he checked his watch – 'three thirty, and I'll wait there ten minutes. If you've not had any luck, we can take it further then, but it's my bet he'll be waiting for you, bright-eyed and bushy-tailed, at the car.'

'I hope to God you're right,' Callum said.

The road back to the field where the cars were seemed endless, and Callum had no compunction in elbowing people aside as he half walked, half ran along it. A stitch dug into his side, but he ignored it, repeating a silent mantra over and over: *Please let him be there, please let him be there.*

Yet when he reached the field and saw row after row of cars, he had a moment of panic, unsure whether he could find the car himself, let alone expect a thirteen-year-old to do so. It took him several agonizing minutes, during which he twice mistook a car for his own, before he came across it. And there was no sign of Josh. By then, he hadn't expected there to be.

Seven

The constable was waiting when Callum, sweating and sick with worry, returned to the village.

'No luck, sir?'

Callum shook his head, bending over to ease the stitch in his side.

'Right, then we'll make an announcement.' He pulled out his walkie-talkie, and minutes later the strident music was interrupted to be replaced by the organizer's voice.

'Attention, everyone! Could I have your attention, please? Will Josh Nelson, aged thirteen, please make his way to the church gate at the north end of the village – that's nearest the car park – where his uncle is waiting for him. I repeat, Josh Nelson, please go to the church gate where your uncle is waiting. Thank you.'

'That should do it,' the constable said rallyingly, and Callum, accepting the relationship conferred on him rather than embark on explanations, nodded.

'Now sir, the rain's coming on and there's no sense in both of us getting wet. The Copper Kettle's just two doors up. Why don't you get yourself a nice cup of tea, and I'll bring the youngster to you when he turns up.'

'I think I should wait here. It said on the announcement—'

'Not afraid of the police, is he, sir, this lad of yours?'

'No, no, of course not.'

'Then do as I say. You look as if you could do with a sit-down. I'll see to things this end.'

Callum nodded again – he seemed incapable of speech – and almost without volition walked the few yards to the café. The windows were running with condensation, but he took a table near them and cleared a space on the glass. By leaning forward slightly, he could just see the blue uniform of the policeman. *Come* on, *Josh!* he was thinking. *You must have heard that! Don't you realize how worried I am?*

He ordered a pot of tea and sat back, loosening his jacket and trying to breathe normally. Then a thought struck him. If Josh didn't reappear within the next few minutes, he'd have to ring home to say they'd be late back. And what else would he say? Oh God, would he have to tell Bob and Elaine that Josh was lost? When he'd been in charge of him? It didn't bear thinking of.

He started to rise, bent on returning outside and somehow hurrying things up, but almost collided with the waitress bringing his tea, and with a muttered apology sank back in his chair. Unbearably hot now, he shrugged out of his jacket and wiped his forehead with the back of his hand. Should the announcement have been more detailed, given a description of Josh? But how to describe him in those surroundings, where all the boys looked much the same?

A splatter of rain rattled on the window beside him, making him jump. For a moment he was afraid he was going to vomit, and looked hastily round for any available rest rooms. But the spasm passed and he drew a deep, steadying breath. Nothing to be gained from panicking, he thought. He poured the tea with a shaking hand, some of it slopping into the saucer, and was raising his cup to his lips when again the music outside was halted.

'This is an announcement for Josh Nelson, aged thirteen. Your uncle is waiting for you at the church gate at the end of the village nearest the car park. Please make your way there as soon as possible.'

He hadn't turned up, then. God, where *was* he? Could he have gone back to the dodgem cars? He might have heard the announcement, but not known how to stop the car in mid-operation – it was remotely controlled, after all. The duration of the ride was fifteen minutes, Callum remembered, in which case he should arrive any time now. A part of his mind questioned why, when they were on the way home, Josh should have returned to the dodgems they'd just left, but he daren't examine it, had to hang on to the possibility.

Suddenly, quite desperately, he needed to hear Judy's voice. She'd have some explanation he'd not thought of – she was bound to have. Feverishly he pulled his mobile out of his pocket and speed-dialled.

'Hello?' How normal she sounded, how safe and ordinary.

'Jude? It's me.'

'Callum? What is it? You sound funny. Where are you? We're expecting you home any minute.'

He swallowed. 'There's been a hiccup, I'm afraid. I – can't find Josh.'

'*What* did you say?'

'I can't find him, Jude. He went for a coke, just a hundred yards away, but he hasn't come back. There have been loudspeaker announcements, but so far he hasn't turned up.'

'Oh, my God,' she breathed. 'How long ago was this?'

Callum looked at his watch. 'Getting on for an hour now.' As he said the words, the frail hope he'd pinned on the dodgems wilted away. 'Jude, what should I do?'

'Have you called the police?'

'I've spoken to the village bobby, and he organized the announcement.' He cleared the window again and peered out at the now wet street and the straggling crowd. The policeman still stood by the gate, now engaged in conversation with another man. 'It's turned wet, and most people have either left or are leaving, but there's no sign of him. He can't have run away, can he?'

'Josh? Of course not. Could he have fallen, sprained his ankle or something?'

'Judy, you don't know what it's been like! The place has been packed all day. I doubt if there was *space* for him to fall, but if he did, he'd have been helped at once.'

'Could he have been taken to a first aid tent or something?'

Briefly, Callum thought of the St John Ambulance at the display field. *Let's hope it isn't needed*, he'd said.

'Callum?'

'Possibly, but he's not a baby. He'd have given them his name and said I was waiting, and if someone did help him, they'd have heard the announcement themselves, and let us know.'

There was a pause, then Judy said, 'Would you like me to tell Bob and Elaine?'

'Do you think we could wait a while?' he asked desperately.

'No, Callum, I don't. Not when he's been missing an hour.'

Missing. It was a word he'd instinctively avoided, even to himself. 'Lost' was somehow much more palatable. 'Missing' had connotations of endless waiting and searching, sometimes lasting for weeks, with tearful parents on TV, and often ending in tragedy. Bile rose in his throat.

'I'll get on to them now, and phone you back,' Judy said.

He closed his phone, fumbled in his pocket for change, and, pushing aside the barely touched tea cup, dropped money on the table, shrugged on his jacket, and stumbled out into the rain.

It was over five minutes before Callum's phone rang, and then it was Bob, not Judy, calling.

'Callum, what the hell is this?'

'Bob, I don't know what to say. He—'

'Is there any news?'

'No. Most people have gone now and it's easier to look, but so far there's been no sign of him. He can't be far. God, he only—'

'I'm on my way,' Bob said.

Callum turned to the policeman, whom he now knew to be PC Dawson. 'Josh's father's coming.'

'Right, sir, that's probably for the best.'

'I just don't understand,' Callum said helplessly. 'He can't disappear into thin air.'

'Seems that's exactly what he has done, sir.'

'You must have known many cases like this. They turn up eventually, don't they?'

'Yes, sir, they usually do. Eventually. And you're lucky in one way; because of the event today, there are more police around than usual – keeping an eye open for trouble, and so on.'

'Has there been any?' Could Josh have been caught up in a fight?

'Not to speak of. The odd fisticuffs outside the pub, but nothing serious. No sign of drugs, which is a blessing in this day and age.'

Callum paused for a minute, the rain sluicing down his face. Then, frantic for action of some kind, he said quickly, 'I think I'll go and have a look at the display field,' and before Dawson could comment, set off, hurrying along the road as hope, that most inextinguishable of human emotions, flared again.

But after trekking the length of the main street and beyond, the deserted field proved a sorry sight, pools forming on the grass and discarded crisp packets blowing in the wind. The last of the motorbikes had gone, spatters of oil and deeply grooved grass the only proof of their existence. A child's woollen glove lay forgotten under the hedge. With a catch in his throat, Callum recalled Josh's glowing face less than two hours ago, and his excited verdict: 'That was awesome!' Oh, God, where was he?

As he walked disconsolately back, he came upon impromptu search parties systematically working their way up and down the road and the turnings that led off it. They seemed to be composed mainly of villagers, but there were several uniformed policemen among them, and he nodded gratefully to them as he passed. He'd have liked to join in himself – anything rather than standing uselessly in the rain – but Bob would be here soon, and, God help him, he had to be there to meet him.

'It's still early days,' Dawson said, as Callum rejoined him. 'We've had someone posted at the car park for the last half-hour, questioning people as they leave. No results so far, but someone may have seen something.'

If only, Callum thought, he'd forbidden Josh to go back for that coke. The boy would have obeyed him, he knew. Or if only he'd gone with him. It was tiredness and the resurfacing headache that had made it too much of an effort. God, if he'd known what that spinelessness would cost him.

The sound of an approaching car pierced his musings, and he turned as Bob's Porsche skidded to a halt beside them, and Bob threw himself out of it and hurried over to them. Automatically, Callum introduced him to the constable.

Bob said briefly, 'I'm grateful for your help,' then, turning to Callum, 'How in God's name did this happen?'

Wearily, Callum went through the episode again – the episode that at the time had seemed so trivial, a minor delay in their return home, but which turned out to have had such unlooked-for consequences.

'He wouldn't have gone off anywhere without telling you,' Bob insisted. 'He's a reliable kid.' Then, with a sharp look, 'You hadn't had an argument, had you? Something that might have upset him?'

'No, of course not. We'd had a great day, he'd been having a ball and kept saying so. He was looking forward to telling you all about it.' Callum's voice cracked and Bob looked away, his hand briefly squeezing his friend's arm.

'Right,' he said, squaring his shoulders and turning to Dawson. 'So where do we go from here?'

'We've laid on a police helicopter, sir. They're scouring the surrounding area for any sight of him.'

Bob voiced Callum's secret fear. 'Could he have been abducted? Forced into a car against his will?'

But Dawson shook his head. 'This road's been closed to traffic all day. From the field where the cars were parked to the display arena at the far end was all pedestrianized – apart from the motorbikes, that is.'

Bob's mobile sounded, and he turned away to answer it. 'No, darling,' Callum heard him say. 'Not as yet, but there's a search in progress and it shouldn't be long . . . Yes, I'm with him now. No, I've heard the whole story. Josh just went to get a coke a few yards away, but the crowds were thick and Callum lost sight of him. That's the last he saw of him. Try not to worry. I'll keep in touch.'

'Excuse me, officer.' All three men turned as one of the search party, dripping rain, approached Dawson, holding out a small object. 'We found this in the gutter at the far end of School Lane, and wondered if it's of any significance.'

Bob, peering over Dawson's shoulder, was shaking his head, but Callum's heart plummeted. 'It's a whale's tooth,' he said in a choked voice. 'Josh bought it earlier.'

'Then what was it doing right down there?' Dawson demanded.

No one had an answer. Slowly, Callum's legs gave way and he sank down on his haunches, covering his face with his hands.

Soon after Bob's arrival, they were taken to the village police station, a converted bungalow halfway up the main street, where they'd been gently dissuaded from joining the search themselves. Instead, they were plied with hot strong tea, feeling a modicum of comfort as the liquid coursed through their chilled bodies. Callum was escorted into the interview room to make a formal statement, repeating the sequence of events while notes were taken, then reading it through and signing it before rejoining Bob in the foyer, which had originally been the main room of the cottage.

Both Judy and Elaine phoned a couple of times, but there was nothing to report. Callum gathered they were all at the Nelsons', waiting for news. Good that they had each other, he thought. Bob had suggested Callum go home to join them. 'You look done in,' he'd said. But Callum had replied that he'd come here with Josh, and he wasn't going home without him. Though he didn't say so, he also felt Bob needed his support, such as it was, as much as Elaine needed Judy's.

The atmosphere in the small room was warm and steamy, and an overwhelming tiredness descended on him. It was an effort to keep his eyes open, but his drowsiness was shot through with shafts of fear that kept jerking him fully awake. Bob said little, sitting forward with his clasped hands between his knees, staring at the floor.

From time to time, groups of policemen, their uniforms sodden with rain, came in to report progress and briefly warm themselves before returning to the search. Radios buzzed, phones rang, and muted conversations were held. Time ceased to have any meaning. Outside, daylight had faded, and their reflections were imposed on the darkness beyond the glass, a mirrored world giving a false impression of normality.

But then, as they were becoming used to the lack of progress, a seemingly routine phone call elicited a quite different response. The man who had taken it rose quickly, went to knock on one of the interior doors, and disappeared inside, closing it behind him. Bob gripped Callum's arm painfully as both men strained unsuccessfully to hear what was being said.

Minutes later, the door opened and a grim-faced sergeant stood there. 'Could we have a word, Mr Nelson?' he said.

Both Bob and Callum had come to their feet.

'Say what you have to,' Bob said harshly.

The sergeant cleared his throat. 'Perhaps you'd like to sit down, sir.'

'The hell I would. Get on with it, man.'

'I have to tell you that the body of a boy has been found just outside the village.'

Bob swayed, Callum's breath was sucked forcibly out of him. They both stared wordlessly at the man.

'Of course, it might not be your son,' the sergeant continued, 'but I have to tell you the description and clothing fit with what you told us.' He paused. 'I'm so very sorry,' he added in a low voice.

'How—?' Bob choked to a halt.

'I'm afraid it's impossible to say at this stage.'

'For God's sake, man! I'm not asking for a pathologist's report! Had he been hit by a car, or what?'

The sergeant struggled for a moment with official caution, but compassion won over. 'We'll be regarding it as a suspicious death,' he said.

Bob stood unmoving, and it was Callum who whispered disbelievingly, 'You mean he was killed *deliberately*?'

'I must go to him,' Bob said, his voice loud in the silent room, but the sergeant shook his head.

'I'm sorry sir, the surrounding area has become a crime scene. Only authorized personnel—'

'Authorized personnel?' Bob's voice cracked. 'I'm his *father*, for God's sake!'

The policeman said gently, 'He'll be taken to the mortuary, sir. You can see him there.'

Buffeted by myriad questions, Bob randomly selected one. 'How long has—?'

'Again, we'll need time to ascertain that, sir.'

He nodded. 'Of course.'

Callum said violently, 'I don't believe this! It *can't* be Josh!'

Bob turned a white face towards him. 'We have to hope to God it's not. But in the meantime, what do I tell his mother?'

The rest of that terrible day and night passed in a merciful blur. The police having decided neither of them was fit to drive, they were taken home in a police car, with officers following in their own vehicles.

Afterwards, Callum retained only a few vague impressions of that homecoming: Elaine's low, despairing cry; Judy's white face; the three children who, having refused to go to bed, were curled up asleep on the sofa, blissfully unaware of the tragedy. But over and above it, his agonizing sense of guilt weighed heavily on him. He had been responsible. He should not have let this happen. Though he gave Elaine a fierce hug of sympathy, he could not meet her eyes. How could she not blame him?

It was Josh, of course. They had known that all along, but final confirmation came when Bob and Elaine went to the mortuary to identify him. In the days that followed, even worse horrors emerged. The boy had been sexually assaulted and strangled, though death might have been inadvertent, resulting from an attempt to silence him.

Bob, good friend that he was, made a point of coming round to tell Callum that he and Elaine did not hold him responsible, that Josh's darting back for a coke could as easily have happened when he was with them. But despite those reassurances, Callum doubted if Elaine would ever forgive him. How would he and Judy feel, if something unspeakable had happened to Luisa in the Nelsons' care?

The following day, Callum was summoned to the local police station, where samples of his blood and DNA were taken – 'just routine', he was assured – and a much more intensive questioning took place, this time conducted by CID.

His account of Saturday was once again gone over minutely, presumably in case he contradicted himself, but fear only kicked in when the senior man said casually, 'You see, Mr Firbank, we're in a difficult position here. As I'm sure you realize, we have only your word for the sequence of events. Is there any way of proving you returned to the main street after the second dodgem ride? Might you, for instance, have gone for a stroll in the opposite direction, where the whale's tooth was found?'

God in heaven, Callum thought, appalled, were they actually putting him in the frame for this? And immediately came the annihilating realization that had they known about his past, they might indeed be looking no further.

He swallowed, forced himself to say, 'Of course we went back. It was looking like rain, and in any case I had a headache and was anxious to get home.'

The detective tried another tack. 'You were fond of him, weren't you? Took him about a lot?'

Callum flushed angrily. 'I've known him all his life. Of course I was fond of him.'

'Perhaps overfond? Perhaps, away from the crowds and suddenly alone with him, your feelings got the better of you? And when he resisted your advances, you lost your temper?'

Callum came to his feet, colour suffusing his face. 'That's a filthy thing to say!'

'It's a filthy thing to have happened. Please sit down, Mr Firbank. Now, take us through what you tell us was your last sighting of Josh. You were on your way back to the car?'

'God, how many more . . . ?' He broke off, and wearily, mechanically, retold his story. 'I should have gone with him, I know,' he ended miserably. 'I fully accept that.'

He looked up, hope dawning. 'The man on the coke stall! He'll confirm I came looking for him.'

'Oh, he did. But he hadn't seen Josh, had he? If he was already dead, you could have been establishing an alibi.'

And so it went on, hour after hour, until, having asked him not to leave town without notifying them, they finally released him. Drained, resentful and frightened, Callum was free to go home. He would, he knew, remain a suspect until the real killer was found. And, among all those crowds, what hope was there of that, especially when the heavy rain must have obliterated vital traces?

The following day he returned to the office, grateful for the familiarity of work surroundings and the scheduled business meeting, which would require undivided attention. The murder had, of course, made the headlines of the local paper, and although Callum's own name didn't appear, his staff knew of his friendship with the Nelsons, and were quick to offer their sympathy.

It was unfortunate in the extreme that Clive Benson happened to be at the meeting, even more so that he had his back to the door as Callum entered the room. In a sudden lull, his voice came clearly.

'The boy was with Firbank, I hear? I always thought there was something unhealthy about that relationship.'

The appalled silence and the frozen look on the faces of his companions must have alerted him, because he spun round to find himself face to face with Callum.

Above the ringing in his ears, Callum heard himself say calmly, 'I hope you're prepared to repeat that in front of my lawyer, Benson.'

Recovering from his initial shock, Benson began to bluster. 'Look, Firbank, it was an off-the-cuff remark. In bad taste, I grant you, and I apologize, but we're among friends, aren't we? No need to take it any further.'

'Your definition of friendship doesn't coincide with mine,' Callum replied. 'That was slander, as you know damn well, and in the present circumstances I've no option but to defend myself.'

'Gentlemen, gentlemen,' the chairman intervened from the other side of the room. 'If we could take our places, please.'

For an instant longer the two men's eyes remained locked, and it was Benson who first looked away. In silence, those present filed to their seats.

Elaine took the cold flannel Bob handed her, and pressed it against her burning eyes.

'Penny was asking me about Callum,' she said. Penny Turner was the family liaison officer assigned to the Nelsons.

Bob frowned. 'What about him?'

'Oh, how long we'd known him, and so on.'

'Bloody cheek. Poor Callum's crucifying himself with guilt as it is. Josh was like his surrogate son — you said so yourself.'

'She asked how I'd describe him. Said she knew he was a friend, but to imagine I'd just met him, and say how he struck me. You know, it was surprisingly difficult.'

'It would be with anyone. What did you say?'

'I tried to be dispassionate. Said he was a bit of a workaholic, that he was devoted to Jude and the kids, that he'd been very kind to Josh.' Her voice trembled on her son's name, and Bob pressed her hand. 'He's quite a complex character, though, isn't he, when you think about it?'

'We all are, I suppose.'

'She also asked how much he saw of Josh, where he took him — things like that.'

Bob shook his head in annoyance. 'She means well, no doubt, but I think we'd be better off without her. I don't like her being here all the time, nosing around and trying to stir things up.'

'That's hardly fair,' Elaine protested.

'Anyway, darling, you should try to get some sleep. Have you taken the pills?'

Elaine nodded. 'I don't like doing, but they seem to help.'

She stood up, tossed the flannel through the open door of the en suite, and climbed into bed. Then, suddenly, she stopped.

'Oh, my God!'

'What?'

'I've just remembered something Josh said last week. I wasn't really listening, but — oh, my God!'

Bob sat on the bed next to her, taking hold of her hands. '*What* did Josh say? Tell me.'

'We were in the car, and he suddenly said, suppose someone likes you — *someone older* — but you didn't want to be with him. What could you do?' She stared at Bob. 'He was talking hypothetically, wasn't he? Not about *himself*?'

Bob moistened suddenly dry lips. 'What did you say?'

'I fobbed him off,' Elaine said aridly. 'I was only half listening, and my mind was on something else. I think I said to make an excuse.'

Bob straightened. 'Well, he couldn't have meant Callum,' he said stoutly, 'because he certainly liked being with him.'

'Yes,' said Elaine doubtfully. 'Of course he did.'

Eight

Callum told Judy about Benson that night. He hadn't intended to – he was too ashamed – but when he got into bed, he started shaking, and she was alarmed.

'Oh, darling, stop blaming yourself,' she implored, holding him close. 'It was the most horrible thing to happen – unbelievably awful – but no one blames you. You really mustn't shoulder all this guilt.'

'You do still love me, Jude?' he demanded urgently. 'Even after all this?'

The old insecurity, she thought, her heart going out to him. '*Of course* I love you! More than ever, after what you've been through.'

Gradually he relaxed against the warmth of her, probing his anxieties like a sore tooth. 'People are saying pretty dreadful things,' he went on after a minute.

'*What* people?'

'Benson, for one.'

She made a dismissive sound. 'Don't take any notice of him; he's in a class of his own.'

'The trouble is, he made his opinion known at the meeting today.' And he related what had happened.

'You must take him to court!' she cried furiously. 'How *dare* he spread vicious rumours like that?'

'But if I do,' Callum said wearily, 'even more people will hear about it, and might wonder if there's something in it. You know what they say: no smoke without a fire.'

'That's just giving in to him.'

'But it's not only Benson; the police were hinting at much the same thing.'

Judy burst into tears. 'I can't bear this!' she sobbed. 'As if it's not bad enough grieving for little Josh and the ghastly thing that happened to him, without other people digging the knife in.'

It was his turn to soothe her, and as his caresses became more urgent and she quickly responded, both of them sought and found some measure of comfort in each other's bodies.

Sandra Lomax watched her seven-year-old son slowly climb the stairs.

'I'm really concerned about Mikey,' she told her husband. 'This murder's hit him extremely hard.'

'Well, it's not surprising,' Tim replied. 'Damn it, it must have happened while we were actually there. They're offering counselling at school, aren't they?'

'Yes, but it doesn't seem to be helping much. Thank goodness they break up at the end of this week, and we'll be away for Easter. It'll help to take his mind off it.' She paused. 'He didn't know this boy personally, did he?'

'I doubt it; Josh Nelson must have been in year eight – they wouldn't have come into contact.'

'That's what I thought; I could have understood it better if they'd been in the same class. I'll have another chat with him after his bath, and try to help him put it into perspective.'

'And just where is the perspective, when a kid at your school gets murdered?'

Sandra sighed, and did not reply.

Why did children always look younger in bed? she wondered half an hour later, as she sat on the edge of her son's bunk. Something to do, perhaps, with the rosiness left over from bath time. She'd read the next chapter of their current book, but she could tell he'd not been listening, and his face had a haunted look that disturbed her.

'Darling,' she began tentatively, 'are you still thinking about Josh? He's safe now, you know. No one can hurt him any more.'

The large grey eyes came back to her, but he didn't say anything.

'Do you talk about what happened, at school?' she probed.

'A bit.'

'You didn't know him well, did you?'

A shake of the head.

Sandra said gently, 'Mikey, is there something in particular that's upsetting you? Something we haven't talked about?'

A look of apprehension flashed across his face.

'Mikey?'

Slowly, he nodded.

'You can tell me, darling. Let me try to help.'

He was plucking at the edge of his duvet now, not meeting her eyes.

'It often helps to talk about things, you know.'

She was about to give up, to kiss him goodnight and return downstairs, when he said suddenly, 'I saw him, Mummy.'

Sandra frowned. 'How do you mean?'

'I saw Josh, at the fair.'

She leaned forward, covering his small hands with her own. 'When did you see him? At the pillion rides?' Though Mikey was below the required age and height, she knew he and Tim had gone to watch.

'Yes, but again later. When me and Daddy were on the way back.'

Sandra's heart started thumping. 'Tell me about it.'

'He was talking to Dave Harris,' Mikey said unwillingly.

'And who is Dave Harris?'

'He plays football for the school, and Dan says he's a prefect.'

Sandra's mouth was dry. Could this be as important as she was beginning to suspect?

'Did you hear what they said?' she asked carefully.

'Only a bit, because it looked like rain and Dad was making us hurry. But I heard Dave say he had his bike round the corner, and he'd give Josh a ride.'

'And – did Josh seem pleased?'

Mikey shook his head. 'He said someone was waiting for him, but Dave took his arm and said it wouldn't take long.'

'So – what happened?' Sandra asked, every nerve taut.

But Mikey was shaking his head. 'I don't know. We'd gone past by then.'

She drew a deep breath. 'Darling, why didn't you tell us this before?'

His eyes were wide. 'He's a *prefect*, Mummy. You can't tell on prefects!'

'Oh, baby!' There were tears in Sandra's eyes as she scooped him up in her arms. 'Don't worry about it any more. Tomorrow, we'll go down to the police station and you can tell them what you saw. I'm sure they'll be very interested.'

'Callum.'

'Bob?' Callum tensed, gripping the phone. 'How are——?'

'Thought you'd like to know they've got someone in for questioning.'

Heat washed over him, but he answered wryly, 'Don't count your chickens; they took me in, remember.'

'But that was just for the background,' Bob said dismissively, and Callum didn't disabuse him. 'This is a senior kid at school; he was seen talking to Josh – must have been when he went back for the coke. As yet, none of this is official, but rumour has it this boy had his own bike nearby, offered Josh a ride, and wouldn't take no for an answer. And that prompted someone to come forward to report seeing a bike roar down the road running parallel to the main street, with a kid without a helmet riding pillion.'

Callum closed his eyes. 'Well, that's great news, Bob. Do you think they'll charge him?'

'No doubt they're processing his DNA as we speak, but it sounds pretty conclusive. Especially since Josh's friends are saying this boy had been pestering him after football.'

Callum frowned. 'You'd think one of the staff would have noticed.'

'I don't suppose it was obvious. But on the bright side – if there is one – it looks as though we're a step nearer getting some justice for Josh. God, if I could lay my hands on that murdering little pervert!'

'I'd be right behind you,' Callum said.

After replacing the phone, he leaned, palms down, on the table, deluged by a enervating wave of relief. Thank God, he thought, oh, thank God! The odds against a breakthrough had seemed a hundred to one; but Fate had intervened. Perhaps now he could grieve naturally for Josh, with no undercurrent of fear. Which, as Bob said, had to be a step forward.

Schoolboy charged with fellow pupil's murder, ran the headlines, but though a detailed report followed, the identity of the suspect was withheld. The alleged killer was a juvenile, and as such, granted anonymity by the law. Phoebe and Luisa, however, under no such restriction, had already supplied their parents with a name; it was common knowledge at school that Dave Harris had been taken into custody.

Callum found it helped to know the killer's identity – the word 'alleged' he ignored, having no doubt this boy was the culprit. It made the arrest more concrete, somehow, to have a name to focus on, and he hoped passionately that the maximum sentence would be imposed. Not only had this boy subjected Josh to unspeakable horrors, he had caused Callum himself to be considered as a suspect.

His musings were interrupted by Judy putting her head round the door, and he told her the news.

'That's wonderful!' she exclaimed, giving him a relieved hug. 'I'm sure it will help Bob and Elaine to know who was responsible. Actually, I looked in to tell you Mother's been on the phone in quite a state, having recognized the name of the school. She was even more shocked to hear you'd been involved, and invited us over for Easter – to get away from it all, as she put it.'

Just as well, Callum thought, that the police had lifted their restrictions on his movements; it would have been difficult explaining to his mother-in-law that not only had he been with the murdered boy, but was suspected of killing him.

'Did you accept?' he asked.

'I said we'd discuss it, and ring her back.' She added diffidently, 'Actually, I'd rather like to. I know it's selfish, but at the moment I dread seeing the Nelsons in their garden, and we're more likely to do that over the long weekend. I think it would be good for the girls, too, to get away for a while. It's all been pretty close to home, in more ways than one.'

Callum nodded. He was well aware that while Bob had been understanding throughout, he had fences to build with Elaine, though that must wait till the initial sharpness of grief had alleviated. For no matter how one looked at it, if he hadn't taken Josh to the motorbike display, he would in all probability still be alive.

'Fine,' he said. 'If you'd like to go, we'll go. I'll have to be back for the Tuesday, because there's a business dinner I can't get out of, but there's no reason why you and the kids shouldn't stay on all week, if your mother would like that.'

Judy brightened. 'I know she would. Are you sure you wouldn't mind?'

'Of course not; I could come over and collect you the following weekend.'

Judy dropped a kiss on the top of his head. 'You're a star! I'll ring straight back and arrange it.'

Callum was surprised, and a little guilty, to find how much easier he felt in his mother-in-law's house. It wasn't that he put Josh and his family completely out of his mind, merely that, at this distance, they weren't constantly at the forefront.

Daphne Leadbetter, small, stout and bustling, had twice been widowed, but she'd made an interesting life for herself in the local community, chairing several committees and doing voluntary work. David, her son by her first marriage, lived nearby with his family, and Daphne had a standing invitation for Sunday lunch, which, of course, would include Easter.

'I checked with them, naturally, before inviting you,' Daphne said, when Judy broached the subject. 'They'd love to see you all.'

So despite everything, Easter was a relatively happy, family occasion, incorporating church, an Easter egg hunt, and a suitably festive lunch. David had been ten at the time of his mother's remarriage, so there was a considerable age gap between him and Judy, and his children were correspondingly older. Giles, the eldest, with whom Callum had played computer games at his engagement party, was now in the army and had a family of his own. The younger two, a boy and a girl, were home from university for the Easter break, and regarded with awe by their young cousins. Nineteen-year-old Emma in particular was the focus of interest, and indulged them by letting them experiment with her make-up. Even Nathan, at twenty-two, was unusually patient, having been apprised by his parents of their recent trauma.

Bank Holiday Monday was taken up with a country walk followed by a pub lunch, and later that afternoon, Callum packed his bag for his return home.

'It's better to leave now, and avoid the heavy traffic later on,' he said.

'I'll miss you,' Judy told him, going out with him to the car.

'And I'll miss you, all of you. I'll phone you tomorrow before the dinner, and I'll see you Friday evening.'

She clung to him for a moment as the children came running down the path to say goodbye.

'Take care,' she said.

The house seemed strangely silent without the hustle and bustle of the family. In happier times, Callum would have phoned Bob and suggested they had a drink together, but it would hardly be appropriate now. Briefly, he considered and rejected his other friends; they'd be tied up with their families on Easter Monday.

Since there was nothing to hold his interest on television, he decided to employ his time in looking over the speech he'd prepared for the following evening's dinner. It was to be a prestigious affair, hosted by his company at a five-star hotel, in the hope of attracting wealthy local businessmen.

He was halfway through it, editing and timing it as he went, when the phone rang, and he reached for it absentmindedly.

'Callum Firbank.'

There was a brief silence at the other end, followed by a click as the connection was broken.

Callum frowned and looked up at the clock. Nearly half past nine. He dialled 1471, but the number of the caller was withheld. Probably a wrong number. He shrugged, and, his mind still work-orientated, returned to his speech.

It was only some hours later, as he climbed into the empty bed, that his mind returned to the aborted call, reminding him of the unknown caller a few weeks ago. Better not start thinking along those lines, he told himself firmly; they'd do nothing for his insomnia. He'd read for a while, and then, when his eyes grew heavy, hopefully sleep would come.

The evening had been a great success. Callum's speech was enthusiastically received, and there were a gratifying number of enquiries to follow up. The managing director made a point of congratulating him, colleagues lined up to buy him drinks, and for the first time since Josh went missing, he felt at peace with himself. This was the milieu in which he was most comfortable, most sure of himself, with none of the doubts and anxieties that, despite Judy's reassurances, bedevilled his private life.

When the formal part of the evening was over, a group of them adjourned to the bar. Several of those who lived at a distance had booked into the hotel overnight, and consequently were unworried about their consumption of alcohol. By the time Callum looked at his watch it was past midnight, and he belatedly realized he shouldn't have kept pace with his fellow drinkers.

He took his leave of them, and, aware of a slight unsteadiness, went to the cloakroom and sluiced his face in cold water. Briefly, he toyed with the idea of ordering a taxi, but it was only a short drive home, and he'd need his car in the morning. Once he was out in the fresh air, he told himself, his head would clear.

When he reached the car park behind the hotel, most of the cars had gone and his stood in isolation at the far end. His euphoria had evaporated, and he wished Judy was at home waiting for him. As promised, he'd given her a call earlier, and all was well. Flora had had her first pony ride, and Judy laughingly warned him that they might be in for an expensive few years if her present infatuation lasted.

He was smiling to himself as he reached the car and bent to put his key in the lock. He'd some difficulty finding the slot – the nearby lamp wasn't lit, and his hand was none too steady. When the key did slide in, he found to his surprise that the door was unlocked, and paused, frowning. Admittedly he'd been in a hurry when he left it – the phone call to Judy had delayed him, and he'd had no wish to arrive late for the pre-dinner reception. But it was careless in the extreme not to have locked it, and he was lucky, he thought feelingly, that it hadn't been pinched.

He slipped inside, registering with annoyance that the courtesy light hadn't come on, thus causing further difficulty as he fumbled for the ignition slot. It would have been helpful had the nearby lamp been lit, but the open door admitted only a cold wind, and he pulled it shut, swearing softly to himself. This hassle he could do without.

It was as he reached to turn the key that something cold and sharp touched the back of his neck, and a voice – oddly flat and toneless – said softly, 'Good evening, Cal. I've been wanting to have a little chat with you, about something that happened twenty-four years ago.'

They didn't find him until the next morning. His throat had been slit and his body strung up on one of the car park's lamp-posts, the bulb of which had been smashed. Curiously, stuck in the pocket of his overcoat, was a blank picture postcard of a town in the Lake District.

PART III – JILL

Nine

She saw him first in the post office – or, at least, in its doorway, since she was leaving as he entered, and they almost collided. In the brief moment they were face to face, she registered the quick flare of interest in his eyes, and smiled to herself as she hurried down the street. It was undeniably gratifying, this effect she had on men, even though Douglas bitterly resented it.

'You should be grateful,' she teased him. 'I'm good for business!'

Which was true. They were the owners of the Bay View Hotel in the Dorset town of Sandbourne, and Jill's easy way with guests, both male and female, was a definite asset. Since her arrival a year ago, bookings had gone up fifty per cent, a large number of them return visits.

It wasn't only her personality that had paid dividends; she'd invested a considerable amount of money in the hotel, redecorating and refurbishing throughout, and persuading Douglas to engage a first-class chef. What was more, she'd infected the existing staff with her enthusiasm, inspiring them to become more motivated, and Douglas, impressed by the results, was happy to give her free rein. It had paid off handsomely.

Sometimes, Jill wondered if it was because of her money that he'd insisted on marriage. With two divorces behind her, she'd not been anxious to embark on what she regarded as another farce, and would have contentedly lived with him without the blessings of the law. But he had pointed out – no doubt rightly – that as the owner of a hotel, his private life must be beyond reproach if he were to attract the clientele he wanted.

She'd warned him frankly that she was easily bored. 'I was the guilty party in both divorces,' she'd said, 'so don't count on my being faithful. I'll marry you, if that's what you want, but on my own terms – though I promise to be discreet.'

That he'd made only a token protest was indication, she'd thought, of the strength of his desire for her. Or possibly her money.

At forty-eight, Douglas was ten years older than herself, and when they met, had been a widower for two years. Jill, recently divorced from her second husband, had come down to the Dorset coast to 'regroup', as she phrased it to herself, and booked into the Bay View principally because of its position. And from their first encounter, an electrical charge had existed between them.

Douglas Irving was a man for whom there were no half measures, as might have been inferred from his appearance. His arms, permanently tanned, were hirsute and muscular, his shoulders powerful under the thin cloth of his shirt. He ate well, drank well – though never to excess – and had a strong sexual appetite, necessarily held in check for the past two years. It had taken no more than a couple of days before they were in bed together, and after the tender, unhurried lovemaking of her ex, Jill was first startled, then aroused, by the ferocity of Douglas's. In the twelve months of their marriage she'd had no wish to look elsewhere, though she continued to flirt shamelessly. It was as natural to her as breathing, and Douglas, though he didn't like it, held his tongue.

She had forgotten about the man in the post office, and when she saw him in the bar that evening, it took her a moment to place him. She assumed he was staying at one of the boarding houses along the front, which were unlicensed, and whose guests frequently came to the hotel for a pre-dinner drink.

It was her practice to hand out menus in the bar, giving guests time to choose and order their meal before going into the restaurant, and she paused when she reached him.

'Will you be dining with us this evening, sir?' she asked, holding up a menu.

He shook his head. 'Not this evening, no.'

She nodded smilingly, and would have moved on, but he continued, 'I hope I didn't startle you this morning.'

She paused, looking back at him. He had the sandy hair and colourless lashes that had never appealed to her, but there was nevertheless something about him that caught her interest, something contained, held in check, and the expression in his eyes made her uncomfortable.

'I'm not easily startled,' she answered lightly, and, ignoring his raised eyebrow, continued distributing her menus. When she next turned round, he had gone.

Jill had never fooled herself that she loved Douglas, nor he her, but their physical relationship was eminently satisfying to them both, and their shared interest in the hotel provided the necessary ballast. It was, she felt, a sounder basis than the emotional roller-coaster she'd experienced in both previous marriages, which she'd entered into blinded with love, and which in each case had ended in bitter recriminations. Though she was aware Douglas could be jealous, she also knew it was his pride rather than his heart that was affected.

She was aware, too, that though most of his friends had made her welcome, some secretly compared her – to her disadvantage, she didn't doubt – with his first wife, Aileen, who had died of cancer. There was a photograph of her in their private apartment, and Jill was happy for it to remain. She had been the love of Douglas's life, and this was all he had left of her.

Sometimes, Jill picked up the photograph and studied the perpetually smiling face, the dark, curling hair and slight figure, which must have been dwarfed by her husband. It puzzled her that this woman was almost an exact opposite of herself, and on one occasion she'd even taken it to a mirror, looking from it to her own reflection, with its spiky blonde hair and brown eyes, its tall leanness. How was it, she wondered, that two such different women could attract the same man?

Among Douglas's friends, the couple with whom Jill felt most comfortable were Bruce and Helen Fanshawe, who were dining with them that evening. Jill, whose keen interest in food had never stretched to cooking it, was more than happy to have her meals prepared and served by the hotel staff, and she and Douglas at their corner table habitually chose from the same menu as their guests.

When they entertained, however, they dined privately upstairs, and she liked to plan the meal herself, a feat accomplished by inveigling the chef, who, like most men, was putty in her hands, to include specific dishes on that evening's menu. On this occasion, the dressed crab, coriander chicken and lemon posset she'd selected would also be on offer in the restaurant.

Their guests were not due till eight thirty, and at seven, Jill did her first menu round in the bar. To her slight consternation, she saw that the man from the post office was there again. Determined not to let him rile her, she treated him to a smile as she passed. But he called her back.

'May I have a menu, please?'

She flushed, feeling wrong-footed. 'I'm sorry, I thought . . .'

He took it with a curt nod, and, gritting her teeth, she continued with her round, harbouring the unworthy suspicion that had she offered him a menu in the first place, he would have declined it. It would be interesting to know if he did in fact stay for dinner.

Before returning upstairs, she went to the restaurant in search of the maitre d'.

'François, there's man in the bar who's not one of our usual run of guests. He asked for a menu, and I'd be interested to know whether or not he does dine with us.'

'If you could describe him to me, madame, I will look out for him.'

'Medium height with sandy-coloured hair, and he's wearing a denim jacket and jeans.'

The mention of jeans raised an eyebrow. 'Has he a tie?' François enquired discreetly. Ties were a requisite in the restaurant.

'Yes, I believe he was wearing one.'

The maitre d' nodded. 'Leave it with me, madame.'

At least her curiosity would be settled on that score, Jill thought. She took the lift to their apartment, and, walking quickly through the sitting room, went out on the balcony and leaned over the rail, letting the evening breeze cool her flushed cheeks. Below her, she could see couples strolling along the prom, some families only just returning from a day on the beach, with tired, wailing children in tow. Beyond them, the sand lay golden in the late sunshine, and beyond that again was the incoming tide, moving slowly and rhythmically like the sleeping giant that it was.

Jill drew a deep, steadying breath and went back into the room, checking the table that had been laid earlier. Their suite did not boast a dining room, consisting simply of a bedroom with en suite, a large sitting room, and a tiny kitchenette with a sink, hob and microwave. When they entertained, a heated trolley containing the food was brought up in the lift, and the first and last courses, invariably cold, were set out on the counter ready for serving. Jill's sole contribution to the meal would be the coffee she'd make in the state-of-the-art machine she'd bought Douglas at Christmas. It all worked very well.

Satisfied that everything was in order, she went to have a shower.

They were finishing their dessert when the subject of murder came up. Douglas flashed an anxious look at his wife, and saw her stiffen; he'd noticed before that she erected an instant mental barrier when any kind of violence was mentioned, refusing point-blank to follow any of the cases reported so avidly in the press or on television.

'He battered that old woman to death,' Helen was saying indignantly, referring to a case that was making the headlines, 'and his defence counsel's trying to excuse him by saying he had a traumatic childhood! I ask you!'

'All the same,' Bruce put in, 'it's increasingly accepted that children *can* be permanently damaged by trauma or abuse suffered when young. Then, later, if something triggers a suppressed memory, it can flare up and transference takes place. If you remember, it emerged that the killer's grandmother used to beat him and shut him in the cellar for hours on end. It's possible something snapped inside him, spurring him to take revenge.'

'On the poor old soul who'd befriended him, and found him odd jobs to do.'

'Mind you,' Bruce continued judiciously, 'children obviously react in different ways; the stronger ones escape relatively unscathed, others might become withdrawn, or psychotic, or simply inadequate, unable to cope with life.'

Jill pushed back her chair. 'If you'll excuse me, I'll make the coffee,' she said, and left the room.

Helen, unaware of any tension, went on: 'Then there are these postcard murders. Now, they're *weird*. A woman in an orchard in Gloucestershire and a man in a Cambridge car park, killed several months apart but in exactly the same way – stabbed, and then strung up, with an identical postcard stuck in their pockets.'

Bruce leaned back in his chair. 'Remind me where it was of?'

'The police wouldn't say at first, but it turned out to be somewhere in the Lake District. I ask you, what possible connection can there be?'

'Search me,' Douglas admitted, with an anxious glance towards the door.

'No doubt a *damaged child* at work again,' Helen said scornfully. 'God, if I thought something I did could have a lasting effect on ours—'

'—you wouldn't beat them so regularly!' Bruce ended for her, and Helen had the grace to smile.

'Talking of your kids,' Douglas said quickly, seeing Jill emerge from the kitchen with the coffee, 'how are they? I haven't seen my godson for a while.'

And by the time she reached the table, the subject of murder had mercifully been shelved.

The Fanshawes left an hour or so later, and their hosts went down to see them off. As they came back into the foyer some guests approached Douglas, and the maitre d', appearing in the restaurant doorway, signalled to Jill.

'The person you referred to did indeed dine with us, madame,' he told her, and she noted with amusement his avoidance of the word 'gentleman'. 'He had booked a table in the name of Mr Gary Payne, and by an odd coincidence, chose the three dishes you'd selected for your guests.'

Jill gave a superstitious little shiver, as if this man had read her mind, and wanted her to know it.

'He settled his bill by cash,' François continued, when she made no comment, 'and I have to say, left a generous tip.'

'Thank you, François. It seems I misjudged him.'

'You can't be too careful, madame,' he said.

So now she had a name, Jill reflected, as she joined Douglas in the lift. If she ever thought of him again – which she didn't intend to – at least she needn't refer to him in her mind as 'the post office man'.

But it seemed he'd gone out of her life as abruptly as he'd entered it. For the next three evenings she'd looked quickly round on entering the bar, but there'd been no sign of him. It was the beginning of a new week; perhaps, his holiday over, he'd returned home. She was surprised by the depth of relief that explanation afforded her.

Having made her financial contribution, Jill's duties in the hotel were not onerous. She wasn't trained in the day-to-day running of the hotel, though occasionally she helped out on reception, took bookings, or made out the bills.

The lack of occupation did not bother her in the least. Having had money all her life, she'd never held down a regular job, and during her previous marriages had amused herself by helping out friends from time to time, fund-raising for their favourite charities, sitting in art galleries to keep a discreet watch on visitors, even doing a stint in an antiques shop. For the rest, she had shopped, met friends for coffee or lunch, gone to theatre matinées, and generally enjoyed herself.

Moving from London had necessarily curtailed her activities, but she'd set about building up a circle of friends, for the most part women like herself, some married, some divorced, who were more than happy to include her in their lunches and bridge afternoons, and who were quite different from the friends she'd inherited from Douglas.

Sandbourne was an attractive little town, catering for a fairly select type of visitor. There were good dress shops, smart restaurants, a three-screen cinema and even a small repertory theatre – enough distractions, in fact, to keep Jill happily occupied during winter months.

Now that it was summer, she was more than content to spend her time lying in the sun with a good book, and in her afternoon wanderings had come upon a secluded little beach, hemmed in by cliffs and accessible only by a tortuous path, that no one else seemed to know about and where, taking advantage of its privacy, she swam and sunbathed naked. Her body had taken on a golden, all-over tan, unsullied by strap marks, that Douglas, though slightly scandalized by its method of achievement, appreciated to the full.

On the Wednesday afternoon of that week, her beach bag slung over her shoulder, Jill set off along the cliffs, glorying in the depth of blue in the sea below her, the wheeling gulls, the breeze that ruffled her hair. Life, she thought, was good.

Her little beach lay waiting for her, its sand glinting almost white in the sunshine. She threaded her way down the cliff path, slipping and sliding a little on the loose stones, and, on reaching the bottom, stepped out of her sandals and made her way to her favourite place beside an outcrop of rock.

Having spread her towel, she slipped off her clothes and ran straight into the sea. The first shock of its coldness took her breath away, but her body soon acclimatized and she waded out until the water was deep enough for her to swim. For twenty minutes or so she lay on her back, splashing lazily, eyes shut against the glare of the sun, enjoying the slap of the water on her nakedness. Then she swam back into the shallows and, dripping water, returned to her belongings and lay down on the towel, allowing the heat of the sun to dry her.

She must have fallen into a light doze, because she was suddenly aware of something coming between her and the sun, and in the same moment a voice above her said, 'Mrs Irving, I presume?'

She sat up with a gasp, pulling her towel round her and knowing, even before she looked up, who her unwelcome visitor was.

'What are you doing here?' she demanded furiously. 'How dare you creep up on me like that? What are you, some kind of voyeur?'

'As far as I'm aware, this is a public beach,' Gary Payne replied calmly. 'The fact that you choose to take your clothes off doesn't automatically confer right of ownership.'

He looked, she saw with sinking heart, as though he intended to stay; he was wearing swimming trunks and an open shirt revealing a pale, hairless chest, and a towel hung over his arm.

'Anyway,' he continued, 'you have a good body. No need to be ashamed of it.'

Deciding to ignore that, she blurted out the first thing that came into her head. 'I thought you'd gone home.' As soon as she said it, she realized it was a mistake, and one he immediately seized on.

'Ah, so you missed me. How gratifying. Sadly, though, the likes of me can't afford your prices every day of the week.'

Jill struggled to hang on to what dignity remained to her. 'Since I was here first, I'd be grateful if you'd go and find somewhere else to swim.'

'But, like you, I prefer to be away from the madding crowd.'

She was in a dilemma, and he knew it. She couldn't move without revealing her nakedness, and she had no convenient swimsuit to slip on. Her beach bag held only her discarded underwear and a cotton dress – hardly suitable for sunbathing. If she wanted to avoid him – and she did – it seemed she must be the one to leave, which, she thought irritably, would involve dressing under the tent of the towel, like a twelve-year-old on a school outing.

Clutching her towel about her, she reached for the beach bag and began the awkward manoeuvre while her companion, unperturbed, removed his shirt, spread his own towel, and proceeded to lie down on it. At least he wasn't watching her – she could be thankful for that, even if, irrationally, his lack of interest piqued her.

When she'd completed the procedure, Jill shook the sand from her towel and, without glancing in his direction, started to walk back towards the cliff, her mind seething.

'See you around,' he called after her.

She did not reply.

He'd spoiled it for her, she thought furiously. Even when he *did* return home, she could never sunbathe nude again, never be sure someone else might not find his way down the path. Though any normal person, coming across her like that, would surely have retreated before she noticed him, saving them both embarrassment. That Gary Payne hadn't been in the least embarrassed did nothing for her own sang froid.

How had he found her, anyway? It wasn't a place you'd easily stumble across. Had he followed her? The thought raised goose bumps on her arms. How much longer, she wondered, tramping up the steep path, would she have to put up with his presence? Two weeks was the norm for a seaside holiday, but she'd no way of knowing how long he'd been around when she first saw him. Surely this week must be his last? She could only hope so.

Jill remained unsettled by the incident for the rest of the week, and every now and then her face flamed as she remembered Payne's assessing gaze and his unnerving comment: *You have a good body; no need to be ashamed of it.*

Odious man! On all three occasions that their paths had crossed, he'd succeeded – seemingly without trying – in putting her at a disadvantage. And though she'd never have admitted it, even to herself, she knew subconsciously that part of her resentment was due to his only too obvious imperviousness to her charms. After that initial flash of interest in the post office doorway, he'd gone out of his way to demonstrate his lack of it.

She determined to put him completely out of her mind, but at the next bridge afternoon, an innocent remark of Kitty's brought him back into focus.

'I envy your glorious tan, Jill,' she remarked as she dealt a hand. 'With my red hair, I have to keep out of the sun, or I look like a lobster.'

'Not only that,' Priscilla added, 'we've seen you in a variety of tops and dresses, but there's never a sign of a strap mark. How do you do it?'

Jill smiled. 'Ah, that's my secret!'

'Come on, now, you're among friends!'

'Isn't it obvious? I don't wear anything that would leave a mark. Anywhere.'

The three of them stared at her for a moment, the game forgotten. Then Angie said incredulously, 'Are you telling us you sunbathe in the nuddy?'

'Got it in one!'

'Good God, Jill! How do you manage that?'

Jill paused, her heartbeat quickening. Should she tell them? Perhaps if she made light of it, it would defuse the impact, put it all in perspective.

'I found a private little bay, where no one ever goes,' she said. 'At least, no one ever had, until last week.'

'You mean someone *saw* you?' Kitty's blue eyes opened wider. 'What happened?'

Jill moistened her lips, trying to keep her voice light. 'I must have been dozing, because I woke up to find someone standing over me.' No need to admit she knew him.

'A *man*?' Angie gasped.

'As you say, a man.'

'Good God, Jill, he could have raped you!'

'I suppose he could.' She made herself add, 'Actually, he didn't seem remotely interested.'

'He saw you naked, and wasn't interested? Was he gay?'

Jill laughed. 'Thanks for the vote of confidence, but I've no way of knowing, have I?'

'So what happened?'

'I asked him to leave, but he said it was a public beach, spread out his towel and lay down on it. So I hastily dressed and left him to it.'

'But Jill,' Priscilla said worriedly, 'that could have been really dangerous. There you were, closed off from everyone, lying naked on the beach. *Anyone* could have come down. You were damn lucky to get off so lightly. Didn't you realize what a risk you were taking?'

'No,' she answered honestly, 'I can't say I did.'

'Well, I hope you do now. For God's sake, don't do it again. Strap marks are infinitely preferable to rape, or worse.'

Jill gave a little shudder, closing her mind, as always, to thoughts of violence.

'Oh, rest assured,' she said. 'From now on, I'll be the soul of discretion.'

And, since there seemed no more to be said, they returned, a little reluctantly, to the game in hand.

The next time she saw Gary Payne was as she came out of a café in Sandbourne High Street. He was standing on the opposite pavement, staring across at her. She came to an abrupt halt, but her view of him was immediately obscured by a double-decker trundling down the road, and when it had passed, he'd disappeared.

With an effort, she pulled herself together. What in God's name was the matter with her? Why was she letting this man get to her? Because of that indefinable something in his eyes that she couldn't put a name to? That sense of something coiled inside him, waiting to spring? Yet he'd been civilized enough in their conversations – more so, in fact, than she had herself. And if – fanciful thought – he'd really been waiting to spring, she'd handed him the opportunity on a plate, and he'd not taken it. Possibly he was following some devious agenda of his own, but if so, she refused to pander to it.

She needed something to do, she thought urgently; something to take her mind off him, and glancing around, her eyes lit on the gilded window of Gina's Hair and Beauty Salon. Perfect! She went purposefully inside and requested a body massage, facial, and cut and blow-dry; and since she was a good customer, they fitted her in without an appointment. This, she thought with satisfaction, should make her feel a great deal better.

When she emerged a couple of hours later, she was more than satisfied with the result. Her bronzed skin was glowing, her hair, in a flattering, layered style, was soft about her face, and she'd taken the opportunity of having her lashes darkened, making them appear longer and thicker. It was time and money well spent, and she looked ten years younger. But now, if she wanted any lunch, she'd better hurry back.

Lunch at the hotel took the form of a self-service buffet, and usually only about half the guests returned for it. Jill pushed her way through the swing doors, glancing to her left through the restaurant door. Douglas wasn't at their corner table; perhaps he was waiting for her.

A man was standing at the reception desk, his back towards her, and something about his stance and the set of his shoulders struck a familiar chord. She stopped short, and was staring unbelievingly at him when he turned, meeting her gaze.

He smiled uncertainly. 'Hello, Jill,' he said.

Ten

'Patrick!' Jill said incredulously. And then, 'What the hell are you doing here?'

'Everything all right, darling?' Douglas had come out of the bar behind her.

'I – yes, I think so. It's just . . .'

The newcomer came forward, holding out his hand, which Douglas, after a moment's hesitation, took.

'I take it you're the proprietor?' he was saying easily. 'I'm Patrick Salter, an – old friend of your wife's.'

'Douglas –' – Jill's voice cut across his – 'allow me to introduce my ex-husband.'

Douglas stiffened and withdrew his hand. 'How do you do?' he said curtly.

Patrick smiled the smile that had made Jill fall for him. 'Look, I don't want to be the spectre at the feast. I'm down here for a few days, but if you'd prefer me to stay elsewhere, I'd quite understand.'

'Jill?' Douglas demanded, his eyes still on Salter. 'This is your call.'

She hesitated, knowing Douglas wanted her to dispatch him; but after the first shock, it was quite good to see Patrick again. Although the end of their marriage had been bitter, it was she who'd been at fault. Patrick had done no wrong, and if he wanted to offer an olive branch, she wouldn't throw it back in his face.

'Oh, I'm sure we can be civilized,' she said evenly. 'It would be too bad to deny him the best hotel in town.'

'That's kind of you, but are you sure it's all right with you, Mr Irving?'

'If my wife has no objection, you're free to stay,' Douglas confirmed briefly. 'Enjoy your visit.' He took Jill's arm. 'Ready for lunch, darling? I've been waiting for you.' And with a nod at Salter, he led her firmly into the restaurant.

'Husband number one or two?' he enquired as they moved along the buffet table.

Jill glanced at him, noting his set face. It might have been wiser to send Patrick packing, but she was curious to know why he'd come. It wasn't pure chance that he'd hit on this hotel; he'd shown no surprise at her appearance, obviously expecting her to be here.

'Number two,' she answered, ladling salad on to her plate.

'Did you know he was coming?'

She turned to him quickly. 'Douglas, of course not! We haven't been in touch since the divorce.'

'A bit odd, him showing up like this, don't you think? How'd he know where to find you?'

'I really have no idea. Why don't you ask him?'

'There's no need to take that tone, Jill,' Douglas snapped.

'Well, I object to being interrogated. I've not seen Patrick for three years, and I resent your insinuating I somehow inveigled him down here.'

'I insinuated nothing of the sort.'

Jill snatched up a roll and butter, added it to her plate, and carried it quickly to their table, her heart beating uncomfortably fast. The restaurant was less than half full, and no one had been near enough to overhear the exchange. She just hoped their body language hadn't given rise to comment.

Douglas, following her, set his plate on the table with a noticeable thump and sat down. He was flushed, and a nerve jumped at the corner of his eye. She felt suddenly sorry for him.

'We're not quarrelling, are we?' she asked.

He looked up, meeting her smiling gaze. 'No, of course not.'

'Patrick is history, Douglas. Don't they say third time lucky?'

She had managed to coax a smile out of him. 'Seriously, honey, I'm quite sure he hasn't any designs on me.'

Douglas shrugged, picking up his knife and fork. 'I still think it's odd, him arriving midweek, out of the blue. He's damn lucky we had that cancellation.' He paused, his fork halfway to his mouth. 'Has he married again?'

'I've no way of knowing, have I?' Jill answered patiently. 'Quite probably, I should think. He's a nice man; as I told you, I was the guilty party.'

'Why were you?'

Jill lifted her shoulders. 'As I also told you, I'm easily bored.'

'Are you bored of me?'

She looked up quickly, meeting his eyes and the sudden uncertainty in them.

'No, of course not.'

'I appreciate you've a lot of spare time on your hands. If you'd like more involvement in the running of the hotel, you only have to say.'

She shook her head. 'I was speaking of emotional boredom. I love my

life here. As you know, I'm bone idle and enjoy being a lady of leisure.'
She smiled. 'And if you're thinking the devil finds work for idle hands to
do, don't worry: he won't pull one over on me!'

He gave a brief laugh, and some of the tension left his shoulders. 'As
long as I don't have to chase Salter off the premises with a shotgun,'
he said.

Jill didn't see Patrick during the afternoon, and although she noticed him
across the room at dinner, they didn't exchange any further words.

It was the next morning, as she walked into town to change her library
book, that he fell into step beside her.

'I hope you're not averse to a bit of company,' he said.

'Why are you here, Patrick?'

'I felt in need of some sea air.'

'You knew I was here, didn't you? How did you find me?'

'Don't worry, I didn't set a private detective on you. I bumped into
Claire Denver at a drinks party, and she mentioned receiving a Christmas
card. Said you seemed to have gone into the hotel business.'

Douglas's card, sent to business colleagues and regular guests, had
boasted a photograph of the hotel, and, having run out of her own, Jill
had used half a dozen of them herself. Obviously one had gone to Claire
and Martin.

'There's no need to ask how you are,' Patrick continued. 'You look
absolutely stunning.'

'How about you? Have you married again?'

He shook his head. 'I have a partner, as they say nowadays, but we haven't
tied the knot. Come to that, I seem to remember you swearing when we
parted that you'd never do it again.'

'I didn't intend to,' Jill admitted, 'but Douglas's position requires
unimpeachable morals.'

Patrick was a good companion, she thought, pleasant and easy to talk
to; he was also attracting interested glances from the women they passed,
which she found gratifying.

'Are you still living in the house?' she asked him.

'No, I didn't fancy it, after you'd gone. Too many memories.'

She said quietly, 'I treated you badly, didn't I?'

'Appallingly.' His smile took the sting out of the word. 'However, I've
got over it, and Lucy and I are happy together.'

'I'm glad.'

She stopped as they reached the entrance to the library, preparatory
to their parting, but he nodded her ahead of him and followed her in,

contentedly moving along the shelves and lifting out the occasional book as she made her own choice; and when they emerged into the sunshine, said casually,

'Fancy a coffee?'

Assuming he'd then tell her the reason for his coming, she agreed, leading him not to her favourite café, where her friends would be gathering, but to one farther along the street. And sitting opposite him at the small table, she had her first really good look at him.

There were perhaps a few more lines round his eyes, but his chin was as firm and his eyes as blue as she remembered, and the lock of hair still fell over his forehead as it had always done. It surprised and slightly disconcerted her that she was still strongly attracted to him.

'Latte?' he queried, and she nodded with a smile.

'So why isn't "Lucy" with you?' she asked, as the waitress moved away.

'Ah.' He smiled crookedly. 'I told her I was coming away on business.'

'She doesn't know you're seeing me.' It wasn't a question, though he answered it.

'Obviously not.'

'Why *are* you seeing me, Patrick?'

He began toying with the cutlery on the table, no longer meeting her eyes. 'I feel pretty rotten about this, Jill. In fact, I wish to hell I hadn't had to come. It's – by way of being a last resort.'

'Thanks very much.'

'Seriously. I really hate doing this. If there'd been any other way . . .'

She leaned back in her chair, puzzled by his embarrassment. Beads of sweat had sprung up on his hairline. Whatever he was about to say, there was no doubt that it wasn't easy for him.

Their coffee arrived, but neither of them made any move to drink it.

'The fact is,' he blurted out, 'I'm in a pretty parlous state. Financially speaking.'

'I see.' So that was it. She was more disappointed than she'd any right to be.

He looked up, pleading in his eyes. 'You remember at the time you left that we were starting to expand the business?'

Patrick and his partner owned a small publishing house, printing limited runs of high quality coffee-table books.

She nodded, drawing the glass of latte towards her and stirring it with the long spoon.

'Well, we've had to tighten our belts considerably of late, and the plain truth is that we've run into debt. Bad debt. The stuff we produce is for a limited market, and people aren't spending as much on luxury goods. Added to which, the bank's foreclosing on our loan, and quite frankly we don't know where to turn.'

'So you thought of the rich bitch,' she said baldly. 'Wasn't that what you called me?'

'Oh, Jill, please don't. We both said some unforgivable things at the end. Look, if you were prepared even to consider it, I must stress it would be on a sound commercial basis, with the going rate of interest, and so on. We should be able to pay back the full amount within two to three years, all being well.'

'And what would that full amount be?'

He took a deep breath. 'About twenty thousand?'

'You don't do things by half, do you?'

'I know it's the hell of a nerve even asking you, but I really am desperate and I know you enjoy speculating. You always have.'

'And exactly why should I even *consider* lending you a brass farthing?'

He smiled ruefully, and something inside her gave a little tug, making her catch her breath.

'Because it would give you a hold over me?' he suggested.

She drank some latte, aware of his tension. 'I take it you're not expecting an immediate answer?'

'At least it's not an outright no!'

'Not an outright one, though frankly I can't see what's in it for me. I haven't set myself up as a charity.'

He winced. 'That's a bit harsh.'

'Is it?' She stared thoughtfully down into her glass. 'Does your girlfriend know of your money problems?'

'That things are a bit tight, that's all.'

'Can't she help?'

He shook his head. 'She doesn't have that kind of money.'

'But, as the ad says, you know a girl who has.'

He didn't reply.

'How long are you down for?'

'Till Friday. Just today and tomorrow, really.'

'Well, I'll think about it, and give you an answer before you leave.'

'Thank you,' he said humbly.

They parted outside the café. 'I suppose you'll want to discuss this with your husband,' Patrick said.

Jill looked surprised. 'Why should you suppose that? As you know, it's my money – family money, that's accumulated through what you call my speculation – and I spend it as I choose.'

'Of course,' he said quietly, 'Silly of me. Jill, I really am terribly sorry to have sprung this on you. I know I've no earthly right to appeal to you, but, well . . .'

'You didn't know where to turn,' she finished for him, and he smiled.

'Exactly. Now I'll leave you to do whatever you have to do, and take a look round this town of yours. It seems a charming little place.'

'Oh, it is, and quite historical. Go to the Tourist Board — they'll tell you what to look out for.'

'I'll do that. Thanks. And thanks again for even entertaining the idea of helping out.'

Jill had known from the first that she'd lend him the money, knew also that one reason for doing so was to keep in contact. Which was odd, she thought, as she continued her shopping; she'd not given Patrick a thought since their divorce, but having seen him, she was reluctant to lose touch again. Douglas and Lucy notwithstanding, there was still a spark between them, and she knew he was as aware of it as she was.

She spent the afternoon in a secluded part of the grounds with her new library book, suitably garbed in a sundress, in case any of the guests wandered by. At five o'clock, since the pool was deserted, she stripped to her swimsuit and passed an energetic twenty minutes swimming strongly backwards and forwards, relishing the cold water on her sun-warmed body.

Wrapped in a towel, she used the staff entrance to re-enter the hotel, to avoid meeting guests on her way upstairs. Instead, along the corridor from the kitchens, she came face to face with Douglas.

'So there you are!' he exclaimed. 'Where have you been?'

Jill looked at him in surprise. He'd never before questioned her whereabouts.

'In the pool. Isn't it obvious?'

'Before that.'

'Reading in the garden.'

'I didn't see you.'

'Why should you have done?'

'I wondered where you were, that's all.'

What he meant, Jill knew, was that he wondered if she was with Patrick, and since she had been that morning, she felt it wiser not to pursue the subject.

'Did you want me for anything in particular?' she asked innocently.

'No, not really. The Beaumont wedding reception has been confirmed, but that's not really your province.'

'Good for business, though. Well done.' She bent forward and kissed him quickly on the mouth, feeling his instant response.

'You'd better go and get some clothes on, Mrs Irving, or I shan't be responsible for the consequences.'

'Yes, sir,' she said, and, knowing she'd defused his anxiety, at least for the moment, she continued on her way.

Patrick was in the bar when she distributed menus that evening, but she treated him the same as the other guests, and he didn't attempt to prolong the contact. She knew he was watching her as she moved around, aware that her brown arms and shoulders were displayed to maximum advantage in the primrose sheath dress she wore.

Douglas was still slightly guarded over dinner, watching her more closely than usual, and she was careful not to glance in Patrick's direction. She kept up a stream of inconsequential chat, but it was an effort, and by the end of the meal she needed to escape from both her husband's scrutiny and the possibility of bumping into Patrick, which would only aggravate it.

On impulse, therefore, she slipped out of the front entrance and crossed the road to the promenade. The families had returned long since to hotel or boarding house, and the beach was empty except for the odd figure or couple, some walking dogs. The tide was quite a long way out, and the darker sand was studded with shining pools reflecting the rosy tint of the sky.

Jill walked slowly along until she came to a set of steps, which she went down, stooping to remove her high-heeled shoes. The sand felt cool between her toes, and she started to move down towards the far line of the water, swinging her sandals by their straps. There was a slight breeze off the sea which lifted her hair and caressed her bare shoulders.

A wet collie dog came bounding up to her, spraying water from its coat, its breathless owner hot on its heels.

'I'm so sorry! He didn't splash your dress, did he?'

'Don't worry, it can go in the machine.'

'I'm sorry – he just took off when I wasn't expecting it.'

Then she was alone again. The sand beneath her was now dark and ribbed by the retreating waves, and the ridges made uncomfortable walking. She was in introspective mood, occasioned by the past and present being brought together in the form of Patrick. And what of Paul, her first husband? If she saw him again, would she want to go to bed with him, too?

Lifting her dress slightly, she stepped into one of the shallow pools, still warm after the day's sunshine, and the sand, turned to mud by the water, squelched up between her toes. Some minute sea creature, stranded by the outgoing tide, swam in small circles round her feet. If she had a bucket, Jill thought, she would have caught it and carried it to the safety of the sea.

She stepped out of the pool and continued her walk until she reached the sea itself, pulsating slowly, retreating steadily. It was almost dark now. She turned and looked back the way she had come, surprised at the distance separating her from the lights of the hotel. In front of it, leaning on the promenade rail, she could just make out a solitary figure looking seawards. Could he see her, whoever he was? Was it Douglas, looking for her again, or Patrick? Or no one to do with her at all?

Suddenly conscious that she was now alone in the great, empty expanse, she started to walk back more quickly, keeping her eyes on the lights along the promenade. What, if anything, had she gained from her solitude? Only the smell of the sea and the coolness of the sand and, perhaps, the sense that she was her own person, and beholden to no one. Which was the most anyone could ask.

That night, Douglas's lovemaking was rough and demanding, and Jill, while she gladly responded, recognized that it was also proprietary. After her meditations on the beach, she smiled to herself at the irony of it.

When it was over and he'd fallen asleep, she lay with the sweat cooling on her body, staring out at the star-speckled sky. Was Patrick awake, in his room on the floor below? Was he too anxious, awaiting her decision, to allow him to relax? Perhaps it was cruel of her, keeping him in suspense. Tomorrow, she must find some way of handing over the cheque without anyone noticing. Living in the public gaze as she did, that might not be easy.

The following morning, therefore, the cheque in her handbag, she set out again to walk into town, expecting him to catch her up as he had the previous day. But he did not. She'd seen him at breakfast, but he'd left the restaurant while she was still eating, and she hadn't seen him since. Suppose he'd gone off somewhere for the day, somewhere recommended by the Tourist Board?

Well, she thought irritably, more fool him! How did he expect to learn her answer if he wasn't there? She loitered about the shops, even sat for a while on one of the promenade seats, so as to be clearly visible if he came looking for her. But he didn't, and after a while, she gave up and returned to the hotel.

Nor was he in for lunch, and Jill began to feel anxious. The morning would have been the best time to meet unobserved; now it seemed he'd be out all afternoon, too, and it would be almost impossible to meet privately in the evening. And tomorrow he was going home.

At four o'clock, seeing opportunities for a personal handover rapidly decreasing, she decided to leave the cheque in his room. It would save him the embarrassment of thanking her – he could phone or write when he got home – and also save her the anxiety of Douglas coming upon them in mid-transaction, which would certainly require explanation, whether or not it was her own money she was parting with. This afternoon, though, Douglas had gone to see his accountant.

She made her way to the housekeeper's room, sure it would be empty at this time of day, and lifted the master key off its hook. She'd already checked that Patrick was in room 10, on the first floor.

It was a hot, cloudless afternoon, and everyone was out enjoying it. Jill didn't see a soul as she went up the wide staircase and along the corridor. The master key turned smoothly in the lock and the door swung open. She stepped quickly inside, closed it behind her, and slipped the key in her pocket.

The room was much the same as all the others in the hotel – television, sofa, en suite. But there were personal touches. Patrick's old leather travelling clock was on the bedside table, and Jill couldn't resist picking up, seeing with a lurch of the heart the red stain on one corner where she'd upset a bottle of nail polish.

On the dressing table was the silver-backed brush that had been his father's, and which Patrick took with him everywhere. Her fingers traced the scrolled monogram – ERS – Edward Roger Salter. She thought briefly of her ex-father-in-law, a small man with a military moustache, who had died of a heart attack the year after their wedding. Patrick's belongings, she saw with a tinge of regret, were as they'd always been, unaltered by her absence, even if she'd left her mark on them.

She was still at the dressing table, the brush in her hand, when, to her horror, she heard a key turn in the lock, the door opened, and Patrick himself stood staring at her.

She felt herself flush scarlet. 'I – was admiring your father's brush,' she said foolishly, hastily replacing it.

He came slowly into the room, pushing the door closed. 'What are you doing here?'

'Well, not looking for something to pinch,' she snapped, furious at being put in the wrong.

'I wasn't suggesting—'

'Time's running out, isn't it? I looked for you this morning, but you were nowhere to be seen, and you didn't come back for lunch. There's no way we could have talked privately this evening, so I thought the best thing was to leave the cheque here.'

She opened her bag, took out the envelope, and held it out to him.

'You mean – you will? You'll lend us the money? Oh, Jill!'

He came forward quickly and caught her in a hug of gratitude, realizing almost at once that it had been a mistake. They drew slightly apart, gazing into each other's faces.

'Oh, Patrick!' Jill said on an indrawn breath. Then her mouth closed on his, and she felt rather than heard his protesting, 'No!' But the word was swallowed as he pulled her against him, kissing her as though his life depended on it. Still clinging to each other, they moved towards the bed, Jill, the hotelier's wife, reaching behind her to pull the quilted bedspread aside.

'Look, we really can't do this!' Patrick gasped. 'I can't make love to you under your husband's roof!'

'I think you'll find you can,' she said.

That night, she dreamed she was back in Patrick's bed, making passionate love to him. Then he reached up and switched on the light, and the face gazing down on her belonged not to him but to Gary Payne.

Eleven

By the time Jill went down to breakfast the next morning, Patrick had already left, and though she knew it was for the best, she regretted that the spark so recently reignited between them had had, so soon, to be extinguished.

His visit had put Gary Payne out of her mind, and as she left the hotel, she was unprepared for the sight of him, reading a newspaper on one of the promenade benches. Her feverish dream, mercifully forgotten, flooded back, bringing a shudder of revulsion. Why couldn't the blasted man go home? she thought irritably. And an appalling thought struck her: suppose he wasn't a visitor after all; suppose he actually *lived* here?

Unable to bear the suspense, she half ran to where he was sitting, and, when he looked up, blurted out, 'You don't live here, do you?'

He smiled, removing his sunglasses. 'Good morning, Mrs Irving,' he said.

'Good morning,' she stammered, already furious with herself, and added foolishly, 'It's just that most people only stay two weeks.'

'Ah, but I'm not most people.' His expression as he looked her slowly up and down bordered on insolence, and she wondered hotly if he was remembering her without her clothes. 'Since you're so interested, though,' he continued after a pause, 'the answer is that I'm a schoolteacher, and we have long summer holidays.'

'A schoolteacher?' she repeated doubtfully. He didn't look in the least academic.

'PE and sport,' he amplified, as though reading her mind. 'But don't fret, I'm not here for the whole six weeks.'

'It's of no interest to me how long you stay,' she retorted, stung as always by his manner.

'You could have fooled me,' he shrugged, returning to his paper.

She hesitated, searching for the most dignified means of retreat, and, looking down at him, realized with a sense of surprise that some women might find him attractive. Apart from his colouring, which didn't appeal to her, his features were good: his nose long and straight, his chin square with a dimple in it, and his eyes a very dark grey – surprising, with his complexion – like black pebbles in the pallor of his face. If he'd spent his holiday sunbathing, there was little to show for it.

Impervious to her presence, he turned the page of his paper, and she felt her temper rise. It was that lack of interest that needled her, making her want to force herself to his notice. That, and the expression at the back of his eyes which, despite herself, intrigued her. Again she remembered the dream, and again shuddered, though not, this time, with the same measure of distaste. Weren't dreams said to reveal hidden longings?

God, no! she thought, recoiling. Her involuntary movement caught his attention, and he looked up with an exaggerated sigh.

'If you're staying, would you mind sitting down?' he said laconically. 'You're blocking the sun.'

'I'm *not* staying!' she replied sharply, and, turning on her heel, walked quickly on towards the town.

Why, she wondered furiously, was she continually making such an idiot of herself in front of this man – she, who had always had the upper hand in her dealings with the opposite sex? How was it that he continually managed to wrong-foot her? And a dangerous little worm stirred in her mind, a resolve to *make* him interested, just to prove she could. After which, her goal attained, she could discard him and get on with her life, while he, thank God, would finally go home.

And though, turning into the bakery, she impatiently dismissed the thought, it remained in her subconscious and slowly, insidiously, began to grow.

It was only when Jill returned to the hotel and found Dilys, Douglas's secretary, busy with accounts, that she remembered it was Friday, and several of their guests would be leaving the next day. So, possibly, might Gary Payne; it was three weeks since she'd first seen him.

She told herself that, were that the case, she'd be well rid of him, but part of her regretted a missed opportunity, a challenge that, the more she thought about it, became increasingly attractive. Contentedly faithful since her marriage, her session with Patrick had reawakened for her the delights of illicit sex, its excitement and sense of danger, and the unlikeliness of her latest prospect merely added to it. He was also, at a guess, five or six years younger than she was, a novelty in itself; her previous lovers had all been older.

Deliberately, therefore, she returned that afternoon to her private beach for the first time since he'd come upon her, and, by way of tempting fate, stripped before lying down to sunbathe. For three hours she remained there, swimming, reading, dozing, but no one came down the cliff path to join her, and it was with a sense of disappointment that she eventually dressed and made her way home.

*   *   *

For the next day or two she kept watch for him – on the benches along the front, in the town, in the bar before dinner – but there was no sign of him, and she concluded he must have returned home at the weekend. Which, she reminded herself briskly, was what, until the other day, she'd been anticipating with mounting impatience.

Then something happened that wiped him completely from her mind. As she came downstairs prior to menu duty, Dilys called to her through the open office door.

'Jill, there's an email for you.'

Jill frowned and went to join her. 'For me? Are you sure?'

She had her own email address, and never used the hotel one.

'Well, it says For the Attention of Jill Irving,' Dilys replied. 'In fact, that's all it says, but there's an attachment.'

'Have you opened it?'

'No; I was going to, then I thought it might be personal. Look, I've finished for the day. I'll leave you to read it in peace, and come back in a few minutes to shut everything down. OK?'

Jill, still puzzled, nodded, and, sliding on to the vacated chair, clicked on the attachment and again, impatiently, to confirm that she wanted to open it. Which was the point at which the nightmare began, as what appeared to be the front page of a newspaper materialized in front of her, a provincial newspaper, dated July 1985.

Time stopped, gripping her in a horror of disbelief as, of their own volition, her eyes moved down the column, and a numb coldness closed over her. Then the screen blurred, and, realizing she was about to faint, she used the last of her strength to click on Delete. Only just in time; as the picture disappeared, she slid off the chair to lie in a crumpled little heap on the floor.

Dilys, returning to shut down the computer, found her minutes later, and Jill slowly resurfaced to find Douglas supporting her head and gently slapping her face.

'She's coming round, thank God. Jill – are you all right, honey? Whatever happened?'

He snapped his fingers at Dilys, indicating the glass of water she was holding, and held it to his wife's lips. She turned her head away but he persisted, and she perforce took a few sips.

'She was fine when I left her,' Dilys was saying, anxiously watching his ministrations.

'I can't think why she was here in the first place,' Douglas muttered testily. 'She's supposed to be in the bar, handing out menus.'

'There was an email for her.'

He looked up, frowning. 'On this computer? Then it must have been hotel business. Why—?'

'I don't know what it was; there was no message, just an attachment.'

'Which was?'

'I don't know,' Dilys said again. 'I didn't open it.'

They both glanced at the blank screen, now on stand-by. Dilys clicked to reactivate it, but the only emails listed were those she'd already dealt with.

'She must have deleted it,' she said.

Jill stirred in Douglas's arms and gave a little moan, and they both turned back to her.

'Help me to get her up on the chair,' Douglas instructed, and they achieved it between them. Jill put a hand out to steady herself, the other going to her bowed head.

'How do you feel, love?'

'I'm all right. It was – the heat. It suddenly came over me, I don't know why.'

Douglas and Dilys exchanged a puzzled glance. Jill had never complained of the heat before; on the contrary, she frequently declared that the hotter it was, the better, sunbathing at every opportunity, even at midday.

As though aware her reply lacked conviction, she added, 'And it's the time of the month, which didn't help.'

'Nothing to do with that email, then?'

A tremor crossed her face. 'I wasn't prepared for it, I admit. It was spam, but of a particularly obscene variety.'

Dilys looked stricken. 'I'm so sorry, I should have opened it myself.'

'What the hell is the point of all these anti-spam devices?' Douglas demanded. He studied his wife's face. She was pale beneath the tan, and he wasn't satisfied that she'd completely recovered. 'Would you like to go and lie down for a while? Rosie can do the menu stint.'

Jill hesitated, aware that she still felt shaky. 'That might be best,' she admitted. 'Just for a few minutes. I'll be down for dinner.'

'See how you feel. We can always send something up on a tray.'

His arm round her, he escorted her to the lift and up to their room. The bedspread had already been turned down, and he settled her on top of the duvet, pulling the pillow down to support her head.

'You're sure you don't need the doctor?'

'Absolutely. Give me a few minutes, and I'll be fine.'

'Right, then I'd better get back downstairs. Ring if you need anything, won't you?'

She nodded, forced a smile, and he left the room, closing the door softly as though she were an invalid. As soon as she was alone, she slipped off the bed and went to the dressing table, sitting on the stool and staring at herself in the mirror.

It didn't happen, she thought. It couldn't have done; it just wasn't possible. She looked about her, seeking reassurance in the familiar surroundings. This room, this hotel, was the here and now, and she was safe in it. The past couldn't touch her. Could it?

She spread her hands on the cold glass, fighting down incipient panic. She'd been so careful. There was nothing, absolutely nothing, that could link her to that other self. But though she wanted more than anything to expunge the whole episode from her memory, it was necessary, just once, to think back to what she'd seen.

In all conscience, it had been little enough before darkness swiftly overtook her, but it was enough to know that the paper was genuine, and not some malicious mock-up. Thank God she'd had the presence of mind to delete it. All the same, it would have been helpful, perhaps, to have studied it more closely – not the content, God help her, but the sender's name and address. Because she needed, quite desperately needed, to know his identity, and whether he was in any position to harm her.

Could she risk asking Dilys if she'd registered it? Would she think it odd Jill should want to know? She'd hoped, of course, to deflect their interest by blaming the heat and the lie about her period, but doubted if either had convinced them.

Oh God, she'd really thought all this was behind her! How, with three name-changes, had they managed to track her down? And *why*, after all this time?

She drew a deep breath. She would not, repeat not, let this destroy her. If the chance rose in the next day or so to question Dilys, she would take it. Otherwise, she'd confine the whole thing to oblivion. It was the only way to survive.

As it happened, Dilys was of little help. The sender's name and address had been something cryptic, she thought, like 'guesswho', and then some numbers. There'd be no way to identify him.

Guess who? Jill thought with a shudder.

'So there's no way to block future messages?'

Dilys shrugged. 'As Douglas said, we should be protected against this sort of thing, but there's always one or two that get through. I'm so sorry I didn't intercept it, Jill. I'd just try to forget it, if I were you.'

'Oh, I will,' Jill assured her.

But though during the day she was able to clamp down on the memory, her subconscious was not so easily deflected, and the nights became a minefield during which she woke repeatedly, drenched in sweat, with the trailing strands of nightmare still clinging to her.

What she needed, she told herself, was something that would occupy her mind so fully that there'd be no room for these intrusive fears. And the perfect antidote was Gary Payne.

It was pure chance that she saw him, ironically enough through the window of the café she'd visited with Patrick. He was seated just the other side of the glass, reading the inevitable newspaper. Without stopping to consider her action, she went in and sat down opposite him.

He lowered his paper and looked across at her. 'Are you going to order me off the premises?'

She shook her head with a smile. 'It's not within my jurisdiction.'

'Nor, I believe, are the beach or the promenade, but it didn't stop you then.'

'I didn't actually—' she began, but he interrupted her.

'Look, my presence obviously offends you, but most of the times we've met haven't been at my instigation. All right, I probably shouldn't have joined you on the beach when you were in the altogether; but it was a chance you took, and I wasn't actually trespassing.'

'I know,' she said, discomfited as always by those dark eyes. 'Actually, I've come to apologize. As a hotelier, it's my business to make visitors to Sandbourne welcome, whether or not they're staying with us. I rather doubt that came across with you.'

He lifted an eyebrow. 'An understatement, I'd say.'

'Then I'm sorry. Let me belatedly make amends.' She glanced round, hoping to order a coffee – since her companion had made no move to do so – but couldn't catch anyone's eye.

Giving up the attempt, she turned back to him. 'Where are you staying, Mr Payne?'

'You know my name.'

A slip there. 'I always check the table reservations,' she replied, less than truthfully. 'So, are you at another hotel, self-catering, or what?'

He was silent for a moment, then said flatly, 'I'm at Sunnyside. It's a boarding house on the front.'

'I'm aware of that. And how do you find it?'

He lifted a shoulder. 'It suits my needs.'

He wasn't helping her, she reflected ruefully; in fact, he was very heavy going. Then an idea came, and with it, a quickened heartbeat. 'Have you been to the Fisherman's Catch, farther along the coast?'

He shook his head, eyeing her curiously.

'You should try it. Basically, it's a fairly unpretentious little pub, but its seafood is out of this world. People travel miles to eat there.'

'I'll bear it in mind,' he said, 'but my time here's running out. You'll be glad to know I leave at the end of the week.'

'Then let me take you there as my guest,' she said quickly, before she could change her mind. 'To make up for my somewhat cavalier treatment of you.'

And on the way home, she thought, blood thundering in her ears, there'd be plenty of opportunity to park overlooking the sea, where she'd entice him into making love to her. That should banish all thought of—

He was staring at her, a strange expression in his eyes, and she had the absurd notion that he'd read her mind.

'Let me get this clear,' he said at last. 'Are you actually inviting me to dinner?'

She nodded. 'I want you to remember Sandbourne as a friendly place.'

Her mouth was dry as she waited for his answer.

'In that case,' he said, 'I accept your invitation.'

Twelve

Jill returned to the hotel with a considerably lighter heart than when she'd left it. Excited by the prospect, she would have preferred their date to be for that evening or the following one, but Payne had previous engagements which he'd obviously no intention of cancelling. So it was fixed for Friday, his last night: which meant any lovemaking that took place would have no chance of repetition. A pity, but then once would be sufficient for her purpose.

She'd suggested they use her car, thereby both giving her the chance to select a suitable spot on the way back, and eliminating any restriction on his drinking, which, she hoped, would make him more susceptible to her overtures.

A week ago, she'd have treated the idea of seducing Payne with ridicule, but ever since her dream lover had metamorphosed from Patrick into his likeness, she'd felt a growing interest that had been fuelled by his continued lack of it. Well, she thought defiantly, she'd show him what he'd been missing.

It was at lunchtime the following day that the trouble started. Rain had set in during the morning, with the result that more guests than usual had returned for lunch, together with several non-residents, opting for a pleasant way to pass an hour or two.

When Jill looked into the office, Douglas was on the phone, and signalled that she should go to the restaurant ahead of him; where he joined her five minutes later, looking very pleased with himself.

'That was the secretary of the Conservative Association on the phone, in quite a flap. Our revered MP is tearing himself away from his Italian villa to visit his constituency, along with an Italian delegation anxious to twin their town with Sandbourne. All last minute, and he's asked her to book a table for ten for tomorrow night, to include the Mayor and various councillors. She was practically on her knees, begging me to fit them in.'

'And can we? Surely we're fully booked?'

'Damn right we can, even if it means moving a table or two into the Garden Room to make more room for them. It's quite an honour, though, isn't it? We're not the only four-star hotel in town.'

'It's a feather in our cap, certainly. I'm sure we can rely on Chef to rise to the occasion.'

'And I've invited them to a champagne reception beforehand. No harm in pressing our advantage. So wear your most glamorous outfit, my love.'

Jill, her mind on Payne, had been only half-listening, and looked up, startled, as his words sank in.

'Tomorrow, did you say? Oh Douglas, I'm sorry! I shan't be here.'

He put down his fork and stared at her. 'What do you mean, you won't be here? You'd bloody well better be!'

'Really; I'm going out for dinner with – a group of friends.'

'Then cancel it,' he said briskly. 'You can do that anytime.'

'As it happens, I can't. It's Priscilla's fortieth, and I promised I'd be there.'

'Jill, I don't think I made myself clear. This is a fantastic opportunity for us. If the twinning goes ahead – and there's no reason why it shouldn't – we'll be quids in from the word go. The Eye-ties will stay here during negotiations, and we'll get plenty of publicity.'

'I know, and I'm really sorry, but this has been booked for weeks.'

'You've never mentioned it.'

'I thought I had. Anyway, I won't be missed.'

'*I'd* miss you,' he said. 'Seriously, this is not negotiable. I need a hostess.'

'Couldn't they come on Saturday?'

He stared at her. 'I don't believe I'm hearing this. You want our MP and his guests to alter their arrangements to suit your convenience?'

His voice had risen, and heads were turning at nearby tables.

Jill leaned forward, hoping that by speaking quietly, he'd moderate his own tone. 'Douglas, please! It's all most unfortunate, and if I'd had more notice—'

His face was stony, and she went on quickly, 'What time are they coming? Perhaps I could look in before I go? To meet them, at least?'

'And then excuse yourself, on the grounds that you've something better to do?'

'I'm trying to be helpful,' she said.

'But you're not, are you?' His voice was rising again, and conversation at the nearby tables had fallen silent. 'On the contrary, you're being totally selfish, as usual. All you ever think of is your own pleasure. God knows, I don't ask much of you, but this is important to me – to us, dammit! I want you there, Jill. End of.'

Her face was burning. 'Thank you for expressing your opinion of me so publicly.'

'It needed to be said. I've put up with a lot—'

Abruptly, she pushed her chair back and stood up, flinging her napkin on to her plate of scampi. Face flaming and looking neither to right nor left, she stalked out of the restaurant.

He caught up with her in the foyer, seizing her arm in a vice-like grip and steering her into the deserted office.

'How *dare* you show me up like that?' he demanded furiously.

'You showed yourself up, with no help from me.'

'God, I can't believe you're behaving like this!'

'All because I won't go to your poxy champagne reception? It's not as though either of us will be present at the dinner, so what the hell is all the fuss about? You expect me to renege on a long-standing engagement for the sake of twenty minutes' chat with a bunch of Italians?'

His face was congested with fury. For a second longer they confronted each other, both breathing quickly. Then his hand went stingingly across her face. She gasped, her own hand going up to it. Then she turned and ran out of the room and up the two flights of stairs, turning the key in the bedroom door as she slammed it behind her, and leaning, panting, against it.

Almost immediately, the handle rattled as he tried to come in.

'Jill, open the door at once!'

She did not reply.

'Look, I'm – I'm sorry. I didn't mean to do that, but you goaded me too far.'

'I might have known it was my fault,' she said quietly. She moved away to the mirror and gazed at the scarlet weal across her cheek and the small cut caused by his ring.

'Jill, please!'

'Go away, Douglas,' she said.

And after a minute, he did.

Jill washed her face in cold water, applied fresh make-up to mask the stinging redness, and went downstairs. There was no one about. Douglas, to her relief, was nowhere to be seen, and the guests were still in the restaurant, the topic of their conversations not difficult to guess. She pushed her way through the swing doors and walked quickly down the path. The rain had stopped at last, but the pavements underfoot were wet, and heavy clouds still hung over the sea. They weren't finished with it yet.

Once clear of the hotel, she took out her mobile and rang Priscilla.

'Jill, hello!' She sounded surprised; they'd had coffee together that morning.

'Are you doing anything at the moment?'

'Finishing lunch. Otherwise, nothing.'

'Could I come round?'

'Of course. Is something wrong?'

'You could say so. Ten minutes be OK?'

'Right. See you then.'

Priscilla was a good choice, Jill reflected, walking on towards the town. Angie and Kitty both had husbands, in whom they might confide; Priscilla was divorced, and could be counted on to keep her own – and anyone else's – counsel.

She lived in an attractive house near the town centre. Jill had been there many times to play bridge, and turned into the gate with a feeling of thankfulness. Priscilla had the door open before she reached it.

'Jill!' she exclaimed, her welcoming smile fading. 'Whatever's happened to your face?'

Jill stepped into the hall. 'It was the immovable object that met the irresistible force,' she said grimly.

Priscilla hesitated, and when she didn't go on, suggested tentatively, 'Coffee?'

'Thanks, yes, I'd love some.' She'd had virtually no lunch, but the thought of food was anathema to her. Coffee, on the other hand, might help to steady her. She was still incandescently angry at what she saw as her husband's unreasonableness and his unforgivable humiliation of her in front of their guests. And the slap had shaken her more than she'd have expected.

Priscilla returned and set down the coffee tray. 'Now,' she said. 'Tell me what's happened? You were fine this morning.'

'Douglas and I have just had a regrettably public row.'

'Oh dear.'

'He told me in no uncertain terms what he thought of me, and rounded it off, as you can see, by slapping my face.'

'So that's . . .' Priscilla regarded her with horror. 'Was that in public, too?'

'No, thankfully. But it – rather shattered me.' Her voice rocked, and Priscilla quickly poured the coffee and handed her a cup.

'I bet it did.' Priscilla paused. 'Do you want to tell me what the row was about, or shouldn't I ask?'

Jill took a quick sip of coffee, burning her tongue in the process. 'He wants me to attend some stupid reception tomorrow evening – the local

MP and his cronies – and I can't, because I'm going out. He expected me to cancel it, and when I refused to do so, blew his top.'

Priscilla said carefully, 'This reception – is it important?'

'Douglas seems to think so.'

'And he wants you with him?'

Jill glared at her. 'Don't you dare take his side!'

'I'm not, honestly. But – what are you doing, that you can't cancel?'

A smile tugged the corner of Jill's mouth. 'Attending your fortieth celebrations.'

Priscilla's eyebrows rose. 'Well, thanks for the compliment, but you're a bit late; they took place two years ago.' She paused. 'And what are you *really* doing?'

'Having dinner with a man. At the Fisherman's Catch.'

Priscilla stared at her. 'You dark horse! The first I've heard of this!'

'There's not much to hear.'

'This the first date?'

'And the last. And, I have to admit, at my instigation.'

'So who is he?'

'No one you know.' Jill hesitated. 'Actually, he's the one who came upon me sunbathing.'

'Ah! Not gay after all! I did wonder if there was more to that than you told us.'

'There wasn't. Honestly.'

'But you've obviously seen him again.'

Jill sighed. 'It's too complicated to explain.'

'But important enough to risk Douglas's wrath?'

'Well, of course, I wasn't expecting that. The MP thing only came up this morning, and he told me over lunch.'

'But couldn't you postpone your date, to keep the peace? Fix another day?'

Jill shook her head. 'He's going home on Saturday.'

'He's a visitor, then? Staying at your hotel?'

'No, one of the boarding houses. Look, Pris, I appreciate this probably doesn't make sense to you, and I really can't go into it all. Sufficient to say I desperately need to see him before he goes, in order to – prove something to myself. It's really important.'

'If you say so,' Priscilla said doubtfully. 'So – what do you want me to do?'

'Give me a bed for the night.'

'Oh, now look—'

'How can I go back there and face everyone, when they heard what he called me?'

Priscilla leaned forward. 'Jill, love, listen to me. Of course you're welcome to stay if that's what you really want, but honestly this isn't the way to play it. The longer you put off going back, the harder it will be.'

'So how do you suggest I play it?' Jill demanded sullenly. 'Meekly trot back, and let him slap me again?'

'Didn't he apologize?'

She nodded reluctantly. 'He followed me upstairs. I'd locked the door, but he called through it that he was sorry.'

'Well, in my opinion, your most dignified approach would be to brazen it out. Behave as though lunchtime never happened.'

'But he'll bring up the reception again.'

'Possibly, though I doubt it. Ironically enough, I think the slap will work in your favour. He's now ashamed of himself, and I don't think he'll risk raising the subject again. You're quite sure you can't give in gracefully and attend the thing?'

'Quite sure.'

Priscilla sighed. 'Well, you know best. But Jill, if he ever hits you again, come straight here, you understand? He's used up all his grace. One more time, and you have to get out. For your own safety.'

Jill gave an uncertain laugh. 'I honestly don't think he's a wife-beater, Pris.'

'He's taken the first step. Don't let there be another. Promise?'

'Yes, all right.' She smiled. 'Thanks for making me see sense. It's not like me to throw a wobbler; I don't know what came over me.'

'You're OK now?'

'Yes, fine. Balance restored, and as you say, the longer I wait, the worse it will get. In which case, I might as well wend my way back.'

Priscilla stood with her. 'Good luck, then. And enjoy yourself at my party!'

Thankfully, Priscilla proved right. When Jill reached the hotel, Douglas was alone in the foyer. He looked at her searchingly and, she thought, with a tinge of relief. Perhaps he thought she'd gone for good. But all he said, gruffly, was, 'You all right?'

'Fine,' she said, forcing her voice to lightness. 'You?'

He nodded, and she nodded back, and, passing him, went on up the stairs. Please God let that be the end of it.

The subject wasn't mentioned again. That evening, she did her usual stint in the bar, handing out menus to all and sundry with a dazzling smile, and though there was a palpable undercurrent, everyone returned it. And when the time came for dinner, Douglas made a point of seeking her out and threading her arm through his as they went together into the restaurant. But that, she feared, was window-dressing. Things had been said that could not be unsaid, and sooner or later, they'd have to be faced.

That night when he came to bed, he made love to her, roughly and in complete silence, as though inflicting punishment. Jill, however, found it stimulating, and even as she responded, wondered how the following evening would compare, remembering the whiteness of Gary Payne's body as she'd seen it on the beach and imagining it above her, those dark, fathomless eyes at last coming alive and blazing with passion.

And that, she told herself, would be worth all the opprobrium Douglas might throw at her.

Throughout the following day she was restless and unsettled, chafing at the slow passing of time. The fine weather had returned; she met her friends as usual for coffee, exchanging a brief, complicit smile with Priscilla, and spent the afternoon in a secluded part of the grounds, topping up her tan in a strapless sundress and trying to concentrate on her novel.

She'd booked a table for eight o'clock, and had arranged to pick up Gary, as she now thought of him, at the far end of the promenade at seven thirty. Suppose, she thought, he wasn't there, had decided not to show up? Would she wait for him? And if so, for how long? She couldn't return to the hotel, since she was supposed to be at Priscilla's party; nor could she arrive alone at the Fisherman's Catch. And it would be too humiliating to seek refuge again with Priscilla, admitting that she'd been stood up. Well, she'd have to face that problem when and if it happened.

At five she went indoors and had a long and luxurious bath, then lay for a while on her bed, watching the hands on the bedroom clock. God, she thought with amused impatience, she was like a sixteen-year-old on her first date!

She was almost ready when Douglas came up to shower and change, and he stopped short at the door, gazing at her. She knew, with a little spurt of pleasure, that she looked good. The hyacinth-blue of the dress accentuated her tan, its lines the contours of her body.

'I suppose you haven't changed your mind?' he said.

'Sorry, no. Hope it goes well.'

'Likewise.' And he went through to the bathroom, stripping as he went.

She looked for a moment at the closed door, heard the shower come on. Then, with a sigh, she picked up her handbag and left the room.

It had turned humid, she realized, as she closed the garage doors, and on impulse she lowered the top on her little sports car. Reckless, perhaps, in that she'd be more easily recognized, but the wind in her hair was justi- fication enough.

People were still strolling along the front – one reason why she'd designated the far end as their meeting place – and she forced herself to drive slowly, wanting to avoid the necessity of parking. It was some time since she'd come in this direction, and she noted odd changes along the way. The retirement home had a new coat of paint; the luxury block of flats was at last finished, with, according to the notice, only three remaining unsold; a new B and B had opened between the Grand and the Belle Vue.

Then she was passing the municipal baths and tennis courts, and the end of the promenade was in sight. She glanced at the clock on the dash- board. It was exactly seven thirty, and as she slowed down still further, a figure that had been leaning against the railings straightened and moved towards the kerb. So she needn't have worried; he had come!

'Smart little number,' he said approvingly, as he opened the door and slid in beside her.

'It suits me very well.'

'Do you always drive barefoot?'

She followed the direction of his glance to her brown feet with their brightly coloured nails resting on the pedals.

'Often,' she replied, 'and always when I'm wearing high heels.'

It was the first time she'd been this close to him, and there was no trace of the aftershave that was almost mandatory among the men she knew. Instead, she detected a faint, pleasing smell of soap and freshly laundered clothes. He was, she saw, dressed a little more formally than usual, in linen jacket and trousers and an open-necked brown shirt.

'I wasn't sure of the dress code,' he said in half-apology, as the car moved off. 'I've a tie in my pocket, but on the other hand, if a jacket's too formal I can leave it in the car.'

'You're fine as you are,' she said.

He was nervous, she realized; almost as much so as she was, and she was again conscious of that quality in him that had first intrigued her and that still gave her a frisson – a sense of watchfulness, of something kept tightly under control. She wondered half humorously if she'd know any more about him by the end of the evening, acknowledging that she didn't care either way, as long as they made love on the way home. And with the thought came an unmistakable tweak of desire, the first she'd felt for him. Perhaps she'd been fooling herself that the planned seduction was simply to prove a point.

The car park at the Fisherman's Catch was almost full, and as they walked round to the front of the building, it was clear that a lot of people had elected to eat outside.

Jill turned to Gary. 'Would you prefer in or out?' she asked him. 'You choose, it's your last night.'

'Inside,' he said promptly. 'I'm allergic to mosquitoes.'

They went together into the low-beamed room, also thronged with people sitting at the bar and moving between the tables, and he followed her through the crowds to the door of the restaurant, where a waiter checked their reservation and led them to a window table overlooking the garden, and, beyond it, the darkening sea.

'Much more civilized,' Gary murmured, as the waiter, having spread napkins on their knees, moved away.

They hadn't spoken much on the drive, and there was still a certain reserve between them, which Jill was unsure how to breach. He didn't seem to have much small talk, and it was she who'd opened every conversation.

'So –' she began brightly, when they'd ordered drinks and been handed large, handwritten menus – 'you're off home tomorrow. Where exactly is that?'

'Manchester,' he replied. 'Not "exactly", as you put it, but near enough, any road.'

The northern phraseology was the first she'd noticed; perhaps he fell into local speech at the mere thought of home. Or, more likely, it was simply that until this evening, she'd spent barely five minutes in his company.

'And you teach sport and PE, you said?'

'That's right. It keeps me in good shape, and since most of the kids enjoy it, I don't have too much hassle with them.'

She glanced at his hands, the fingers square-tipped and ringless.

'Married?' she asked casually. Not all husbands wore rings.

'No.' He half smiled. 'I've managed to avoid that so far.'

'Girlfriend, then?'

'Yep, I've got one of those.' He met her eyes. 'You ask a lot of questions, Mrs Irving.'

'Jill, please.'

'Jill does, and all.'

'I'm sorry, but we can't sit in silence all evening.'

'Do I get a turn, then? Quizzing you?'

She looked at him quickly, felt a tug of alarm. 'Of course,' she said steadily, 'though what you see is what you get. You probably know quite a bit about me already.'

'Aye, I do,' he said.

She waited uneasily, but no questions were forthcoming. Perhaps, after all, he thought he knew enough.

'All right' she said quickly, 'if you don't like personal questions, tell me what books or films you enjoy.'

He held her eyes, his own as always unreadable. 'I go for murder, every time,' he said.

She shuddered, shaking her head quickly. 'I'm quite the opposite; I hate anything to do with violence. My husband laughs at me, because I refuse to follow cases in the news. I just try to – block them out.'

Their drinks arrived and, driving or not, Jill felt in need of hers. Perhaps this wasn't such a good idea after all. She thought briefly of Douglas back at the hotel, entertaining their MP and the Italians; almost wished she was there. She gave herself a little shake, and, seeming to realize he was proving a poor companion, Gary picked up his menu and said, 'Well, then, what do you recommend?'

After that, it was easier. Though conversation didn't exactly flow seamlessly, it was less stilted, and they discussed various topics, including education today, global warming and the economic climate – none of them Jill's favourite subjects, but he seemed to find them interesting.

The waiter returned for their order, and though she'd recommended several dishes, Gary selected the same as she did – potted shrimps, sea bass and crème brûlée. As, Jill recalled, he had done at the hotel. Was he trying to make a point? This was turning out to be an evening unlike any other, and she was beginning to have serious doubts that her plan would succeed.

'You weren't always blonde, were you?' he said suddenly, as they drank their coffee.

Startled, she forced herself to laugh. 'Don't tell me my roots are showing?'

He shook his head, and, after a minute, said in explanation, 'You haven't a blonde's complexion. Brown eyes, and so on.'

'Plenty of blondes have brown eyes.'

He made no further comment, but she could see he wasn't convinced. And he was right, damn him, though she'd been a blonde longer than she cared to remember.

'They tell me gentlemen prefer them,' she added flippantly, and he gave a short laugh.

The evening was winding down. People at nearby tables had left and the restaurant was beginning to empty. Jill called for the bill, unsure now whether to proceed with her plan, even though, with the possibility of its abandonment, her desire for him was strengthening.

They walked together into the warm darkness, and as they reached the car, Gary said, 'There must be an inland road to Sandbourne, surely? Shall we go back that way? Might as well see a bit of the countryside while I'm here.'

'You won't see much in the dark,' she answered, her heartbeat quickening. Because although most of the inland road wound over moorland, it also passed through copses that would afford ample privacy for lovemaking. 'But by all means,' she added, 'if you'd like to go that way, of course we can.'

There was no moon, and once they'd turned off the coast road with its various attractions, the only light came from their headlamps. Neither of them spoke, both staring straight ahead at the narrow road. Every now and then, a rabbit scuttled out of the way of their wheels, and an occasional call of an owl reached them as it hunted overhead.

The breeze had strengthened, cool on her bare back and arms, blowing her hair across her face. Jill shivered, wishing she'd replaced the top on the car before setting off, but Gary's suggestion of an alternative route had distracted her. Beside her, there was a tenseness in him that increased her hopes, after all, for a successful outcome.

And now the first of the copses showed up ahead of them, thinly spaced trees, permanently bent against the prevailing wind. Should she slow down, or—?

His voice broke the long silence. 'How about stopping for a while? You're not in any hurry, are you?'

Her heart leaped. *Yes! she exalted silently, oh yes!* And 'None at all,' she answered from a dry mouth, steering the little car off the road. She switched off the lights and they both sat unmoving, conscious of the stillness all round them as they waited for their eyes to accustom to the almost-dark. Then Jill said tentatively, 'There's a rug in the boot, if—?'

'Might as well bring it,' he said, and his voice shook slightly. He got out of the car and slammed the door.

When had she last made love under the stars? Heart thundering, she retrieved the rug and followed him into the trees, almost bumping into him as he came to a halt in a small clearing. Without the branches overhead, the sky was visible and the stars did indeed sprinkle it, lending the night a phosphorescent glow.

'Here?' Jill said.

He didn't reply, but she bent down and spread the rug on the moist ground among the fallen leaves. Still he didn't move. Well, she thought philosophically, she'd had to make the running all evening; might as well continue in the same vein.

She kicked off her sandals, bringing herself down to his height, and, turning to him, put her hands on his shoulders. He stiffened, but the semi-darkness obscured his face.

She said softly, 'Gary?' and, pressing herself against him, kissed him on the mouth.

His reaction was instantaneous, and not all what she expected. He flung her off so violently that she stumbled, and rubbed his hand vigorously across his mouth.

'*Not* the point of the exercise,' he said.

Tears of humiliation filled her eyes. 'I don't understand.'

'You soon will. Sit down.'

He gestured towards the rug and, trembling now, desperately wanting to go home, she obeyed.

'There's something I want you to hear,' he said, taking a small object from his pocket and further confusing her. Had she rushed him? Did he want to set the scene, play background music, for God's sake?

She moistened her lips as he sat down on the rug beside her. 'What is it?'

'A tape recording. Or two, to be precise. Of conversations I had with your brother and sister. I think you'll find them interesting.'

They found her car the next day, and, following a beaten-down path, came across her body strung from one of the saplings. Her throat had been cut, and a picture postcard was tucked down her cleavage.

Subsequent enquiries established that she'd dined with a companion at the Fisherman's Catch, but extensive searches failed to trace him, and forensic examination could find no evidence of anyone else having been in the car. It had, the scientists reported, been thoroughly, and possibly professionally, wiped clean.

The postcard killer had claimed his third victim.

PART IV – THE PAST

Thirteen

Beth Sheridan walked slowly up the path to the house, trailing her fingers against the rosemary bushes and breathing in their perfume. Behind her, the lake was a sheet of steel under the leaden sky, while ahead the crag rose steeply, criss-crossed with bridle paths.

To be truthful, she wasn't looking forward to Harold's return. He'd been away on a course most of the week, and in his absence the atmosphere in the house had noticeably lightened, as though they'd all relaxed and breathed a sigh of relief. And that, she chastised herself, was not only disloyal but unfair, since he was a good man – honourable, conscientious and dependable. Which sounded more like a job reference than the attributes of a husband. Yet he loved her, and she supposed she loved him. The main obstacle, from the beginning, had been the children and their implacable hostility. Because, of course, he wasn't Simon.

The familiar pain twisted her heart. Simon, the love of her life, to whom she'd been married for fourteen happy years; Simon, whom the children had idolized; handsome, laid-back, fun-loving Simon, whose flair for facts and figures had made him, by the age of forty, a very wealthy man, and who, two years ago, had died in a freak boating accident on the lake behind her.

Sometimes Beth wondered how she could continue living here, with the treacherous waters constantly in sight. But he had loved both house and lake, and some part of him lingered here, making it impossible for her to leave. Though, as she reached the house and let herself in, she accepted that she couldn't have come through that wretched time without Harold, who'd been the family's accountant.

'Anybody home?' she called.

'Only me!' came Liza's voice from the kitchen. Liza Jenkins had been with them since Jilly was a baby, when Beth had broken her arm and she'd come to 'help out'. By the time Beth was fit again, neither of them wanted the arrangement to end. A valued member of the household, she had almost single-handedly kept the family afloat during the dark times.

Beth pushed open the door, and a smell of baking met her. She raised enquiring eyebrows.

'Cranberry cake,' Liza informed her, 'to welcome Mr Sheridan home.'

Beth shot her a glance. She knew instinctively that Liza, who had adored

Simon, disliked her new husband as much as the children did, though she'd been careful not to show it.

'His favourite; that's kind of you,' she said. 'Where is everyone?'

'Jilly's playing tennis, Cal's at William's and Abby has gone for a hack. I reminded them you'd said to be back by five.'

Beth glanced at the wall clock. It was four thirty. 'Then I've time for a bath. It's really humid out there.'

'Thunder's forecast,' Liza commented. 'That should clear the air.'

But not, unfortunately, that in the house, Beth thought as she went upstairs.

Minutes later, her hair pinned on top of her head, she lay back in the scented, bubble-filled water and allowed her mind to wander. Was she to blame for all this tension? Had she been selfish in agreeing to marry Harold, barely a year after Simon's death? In her darkest moments, she still wondered why she had. Yet at the time he'd seemed a rock, someone she could lean on, entrust with her worries, and who would always be there when she needed him.

His declaration of love, made over lunch one day, had come as a total shock. She'd assumed, without really considering it, that he was not the marrying kind, had even half wondered if he were gay. He was generally regarded as a confirmed bachelor, being fifty-four years old – twelve years her senior – thin, balding, and, as Simon had once laughingly remarked, as dry as his ledgers. But in her darkest hour he'd been exceptionally kind.

Though remarriage had never occurred to her, the long, dark evenings had become unbearable, and, unable to face the empty bedroom, she'd taken to spending the night on the sofa. Until the morning Liza found her, when embarrassment had driven her back upstairs. The prospect of having someone to advise on the host of decisions now demanded of her, to support and – yes – love her, appeared, the more she'd considered it, increasingly tempting. And it would be good, she'd told herself, for the children to have a father figure. In those early days, they'd seemed to like Harold. The trouble started when she told them of the proposed marriage.

The three of them had stared at her aghast, nine-year-old Abby being the first to find her voice. 'But he's *old!*' she'd objected. 'He's like a *grandfather!*'

Compared to athletic, still-boyish Simon, this couldn't be denied. Beth had forced herself to speak lightly.

'Well, since you haven't any grandparents, that would be a bonus. And he wouldn't expect you to call him Daddy,' she added gently.

'I should flipping well think not!' Twelve-year-old Cal. 'But we don't *need* anyone else. We're managing, aren't we? As well as we can, without—' His eyes had filled, and he'd turned hastily back to his computer.

'He'll never take Daddy's place,' Beth assured him, fighting her own tears. 'But you're growing up, Cal, you'll need a man in the house.'

'Not him!' Cal muttered, his back still turned.

'Jilly?' Beth appealed to her elder daughter, who was staring moodily at the floor. 'What do you think?'

'It doesn't really matter, does it?' she'd answered, in that offhand tone Beth so disliked. 'You've made up your mind, and nothing we say will make any difference.'

'But I want you to like him!' wailed Beth. 'Please, darlings, try to understand.'

But that was something they weren't prepared to do, either then or later; which was why she'd never even suggested changing their names from Poole to Sheridan, though it seemed, to her distress, to create a 'them-and-us' division in the family.

In the hall below, the old clock wheezed into its three-quarter chime, recalling her to the present. Abandoning her introspection, she stepped out of the bath and reached for a towel.

The storm broke an hour later, thunder rolling between the hills and rain sluicing down the windows. The children were all home, but Harold, having parked his car in the garage, had to make a dash for the front door, head down, his grip clutched to his chest. By the time he reached the hall, his thin hair was plastered to his head and his suit drenched.

'God, what weather!' he exclaimed irritably, allowing Beth to kiss his wet cheek. 'I'd better go and change out of these things.'

'Welcome home, anyway!' she said. 'Liza's made you a cranberry cake.'

'That's good of her. Pour me a stiff whisky, will you, love? I'll be down in a minute.'

A deafening crash sounded directly overhead, and Abby came flying down the stairs, nearly cannoning into her stepfather and burying her face against Beth.

'Look where you're going!' he admonished, smoothing his dripping hair. Then, as Beth's arms went comfortingly round her, 'Come along, now. You're not a baby, to be scared of a bit of thunder.'

The dark hallway lit up in a garish gleam, followed instantly by another deafening peal, reverberating around them in a series of diminishing echoes. Abby clenched her mother's skirt and Harold, with a disapproving click of his tongue, picked up his grip and went on up the stairs.

'He always hates it when you hold me,' Abby said, her voice muffled against the cloth.

'Don't be silly, darling. He's only telling you there's nothing to be afraid of.'

But the child's words struck home. Beth herself had noticed that displays of affection between her and the children tended to call forth a caustic comment. Perhaps, she thought tiredly, that was the root of the trouble: Harold was jealous of the children's claim on her, and they of his. Pulled in two directions, she felt a helpless resentment, and gave Abby a little push.

'Go on, now; the storm's moving away. Supper won't be long, so if you haven't washed your hands since your ride, please do so.'

'I wish he hadn't come back!' Abby said under her breath, as she ran upstairs.

Another flash lit the hall, exacerbating the headache such storms invariably engendered. With a grimace, Beth went to pour her husband's drink.

Upstairs, Harold stripped off his wet clothes and went into the bathroom. It smelled of flowers – Beth's bubble bath, he assumed, since her towel was damp. He washed quickly and rubbed his hair dry, annoyed with himself for snapping at Abby. But Beth did tend to baby those children; she should be firmer with them, make them stand on their own feet.

Still, he had more pressing matters to consider. While in London, he'd received a call from his sister to say their mother'd had another fall.

'I really haven't the time to keep going over to check on her,' she'd said, 'and you know she refuses point blank to consider sheltered housing. You'll have to speak to her, Harold. It's all very well for you, up there in the Lake District, you're well out of it. I'm the one who has all the hassle.'

'All right, I'll have a word,' he'd said, surreptitiously checking the time of the next session.

'Well, you'd better. She's more likely to listen to you, God knows why. But get one thing very clear: there's absolutely no chance of her coming here. She'd drive us insane within days.'

'Understood,' he'd said crisply, and switched off. Margaret had a point, though, he'd admitted as he hurried down to the lecture room. Two points, in fact. He *was* well out of it, and his mother, a cantankerous eighty-nine, *would* be impossible to live with. The least he could do was offer his sister some support.

Supper was a less than scintillating occasion, Jilly – Beth suspected deliberately – having set the tone.

'Felicity's had her ears pierced,' she announced. 'Can I have mine done?'

'No!' said Beth and Harold as one, and Beth felt a spurt of irritation. The question had been directed at her, and surely she was responsible for the children.

Jilly glared at Harold, and turned back to her mother. 'Please, Mum.'

Beth put a hand to her head. 'Let's not start an argument, Jilly. Daddy and I always said not until you were sixteen.'

'Well, I will be, in March!'

'But it's only June,' Harold pointed out pedantically, the mention of Simon, as always, discomfiting him.

'This has nothing to do with you!' Jilly flared.

Beth's head pounded. 'Jilly! Apologize to Harold at once!'

'Why should I? He's always butting in! No one asked for his opinion!'

'Apologize, or go to your room. You have the choice.'

There was a taut silence while Jilly stared down at the table, her cheeks flaming. Then she said, barely audibly, 'Sorry.'

Beth glanced at Harold, mutely beseeching him to accept the apology, grudging as it was, and though anger churned inside him, he gave a curt nod. Ignoring the girl, he turned to his wife.

'I had a call from Margaret while I was away,' he told her. 'Mother's had another fall.'

With an effort, Beth switched her attention from daughter to husband. 'I'm sorry to hear that. Did she hurt herself?'

'I don't think so, but it raises concerns. Margaret feels she's no longer fit to live alone.'

Beth felt a clutch of panic. 'You don't—?'

'No, no,' Harold said hastily. 'There's no question of that. Nor can she go to Margaret. It's just a matter of getting her to agree to move in somewhere.'

Beth was silent. Martha Sheridan was a difficult woman, who still ruled her children, middle-aged though they were, with a rod of iron. Beth and Harold had held their wedding down south for her convenience, during which she'd confounded them by demanding loudly why he wanted to get married at his age. But on a brighter note, Beth's sister and her husband also lived in Surrey, and had taken the children back with them when she and Harold left on their honeymoon.

Their honeymoon. Her mind slipped back to the first days of their marriage, when they were still virtual strangers. There'd been no mention of sex before the wedding, and Beth guessed that her husband was a virgin. Consequently, she'd expected little of their love life – possibly a dutiful coupling every month or so – and consoled herself with the thought that

she wouldn't be betraying Simon; it would simply be a case of lying back
and thinking of England.

But after the first fumbling and embarrassing coming together, Harold
had astonished her by his passion and increasing dexterity, to which her
love-starved body had instantly responded. It was as though his desires,
having been damped down all his life, had at last found expression, and he
exulted in the experience. No doubt, after several days' abstinence, he would
want her tonight. She could only hope her headache had lifted by then.

Cal's voice broke into her musings. 'What's for pudding?'

'Cranberry cake.' It was Liza, in the act of clearing away the main course,
who answered him.

'Especially for Harold,' Beth said quickly, willing him to show some sign
of appreciation. But, his mind presumably still on his mother, he merely
nodded with a slight smile, and Beth, with sinking heart, saw Liza's lips
tighten.

'Can I have ice cream instead?' Abby asked. 'I don't like cranberries.'

'No, you can't.' Beth spoke sharply, her annoyance with her husband
transferring itself to her daughter. 'This isn't a hotel. Tonight's pudding is
cranberry cake, but you may ask for a small slice.'

Abby's face took on a mutinous expression, Harold's one of satisfaction.
Beth didn't know which irritated her the most. It was a relief to all of
them when the meal was over.

The thunder had indeed cleared the air, and the next day dawned fine and
dry, with a breeze to temper the summer heat. At eight thirty, Harold
having already left, Beth stood at the front door to see the children off to
school. Beyond them the lake, now shining blue and gold in the sunshine,
hurt her eyes, still weak after the headache, which always left her drained.

At the bend in the path they turned to wave, a daily ritual, and she reci-
procated before going back inside, reflecting yet again how fortunate they
were that the school was so close. King Edward's and its excellent reputation was one of the reasons she and Simon had come to Scarthorpe. Though
primarily a boarding school, there was a small number of day pupils, and
the fact that it took children from kindergarten right through to eighteen
was another advantage. The handsome building, surrounded by its playing
fields, was at the foot of the hill on which their house stood, and Beth passed
it several times a day as she went about her business. Which today would
consist of driving the mobile library to outlying farms and villages.

Scarthorpe itself lay half a mile from the school gates, the road running
alongside the lake and passing the local sailing club en route. Largely thanks
to the school, it was saved from depending solely on the tourist trade,

boasting a bank, library, up-to-date health centre, restaurants, a hotel where visiting parents stayed, and a larger range of shops than its neighbours. Not to mention a firm of accountants, of which Harold was a partner.

In the breakfast room, Liza had replenished Beth's coffee and laid out the daily paper, both of which she took to an easy chair for a brief relaxation before her working day.

The time she'd allotted was almost up, and she'd made a start on the crossword when the telephone interrupted her, and she lifted it to hear her sister's voice.

'How's the northern tribe this sunny morning?'

'Pam! Lovely to hear from you! We're fine, how are you?'

'Somewhat harassed. I'm trying to organize a trip to Scotland, which, of course, includes arranging for people to come in and feed the animals. Actually, that's why I'm ringing.'

'To ask us to baby-sit your horses?'

Pam laughed. 'Hardly, though no doubt Abby would love to. No, I'm wondering if we could scrounge a bed next weekend? It would be a lovely way of breaking the journey.'

'Of course you can. We've not seen you since the wedding.'

'True enough. How's the bridegroom?'

Beth bit her lip. Though Pam hadn't said as much, Beth knew she'd been dumbfounded by her choice of husband.

'Very well. He's just back from a few days in London, attending some course or other.'

'A long way to go. He didn't drive, surely?'

'No, he gets the train to Manchester, and flies from there.'

'Still a long way. And the kids?'

'Stroppy, as usual.'

'Seriously, are they settling down?'

'Oh God, Pam, I don't know. They and Harold continually wind each other up. Sometimes I could knock their heads together.'

'Like us to have them for a while during the summer hols?'

'Would you? They always love staying with you.'

'And we love having them.' It was a continuing sadness to Pam and her husband that they were childless.

'Well, there's time enough to discuss that. As to next weekend, when should we expect you?'

'Stephen's taking Friday off, so – a week today, in time for dinner?'

'Great. Till the Monday morning?'

'If we don't outstay our welcome. And perhaps at some stage you and I can slip away for a while and have a good old natter.'

'I'll make certain of it.'

Beth replaced the phone, feeling all at once more cheerful, and, putting the paper aside, went into the hall and put her head round the kitchen door.

'I shan't be in for lunch, Liza, so feel free to go out earlier, if you'd like to.'

Liza turned from the sink. 'I might, at that. Thanks, Beth.'

'See you later, then.'

When the front door had closed behind her, Liza went into the hall and lifted the phone.

'Cora, it's me. I can manage lunch, if you're free? . . . Fine; I'll catch the twelve thirty, and be with you about quarter to one.'

She put down the phone, felt in her pocket and extracted a few coins, which she laid on the small table beside it. At first, there had been arguments when she'd tried to pay for her calls, but once Beth understood how strongly she felt, she tacitly accepted the occasional offering. From Liza's viewpoint, it meant she needn't feel guilty about using the phone as and when needed.

She stood for a moment, drawing a deep breath and enjoying the peacefulness of the now-silent house – lozenges of sunshine on the floor, richly gleaming wood and tapestry-seated chairs. How lucky she was to be living here, and with this family, even though things weren't as happy as they had been.

She sighed, manoeuvred the vacuum cleaner out of the cupboard, and set off with it up the stairs. No thanks for the cranberry cake, she reflected, despite Beth's prompting, bless her. Not that she'd really expected any, the sour-faced old stick. (That Mr Sheridan was roughly the same age as herself was irrelevant.)

She knew he resented her familiarity with the family – calling Beth by her first name, for instance. But Beth and Simon had insisted on it when she first came, which admittedly had been unusual in the seventies, though things were becoming less formal now. Beth had even suggested Liza continue the practice with her second husband, but the name had stuck in her throat – nor, she was sure, would it have been well received. When Simon was alive, she'd known the accountant as Mr Sheridan, and that was how she continued to address him. Beth, perhaps understanding, hadn't pressed the point.

But names and cranberry cake weren't really the issue. What did upset her was the way he was with the children, and they with him. Poor mites, they still missed their father. A less stiff-necked man would have seen that, though to be fair, it had to be said they played him up, particularly Jilly, who cheeked him as often as she dared. So the chasm between them widened daily, while she and Beth stood helplessly on the sidelines, seemingly power-less to intervene.

There was a request stop outside the gates of The Lodge, and Liza flagged down the bus and climbed on board. The ten-minute drive beside the lake was always interesting; in winter, the water lay darkly brooding, strong winds whipping up white ruffles and gulls swooping and crying. In summer, as now, it was serenely blue, dotted with small craft of every description. She'd had to learn to block its connection with Simon's horrific death – though her dreams were still troubled by it – as she'd also buried her shock at Beth's second marriage. It wasn't her place to criticize or condemn. Having no experience of marriage, or even of the love between a man and a woman, she was in no position to judge, and whatever she felt privately, she'd fiercely defended Beth's actions against anyone who questioned them – Cora, for instance. And Cora, good friend that she was, had subsided and said no more.

Cora Selby was the proprietor of one of the cafés on the lakeside of Scarthorpe's main road. A widow with a son in his twenties, they had met when Liza first came to work for the Pooles, and had popped into the Willow Pattern on her afternoon off. Fifteen years on, though both were forthright women, there'd been scarcely a wrong word between them. They had shared confidences, discussed problems, helped each other through good times and bad, and for several years now had gone on holiday together.

Cora was, in fact, her first real friend. Liza had been a large, ungainly child, not popular at school, where she was teased because her parents were so much older. Though come to think of it, her younger brother, Ted, had managed to escape such baiting – just as, years later, he'd escaped to marry Freda, leaving Liza to stay home and care for their increasingly frail parents. Ted the escapologist, she thought now, with wry amusement. The domestic science course she'd taken with a view to teaching, had, instead, been utilized in running her parents' home, and any hopes of marriage and a home of her own were stillborn.

Mother had been the first to go, and thereafter Father became increas-ingly difficult, finally refusing to leave his bed. When he too died, Liza's grieving was mixed with a guilty sense of relief. Free for the first time to make her own decisions – she was then thirty-seven – she was at a loss to know what to do.

Her parents, after a discussion with Ted and Freda, had left their house and its contents outright to their daughter, in recognition of her care for them. It was, after all, the only home she had, and Ted hadn't argued the point. Money was not a problem for him; he was doing well in his job, had recently been promoted, and did not grudge his sister her reward. But Liza had no desire to continue living in the small, cluttered house, reminiscent of old age and sickness, and lost no time in putting it on the market. And because it was on a main road, close to shops, schools and station, she'd had no trouble in getting a good price for it. On completion, she'd moved into temporary accommodation, to allow herself time to take stock.

Her original goal of teaching was no longer feasible. Domestic science had evolved into food technology, and everything she'd learned was hopelessly out of date. On one thing, however, she was determined; she would not apply as housekeeper-companion to some elderly lady, even though, by default, she was qualified for little else. Enough, she told herself, was more than enough. But though retraining courses of all kinds were widely advertised, none stirred so much as a flicker of interest, and the months slipped by without any decision being reached.

It was at that point, when she was beginning to despair, that, idly scanning the advertisements in a newsagent's window, she'd seen Beth's plea for help. The idea of being with young people – especially a baby – had appealed at once, and it would at least be a stopgap while she continued to deliberate her future. But she and Beth had immediately taken to each other, and Liza had fallen completely for the sloe-eyed baby girl in her charge. As Beth's broken arm mended, she kept finding excuses for Liza to stay on a little longer, and without any conscious decision, it had gradually become apparent that her position in the household was to be a permanent one. In those days, she was, she supposed, a cross between children's nurse, cook and general help – not a million miles from the post she'd sworn not to take. The mitigating factor was the charm of the young couple and their baby, not to mention their beautiful home overlooking the lake, and Liza, for the first time in her life truly happy, felt that the gods had at last smiled on her.

The bus came to a halt and, jolted from her reminiscences, she realized they'd reached her stop, directly opposite the Willow Pattern. She waited for a gap in the traffic, then crossed the road and went through the curtained door into the buzzing, familiar interior. All the tables were occupied, and Alice and Shelley, the two waitresses, were moving quickly and efficiently between them, carrying plates of food, removing empty dishes, replenishing water jugs. The Willow Pattern had a reputation for good food which it guarded jealously, and was usually filled to capacity.

Cora, with supreme confidence in her staff, took her own lunch in her flat above the café, and it was there that Liza, climbing the stairs behind the door in the corner, found her, standing at the window and gazing over the lake. Hearing her friend's footsteps, she turned with a smile.

'Just enjoying my wonderful view,' she remarked.

'And why not? I was thinking on the bus how lucky we are to have it. I now can't imagine living anywhere else.'

Cora's brow creased, and she turned to pour them each their customary glass of sherry. She was a small, neat woman, with frizzy brown hair which she described as looking like a bad perm, though it was, in fact, completely natural. Liza, watching her, felt a faint unease. Knowing Cora so well, she could tell there was something on her mind.

As they sat down with their drinks, she asked lightly, 'How's Wayne? He was a bit unsettled last time you mentioned him.'

Cora gave a short laugh. 'Finger on the pulse, as usual.'

Liza frowned. 'Meaning?'

'Meaning that you've hit the nail on the head. Or am I mixing metaphors?'

'He's all right, isn't he?' Liza asked anxiously. Cora's son was her pride and joy, and, having been brought up in the ambience of the café, had gone in for a career in catering.

'He's fine.' Cora sipped her sherry. 'I wasn't going to bring this up till after lunch.'

Liza waited, a cold feeling in the pit of her stomach.

'Actually, he's thinking of opening a small restaurant of his own.'

Liza felt a surge of relief. 'Well, good for him! That's wonderful news!'

'In France,' Cora said flatly.

After a pause, Liza said tentatively, 'Wouldn't that be like taking coals to Newcastle?'

'It seems not. As you know, he's spent his holidays there for the last couple of years. What you didn't know – and I didn't either – was that he was sounding out the ground, making enquiries, speaking to the locals. Now he reckons he's found the ideal place in Normandy, and a property has just come on the market. It'll be a major investment, of course.'

Cora glanced at Liza, then away. 'He'll need help raising the capital, so he – suggests I sell up here and go in with him.'

'Sell the Willow Pattern?' Liza repeated stupidly, the cold feeling spreading.

Cora nodded. 'I've been here for twenty years, Liza. Perhaps it's time for a change. I think I told you several people have approached me, asking if I was interested in selling.'

'And you've always said you weren't,' Liza reminded her from a dry throat.

'Nor was I, then.'

'You're seriously considering it?'

Anthea Fraser

'I'm considering it, yes, but I haven't reached a decision. It's a big step to take, particularly at my age, but if Wayne needs my help . . .' Her voice tailed away.

'I'd miss you,' Liza said inadequately.

'And I you. But it goes without saying you'd have an open invitation to come and stay, and we'd still have our holidays together. Anyway –' she straightened – 'that's enough about me. Tell me your news. How's the dreaded Mr S?'

With an effort, Liza closed her mind to Cora's earth-shattering news and took a gulp of sherry. 'He was away for most of the week, thank God. The difference was unbelievable; the children behaved like angels, and all was harmony. Then he arrived back last night, appropriately enough in the middle of the thunderstorm, and all hell broke loose again.'

'In what way?'

'Jilly giving cheek, Abby refusing her pudding, and His Lordship putting his oar in. No wonder poor Beth had a headache. She was pale as a ghost at dinner. I'd made one of his favourite cranberry cakes, hoping to soften him up, but I could have saved myself the trouble, for all the notice he took of it.'

'That's too bad.' Cora glanced at her watch. 'I'd better ring down for lunch. I told them one-fifteen, so it should be ready.' She glanced at her friend and, although not a demonstrative woman, leaned forward suddenly and patted her hand.

'Don't worry,' she said. 'It might never happen.'

Fourteen

'I could have got round Mum about piercing my ears,' Jilly said resentfully, 'if old po-face hadn't butted in.'

They were comparing grievances in Cal's bedroom after school.

'Blow your ears!' retorted her brother. 'You know the latest? He won't let me ride down Lake Road – says it's not safe with all the traffic. And as the garden's too hilly, it means I can't cycle at all. That bike was the last thing Dad gave me.'

'Ignore him,' Jilly advised. 'He'll be at work, so how will he know?'

'He'd know at weekends,' Cal said gloomily, 'and that's the best time.'

Jilly slammed down her hand in a burst of irritation. 'Mum must have been out of her mind! Couldn't she *see* he was marrying her for Dad's money? He was their accountant, he knew exactly how much they had.'

'He can be quite soppy, though, when he thinks they're alone.'

'Ugh!' Jilly gave an exaggerated shudder. 'Imagine him slobbering all over you! But it's just a screen, it has to be; people his age don't fall in love.'

'Remember all that about me being the man of the house when Dad died?' Cal asked resentfully. 'Didn't last long, did it?' He glanced at his sister. 'If Mum knew how we felt, d'you think she'd divorce him?'

'Not a chance. She knew right from the start, didn't she, but it didn't stop her marrying him.'

'She *can't* love him, can she? Not after Dad?'

'Of course not. She just wanted someone to lean on.'

'I wish there was some way we could get back at him.'

'Yes; laxative in his tea, or something. He's got Abby's back up, too; he's stopped her watching that TV programme – says it's not suitable. She was in a right strop – she's always watched it, and it's on at five thirty, so it can't be that bad.'

'I saw a bit yesterday, when I went in for my CD. Something about a schoolgirl having a baby.'

Jilly gave a snort. 'Does he think Abby will go off and have one?'

They both laughed, then stopped abruptly, turning simultaneously as a sound reached them from outside the door. Jilly slid off the bed and flung it open.

'Who was it?' Cal asked urgently.

'No one there. But someone must have been; that board always creaks when you tread on it.'

'Were they just walking past, do you think, or standing listening? How much could they have heard?'

Jilly shook her head. 'The only person who'd eavesdrop is Harold, and he's not home yet. All the same, it's a warning; if we're going to do anything, we can't discuss it in the house. The bottom of the garden would be safest, well out of earshot.'

'Down by the swings, you mean?'

'Yep. We could hold a daily conference after school, until we come up with something.'

'Good idea!' Cal looked more cheerful. 'What about Abby? Is she included?'

'I don't see why not. She hates him as much as we do. She'd have to be sworn to secrecy, though.' Jilly glanced at her watch. 'I've got some prep to do. See what you can come up with, and we'll have our first meeting tomorrow, and exchange ideas.'

Cal watched her leave the room with a glow of pride. It wasn't often his elder sister took him into her confidence – she was usually too busy being superior. He supposed it showed how desperate she was. He must come up with something really good, to prove his mettle.

Liza said, 'Cora's thinking of moving to France.'

Her sister-in-law gave her a quick glance. 'That's a blow. You'll miss her, won't you?'

'Terribly.' Liza bit her lip, looking down at her folded hands. This was the first time she'd mentioned Cora's news, and she was hoping that discussing it with her family would make it somehow less momentous. Free every afternoon between two and four – earlier, if Beth was out to lunch – she'd caught the bus to Crosthwaite on impulse, and landed unannounced on Ted and Freda's doorstep. Ted wasn't home, of course, but it was Freda she'd wanted to see.

'What brought that on, all of a sudden?' Freda enquired, refilling Liza's teacup. 'Or has she been thinking of it for a while?'

'No, her son has set his heart on opening a restaurant there. He's short of funds, and wants her to sell up and go into partnership with him.' She looked up, meeting her sister-in-law's sympathetic gaze. 'Cora's been my lifeline, Freda, especially this last year. Things haven't been easy at The Lodge – I've mentioned that before – and being able to talk it over with her has calmed me down, helped me to keep my perspective.'

'It's no better, then?'

Liza shook her head. 'That bloody man – he's poisoning the whole atmosphere.'

Freda gave a protesting laugh. 'That's a bit strong, isn't it?'

'No, it's the truth. It was sheer bliss when he was away last week – just like old times. What worries me most is the effect he's having on the children. They've become sulky and disobedient, always whispering among themselves and stopping if anyone goes near.'

'Sounds familiar! It's their age, Liza, that's all.'

'No, it's hard to put into words, but this is something different.'

'Well, if you're no longer happy there, you don't have to stay, do you?'

Liza stared at her. 'You mean I should leave?'

'It's not unheard of, you know! I seem to remember you originally went as a temporary home help. Well, the children aren't babies any more; they don't need you to look after them, and if Beth still wants a housekeeper, she could always find another.'

'But – where would I go?'

'Heavens, woman, the world's your oyster! You've got a nice little nest egg, haven't you, from the sale of the house all those years ago? It'll have been piling up interest for you, and you can't have spent much in the meantime, getting your board and keep at The Lodge, as well as a good wage. I bet you've never even touched your capital. You could go on a world cruise or something.'

Liza laughed. 'Imagine me on a world cruise!' She shook her head. 'No, I won't desert Beth. It's my belief she's not as happy as she tries to make out.' She straightened her shoulders. 'Pay no attention, I'm just being selfish, wondering how I'd manage without Cora.'

'Well, we're still here. You could come and see us more often. I only work mornings, you know, and sometimes time hangs heavy, with the boys away, and Ted not home till six at the earliest.'

Ted was a salesman for a firm making agricultural machinery.

'That's good of you,' Liza said. 'I might well do that. Sorry for crying on your shoulder.'

'What are families for?' Freda answered placidly.

Whether or not Harold Sheridan's ears were burning as he drove home, he was not unaware of his unpopularity, and wondered gloomily what confrontation awaited him that evening. He'd had a difficult session at the office, with Sidney Lester ranting and raving and accusing him of God knew what after the company he invested in went bust. What he needed above all was Beth's sympathetic ear and a peaceful evening with just the two of them. Small chance of that.

This, he thought resentfully, should be the happiest time of his life, but it wasn't turning out that way, and it was all due to the children, and in particular Beth's leniency with them. Though he naturally didn't expect her to be as strict as his own parents, she was spoiling them, allowing them to become more and more undisciplined, and it was therefore left to him, in loco parentis, to rein them in.

Such reflections inevitably recalled his own childhood, and it struck him for the first time that there'd not been much evidence of love in that house, either between Mother and Father, or towards their children. He and Margaret had been adequately fed, clothed and educated, but there'd been none of the spontaneous hugging Beth and her children seemed to think natural. And there were punishments for real or imagined bad behaviour, something singularly lacking at The Lodge. If he was late home from school, or forgot his homework, he got the slipper – admittedly painful only to his dignity – and was sent to his room without supper. Margaret, though spared the beating, suffered similar banishment and had her privileges withdrawn. Thinking back now, he could remember neither resentment nor affection towards his parents; he'd merely accepted them, assuming this was the norm.

At school he'd been regarded as a swot, but his diligence earned him a scholarship, and university had followed. There, he'd expected to study even harder, but it was soon apparent that his companions' ambitions centred on girls, and stories of their conquests, luridly detailed, made Harold's face burn. For the first time, the opposite sex was brought forcibly to his notice, and he accepted that if he wasn't to be odd one out, he must follow suit.

Not that he met with much success. Though a few girls agreed to go out with him, such relationships were short-lived, nor did they respond to his advances in the way – if the stories were to be believed – that they did with his friends. So he resigned himself to going around in a crowd, often the only one without a partner, and, his interest belatedly aroused but unsatisfied, was reduced to fantasizing about girls in the films they saw, well aware he should have outgrown such practices in his teens.

After graduating, accountancy exams entailed further studying, and there was less opportunity to socialize. It wasn't until he was qualified and settled in a job that he realized all the young men he'd grown up with were now married with homes of their own, while he continued to live with his family. Restlessness began to build, but the fact that the firm he worked for was within walking distance of his parents' house, made it difficult to announce suddenly that he was moving to a place of his own, which was bound to be less convenient.

Margaret's marriage finally spurred him into action. Overtaken by panic that he'd never get away, he began searching the Situations Vacant columns, and almost at once found what he was seeking – a post in a firm of accountants based in Westmorland, as it then still was, more than two hundred miles away. He wrote after it, went up for an interview, and was immediately accepted. His parents neither questioned his decision, nor offered congratulations, simply nodding acceptance of the news, and leaving him to wonder if they'd been waiting for years for him to leave home.

So he had come to Scarthorpe as, a few years later, had the young Pooles. He still remembered his first sight of Beth – indeed, it was branded indelibly on his memory – when, shortly after their arrival, she and Simon had come to his office. With her windblown hair and her wide, candid eyes, she'd seemed little more than a girl; but her stomach was gently rounded with her first child, and for some reason, this had a profound effect on him. He had immediately and irrevocably fallen in love with her.

After a lapse of years, he started fantasizing again, Beth now playing the role of the screen goddesses, and, fuelled by as frequent meetings as he could engineer, this had continued on and off until a couple of years ago, when, though he'd been genuinely shocked and appalled by Simon's untimely death, it did seem that Fate at last was playing into his hands.

So he had no intention, Harold thought grimly, turning into the gateway of The Lodge, of letting those children jeopardize the precious relationship he now enjoyed, and for which he had waited so long.

Cal said, 'I've just seen that creepy kid that comes with Spencer. He was hanging round at the bottom of the garden.'

'He'll soon scuttle off when we arrive.' Jilly smiled. 'I used to think Spencer was a miserable old goat, but I have to hand it to him – he knows how to annoy Harold.'

Cal nodded. 'He was going on to Mum about him at the weekend. Where's Abby, by the way?'

'Skipping on the front path. I said we'd collect her on our way down.'

Abby dropped her rope as they appeared, not sure why her presence was required, but gratified to be included in whatever it was. As the youngest, she was used to being sidelined by both her brother and sister.

'Why are we going down the garden?' she asked for the second time, having received no satisfactory reply.

'Because it's the only place we can talk without being overheard.'

It wasn't a full answer, but for the moment Abby accepted it, skipping beside them as they went down the slope of the lawn, the afternoon sun hot on their backs. Over to their left, they could see Spencer raking some leaves, but there was no sign of his son. Then, as they rounded the corner into the play area, they saw his pale, startled face peering up at them from beneath the slide.

'What are you doing?' Jilly demanded sharply.

'Playing.' He scrambled out and stood looking fearfully up at them. There was a flimsy wooden construction behind him, forming, she presumed, some kind of den.

'Well, this is our place,' she said, 'and it's private. We need to talk, so if you must come to our garden, go and play somewhere else.'

The boy ran off, and Cal said admiringly, 'That's telling him!'

Jilly kicked scornfully at the wooden structure, which collapsed in a pile of twigs. She seated herself on one of the swings, rocking it slowly back and forth with the toe of her shoe.

'So,' she began, 'for Abby's benefit, the reason we're here is to agree on a way of getting back at Harold for being such a toerag.'

Abby giggled. 'How?'

'That's what we have to discuss. Cal and I have been thinking.' She looked down at her brother, who, having flung himself to the ground, was propped up on one elbow, chewing a blade of grass. 'What have you come up with?'

'Nothing, really,' he admitted reluctantly. 'I mean, he's out at the office all day, and evenings and weekends he's usually with Mum.'

'Well, that's not much help, is it?'

'How about you, then?' Cal retorted 'What brilliant ideas have you had?'

'I did suggest laxative in his tea.'

'And how exactly do we manage that, when Mum always pours it? Distract them both, while we drop something in? Anyway, he'd be bound to taste it.'

'Make him an apple-pie bed,' Abby suggested, anxious to be part of the conspiracy.

'Just on his side, you mean?' Cal jeered, and she flushed.

'Superglue in his briefcase?' Jilly proposed.

'That's a thought. Don't know if it would be worth it, though; there'd be a mega row.'

'There will be, whatever we do. We have to accept that, if we're to make Mum see how we hate him.'

'Or,' Cal suggested, 'we could just remove something from his brief-case, so that when he goes into a meeting, he'll find he hasn't got what he needs, and look a prat.'

Jilly slid off the swing and smoothed down her skirt. 'OK, we've got a few possibilities: laxative – if not in his tea, somewhere else – pinching his papers, and superglue. I suppose that's a start, but we need more to choose from. Rack your brains, both of you, so when we meet at the same time tomorrow, we can form a plan. Agreed?'

'Agreed,' they echoed, and all three made their way back to the house. They'd not achieved as much as they'd hoped, but it was their first meeting, and, as Jilly said, they'd at least made a start.

Sometimes, when his mum worked the afternoon shift, Bryan Spencer let himself into his home with the key hidden under the flowerpot. He liked having the cottage to himself, and had argued forcibly against going back with one of the other kids till he could be collected, as his younger sister did.

More often, especially in summer, his dad, who was a gardener, picked him up at the school gates and took him along to wherever he was working, so he could be in the fresh air instead of watching TV.

Jack Spencer, who was claustrophobic, was, in fact, a great exponent of the outdoors, and though he couldn't be regarded as a conversationalist, a bond had developed between father and son, forged among the plants and trees of the gardens of Scarthorpe. He taught the boy to identify birds and flowers, and if there was planting to be done, encouraged him to dig his hands in the soft, moist soil and hollow out space for tender stems.

Jack's favourite among the gardens he tended was that at The Lodge, down Lake Road. In his opinion, it was what every garden should be – not too formal, lots of colour and scent, and a wild patch near the bottom, to encourage birds and insects. There was also a corner, screened by shrubs, containing a slide, a pair of swings and a seesaw, where the Poole children had played when they were younger. When Mr Simon was alive, he'd sometimes push young Bryan on the swing, and even sit at one end of the seesaw to bounce him up and down. If he was working from home, he'd wander down the garden for a chat with Jack, and as often as not fetch an extra spade from the shed and dig beside him. A rare one was Mr Simon. Not like him she had now, never missing a chance to criticize.

What made the garden so special to Jack, almost like his own, was that it had been left to him to choose what to plant, and the colour schemes for each season. He'd spent hours at the kitchen table, meticulously drawing plans and crayoning in colours, till he had just the effect he wanted. The Pooles had never failed to approve his choice, nor make a point of complimenting him.

Not so Mr Sheridan. From the first, he had queried the bills Jack submitted from the garden centre, maintaining he was being unduly extravagant.

'It's not even his garden!' Jack had fumed to Molly. 'He landed on his feet all right, that 'un, moving in with Mrs Beth. Gone to his head, like as not. Well, he's not going to boss me about, and that's flat!'

'Don't take on so, Jack,' Molly had soothed. 'He might have landed on his feet, but he still needs to find them, assert his authority. It can't be easy for him, stepping into Mr Simon's shoes. He'll calm down, given time.'

Bryan, though he'd said nothing to his father, resented the sudden and unwelcome reappearance of the Pooles. They were all older than he was – Abby ten to his eight – and he couldn't see why, all of a sudden, they'd returned to the play area, unless it was to keep him out. He said as much to his friend Pete in the playground.

'It's a great place to go, 'cos there are bushes all round, like, and no one can see you. But they told me to naff off, said they wanted to talk private.'

'Why not spy on 'em?' Pete suggested, scuffing the toe of his boot in the dust. 'Get your own back, like.'

Bryan stared at him. 'How?'

'Well, if there are bushes all round, they wouldn't see you, would they? So creep up close and listen. Pretend as how you're 007,' Pete continued, his imagination quickening, 'and you catch 'em planning to blow up the Houses of Parliament, or summat.'

'You reckon they are?' Bryan asked, wide-eyed.

'Course not!' Pete scoffed. 'Don't be daft! They just don't want you using their things, that's all. But you'd be one up on 'em, even if they didn't know it.'

It was a good idea, Bryan conceded. He'd never have thought of spying, but it would add a spice of danger to the game, 'cos he sure as eggs couldn't risk being caught.

'OK, I'll have a go,' he said, and as the bell went for the end of break, he made his way thoughtfully into the school building.

Harold watched his elder stepdaughter as, with a defiant glance in his direction, she went out of the room.

'You won't let her go, surely?'

Beth flushed. Jilly had just announced her intention of going to the dance hall in Scarthorpe on Saturday, and Beth had made no demur. Admittedly she'd been taken by surprise, but she resented Harold's immediate interference.

When she didn't reply, he continued, 'She's far too young. There'll be drinking and God knows what else going on.'

'She'll be all right. There's a crowd of them going, including Jane and Felicity—'

'The child with pierced ears? That says it all. In any case, Pam and Stephen will be here; she can't go waltzing off when we have visitors.'

'Oh Harold, they're our visitors rather than hers, and they're here for the whole weekend. There'll be plenty of time for them to see her. They certainly wouldn't want her grounded on their account.'

'Well, you know best, of course,' he said, in a tone that implied she didn't.

Beth bit her lip. Lately, they'd several times come perilously close to quarrelling, and it was always about the children. She and Simon had presented a united front when dealing with them, but it was becoming increasingly difficult to maintain this with Harold, and to her distress, she often found herself wondering what Simon would have done.

Perhaps her anxiety reached him, because he suddenly rose and came over, bending down to kiss her. 'My darling, I'm only trying to help, you know. It's natural that they should try it on, but they must realize I'm here now to back you up and see that you're not manipulated.'

She put up a hand to touch his face. 'I know, Harold, but we have to give them a little leeway, not be continually putting the damper on, or they'll just build up resentment.'

He straightened. 'You mean let them have their own way?'

'In moderation, that's all.'

'You're spoiling them, Beth. Letting Abby ride so often, is a case in point. It's an expensive pastime – she doesn't seem to appreciate that. They should be taught the value of money, even if there's no shortage of it.'

'But it's good for her, Harold; I loved it myself, when I was younger. We resisted her pleas for a pony till she'd old enough to look after it, but in the meantime, she's out in the open air and having some exercise. The country round here is excellent for riding, and it's a bonus that the stables are so near, with no roads to cross.'

We. She was bracketing herself with Simon again. Harold wondered whether to revert to the subject of Jilly, but thought better of it. If she was determined to let her children run wild, he would just have to step back, and be ready in due course to pick up the pieces.

Pam Firbank tossed her handbag on to the bed and walked to the window, gazing over the sloping garden to the waters of the lake and the mountains beyond.

'There can't be many better views than this,' she said.

Stephen smiled. 'You've always loved this house, haven't you?'

'It's my ideal, yes. Not just its position, but all of it – the high ceilings, the spaciousness, the décor.'

She turned, suddenly sober. 'It's still very much Simon's, though. Lord knows how Beth can bear to stay on without him. I see him everywhere I look – at the dining table, playing croquet on the lawn, pouring drinks.'

Stephen slipped a sympathetic arm round her shoulders. 'We had some great times together, the four of us.'

Pam nodded. 'I don't quite know what to make of Harold,' she confessed in a low voice. 'Admittedly the only time we met was at the wedding, which was fairly stressful all round, what with the children being bolshie and his old mother shouting the odds.'

Stephen grimaced. 'A laugh a minute, wasn't it?'

'But he seems very – formal, doesn't he?'

'Probably because he doesn't know us, either. No doubt we'll all relax over the weekend.'

'Beth was saying on the phone that things are still difficult with the children, that they wind him up.'

'It can't be easy for him, poor devil, stepping into Simon's shoes.' Stephen patted her behind. 'Anyway, enough of that; it's hardly etiquette to start analysing our hosts the minute we arrive.' He loosened his tie. 'Are you going to have a shower before dinner?'

'Most definitely; I'm hot and sticky after the journey.'

'You go first, then. We've half an hour before we all meet for drinks.'

Pam was still undecided about her brother-in-law the next day. During dinner the previous evening, though the conversation had flowed fairly freely, it had seemed to her heightened sensibilities to lack spontaneity, as if they were all thinking before they spoke. Beth, though she sparkled determinedly, looked a little pale, and it was noticeable that none of the children addressed themselves specifically to Harold. Even dear Liza, stalwart of many a past visit, seemed subdued.

And today's lunch, even in the children's absence, was proving little better. They had driven round the lake to the Green Man, a pub well known for its food, and from the terrace where they sat, had a clear view of The Lodge perched on its hill, with the school buildings spread out below it and the cluster of Scarthorpe close by. Nearer at hand, gulls floated high above the water like scraps of white paper thrown up in the air.

'Why did I ever move south?' Pam asked rhetorically, sipping her ice-cold wine.

'To earn your living,' Beth reminded her. 'At the time, there was nothing sufficiently high-powered for you up here.'

'And if you hadn't, you'd never have met me,' Stephen added. He glanced at Harold, who'd been sitting silently, staring into his glass. 'You're originally from southern parts too, I believe?'

Harold started at being addressed. 'That's right; I was born in the Surrey town where my mother still lives.'

'So what brought you here? Pam's migration in reverse?'

'Work was my motive, too. That, and a feeling I'd stagnate if I never moved from my birth place.' He gave a strained smile. 'And I, too, owe my marriage to the move, although some considerable time later.'

Their food arrived, and they settled down to enjoy it.

'Where are the children this afternoon?' Pam asked, squeezing lemon juice over her smoked salmon.

Beth avoided her husband's eyes. 'Liza's in charge, but as far as I'm aware, Abby's riding, Cal is going to William's, and Jilly no doubt is conferring with her friends about what they should wear this evening.'

Pam smiled. 'Is it her first dance? I remember mine, at the church hall. I went with Annabel Brown – God, I haven't thought of her in years! – and spent most of my time avoiding Ronnie Wood, who I seem to remember had a crush on me. He also had spots and bad breath, which did little for his prospects!'

'I'd no idea I'd such formidable competition!' Stephen joked.

Beth said in a low voice, 'At *my* first dance, I met Simon.'

There was an embarrassed pause – though why, thought Pam with irritation, should anyone be embarrassed? She said, rather more loudly than she'd intended, 'I remember you coming home and telling me about him.'

Stephen came to her assistance. 'At that time, I believe, a large percentage of people met their future partners at dances. Now, it seems more likely to be at places of work.'

'Not nearly so romantic!' Beth commented, sending him a grateful smile. 'How did you and Pam meet – I forget?'

'At a New Year party,' Pam supplied. 'I saw this gorgeous fellow across the room, and edged my way closer so he couldn't avoid kissing me at midnight!'

And, as she'd intended, the potentially difficult conversation ended in laughter.

After lunch, they walked for a while along the shores of the lake, enjoying the sunshine and watching the activity on the water. The narrowness of the path permitted only two to walk abreast, and the men had fallen slightly behind.

'Whereabouts in Scotland are you going?' Harold asked Stephen.

'We'll spend the first night at Callander, then on to Fort William and Skye. Pam wants to see the tropical gardens at Inverewe, after which, if all goes according to plan, we move on to Strathpeffer, Inverness, Nairn, and back down the east side.'

'Pretty comprehensive.'

'It's bed and breakfast mostly. We've only booked into a hotel for our first and last nights.'

'And how long is the trip?'

'Ten days, which means there'll be a fair mileage to cover each day.'

'That's something I'd really enjoy, but it'll be years before we've a hope of doing it. The children would draw the line at so much time in the car.'

'A problem we don't have,' Stephen said quietly and Harold, cursing his thoughtlessness, lapsed back into silence.

Having stopped at a café for tea, it was almost five o'clock when they drove back down their own side of the lake, and as they came to their turn-off, they were startled to see Liza come running down the drive towards them.

Harold screeched to a halt, and Stephen wound down the window as she stumbled, panting, up to them.

'Oh, thank God you're back!' she gasped breathlessly. 'I didn't know what to do – Mrs Telford's just phoned to say Cal and William have got into difficulties out on the lake. They took—'

Beth's hand flew to her mouth, as Harold demanded urgently, 'How far out are they? Has anyone reached them?'

Liza tried to steady her breathing. 'I don't know, but, Mr Telford's taken the speed boat.'

Not again! Pam thought with cold dread. *Oh, please God, not again!*

Harold was already turning the car. 'Get in,' he said tersely, and she opened the rear door for Liza, who'd barely time to fall on to the seat before he took off again. Beth, her face like wax, whispered, 'Oh God!' And then, again and again, 'Oh God!' in an endless litany. Liza reached across Pam to grasp her hand.

'They've probably been rescued by now,' she said hoarsely.

'Cal's a good swimmer,' Stephen put in rallyingly from the front seat. 'I remember being surprised how strong he was.'

The Telfords' landing stage was several hundred yards down the road. As their car swung into the approach, Pam could see figures down on the lakeside, staring out across the water. One of them, a woman, turned on hearing the car, and came running towards them as they piled out of it.

'Oh Beth!' she cried, on a half-sob. 'I'm so desperately sorry about this, but the panic's over now.'

Beth gripped her arm, and Pam saw the woman flinch. 'What's happening?' she demanded, her voice cracking.

'It was all pretty confused, but several boats dashed to the rescue, and from what we could make out, one had already reached them by the time Jeffrey got there. I think they're starting back now.'

'But they're – all right? The boys?'

'They seem to be, thank God. We were watching from the veranda –' she nodded towards the boat house, and Pam saw the little platform outside, with a couple of deck chairs. 'We always keep a lookout when William's on the water.'

'Weren't they wearing life jackets?' Harold demanded.

Sally Telford glanced at him. 'It seems not. They'd been swimming over the side, I think. Anyway, one of the speed boats went too close, and its wake overturned the dinghy. It all happened in seconds. Our boat was in the water, thank God, and Jeffrey was off within a couple of minutes. I – I felt I should let you know, but perhaps it would have been better to wait till I knew Cal was safe.'

'Of course I had to know,' Beth said. She swayed slightly, and as Stephen moved to support her, Harold shoved him unceremoniously aside and took her arm.

'It's all right, my darling, it's all right.'

One of the speedboats was now detaching itself from the cluster and making for the shore. Someone pushed a pair of binoculars into Beth's hand, and though they were out of focus, she could make out three figures huddled in it, and released her breath in a long, shuddering sigh.

Harold said under his breath, 'I'll have something to say to that young man, putting you through this.'

'It was an accident, old man,' Stephen protested. 'Could have happened to anyone.'

'Well, it won't happen again,' Harold said tightly. 'I shall personally see to that.'

For a moment longer they all stood watching as the approaching boat drew nearer. Then Sally said, 'I'll get towels,' and hurried away towards the boathouse, and Beth, with Harold's arm round her, walked down to the water's edge. Liza was still standing by the car, and Pam and Stephen, by tacit agreement, went back to join her.

'A happy outcome, thank God,' Stephen said.

'I feel responsible,' Liza replied, her face drawn. 'He was left in my charge, but he *always* goes to play with William. Nothing like this has ever happened before.'

'It was a fluke,' Pam assured her. 'A strong wave overturned the dinghy. No one could have foreseen it.'

'A freak accident,' Liza commented flatly. 'That's what they said about Simon. When I saw Beth's face just now—' She broke off, and turned away.

'All's well that ends well,' Stephen said, aware how fatuous it sounded. But now helping hands were pulling the boat out of the water, and Sally was waiting with towels to wrap round the shivering boys. They watched as Beth clutched her son to her, holding on to him until Harold gently disengaged her arms and they started back towards the car.

'Do you realize what you put your mother through?' Harold was saying as they reached the others. The boy, white-faced, was shivering violently, and obviously close to tears.

'I'm sorry, Mum,' he said through juddering jaws.

'Darling, all that matters is that you're safe,' Beth answered unsteadily.

'No,' Harold corrected her, 'that's not all that matters. I shall have more to say about this later.'

The boy turned his head and looked at him, and something in his expression made Pam catch her breath: it was a look of pure hatred. But before she could adjust to it, they were all squeezing into the car, Cal – illegally, no doubt – on Stephen's knee in the front, and, back on the road, they headed once more for home.

Fifteen

Since dinner that evening was to be a more formal affair, the children had eaten earlier. Jilly was duly collected by Jane's father and transported to the dance, and Harold, with bad grace, had agreed to bring both girls home.

'Which means I shan't be able to enjoy the wine,' Pam heard him complain to Beth, who'd promptly offered to go herself. But as Pam had known he would, Harold dismissed the suggestion, aware it would reflect badly on him in front of their guests. She was regretfully concluding that the more she came to know her brother-in-law, the less she liked him.

All four of them were subdued as they took their places at the candlelit table and Liza, still tight-lipped, served them with lobster mousse, one of her specialities. The raised voices when Harold took Cal into his study earlier had been heard by everyone in the house, and the stilted conversation round the table was indicative of a general desire to avoid the subject.

Such circumvention carried them through the mousse and the main dish of duck breasts with mango and coriander, but halfway through the cheese course, traditionally served before dessert, Harold, whether perversely or to elicit approval, himself referred to it.

Spearing a slice of Stilton, he said suddenly, 'I must apologize for subjecting you to a display of family drama earlier. Cal needed a reprimand, but I'd not intended the whole house to partake in it.' He flicked a glance at Beth, who sat with downcast eyes at the other end of the table. 'Unfortunately, the boy isn't used to being taken to task, and reacted accordingly.'

There was a pause, and Stephen said awkwardly, 'Well, thankfully he's none the worse for his adventure.'

'Nor will he repeat it. I've forbidden him to go on the lake till he's learned some common sense.'

Beth looked up at that. 'Oh, but Harold,' she exclaimed, 'he loves being in boats – he spends the whole summer in them! You can't just ban him!'

'I can and I have, my dear. I'm aware how you feel about the lake, and I won't allow you to be subjected to such anxiety again.'

Beth leaned forward, her eyes willing him to understand. 'But I can't impose my fears on the children! All I can do is teach them to look after themselves, then allow them to assess the risks. How else will they learn to cope with life?'

'My point,' Harold replied evenly, 'is that he *doesn't* know how to look after himself, or the upturned dinghy wouldn't have found him without a life jacket.'

'All right, but he's had a fright and he'll know better in future. He doesn't need additional punishment, and Simon certainly wouldn't want what happened to him to rebound on his son!'

'Well, Simon isn't here now,' Harold said, with unaccustomed sharpness. 'And since he isn't, it's *my* duty to look after your welfare and that of your children. Now please, Beth, the subject is closed.'

Beth stared at him a moment longer. Then, with an exclamation, she pushed back her chair and ran from the room. Pam, with a murmured apology, went after her, almost colliding with Liza, who was standing in the hall with a tray of desserts, gazing up the stairs after Beth's vanishing figure.

Pam caught up with her at the bedroom door. Beth spun round, fists clenched at her side, supposing it was Harold who'd followed her. Seeing her sister, the defiance drained out of her and her eyes filled with tears.

'You see how it is, Pammy. They hate each other. What can I *do*?'

'Everyone's overreacting,' Pam said. 'Cal resents having to be rescued – it hurt his pride, if nothing else – and Harold, however strict he seems, is acting on what he thinks is your behalf.'

'Well, I wish he wouldn't. His way of dealing with the children is so different from Simon's and mine.' At the mention of her dead husband, the tears spilled on to her cheeks, and she brushed them angrily away. 'Perhaps I shouldn't have been in such a hurry to marry again.'

'He loves you,' Pam said. It was undeniably true, and the only comfort she could offer.

'Too much, I think,' Beth acknowledged in a low voice.

'Can't you just sit him down over a drink, and calmly and reasonably fix some parameters?'

'I've tried. It doesn't work. He thinks I let them run wild.'

Pam sighed. 'Well, we've still not had that tête-à-tête we promised ourselves. Let's postpone any further discussion till then. In the meantime, we'd better make a dignified return to the dining room.'

Beth looked at her quickly, and, seeing her smile, returned it. 'Or they'll think I'm running wild myself,' she said.

Both men rose as they made their reappearance. Beth said simply, 'Sorry about that,' and turned to smile at Liza, who had followed them in with the dessert.

'Thanks, Liza. It's been a delicious meal. We'll have our coffee on the patio.'

Pam, seating herself, glanced across at her husband, who closed one eye in a slow wink. They might not have children, she thought, but at that moment she certainly wouldn't have changed places with her sister.

'Too bad we're not leaving today,' Stephen remarked, as they dressed the next morning. 'I'm not sure I can stomach Harold for another day.'

'I'm afraid you'll have to; I intend to winkle Beth away for a good, sisterly chat.'

'Do you think she's happy?' Stephen asked curiously.

Pam considered a minute. 'On the whole, yes, but this war between Harold and the children needs to be settled, without either side seeming to give way.'

'And how exactly will that be achieved?'

'I've suggested to her that we have them for a spell in the holidays. That'll give her and Harold a time by themselves, when hopefully they can thrash out any problems without interruptions.' She leaned forward to apply her lipstick. 'Did you notice yesterday that he wasn't nearly as worried about Cal's safety as the effect it was having on Beth?'

'That's hardly fair, darling; it's difficult to distinguish where one ended and the other began.'

Pam shook her head. 'He didn't say, "Don't you realize you could have been drowned?", as any normal parent would; he said, "Don't you realize what you put your mother through?"'

'Probably understandable in the circumstances,' Stephen said uncomfortably.

After breakfast, Pam suggested that she and Beth should climb the scar behind the house.

'I've meant to, every time we've been here, but never got round to it. Are you game?'

'It's pretty steep going,' Harold warned, 'though admittedly there's a marvellous view from the top. You'll need the right shoes, though.'

'She can borrow a pair of mine,' Beth said. 'We take the same size. But we'd better leave soon, before it gets too hot. The forecast's for soaring temperatures today.'

It was a wise decision; though still quite early, the heat was already gathering, the sky a milky blue and no breath of wind. At first they chatted lightly, by mutual consent postponing a more serious discussion, and indeed as the climb grew steeper, neither had breath to spare for talking. It felt to Pam as if they were in a world of their own up there, the only sounds apart from their laboured breathing the song of birds and, far below them, the whistle of a train.

At last the ground flattened out, and with a gasp of relief, they collapsed on to a convenient rock and turned to look back the way they'd come. In the distance, the far mountains were a purple smudge in the heat haze, their peaks melding into the sky, and between them, glinting silver in the sunlight, lay a tiny prism of Morecambe Bay. Nearer at hand stretched fields, neatly divided by stone walls, their different-coloured crops like an artist's palette, and closer still the lake lazily spread its length for a blue mile or two. Beth pointed out the pub where they'd lunched the day before, and the scattered farms round the water's edge.

The Lodge itself, immediately below them, was hidden by outcrops of rock, but as they watched, three foreshortened figures emerged and began to walk down the slope of the garden to the corner that held the swings. From this height, they were still visible once they'd entered the clearing; the largest figure – Jilly – perched on one of the swings, the other two leaning against the slide.

'They're spending more time together than they've done for years,' Beth remarked. 'I don't know whether to be glad or suspicious.'

'United we stand?' Pam hazarded.

'Exactly.'

'Why don't you approach this from a different angle?' Pam suggested 'Try talking to *them* rather than Harold, preferably individually. Ask them, for your sake, to make a special effort to get on with him, not deliberately annoy him, as you say they do at present. If he sees they're trying to be amenable, he'll probably calm down and be prepared to meet them halfway.'

'I suppose it might work,' Beth said doubtfully. 'Worth a try, anyway.'

'And if it's still necessary, you can tackle Harold while the kids are away,' Pam added. 'We can take them as soon as they break up, if you like – the end of July? It's only about a month away.'

Beth patted her knee gratefully. 'Thanks, sis. That would be a great help.'

She slipped the rucksack off her shoulders, extracted two bottles of water, and passed one to her sister, together with a slab of Kendal Mint Cake.

'In the best mountaineering tradition!' she said with a smile. 'Remember how proud we were, when Hillary and Tenzing ate it on top of Everest?'

Pam laughed. 'I do indeed.'

Further reminiscing led to shared memories of watching the Coronation on a neighbour's television set, and from there, to various other events of their childhood. Sitting together on the warmed rock, with the glorious view stretched before them and the familiar taste of mint in her mouth, Pam felt closer to her sister than she had for some time.

Beth was not the only one to wonder at the children's sudden together-ness. Liza also saw them set off, as she had several times in the past week, and, giving in to curiosity, she hurried up to Abby's room at the side of the house, where, from the window, she watched them enter the play area.

From this position, she, too, could see inside the enclosure, and was further puzzled to find they weren't using the apparatus; though Jilly was on a swing, it remained stationary. For the life of her, Liza couldn't make out what game they were playing. She watched them for a while without enlightenment, until, realizing it was time to put in the joint, she aban-doned the exercise and returned downstairs.

Over the past week, the proposed daily meetings had fallen by the wayside, thanks to continuing lack of a plan of action. They'd met a couple of times after school, only for the same ground to be gone over with waning enthusiasm, and the meetings themselves had degenerated into a diatribe of their stepfather's shortcomings.

Today, however, interest had been revived by Cal's experiences of the day before.

'In front of *everyone*!' he was complaining again. 'Talking to me as though I was a kid who didn't know what I was doing!'

'Well, you did nearly drown,' Jilly reminded him.

'I did *not*! We were already trying to right the dinghy when the first boat came alongside.'

'But you should have had your jacket on. That's what really riled him.'

'Ever tried diving in a life jacket?' Cal demanded scornfully. 'We were just about to put them on again when the wave hit us. And now he has the nerve to say I can't sail again until he says so! Who does he think he is?'

'Mum'll get round him,' Jilly said.

'Well, as far as I'm concerned, this is the crunch. I'm jolly well going to find a way of getting back at him, so any suggestions would be welcome.'

Jilly nodded. 'We've faffed around long enough; it's time we thought of something.'

'We could stick nails in his tyres,' Abby said suddenly, and the other two looked at her in surprise.

'Good thinking, Abs!' Cal said, and she flushed with pleasure. 'That's the best any of us has come up with yet.'

'Yes, well done, Titch.' Jilly slid to the ground. 'I'm thirsty,' she announced, 'and it's getting too hot down here. We've something definite to work on now, so let's end the meeting and see if Liza's made any lemonade.'

The rest of the day passed without incident. They ate a substantial lunch, managing to keep the talk non-confrontational, after which the children played clock-golf on the lawn and the adults spent a lazy afternoon dozing and reading the Sunday papers on the now-shaded patio.

Supper, as always on Sundays, was cold meat and salad, and the evening ended pleasantly enough with a game of bridge. Stephen and Pam finally reached their bedroom with the feeling of survivors.

'You see,' Stephen commented, 'Harold can be quite pleasant after all. We had an interesting talk this morning, while you girls were out climbing.'

'Good. Heaven knows, I want to like him, for Beth's sake.'

'They'll work it out between them,' Stephen said comfortably, 'See if they don't.'

The next morning, Harold left as usual for the office, and shortly afterwards the children, ready for school, came to say goodbye to their relatives.

'We're wondering if you'd like to come and stay for a while during the summer holidays?' Pam said, and was gratified to see their faces light up.

'That would be super! Could we, Mum?'

'Of course.'

'Perhaps as soon as you break up? There's a gymkhana at the end of July, Abby.'

'Oh, *lovely*!' Abby clapped her hands in excitement.

'Fine; then it won't be too long till we see you.'

They dutifully kissed Pam, Stephen handed them each a pound coin, and Beth went to watch them down the path.

'I wish Mummy had married Uncle Stephen,' Abby said as they set off.

'She couldn't, silly,' Jilly told her, 'but I know what you mean.' And on a rare impulse of fellow feeling, she slipped an arm round her young sister's shoulders.

Beth, watching, chided herself for her reservations, raising her hand as the children turned to wave before rounding the curve of the drive.

'We should be going too,' Stephen said, as she rejoined them.

'Stay for one more cup of coffee,' she coaxed. 'I always pause to draw breath once the family's departed. It's the best time of the day!'

If she could have delayed them longer, she would have done, but Stephen was adamant that if they were to make their destination for the night, they would need to leave. So once again Beth stood at the door as her family set off, and again she returned a wave as, at the bend in the drive, Pam leaned out of the car window. Then, with a final toot, they were gone, and, feeling flat and oddly depressed, she went back into the house.

On their return from school, Jilly had a long phone call from Felicity, about some boy she'd met at the dance. It entailed a lot of giggling and shrieking, and Cal, disgusted, retired to his room and made a start on his homework. It was therefore later than usual when they set out to keep their tryst.

Jilly put her head round the door of the sitting room, where Abby was watching television.

'OK, we're going now.'

'I'll be down in a minute – this has nearly finished.'

Jilly glanced at the screen. 'I thought you weren't supposed to be watching it?'

Abby merely grunted in reply, and Jilly shrugged and withdrew.

'She'll see us down there,' she told Cal.

They were discussing Abby's idea of nails in tyres when Abby herself came flying into the enclosure, tears streaming down her face.

'I hate him, I hate him, *I hate him*!' she cried, and hurled herself on to the grass, her face buried in her arms.

'What is it? Whatever's happened?'

'He came back early, that's what happened.' Abby's voice was muffled, punctuated by sobs. 'He caught me watching *Teen Times*, and now I can't go riding *for a month*, as a punishment! I wish he was *dead*!'

'You were taking a risk,' Cal said judiciously. 'You know what he's like.'

Jilly was more practical. 'Sit up, Abby, we need your input. We were discussing what you said, about nails in his tyres.'

'I'd rather put nails in *him*!' Abby said, but she sat up, wiping away her tears. 'I *can't* go a whole month without riding! I just can't!'

'Nor can I, without sailing,' Cal said gloomily.

'We could go and see Mum all together,' Jilly said. 'Explain how we feel.'

'And what would that achieve? You know how she and Dad always backed each other up, no matter what. She's doing the same with *him*. No, we're on our own on this. Abby's idea about the car's good, though.'

Suddenly Cal's face lit up. 'Eureka!' he shouted, punching the air. 'I know what we can do! Why didn't I think of it before?'

'What?' the girls asked in unison.

'You know how I used to watch Dad, when he was working on *his* car? I've just thought of something. It ought to work.'

'*What?*' his sisters demanded again.

'Well, every now and then he had to top up the brake fluid. He kept a bottle of the stuff on a shelf in the garage.'

'So?' Jilly demanded impatiently.

'You have to be very careful with it, or it could seize up the brakes. Dad showed me how to unscrew the top of the chamber where it goes, and pour it in very carefully so there are no air bubbles. He said if any contaminants got in, they could gum up the works.'

'What's contaminants?' Abby asked.

'Dirt of any kind. *So,*' Cal ended triumphantly, 'we could deliberately put something in – soil, for instance – and scupper it.'

He looked expectantly at their doubtful faces. 'Don't you *see?*' he demanded. 'It's a perfect solution! Dad said there wouldn't be any warning – nothing leaking on the floor or anything – but the pipe would be blocked. His lordship would be well and truly stuck, hopefully on his way to work. He always prides himself on his timekeeping; well, with luck this would hold him up for hours, and take time – and money – to fix.'

'You know how to do this?' Jilly asked.

'Yes, I told you. It's easy. And afterwards, it would never occur to him we'd had anything to do with it.'

Jilly said, 'Wouldn't it be dangerous, tampering with the brakes?'

'It's not really tampering; not as if we were cutting the cable, like you see on TV. Dad never said it'd be dangerous, just that you must be careful with it.'

'Did he say what would happen, if dirt or something did get in?'

'Only that it would block the pipe so the fluid couldn't get through.' Cal shrugged, implying he knew more than he did. 'No big deal, just like putting sugar in the petrol.'

Jilly considered while Cal and Abby watched her in silence, trying to gauge her thoughts. Then she looked up.

'OK, let's go for it; we've not come up with anything better.'

'Great!' Cal rubbed his hands together. 'Now the question is, when?'

'Tomorrow? That'll give us time to work out the details. We'll meet here after school to finalize the arrangements.'

'He'll soon be laughing on the other side of his face,' said Cal with satisfaction.

Jack Spencer had been in a bad mood all day. He'd not slept well the previous night – even with door and window wide open, the walls had seemed to close in on him, and when he did sleep, he dreamed he was trapped in an underground tunnel. He'd woken drenched in sweat, and had had to lean out of the window drawing in breaths of cool night air before he was composed enough to return to bed.

And it was Tuesday, his day for The Lodge. Previously, it had been one of the highlights of his week, but that had ended with the advent of Mr Sheridan and his continual carping. What was more, with Jack's hours being three forty-five (on account of picking up young Bryan) till five forty-five, more often than not Sir came home while Jack was still there. In order to check up on him, Jack suspected darkly.

'Honest, Moll,' he said over breakfast, 'I'm in two minds about carrying on there. If it wasn't for Mrs Beth, I'd have given up months since.'

Molly laid a sympathetic hand on his. 'Don't let him drive you away, love. You'll only cut off your nose to spite your face.'

'I didn't get them chrysanths he wanted,' Jack confessed, with a tired grin. 'Can't abide the things, no more could Mr Simon. "Only fit for funerals, Jack," he used to say.'

'Oh Jack, won't that get you in trouble?'

'Happen he'll not notice. He says things off the top of his head to annoy me, and likely forgets them straight after. More'n once I've not done as he said, and he never came back to me.'

'All the same, love, like it or not, as master of the house, he's entitled to choose his own flowers.'

'He's not master of *me!*' Jack declared illogically, and Molly, with a sigh, gave up.

'Liza? It's Pam Firbank. Is Beth there?'

'Sorry, Mrs Firbank, they're all out. Can I take a message?'

'Yes, you could, actually; I'm afraid Stephen left his pyjamas in the bathroom. He didn't realize till he looked for them last night. I'm so sorry.'

'I saw them just now, hanging on the back of the door.'

'That's how I came to miss them. Could someone possibly post them on to us?'

'Of course. Where will you be?'

'If you send them Next Day Delivery, we'll be care of Mr and Mrs Strachan, at Cairn View, Nevis Road, Fort William.'

'Just a moment, while I find a pen. Right, now: Cairn View, you said?'

Pam repeated the address as Liza wrote it down. 'Sorry to be such a nuisance,' she finished.

'That's all right. Beth will be back for lunch, and I'm sure she'll get them straight off to you.'

'Thanks so much, Liza. And thanks again for all those lovely meals.'

'A pleasure, Mrs Firbank,' Liza said.

There was an air of excitement when they met by the swings that afternoon, mixed, in the case of the girls, with slight trepidation.

'You really think it's OK, doing this?' Jilly asked.

'Depends what you mean by OK,' Cal answered impatiently. 'We want to get back at him, don't we?'

'Yes, but – wouldn't it be better to stick to nails?'

'Don't be so *wet*, Jilly. Anyway, if he found nails in his tyres, he'd have a pretty good idea who put them there, and there'd be hell to pay. This way, we'll be anonymous.'

'And you're sure it's not really dangerous?'

'Of course it isn't.'

'OK. So let's recap then. As soon as we leave here, we'll collect some soil—'

Cal held up a jam jar. 'Already done. The shed was open and I could see a sack of gravel, so I took a handful. Probably better than just soil.'

'OK. So now what?'

'We wait till they're settled in the sitting room after dinner, then we let ourselves in to the garage and – do it. It'll only take a couple of minutes, but someone will have to stand guard.'

'Will we be able to open the bonnet?' Abby asked.

'Yep – the car's never locked when it's in the garage.'

Cal shifted his position, and there was a sudden snapping sound. They all froze, then he reached beneath him and held up a broken twig. 'OK, it was only this; it was digging into me, that's why I moved.'

'We'd better put a definite time on this, so we know where we are,' Jilly said. 'Eight thirty?'

'Eight thirty it is. Synchronize watches, everyone.'

Abby looked blank, and Jilly showed her what to do. Then, hugging their secret, they returned to the house.

Jack's last job on a Tuesday afternoon was to wash Beth's car, a task Bryan enjoyed helping with. She always left it on the drive for them, and when they'd finished, Jack would garage it and, if no one was about, drop the keys through the letter box.

'It's been playing up a bit, Jack,' she'd said earlier. 'Perhaps you'd have a look at it, and see if you can spot the trouble.'

He and Bryan were hosing the car down when Mr Sheridan drove past, straight into the open garage.

Jack checked his watch. Barely five-forty, which meant he'd left work early again. Bastard! he thought. His mood had not improved during the day, and when he saw Sheridan walking purposefully towards him, he could feel anger building up inside him.

'Spencer,' the man began imperiously, when still several feet away, 'I thought I told you I wanted chrysanthemums in that far bed?'

Jack gritted his teeth. 'We never have chrysanths in the garden, sir,' he muttered.

'I'm not interested in what you've done in the past. I specifically asked you to get some, and since you've deliberately ignored me, I'll see your pay's docked this week.'

Jack dropped the hose, and water spurted over Harold's trousers and shoes, causing him to jump back with an expletive.

'I've had enough o' this!' Jack declared, his voice shaking. 'Ever since you come 'ere, you've done nowt but criticize – "do that", "don't do that". When Mr Simon were alive, he left me to do as I thought fit, and he were allus right pleased wi' it, and all.'

Sheridan's voice was steely. 'As you might have noticed, Spencer, Mr Simon, as you call him, is no longer with us; but I'm willing to bet even he wouldn't have stood for being addressed in that tone.'

'There weren't never the need of it, that's what I'm saying. Mr Simon were a gentleman, and—'

'I'm not?'

Jack was aware of Bryan tugging nervously at his sleeve, but there was no stopping him now.

'Not the way you talk to me, you're not, bossing me around all t'time as though I'm not good enough to tie your laces. And it's not even your garden, it's Mrs Beth's! If *she* wants chrysanths, I'll get 'em and gladly, but I know damn well she don't!'

Sheridan's face was white, and a tic jumped at the corner of his mouth. 'That's quite enough. Take your things and go. And you needn't bother coming back.'

'Don't worry, I won't. But I'm not going afore I've finished cleaning yon car.'

And he picked up the hose, relishing Sheridan's instinctive skip backwards, and continued with the rinsing. After a moment of total immobility, his employer turned on his heel and strode away.

'Arrogant bugger!' Jack said, loud enough for him to hear.

'Oh, Dad!' Bryan whimpered. 'Have you got the sack?'

'No, son,' Jack replied loftily, 'I resigned. And not before time, neither.'

*   *   *

Jack was still shaking when, having recoiled the hose, he climbed into Beth's car. A turn or two of the ignition showed the battery to be totally flat.

He climbed out again and turned to his son. 'Get in, lad, and steer t'wheel while I push 'un inter t'garage.'

Between them, they managed to roll the car inside. Jack took out the keys and handed them to the boy.

'I'm not goin' within fifty yards of any of 'em, Bry. But you knock on t'back door and hand these to Miss Jenkins. Ask her to tell Mrs Beth as her battery's flat. It'll need chargin' afore she can shift it.'

The boy looked at him anxiously. Then he nodded, took the keys, and ran round the back of the house. Jack stared malevolently at Sheridan's large black car. For two pins he'd have run his keys along the gleaming paintwork.

Smiling grimly, he walked back outside and pulled down the door.

The deed was done. Hearts hammering, the three children had crept out of the house, and as arranged, Abby took out her rope and began skipping outside the garage, ready to warn of anyone's approach. Jilly watched with bated breath as Cal propped open the bonnet and, after a moment's scrutiny, unscrewed the cap of the relevant container. Slowly, careful not to spill any, he dropped a handful of gravel into the fluid and replaced the cap.

Then, breathing heavily, he looked across at his sister and gave her the thumbs up.

'Geronimo!' he said.

It was past eleven when Molly, dozing in front of the television, became aware of knocking on the front door. She looked up at the clock, and frowned. Jack should have been back before this.

She hurried to the door, to find her husband on the step, supported by two of his friends.

'He's all right, missus, had a drop too much, that's all,' Stan Blenkinsop told her.

'More than a drop, by the look of him,' Molly said sharply.

Stan grinned. 'Sounding off he were, all evening, about what he'd like to do to him up at t'Lodge. There was no holding 'im.'

Molly flushed. 'His bark's worse than his bite,' she said. 'Thanks for bringing him home.'

'Reckon we'd better give you a hand wi' him up t'stairs, and all,' said the other man. 'He's no light weight for a slip of a thing like you.'

'Well, I—'

'No bother,' they assured her. And as she helplessly followed in their wake, they half lifted, half dragged Jack up the steep staircase to their room and heaved him on to the bed.

'He'll be right as rain come morning,' they assured her, as they took their leave with her renewed thanks.

Molly could only hope they were right.

Sixteen

The children were surprised to find Harold still at the breakfast table when they came down the next morning.

'He has to see a client, so he's leaving a bit later,' Beth explained.

Great! Cal exulted; thanks to them, he'd be late for an important meeting. He glanced at his sisters, but their eyes were fixed on their plates. They'd not expected to see Harold, and guilty consciences made it hard to look at him. It was a relief when it was time to leave for school.

At the bend in the drive, they turned to wave to their mother.

'Are you sure they won't know it was us?' Abby asked, as they continued on their way.

'Positive,' replied Cal confidently.

It was almost lunchtime when one of the prefects came into the classroom and spoke quietly to the mistress in charge. Jilly, who was translating a French poem, jumped when she heard her name.

'Jilly Poole! Mr Graham would like to see you in his room.'

Jilly stared at her, her mind racing back over past misdemeanours. She couldn't recall any recent ones, but it was rare to be summoned to the head's study, especially in the middle of a class.

'Off you go, then!' Miss Davis prompted, and Jilly, still wondering what she'd done wrong, rose obediently from her desk.

The head's study lay on the far side of the glass entrance doors, and glancing through them, she was surprised to see a police car outside. Then, as she turned into the corridor, she saw Cal and Abby, accompanied by another prefect, waiting for her outside the head's door. A wave of coldness washed over her. Had Harold discovered what they'd done, and reported them to the police? She wouldn't put it past him.

Feeling slightly sick, she hurried to join them. Cal and Abby looked equally worried, but the prefect gave her a sympathetic smile, and knocked on the door. It was opened by Mr Graham himself.

'Ah, there you are,' he said distractedly. 'Come in, all of you, and – sit down.'

This wasn't the usual opening to a reprimand, and their surprise increased when, as the three of them entered the room, the headmaster left it, closing the door behind him. Then they promptly forgot him, for standing by his desk were a man and woman in police uniform, and next to them – unbelievably – was Liza, with tears streaming down her cheeks.

Jilly's heart set up an uncomfortable, thudding beat.

The WPC gave them a strained smile. 'Hello,' she said. 'My name's Sue. Would you – like to sit down?' She indicated three chairs that had been set against the wall.

Cal, speaking for all of them, said in a strangled voice, 'We'd rather stand.' His eyes were fixed on Liza.

'Just as you like.' Sue replied. 'But – I'm afraid we have some very bad news.'

The children, rigid, stared at her in silence. She moistened her lips. 'I'm very sorry to tell you that your parents have been involved in a car crash – a serious one. And – unfortunately, they – didn't survive.'

There was total silence. Then Jilly said in a croak, '*They?*'

Sue nodded. 'Your mother and – stepfather, wasn't it?'

'*Mummy?*' Abby asked, her voice rising.

'I'm afraid so, yes. I'm so very sorry.'

'But – it can't be! There must be a mistake!' Cal said rapidly. 'Mum has her own car, she doesn't—'

The policewoman glanced at Liza. 'Miss Jenkins says her battery was flat, so your stepfather gave her a lift.'

Jilly's hands flew to her head. 'No!' she gasped. 'No, no, no!'

'Oh, my poor lambs!' Liza cried on a sob, and held out her arms. Abby ran to her, hurling herself against the familiar body, but Jilly and Cal stood immobile, ashen-faced.

'This,' Cal said distinctly, 'isn't happening. Please say it isn't.'

The policeman came forward and took his arm. 'Sit down, sonny. You've had a nasty shock.'

Cal shook him off. 'It's not true – is it? Not Mum?' He stared beseech-ingly at Liza, but her distress was answer enough. She wouldn't have wept for Harold. Cal suddenly crumpled to the floor, hands linked behind his bowed head. Jilly dropped down and held him to her, as the two of them rocked backwards and forwards in an agony of grief.

The police officers watched them helplessly for a moment, then, taking control, raised them gently to their feet. 'We'll run you all home,' Sue said.

Somehow, the hours passed. Since Liza was still distraught, the police offi-cers stayed on, making hot, sweet tea as they all sat, frozen with shock, round the kitchen table.

'Your aunt and uncle are on their way,' Liza said at one point, mopping her eyes. 'It must have been providence made Mr Firbank leave his pyjamas.'

And, at their blank faces, she explained about Pam's call, giving their address. 'Otherwise, with them touring Scotland, we'd have had no way of contacting them.'

Finally bracing herself, Jilly asked fearfully, 'What caused the crash? Does anyone know?'

The policeman shook his head. 'Too early to say. There'll be an investigation, but it seems no other vehicle was involved. The car took a corner fairly fast, then must have spun out of control. It veered into a wall, bounced off it across the road on to the grass verge, and – turned over on to its roof.'

He hesitated, looking at four horrified faces and wondering if he'd said too much. They'd a right to know, though. He added gently, 'It all happened very quickly. They – wouldn't have suffered.'

Cal stood up abruptly. 'If you don't mind, we'd like to be alone for a while,' he said, his voice cracking. 'We'll be down the garden if you need us.'

Liza made a protesting gesture, but without glancing at the adults, the three children quickly left the room.

Once in the privacy of the enclosure, they instinctively held on to each other in a closed circle, all of them trembling.

'We killed Mummy!' Abby sobbed.

'It was an accident,' Cal said harshly. 'The police said so.'

'But we made it happen!'

'No! The gravel couldn't have caused it.'

'You said it wasn't dangerous,' Jilly accused him through her tears.

'It wasn't. It shouldn't have been. Something else must have happened.'

'Perhaps we should—'

'*No!* That's why we came down here – I thought one of you might blurt something out.'

Cal disentangled himself from his sisters' arms, felt in his pocket, and extracted a penknife.

'Nothing we say can help Mum now,' he said unsteadily, 'but in case they try to blame us, we must *never* breathe a word of what we did.'

The girls watched him wide-eyed as he made a small cut in his finger, and a bright spot of blood oozed out. 'Give me your hand, Jilly.'

Jilly recoiled. 'So you can cut me? Not on your life!'

'We have to do this.' Cal spoke in a low, urgent voice, and although she was the elder, she sensed his authority. 'We have to mingle our blood and swear on pain of death that as long as we live, we will never breathe a word of what happened. *For as long as we live!*' he repeated forcefully.

Reluctantly, first Jilly, then Abby received a nick. Then, under Cal's direction, they placed their fingers together, moving them gently so that the blood of all three intermingled.

'Now, repeat after me: "I swear I will never tell anyone what we did last night."'

The two girls did so.

Cal wiped his penknife down the side of his shorts and replaced it in his pocket. 'Remember that's a binding oath,' he said solemnly. 'Blood is thicker than water.'

The diversion over, Abby burst into a storm of tears. 'I want my Mummy!' she sobbed. And as the enormity of their loss overcame them, they huddled together, seeking a comfort none of them could give.

Once they'd absorbed Liza's terrible and incoherent call, Pam and Stephen were faced with choices that would change their lives.

'There's really only one course,' Stephen said, as they hastily repacked their cases. 'We must adopt them.'

And Pam, her tears starting again, flung her arms round him. 'Oh darling, I was praying you'd say that!'

So, heavy-hearted and unsure how the children would respond, they returned to the house by the lake.

Pam, who had always loved the house, could now scarcely bear to be in it. She'd felt Simon's presence on her last visit; now, there were two beloved ghosts, hovering just outside her line of vision. And adding to her unease was the reaction of the children. Though clearly devastated, they were proving resistant to her attempts at comfort, spending most of their time by themselves down the garden. In another world, she and Beth had watched them retreat there from the top of the scar. *United we stand*, she'd suggested then. Perhaps the same thing applied.

As soon as they felt it appropriate, she and Stephen had broached the idea of adoption.

'It would be so wonderful for us to have you,' Pam had ended. 'You know we've always loved you. So what do you say? Would you like to come and live with us?'

Abby's lip trembled. 'We wouldn't have to call you Mummy, would we?'

'Oh darling, of course not! I could never be that. We'll still be Auntie Pam and Uncle Stephen, like we've always been.'

The children glanced briefly at each other. Then Jilly said tonelessly, 'All right. Thank you.'

And that, it seemed, was that.

* * *

Pam related the decision to Liza.

'There's no way they can go on living here,' she said. 'Nearly every day, they'd pass the place where their mother died – not to mention the lake that claimed their father. They know our home, and already have a few friends from when they've stayed with us. We're hoping it will give them a fresh start.'

She looked at the red-eyed woman across the table, and impulsively reached for her hand. 'How selfish of me, Liza! I've never asked what you're going to do. This has been your home, too.'

'I'll go to my friend Cora,' Liza replied. 'Her son's about to open a restaurant in France, and she's moving out there to help him. She's asked me to go with her, and I've offered to put some capital into the business.' Her eyes filled with tears. 'I'm hoping for a fresh start, too.'

'You know you'll always be welcome to visit us,' Pam said.

'Thank you, that's very kind. Perhaps, when some of the healing has taken place, I'll do that. When – how soon will you all be going?'

'As soon as the funeral's over. The police will keep in touch about the investigation, but they don't need us to stay. The house'll go on the market, of course; if there's any little thing you'd like as a keepsake, please feel free to take it.' She hesitated. 'I'm in no position to know how children cope with grief, but doesn't it strike you that they're rather – withdrawn?'

Liza nodded. 'I've been worried about them from the word go. Of course—' She broke off, then went on rather diffidently, 'they didn't particularly care for Mr Sheridan, I'm afraid. I'm wondering if they somehow blame him for the crash.'

'That could be it,' Pam agreed, with a feeling of relief. 'Well, they say time's a great healer. We'll just have to hope that's true.'

So the funeral was held in the little church down the road, which was filled to capacity. There was an unreal quality about the day that helped Pam experience it from a distance, maintaining the self-control she'd been so afraid of losing. Afterwards, only a few disparate memories remained lodged in her mind – the sun shining on to the coffins at the chancel steps as though bestowing blessing; the continuous, silent weeping of the girls and Cal's stony face; the piercing sweetness of the hymns.

There was added poignancy in that Beth was buried not with Harold but in the same grave as Simon, whom they had laid to rest two brief years ago. Pam, glancing at Harold's sister and her husband, wondered if they'd been prepared for that, but their faces gave nothing away. The sun was warm on their backs, the soil flung into the graves dry and crumbly. And across the road on the blindingly blue lake, boats sailed and children shouted, as though it were just another summer day. Which, perhaps, was as it should be. It was a cliché that life went on, but one they had to cling to.

During the next few weeks, the new order gradually took shape. The Lodge went on the market complete with most of its contents, and sold almost at once. In Surrey, the children were enrolled into a new school, which they'd start in September, only weeks remaining of the summer term. And the adoption procedure was initiated. Over supper one evening, Stephen casually suggested it might be easier if they took the name Firbank – a point he and Pam had agonized over – and to their relieved surprise, there was no protest.

'We have no one left called Poole,' Cal remarked, 'so why not?'

It seemed a cold-blooded reaction, but Pam was grateful for it nonetheless. Meanwhile, Abby rode daily, Jilly joined the tennis club and Cal struck up a friendship with the boy next door, who was much the same age. Pam and Stephen were just allowing themselves to breathe more easily when another blow fell.

It was Pam who answered the phone, one evening as she was preparing dinner.

'Mrs Firbank? This is Detective Inspector Hargreaves, of the Cumbria Constabulary.'

'*Detective* Inspector?' Pam repeated, frowning.

'That's right, ma'am. There's been a development in the investigation into the deaths of your sister and her husband. It appears a foreign substance had been added to the vehicle's hydraulic fluid chamber.'

Pam stood stock-still, her hand gripping the receiver. 'A foreign substance?'

She must stop repeating what he said.

'Some kind of gravel, or shale, that caused a blockage in the pipes. A witness stated that Mr Sheridan drove past him, taking the corner ahead without slowing down. If he'd belatedly tried to do so, he'd realize the brakes weren't responding, pump the pedal, then yank the handbrake, causing the rear wheels to lock. By the time the witness rounded the corner, the car had ricocheted off the wall and overturned on the far side of the road.'

'But how could this – shale – have got into the pipes in the first place?'

'That, madam, is what we're trying to ascertain.'

Pam gasped as a new and horrifying possibility took shape. 'You're not saying it was put in deliberately?'

'On the evidence, it would seem so.'

'But that's just not possible! It must have been when the car overturned on the grass.'

'That possibility was examined, and, I'm afraid, discarded.'

'You mean someone deliberately tried to kill them?' Pam's voice rose hysterically, and Stephen, coming into the house at that point, hurried over to her, incredulous horror on his face.

'Possibly not to kill them,' Hargreaves replied, 'but certainly to cause an accident.'

'But who——?'

Stephen took the phone from her hand, swiftly identified himself, and listened intently to what the detective was saying.

Pam, watching his face, saw him frown. 'Is that really necessary? They're just beginning to settle down, and . . . Yes, I see. Very well. No, they're not attending school at the moment. Yes, of course. Two thirty tomorrow? Very well, I'll prepare them.'

He put the phone down and turned to his wife.

'They're not going to interview *the children?*' she whispered.

'Just ask if they heard or saw anything suspicious the previous evening. Harold had driven the car that day, and it had been fine then.'

'Oh, Stephen, why do they have to rake it all up again?'

'It's a serious allegation, darling. If they can nail someone for this, they could be facing a murder charge.' He glanced at her stricken face, and added, 'Someone from the local police will be round tomorrow.'

Pam sat down suddenly on the stair, looking whitely up at him. 'You don't seriously think someone wanted to kill *Beth?*'

'Not Beth, no, but she didn't normally go out with Harold, did she? If her battery hadn't been flat, she'd have used her own car.'

'So he was the target?'

'*If* this was a deliberate act, it seems possible.'

She shook her head. 'This is a nightmare.'

'I agree. And I'm not looking forward to telling the children.'

The following afternoon, a plain-clothes man and woman came to interview them. The three children sat side by side on the sofa, as expressionless as a row of wooden dummies, Pam thought, frightened for them. She noticed they were all holding hands, and felt her heart contract.

'Did you know anyone who had a grudge against either of your parents?' the woman, who'd introduced herself as Sarah, began.

'*He* wasn't our parent,' Cal said stiffly. 'And no one *ever* had a grudge against Mum.'

'Your stepfather, then?' Sarah pursued.

'A lot of people didn't like him,' Jilly said.

'Anyone in particular?'

She shrugged.

'The housekeeper, for instance?'

'You can't possibly suspect Liza,' Cal said scornfully. 'She doesn't know anything about cars.'

The male officer intervened for the first time. 'Do you?' he asked.

Cal stared at him, a small pulse beating at the corner of his eye. 'What?'

'Do you know much about cars?'

'Not really.'

'About brake fluid, for instance?'

Cal's hand tightened fractionally on Jilly's. 'Is it what makes the brakes work?'

'Do you know where it's located?'

Cal shrugged. 'Under the bonnet?' Then, meeting the policeman's eye, he added, 'Actually, I'm more interested in boats.'

Sarah picked up the questioning. 'Was anyone else at the house that evening?'

'Only the gardener,' Jilly said after a minute.

'Did he get on with Mr Sheridan?'

Abby looked suddenly frightened. 'Spencer's always worked for us, for as long as I can remember.'

'When your father was alive?'

She nodded.

'And did he like your stepfather?'

Abby dropped her eyes and did not reply. After several more minutes of unproductive questioning, the children were allowed to leave the room.

Stephen asked with a frown, 'What's this about the gardener?'

'Just following a line of enquiry, sir,' Sarah replied, as she and her companion rose to their feet. 'Thank you for your time. You will, of course, be advised of any developments, and in the meantime, if the children remember anything, however unimportant it might seem, do please contact us.'

A few days later, news reached them that Jack Spencer had been arrested on suspicion of double murder.

Pam broke it to the children as gently as possible, but was not surprised when they retreated to the paddock, their replacement for the play area.

Abby was the first to speak. 'We *have* to tell them!' she cried. 'We can't let poor Spencer take the blame! And it *was* the gravel, Cal! We *did* kill them!'

'Shut up, Abby!' Cal said fiercely. 'Don't be daft – of course we can't tell them.'

'Well, I will!' Abby said wildly. 'I—'

Cal seized her wrist in a grip that made her cry out. 'Oh no, you won't! Have you forgotten the oath we swore with our blood?'

She stared at him, frightened. 'But that was when we didn't think it was our fault!'

'It was still an oath, and it still holds. Anyway, Spencer didn't do it, so they can't prove he did. They'll have to let him go.'

Abby subsided a little. 'Are you sure?'

''Course. Stands to reason.'

Abby turned to her sister. 'What do you think, Jilly?'

Jilly, who'd initially panicked when she heard the news, said slowly, 'I agree with Cal. They'll have to let Spencer go. All we need do is sit tight.'

'The children have changed,' Pam said a little sadly, a week or so later. 'They've grown up too soon and too quickly.'

'That's what bereavement does,' Stephen replied.

'And another thing: you know how close they were, around the time of the accident? That seems to have changed; they don't spend so much time together now.'

'Well, it was the tragedy that brought them together; they never struck me before as being particularly close. Perhaps it's a sign things are reverting to normal.'

'But Jilly's even saying she'd like to board when school starts. Did she tell you?'

'No, that's the first I've heard of it; but provided there's a vacancy, there's no reason why she shouldn't. They've accepted her, after all; she'd only have to switch from being a day girl.'

'It's as though she doesn't want to be with the rest of us,' Pam said forlornly.

Stephen put an arm round her. 'I'm sure it's not that, sweetheart. She needs to find her feet, that's all, and if she thinks this would help, we can't deny her the chance.'

The item was at the foot of the front page, and it was Jilly who, having retrieved the newspaper from the mat, was the first to see it.

Pam looked up sharply at her strangled gasp. 'What is it, darling?'

When she didn't reply, the rest of them crowded round, peering over her shoulder. *CUMBRIA DOUBLE-MURDER SUSPECT FOUND HANGED IN CELL*, they read.

Jack Spencer, 49, on remand for the murders of Elizabeth and Harold Sheridan, was found hanging in his cell last night, despite the suicide watch that was being kept on him.

Pam snatched the paper out of Jilly's hand before they could read more. Glancing anxiously at three deathly-white faces, she said rallyingly, 'That seems to clinch it, wouldn't you say? He couldn't bear the guilt any longer.'

PART V – THE RECKONING

Seventeen

It all started with Mum's death. Funny, in a way; death's always thought of as the end, but it proved a beginning for me – the beginning of something Mum could never have foreseen – nor me, neither, come to that.

At that time I'd been at Stockford Grammar three years, and liked it well enough. I got on with the other PE staff, and on the whole the lads I coached were fairly biddable. And I'd hooked up with Patty, who taught modern languages. It wasn't a grand romance or anything, and though she hinted often enough that she'd like to move in with me, I'd managed to fend her off. The flat was my private domain, and if I had my way, that was how it'd remain. Granted, she stayed overnight at weekends, but I wasn't ready for anything more permanent. Valued my independence too much.

Mum hadn't been well for a year or two. Nothing specific – leastways, nothing she let on about – but she was in her sixties and she'd not had an easy life. So my sister Hayley took to visiting more often – did her shopping, drove her to bingo, that kind of thing, and I'd look in from time to time and take her for a pub lunch. Then she had this fall, and after that, she went rapidly downhill.

It was a Saturday morning the call came – early, about seven. Me and Patty were still in bed, but the tone of Hayley's voice brought me quickly awake.

'Bry, you have to come to the hospital at once! It's Mum – she's taken a turn for the worse.'

'The General?' I asked quickly, through the constriction in my throat.

'Yes. Ward Nine. Please hurry.'

'Fifteen minutes,' I said, and rolled out of bed.

Patty's head appeared above the sheet, tousled, eyes half-shut. 'What is it?'

'Mum. I have to go.' I was already on the way to the bathroom.

I hate hospitals. Always have. Something about the endless corridors and the smell of disinfectant and past meals, and the trolleys rushing round corners.

Mum's bed was at the end of the ward, screened by a curtain, and I pushed it aside to find Hayley sitting holding her hand. Mum was propped up on God knows how many pillows, and her face was as white as they were. I felt a stab of foreboding as I bent over to kiss her cheek. It was cool and damp.

'What have you been doing with yourself?' I asked, with forced jollity.

Mum smiled weakly, but Hayley said, 'She has something to tell us, Bry. Something important.'

'OK.' There was a chair on the far side of the bed, and I went and sat down. 'Shoot.'

'This isn't easy,' Mum began, and her voice was so faint we had to lean closer. That alarmed me some more, but I hoped it was just that she didn't want anyone else to hear. 'It's – about your dad.'

Hayley and I exchanged a puzzled look. Dad had died when we were kids; I'd have been about eight, Hayley only six.

'I don't know how much you remember,' Mum went on, in that thread of a voice, and Hayley seemed to realize this was a question.

'Well, just that he was taken ill, and went to hospital, and – died.'

Mum half-lifted her hand, as though in contradiction, then let it fall, and Hayley went on more uncertainly. 'We left home soon after, and went to live with Uncle Bill and Auntie Madge. And wasn't that when we changed our name, from Spencer to Reid?'

Mum closed her eyes. 'Did you ever wonder why? Later, I mean?'

We looked at each other, but found no answer in each other's faces.

'Couldn't afford the rent?' I ventured.

'I meant – the name change.'

'Well, Uncle Bill's name was Reid. Living with him, it made things – tidier.'

'And it used to be your name, and all,' Hayley added. 'Before you were married.'

Mum shook her head feebly. Seemed we weren't doing too well. She tried another tack. 'What do you remember about Dad himself?'

'He was a gardener,' I said promptly. 'Used to take me with him sometimes, after school.'

'You remember going to the Big House?'

'Yeah.' I had a mental picture of a long, sloping garden, with a playground in the far corner. 'We used to clean the lady's car,' I added. Memory stirred. 'Didn't something happen to them, the family? A car crash, or something?'

Mum let out her breath in a long sigh. 'That's right. Mr and Mrs Sheridan were killed. Someone had tampered with the car, and it went out of control on the lake road.'

Her hand tightened round Hayley's, gripping it so that her knuckles stood out like pebbles. 'And your dad was accused of their murder,' she finished in a rush.

The shock went through me like a lightning bolt, and I saw it reflected on my sister's face. There was a long silence, while we tried to get our heads round this totally unbelievable statement. Mum was lying back against the pillows, her eyes closed again, as though that last sentence had sapped all that remained of her strength.

Then Hayley said incredulously, for both of us, '*Dad?*'

Mum's eyes trembled open. 'A more mild-mannered man than your father would be hard to find, and there wasn't many he didn't get on with. But Mr Sheridan was always one for criticizing and finding fault. Months it had been going on, and that last day, Jack finally lost his temper. You were there, Bry, though you probably don't remember. Any road, there were words – some of them overheard by the housekeeper – and the upshot was he got the sack. That night in the pub, he drank too much, started mouthing off about what he'd like to do to Mr Sheridan. And the very next day, the man died.' She drew a deep breath before adding flatly, 'They found gravel from your dad's shed in the brake fluid.'

'But that doesn't mean anything!' Hayley objected, indignant tears in her eyes. 'Anyone could have put it there!'

'Point is, love, they couldn't. That shed was kept locked, so the kids couldn't get at the weed-killer and such. Your dad had the key.'

My heart was pulsing in my throat as I put in my own two penn'orth in Dad's defence. 'But he'd never have done a thing like that.'

'Course he wouldn't.' Mum's voice was briefly stronger. 'But the worst part – the absolutely worst – was that they locked him up, and you know he couldn't stand that. Remember how we could never shut doors in the house, no matter how cold it was?'

She smiled briefly. 'Even at the pub, his pals grumbled they had to sit outside till they were near frozen, and when forced to go in, he always sat by the door, so he could get out quick if need be. Claustrophobia, they call it. I tried to tell them at the police station, but they thought I was making excuses.

'He was never charged, mind you, only on remand, but it was double murder so they wouldn't grant him bail. And he'd made a scene when they took him to the cell, lashing out, like. It was panic, of course, but they called it "assaulting a police officer". I swore to him it wouldn't be for long, that I'd get up a petition, but he was near out of his mind, shut up like that. And next thing, he – he went and hanged himself.'

We both stared at her, our world falling apart and reforming in a totally unfamiliar pattern.

'They'd taken away his belt,' Mum went on in a whisper, 'even the laces from his shoes, but he were that desperate, he ripped the sleeve out of his shirt and tore it into strips. Didn't take much – his feet were only two inches from the floor.' She drew a deep breath. 'Well, they took that as proof, didn't they? Remorse, they said, and no matter how often I explained, no one believed me. They closed the case and never even looked for no one else.'

'You mean—' Hayley's voice croaked and she started again. 'You mean the real killer never came forward? Let Dad take the rap for it?'

'That's exactly what I mean. One thing's for sure: whoever killed the Sheridans also killed your dad. As surely as if they'd knotted that sleeve round his neck.'

Her words hung on the air, bitter and accusatory. Then, heavily, she went on. 'So – we packed up and left Scarthorpe. I wasn't having people pointing you out as a murderer's kids, and I changed our name for the same reason, apologizing in my heart to Jack. But "Spencer" was on everyone's lips, and I had to protect you.'

'Oh, Mum!' Hayley said softly, tears raining down her cheeks.

'I tried to get Bill to do something . . . clear Jack's name . . . but he didn't want the bother.' She was speaking less fluently now, with pauses between words, as though she needed to keep building up her strength. 'Said he was . . . doing his bit . . . giving us a home . . . and anything else . . . was a waste of time . . . and wouldn't help Jack any road. He might have been . . . my brother . . . but him and Madge made it . . . clear . . . we were a nuisance. As right enough we were . . . the three of us, landed on them. But it weren't for charity. We paid our way . . . even though it meant keeping two jobs going.'

Her words brought back those cramped quarters over my uncle's pub, the noise in the evenings when we were trying to sleep – bellows of raucous laughter, singing, and sometimes raised voices and the sound of crashing glass. Mum worked day shifts in a shoe factory, and as she helped out in the pub in the evenings, we hardly ever saw her. She'd come late at night into the room we all shared, white with exhaustion, and just fall into bed. As kids, we'd accepted it as part of our changed lives, never realizing the agony that lay behind it.

I put my hand over her free one. 'You did us proud, Mum,' I said, my voice choked, and she gently squeezed mine in acknowledgment.

The curtain was pulled aside and a nurse stood there, frowning down at us.

'Your mother's tired,' she said briskly. 'She needs to sleep now. We'll let you know if there's any change.'

Reluctantly, since we couldn't argue the point, Hayley and I stood, bending from opposite sides of the bed to kiss Mum goodbye. I glanced back as the nurse held the curtain for us, but her head was turned away and her eyes shut.

Realizing Hayley was sobbing quietly, I took her arm and led her down the long ward past the rows of beds, some of whose occupants stared at us curiously. Out in the car park she dabbed her eyes.

'Can you come back to ours, Bry?' she asked. 'We need to talk this through.'

I'd been thinking the same thing. I pulled out my mobile, pressed the button for Patty's, and her still-sleepy voice answered me. Patty would have stayed in bed all weekend, given the chance.

'I'm not coming straight home,' I said. 'I'm going back to Hayley's. Can you let yourself out? I'll give you a bell later.'

'OK.' Always acquiescent, was Patty, accepting anything I said. Most of the time I liked it, sometimes it irritated me. 'How's your mum?' she added.

'Not good,' I said briefly, and rang off.

My mind was spinning as I followed Hayley's blue Focus out of the hospital car park and along the crowded Saturday streets, where market stalls narrowed the pavements, and people wandered heedlessly on to the road. We'd been hit with two shocks in the space of as many minutes – a double whammy. First, Dad had been accused of murder – shy, quiet Dad – and second, he'd topped himself. Neither seemed even remotely possible. And added to all that was a gnawing worry about Mum; she'd looked so much worse than when I'd last seen her, some ten days since.

Ten minutes later, we were drawing up outside the little semi where my sister lived with her husband and kid. There was a trike in the small front garden, and an abandoned doll. Hayley, going up the path ahead of me, stopped and retrieved the doll, carrying it with her into the house.

As we came into the hall, Gary appeared from the kitchen, a tea towel in his hand. Good about the house, was Gary; Hayley always said so.

'How is she?' he asked, putting an arm round his wife as she stumbled against him.

'Pretty poorly,' she replied, 'but that's not the half of it.' She looked at me over her shoulder, and I knew she was asking permission to tell him what we'd learned. I nodded; Gary had been part of the family for the past seven years.

'Where's Jade?'

'In the back garden, playing with Jasmine.' The kid next door, and Jade's best mate.

We moved by mutual agreement into the kitchen. Through the window, we could see the two little girls in the Wendy House, having what appeared to be a toys' tea party. Gary and I sat at the table while Hayley made instant coffee. None of us spoke until she joined us at the table, distributing mugs.

Then Gary, looking from one of us to the other, said, 'Well, what is it?'

Hayley reached for a handkerchief. 'You tell him, Bry.'

So I did, watching his brows draw together and his eyes darken with concern.

'What a God-awful thing to have happened,' he said, as I came to the end.

We nodded sombrely.

'And you never had an inkling? Wonder why she told you now, after keeping it quiet all these years?'

'It's because she thinks she's dying,' Hayley said unsteadily, 'and she wants to set the record straight.'

Gary looked sharply at her, then at me. 'And is she?'

I nodded wordlessly. There wasn't much doubt.

'Sorry to hear that. Still, not wanting to criticize or nothing, I reckon it's a bit hard, lumbering you with it all when there's nothing you can do. You'd be better not knowing.'

Hayley started to cry again, and Gary comforted her as I stared into my coffee. *Whoever killed the Sheridans*, Mum had said, *also killed your dad*. Not only that, I thought; he'd completely sabotaged our lives. If Dad hadn't been wrongly accused, we'd have gone on living happily in the little house in Scarthorpe. Mum would have continued doing shifts at the supermarket, not injuring her health by working all the hours God sent and having to be grateful to Bill and Madge. Now memory had been stirred, I recalled often hearing her softly crying in the night.

Nothing you can do about it, Gary said. Those two sentences, Mum's and Gary's, kept repeating themselves in my head. And I thought that it wasn't right this unknown killer should get away with it, not only the car crash and making those kids orphans, but with causing Dad's death and Mum's ill health, and a totally changed life for me and Hayley.

The hospital's second call came that evening, as we were preparing for another visit, but by the time we got there, it was all over. We were told Mum had slipped into a coma soon after we left, and never regained consciousness.

'So the last thing she knew,' said the kindly doctor, 'was the two of you by her bedside. That would have been a comfort.'

How could we tell him that her last thoughts would have been far from comfortable?

Over the next week or two I felt somehow suspended, on a different plane from everyone else. People made allowances, putting it down to bereavement; as, of course, it was – partly. But as well as grieving for Mum and shedding tears at her funeral, I reckon me and Hayley were also crying for Dad, knowing what we now did.

And all the time, below the level of consciousness, a resolution was hardening inside me, a resolve to find out who really did cause the crash and all the devastation that followed. And if he was still alive, to track him down and force a confession, clearing, however belatedly, my dad's name.

By the time these internal workings came to the surface, they'd evolved into a firm commitment. I didn't mention it to Hayley, not wanting to get her hopes up; in all probability the real culprit was dead by now, and beyond my reach. Twenty-three years is a long time, especially if he was a hardened criminal. For all I knew, he might have been caught and served time for something completely different.

Yet, on reflection, that seemed unlikely. The more I thought about it – and I did, constantly – the harder I found it to fit the crime into any category. That it was personal was beyond doubt, but it was also frighteningly haphazard: it could so easily have caused more deaths – the car crashing into another, or mounting the pavement and hitting a pram, a group of kids, old-age pensioners. Most personal grudges were settled more immediately, by mugging or a knife in the guts. This one was curiously remote-controlled; in fact, hardly controlled at all.

And something else occurred to me; the police had assumed Dad targeted Sheridan, because of the bad feeling between them. But since Dad hadn't been the perpetrator, there was no knowing whether in fact it had been Mr Sheridan or his wife who was the intended victim. Admittedly it had been his car, but she might also have driven it. So who was meant to die – him, her, or both of them?

Pondering motives had become an obsession, but there came a point when pondering wasn't enough. Half-term was approaching, bringing with it a week's freedom. Patty and I had talked of going away, but nothing was finalized, and when she brought it up, I told her I'd made other plans, firmly ignoring her disappointment.

And I wasn't lying – I *had* made plans; I'd decided that the place to start my search was where it all took place – up in Scarthorpe. The thought of going back there after all these years was exciting, unsettling. Would anyone we'd known still be there, some of the kids from school – Pete, for instance? Even if he was, would we recognize each other?

Alone in the flat in the evenings, I began to make lists of who I should contact for information. The local newspaper was the first step; their archives would contain reports of the crash, the inquest, and so on. Next, the people now living at the Big House. I still thought of it as that, couldn't for the life of me remember its real name. There might have been talk at the time they bought it, which could contain a germ of truth.

In any case, I'd a hankering to see the place again, try to recreate it in my mind as it had been all those years ago, and at the same time check, for instance, if there were other means of access to the locked shed. It was a faint hope, but might give me a push in the right direction, and it would be a nostalgia trip at the very least. Then there was the local vicar; he might know what had happened to the kids, who might, in turn, have some memory that hadn't been thought important at the time.

I'd need a cover story; a journalist, say, doing a piece on old crimes and their effect on those left behind? That could be tricky, though, if I was asked what paper I worked for. Research for a book was safer.

The more I thought back to those distant days, the more I found I remembered. The housekeeper, for instance; she'd always been kind to me – given me biscuits. What was her name? It would come back. All in all, she'd probably be the best bet, if I could trace her. She'd know who the family were friendly with, and who not. Though according to Mum, she'd helped to nail Dad, with her talk of the row she'd overheard.

That row – Mum also said I'd been there. I tried to recall it, but the memory had been buried under all that came after – Dad's death and the move to the pub. Perhaps a return to Scarthorpe would unearth it.

The church clock across the road started to strike, and I counted the chimes. Midnight. Another day nearer. I closed my notebook and went to bed.

Sunday lunch with Hayley and Gary, the week before half-term. We'd seen more of each other since the funeral; the only two members of the family left, privy at last to its secrets, and needing the comfort of each other's company as we found ourselves mourning both our parents.

We'd cried, of course, when told of Dad's death, but what with the bustle of moving to a new home and a different school, together with kids' natural resilience, he soon faded from our thoughts. And a contributory factor, I remembered now, was that our uncle and aunt had forbidden us to speak of him, on the pretext that it would upset Mum. In effect, he'd been metaphorically swept under the carpet, and twenty-three years on, I bitterly resented the fact that he'd gone to his grave believing his children would think him a murderer.

'You and Patty going away next week?' Hayley asked, stirring the gravy at the stove.

I was prepared for that. 'I am, though not with Patty.'

She turned then, eyebrows raised. 'You two had a row?'

'No, it's not that. I just need a bit of space at the moment, time to clear my head.'

She nodded in understanding. 'Me too, but chance is a fine thing.' She paused, not looking at me. 'Could you manage one evening next week, to go over Mum's house with me? It'll have to be cleared.'

'God, Hayl,' I said, taken unawares.

'I know; I've been putting it off. Seeing all her clothes and that—' Her voice broke.

'Of course I'll come,' I said, dreading the prospect.

'Dinner nearly ready?'

Our depressing conversation was interrupted by Gary, coming in with Jade. She was a skinny little thing with plaits, much as Hayley had been at her age, but cheekier.

'Yes, you can start carving,' Hayley replied.

We took our places round the table; comfort food, I thought, surveying the heaped plate of roast beef and Yorkshire, crisp roast spuds and buttered carrots. Funny how you always felt better on a full stomach.

Jade was regarding me from across the table. 'There's a boy in my class called Brian,' she said. 'But he doesn't spell it with a "y".'

Hayley laughed. 'Your nan was very proud of that "y".'

I smiled, remembering the embarrassment it had caused me in childhood, the accusations of being a toff, or, even worse, a poof. Mum had insisted on the spelling, Dad told me once.

'Bit fancy to my way of thinking,' he'd said, 'but she'd set her heart on it, and nowt would shift her.'

'You should add a "y" to your name, and all,' I teased Jade. 'J-A-Y-D-E. It'd make you special, like it does me.'

'Don't put ideas in her head,' said Hayley.

We went to Mum's house that Tuesday after school, a two-up, two-down on the Sale Road council estate, where she'd been for ten years or more, since Bill and Madge retired from the pub. And though it was tiny, she'd made it home, delighted to have her own place again. At least we'd be spared the headache of trying to sell it, I thought gloomily.

The process was every bit as bad as we'd feared, everywhere we went, everything we touched, poignant reminders. In the desk in the living room we found school reports dating back to kindergarten, childish drawings in felt pen, a few photographs. She must have taken them with her to the pub, kept them all these years despite chronic lack of space.

'If there's anything you want, just say,' Hayley instructed, tears streaming down her face. 'Otherwise, we'll pack up everything for Oxfam. Mum always supported them.'

In the end, that was what we did. Hayley kept a couple of brooches – there was nothing of value – and I took an ornament that had travelled with us from the house in Scarthorpe, an otter with a fish in its mouth. Dad had won it at the fairground in Blackpool, when they were engaged.

We were both of us drained by the time we'd finished, and as we were about to leave, we exchanged a prolonged hug, holding on to each other as a part of our lives came to an end.

'We've still got each other, Bry,' Hayley whispered through her tears. 'And as Mum always said, blood is thicker than water.'

I nodded, though at the time it was small consolation. I drove home wrapped in a shroud of misery, to find Patty waiting on the step.

She regarded me anxiously, unsure of her welcome. 'I know where you've been,' she said. 'I thought maybe you'd like a bit of company?'

I didn't trust myself to speak. I nodded, and we went together up to the flat. I had the ornament in my hand, and went straight to the mantel-piece, pushing aside the clock and an old ashtray to make room. For a moment I stood looking at it, then it blurred before my eyes as, to my intense embarrassment, the tears came – tears I'd so far managed to suppress except for a few at the funeral, and which now demanded release.

Patty's arms came round me, and she held me while I sobbed like a kid, giving way at last to all the trauma of the last few weeks. And gradually, as the tears lessened, she began to kiss me, my face, my ears, my mouth, gently pressing herself against me, comforting me in the only way she knew. And I felt myself beginning to respond, my thoughts shifting from the past to the present and its needs as she took my hand and gently led me to the bedroom.

Eighteen

It would be around an eighty-mile drive, I reckoned, virtually all of it M6. Realizing how near it was and how easy to get to, I wondered why I'd never thought to go back. No reason to, I suppose.

I'd booked a B and B on the Internet, feeling a twinge as I recognized so many of their addresses – roads Pete and I had cycled down, the street where his Auntie May lived – but realized I was not, after all, anxious to renew old friendships. Everyone I'd known all those years ago believed my dad to be a killer, and would go on doing so till I proved different.

Nor did I want to use my real name; while 'Reid' wouldn't mean anything, Bryan with a 'y' just might, so without so much as a by-your-leave, I hijacked Gary's. I'd confess later, but old Gar wouldn't mind. All in a good cause, and it wasn't as though I was going to rob any banks. And since my email address bore my real name, I invested in another, with the anonymous handle of 'guesswho'. I was rather pleased with that.

So Saturday finally arrived, and, throwing my grip in the boot, I set off for the Lakes.

'Send me a postcard,' Hayley had said. Whether I would or not depended on the success of my mission.

It was a glorious spring day, and the roads were busy on this bank holiday weekend. However, the traffic, heavy until the Blackpool turn-off, eased considerably the farther north I drove, and my excitement grew as hills began to appear ahead, and open countryside, freshly green, stretched as far as the eye could see. The sky was wide and blue, vast expanses of it, unmarred by roofs and chimneys and television aerials, and after the clutter of my usual environment, unconsidered till now, I felt suddenly freer; wondering whether Dad, with his claustrophobia, could ever have survived in Stockford.

I caught my first glimpse of the lake soon after leaving the motorway, and was buffeted by a welter of emotions. God, I'd never realized how much I'd missed this! I slowed down, savouring every minute of the approach to Scarthorpe, nestling along the lakeside with its backcloth of hills. It was windier here, white clouds racing across the sky, creating dark blue shadows on the surface of the water. A few boats bobbed at their moorings, and a motorboat roared down the far side, creating a creamy wake of spume.

I rounded the corner into the town and made my way from memory to Church Road. At first glance, not a lot seemed to have changed, though a municipal playground I remembered had given way to a cluster of houses, some bearing vacancy signs in their windows.

I found White Gables at once, thanks mainly to its living up to its name. I'd been warned in advance there was no parking and I'd have to use the long-stay car park, but that was no problem; I'd be on foot most of the time. I stopped briefly at the gate to announce my arrival, leave my bag, and ask directions to the car park, new since my time.

Mrs Bunting, the owner, was a round-faced woman in her fifties, with prematurely grey hair and rosy cheeks.

'Have you been to Scarthorpe before, Mr Payne?' she asked, pushing the register towards me.

It was a timely reminder; I almost looked over my shoulder, before remembering that was my name for the next week and signing it with a flourish.

'Yes, I grew up here,' I told her.

'Really? So you have relatives nearby?'

'Not any longer,' I said steadily. 'Have you lived here long yourself?'

'Born and bred,' she answered with a smile. 'Met my husband at primary school. We feel, sometimes, that we've stagnated rather, but as Bert says, if you've found the perfect place to live, why bother moving?'

Her accent, so familiar, was different from the one I'd become used to, an echo of my childhood. I'd have to expect plenty of those. She showed me to my room, which was clean and bright, and boasted twin beds and a wash basin.

'The bathroom's just across the landing,' she told me. 'You'll be sharing with Mr and Mrs Crossley, our other guests. We haven't the space for en suites, I'm afraid, but with only two rooms let, there's usually no problem.'

I dumped the grip, enquired the way to the car park, and followed her back downstairs.

'There are plenty of pubs and cafés around, if you need a late lunch,' she said. 'Perhaps you remember some of them?'

'I might, at that,' I said. And five minutes later, having parked the car, found myself on the corner facing the Pig and Whistle, Dad's old haunt. I took a deep breath, went inside, and ordered a pint of bitter and a Ploughman's. It was close on two o'clock, and the place was almost empty, but two old men, seated at a corner table, looked faintly familiar, and as I waited for my pint, I cudgelled my brains.

The fact that they were in Dad's old pub made it likely he'd known them – and then, in a flash, I had it: they were the pair who used to come with us to football matches. One of them had a boy my own age. To think they were still here, drinking in the same pub, when Dad had been dead over twenty years! Talk about life goes on.

I looked across at them, hesitating. Already adult when I'd known them, they'd not changed that much – older, heavier, perhaps; greyer. But I doubted they'd know me in a month of Sundays. I'd been a young kid, one they'd taken scant notice of, and must have changed beyond recognition. Added to which, they wouldn't be expecting to see me, while their presence here had helped my own remembering.

Well, nothing ventured, nothing gained, and what better place to start my search? Before my nerve failed me, I walked across to them, heart hammering. They broke off their conversation and looked up, surprised at my approach.

'Would you think me very rude if I joined you?' I asked with an ingratiating smile. 'I'm hoping to do some research for a book I'm writing.'

That impressed them, as it was meant to.

'Oh, aye?' said one cautiously.

Taking that for consent – or at least, not refusal – I set down my glass and pulled out a chair. 'It's about crime and its aftermath,' I explained.

'Too much writ about crime already,' vouchsafed the second man. Stan, was it?

'But perhaps not enough about the people affected by it,' I went on swiftly. 'The husbands, wives or children left behind.' I took a sip of beer, choosing my words carefully. 'No doubt there've been crimes here over the years?'

They could have asked why I'd come, apparently on spec, to this small Lakeland town, when there must be much richer pickings elsewhere. But they didn't. Almost despite themselves, they were interested, which was what I was banking on.

I nodded to the barman as he set down my Ploughman's. 'You must have known of quite a few in your time, gentlemen. Any you can regale me with?'

'Don't rightly know as we can,' mused the first man, stroking his nicotine-stained moustache. Fred! His name came to me suddenly; Fred Barnes, never seen without a pipe in his mouth. Now suffering, no doubt, from the No Smoking rule.

'There were that robbery over at Blackwell's, Fred,' said his companion, helpfully confirming my memory.

'Aye, but robberies are two a penny, that not right, Mr——?' He looked at me enquiringly.

'Payne. Gary Payne.'

He reached over a gnarled hand. 'Fred Barnes, and this here's Stan Blenkinsop.'

Stan also extended a hand. I'd been accepted. I hid a relieved sigh and started on my Ploughman's. 'I admit murder's more my line.'

'Ah. Not so many of them, glad to say.'

'But there have been a few?'

'Well, there were that young lass stabbed on her way home from a dance. Bad business that were, but they got the lad straight off. Turned out to be ex-boyfriend.'

'And that farmer, found dead among his chickens,' put in Stan. 'Burglary that went wrong, they said.'

'Nothing a little more – unusual?' I probed hopefully. 'Family feud, that kind of thing?'

The two men exchanged glances, and were silent for a moment. Then Stan said, 'Not what you'd call family, but feud of a sort. Folk up at the Big House, twenty year or more back.'

Bingo! 'What happened?' I asked carefully.

'You're talking out o' turn, Stan,' Fred warned him.

'Well, someone's bound to say summat; might as well be us.'

Fred shook his head dolefully, his eyes on his beer, and Stan went on, 'Point is, mister, it concerned a pal of ours. Struck close to home, you might say. Still hard for us to speak on it.'

'I'm sorry,' I said, and waited, holding my breath.

'This pal worked up there. Gardener, like. Straight a feller as you'd care to meet, was Jack. Or so we thought. But governor up there gave him a hard time.'

'So – what happened?'

'That's what we can't get our heads round. But old Jack tinkers with his car, result being not only the man killed, but his missus, too. Real tragedy.'

I moistened my lips. 'Did he admit that, your friend? Tinkering with the car?'

'No, course he didn't.' Stan sighed. 'But he didn't do hisself no favours, neither. In here he was, the night afore – leastways, on the bench outside, on account of him not liking indoors. In a right blether over some set-to they'd had up at t'Lodge, sounding off about the governor, and how he'd get his own back, see if he didn't, and there were plenty heard him. Fred and me didn't pay no heed; thought it was the drink talking. Had to help him home, and all.'

He took a drink of beer, and wiped his mouth with the back of his hand. 'Then, next day, caput. Man was dead, and his wife wi' him.'

My heart was hammering. 'But perhaps it *had* just been the drink, and someone else—'

Stan was shaking his head sorrowfully. 'Oh, he done it, right enough. Must have – no one else it could have been, and like I said, they'd had that row.'

'Worse to follow, though,' Fred put in. 'Couldn't stand being shut in, could Jack, as Stan here told you, and being put in t'cell did for him. Took his own life.' He shook his head. 'Tragic,' he said, 'though thinking on it, mebbe it were for the best. Leastways he didn't have to suffer years of it.'

I pushed away my half-eaten Ploughman's, forcing myself to ask, 'What happened to the families?'

'Moved away, the lot of 'em. Can't blame 'em. Jack's Molly and kids went to live wi' her brother, over Kendal way. And the young 'uns from the Big House, their aunt and uncle took 'em down south somewheres.'

'It would be good to talk to them,' I said from a dry mouth.

'Aye, well, can't help you there.' Stan took a swig of his beer, emptying his glass. I offered to stand him another, but he shook his head. Clearly, my presence had put a blight on things.

'You've no idea how I could contact them?'

They both shook their heads.

'Know someone who might, though,' Fred said suddenly. 'Eileen at Willow Pattern – that's a café down by t'lake. Bought the place from Cora Selby, when she moved away wi' yon friend of hers. And,' he added significantly, 'that there friend were housekeeper up at Big House. Still in touch, Eileen and Cora, that I do know, Eileen being a pal of my missus. Says she often speaks of her.'

I could hardly believe I'd struck gold so soon. 'Thank you,' I said. 'You've been very helpful.'

The two old men rose to their feet. 'Send us a copy of yon book,' said Stan, and I smiled and nodded. Then they were gone, and I was left with three empty glasses and a half-eaten Ploughman's, finding it hard to breathe.

My mission had begun.

*   *   *

I left the pub on a high, in search of the Willow Pattern café, but there my luck ran out. The owner was not at home.

'Gone to her daughter's for t'weekend,' the waitress told me laconically.

I hesitated, uncertain what to do next. It was after three, and though I'd just finished lunch, the tables were filled with people enjoying cream teas. Since I was here, I decided to have a cuppa myself, and sat down to go over what I'd learned. Which, basically, was very little I'd not known already. What it did prove, though, was that the crime was still remembered locally, and hopefully the absent Eileen might be really useful.

The unexpected meeting had caught me on the hop, and though I'd brought a recorder to save having to write notes, I hadn't thought to use it. This evening, back at the B and B, I'd make good the omission, and from now on keep my wits about me.

Twenty minutes later, I emerged from the café and paused on the pavement, the freshening breeze cool on my face. A group of girls went by, giggling, and I caught fragments of their conversation. Their homely accents, like those of Stan and Fred, were a reminder of how much I'd lost of mine, the rough corners being painlessly smoothed during my time at college. A schoolteacher, even a PE one, ought to 'talk proper', I thought with a wry grin.

Nonetheless, this was where I'd sprung from, where my roots still were, and I found it mind-blowing to think that the last time I'd been here, stood by this lake, walked these streets, I'd been eight years old and my dad had just died.

I started to walk, wondering what to do next, and paused to rotate a stand of postcards outside a newsagent's. On impulse, I selected two local views for Hayley and Patty, and a couple to keep as souvenirs. Whether I'd post them was a moot point, but at least they'd be to hand if I decided to.

Without conscious intent, I headed in the direction of our old home, a cottage behind the High Street. My heart was thundering as I turned the corner, suddenly afraid it might have been demolished and another built in its place; but there it was, number seven, looking much as it had always done, with its wooden gate and short path, and even a stone pot by the door, like the one Mum left the key under.

And there, just visible round the back, was the twisted apple tree me and Pete used to climb, and which he'd fallen from and broken his arm. A right to-do there'd been about that, and all.

Having set the tone, I spent the rest of the afternoon revisiting old haunts, awash with memories, and that evening treated myself to dinner at the Swan, the hotel that, in the old days, had seemed on a par with Buckingham Palace. What *would* my parents have thought?

It was just on ten o'clock when I returned to White Gables. A middle-aged couple were sitting in the lounge watching the News – the Crossleys, presumably – and they nodded and smiled at me as I passed. Back in my room, I dictated the pub conversation into the recorder, then summarized the rest of the day's activities. It could double as a diary, I thought, a reminder for checking things later. (And it's proving its worth as I write this.)

There were muted voices on the landing, a floor board creaked, a door closed quietly. The Crossleys had retired.

I stretched, deciding I, too, would call it a day. Having sluiced my face and brushed my teeth at the corner basin, I undressed and, with some trepidation, tested the bed. Fortunately, it proved comfortable. I settled into it with a sigh of satisfaction, and despite my teeming thoughts, soon slid into a dreamless sleep.

Sunday was, by and large, a frustrating day. The newspaper offices were closed, and the vicar – who might, just possibly, have conducted the Sheridans' funeral service – would be too busy to speak to me. I took a boat out on the lake, climbed one of the neighbouring hills, and finally took refuge in a voluminous bundle of Sunday newspapers.

That night, I ate in a pub restaurant – not the Pig and Whistle – and on returning to the B and B, again went straight upstairs, having no wish to make small talk with my fellow guests. In my room, I took out the notes I'd made before leaving home, and sketched out a plan of campaign for the next day.

During a carefully casual chat, Hayley and I had agreed the car crash must have occurred at the end of June '85, and since the local paper, the *Cumberland and Westmorland Post*, was a weekly, it should be easy enough to track down the story. Their office would therefore be my first port of call, and having located contemporary reports in their archives, and hopefully managed to obtain copies, I'd have lunch at the Willow Pattern, and attempt to waylay the proprietor.

Life, however, is seldom straightforward. I discovered the next morning that the newspaper office didn't keep archives, and I'd have to visit the library in Kendal. Which meant retrieving my car from the long-stay, and a twenty-mile round trip.

Still, it proved more than worthwhile. Having been informed that the paper came out on Wednesdays, I requested the copy dated 26th June '85, and all five July editions. The films were loaded for me by the helpful staff, but after scouring the June issue from cover to cover, I concluded the crash must have occurred after publication.

Sure enough, the next week's edition devoted its front page to the tragic death of 'two well-known Scarthorpe residents', together with slightly grainy photographs which, to my surprise, I recognized. Inside, there was a rehashed account of the crash and obituaries of both the Sheridans.

A week later, a detailed account of the funeral was given, with references to the packed church, the presiding vicar's poignant eulogy, and sympathetic references to the couple's three children, who were being 'comforted by relatives'.

By the following week, it had been established the crash was no accident, and a murder investigation had begun. There were appeals from the police for any information that might be useful.

The next issue had little of interest and, with no further development, the story had been banished to the inside pages. But the final paper I'd selected, dated 31st July, bore a single relevant sentence in the Stop Press: 'Man arrested in connection with Sheridan murders.'

I sat staring at it for long minutes. I could, of course, have requested the August papers, but my heart was no longer in it. Basically, I couldn't bring myself to read in black and white of the death of my innocent father.

I ran a hand over my face, returning with some difficulty to the present. I needed at least some of this material to study at my leisure, searching for elusive clues, but after painstakingly going through it again, decided the only report of real value was the first, which included photos and obits.

I pushed back my chair and went to order a copy.

It was after twelve when I left the library, and I'd given up all thought of lunch at the Willow Pattern; by the time I got back to Scarthorpe, reparked the car and walked down to the lake, they might well have stopped serving it.

Instead, I went to a nearby pizzeria, where I took out my photocopy and read through the report again. It seemed Mrs Sheridan's death, at least, had been unintentional; an interview with the housekeeper, Miss Liza Jenkins, revealed that she'd asked her husband for a lift because her own car had a flat battery. The wrong place at the wrong time, with a vengeance.

Which brought us firmly back to Mr S being the sole target, and the vital question of who had wanted him dead. That, in a nutshell, was what I had to find out, because, despite all talk to the contrary, it sure as hell hadn't been my dad.

The same waitress was on duty when I reached the Willow Pattern, and, since Fred hadn't furnished me with a surname, I again asked for the proprietor. This time, she nodded me in the direction of a small, spry woman talking to the cashier.

I went over to her, and she broke off her conversation to smile at me.

'Can I help you?' she enquired.

'I hope so,' I replied, 'though perhaps not in the way you mean.' She raised her eyebrows, and I added, 'Your name was given to me by Fred Barnes.'

My implied exaggeration of our acquaintance secured her attention.

'Is there somewhere we could talk?' I asked, and after a quick nod, she led me to a door that opened on to a flight of stairs.

At the top was a pleasant sitting room overlooking the lake. It seemed that 'Eileen' lived above the shop.

She motioned me towards a chair, sat down herself, and began brightly, 'Now, tell me how I can help you, Mr——?'

'Gary Payne,' I supplied, beginning, by this time, almost to believe it. I smiled apologetically. 'I'm afraid Fred referred to you simply as "Eileen" . . .'

'Morgan,' she said. 'Mrs Eileen Morgan.'

I nodded. 'Well, the point is I'm doing research for a book on the aftermath of crime – the effect it has on those left behind.'

'Oh yes? Very interesting, I'm sure, but I don't quite see——'

'And what brings me to Scarthorpe is the Sheridan case, back in the eighties.'

She shook her head. 'I really can't help you. We heard of it, of course, but we hadn't been here long at the time; I never met the victims or their family.'

I drew a deep breath. 'But you did, I think, know their housekeeper, Miss Jenkins?'

Enlightenment flooded her face. 'Oh, that's why you . . . but I didn't know her well, only through Cora – the lady I bought this café from.'

Not what I wanted to hear. 'But did she speak of the tragedy? What happened to the children, and so on?'

Eileen Morgan thought for a few moments. 'She was desperately upset, of course. She'd been very fond of Mrs Sheridan and her first husband.'

The obituary had mentioned a second marriage.

'He was drowned in a boating accident,' she added.

'And the second husband, the one in the crash?'

Eileen Morgan pursed her lips. 'Miss Jenkins was always discreet, but I don't think she cared for him. Said he was very strict with the children.'

'What happened to them?' I asked again, still hoping they might remember something vital.

'Their aunt and uncle took them away. That's all I know.'

'Do you by any chance remember their name – the uncle and aunt's?'

Eileen Morgan shook her head. 'Liza would know, mind,' she said suddenly. 'She could tell you far more than I can.'

Just what I'd been angling for! 'That would be most helpful. Do you happen to have her address?'

'Yes, yes, I have. She still lives with Cora and her son, in France.'

'In *France?*' I repeated blankly. I'd been intending to go straight on to see her.

'That's right; that's why Cora sold the café. Her son's a chef, and he was opening a restaurant over there. They went out to join him.'

She'd opened a small desk and taken out an address book. 'In Normandy, it is,' she said, leafing through the pages. 'Here we are. *Le Bon Gout*, if that's how you pronounce it.'

It wasn't, but I didn't correct her. My own French was nothing to write home about. She passed me the book and I took down the address, though France might be a step too far on what was after all a slender off-chance.

'Have you got a phone number?' I asked, thinking that might be the easier option, but she shook her head, surprised anyone should think of phoning France.

I slipped my diary into my pocket and stood up. 'Well, thanks very much, Mrs Morgan, you've been a great help.' I paused. 'One last question, if you don't mind: do you know who's living up at the Big House now?'

'The Lodge, you mean? It's a family called Harrison. Two grown-up sons. He's a dentist in the town.'

We walked together down the stairs and through the café to the entrance.

'Thanks again for your help,' I said.

She nodded, and, as I went through the door, called after me, 'Good luck with the book!'

*   *   *

Out on the pavement, I looked round for a public call box, but in this age of mobiles they were few and far between, and I reached the High Street without spotting any. In the post office, though, I struck lucky; they had a public phone complete with directory, and I ran my finger down the list of Harrisons, coming to rest on one JB, whose address was given as The Lodge. I added his number to my mobile and went outside to phone. At three thirty on a Monday afternoon, Mr Harrison would be at his surgery, but his wife—

'Hello?'

'Mrs Harrison?'

'Yes?' She sounded in a hurry.

'My name is Payne, but you don't know me. I wondered if I might have a word with you about the Sheridans, who used to live at your house?'

There was a pause. Then she said, 'I never met them.'

'Even so, I'm writing a book—'

'My Payne, I'm sorry, but I have an appointment—'

'I won't keep you long,' I said quickly, unwilling to postpone my visit. 'I can be with you in five minutes.'

'Well . . .'

'Please. I'll only take ten minutes of your time.'

'Very well, then. Ten minutes.'

'I'm on my way.'

The gods had been with me; anxious to speak to Eileen, I'd parked in the town centre, only yards from where I now stood. I ran to the car, and within minutes was driving along Lake Road, conscious of the lake itself on my left, dull and brooding under a cloudy sky.

Then I was turning off the road into The Lodge driveway, following it uphill to the house, as I had so many times with Dad. There was a car parked outside, proof, I guessed, of Mrs Harrison's anxiety to be off.

She opened the door immediately I rang, a tall, thin woman in her fifties, formally dressed in navy suit and white blouse.

'Gary Payne,' I said, holding out my hand. 'It's good of you to see me.'

'I really don't see how I can help.'

It was becoming a familiar refrain. However, she led me into a drawing room – no other word would do it justice – and as she didn't invite me to sit, we stood facing each other.

'I've already told you I never met the Sheridans.'

'I was wondering, though, if there was talk of them when you bought the house – gossip, if you like. Whether people talked about the crash, and what might have happened?'

'What happened was clear enough,' she answered crisply. 'They were murdered by their gardener, in retaliation for sacking him.'

I held myself in check, saying merely, 'An extreme reaction, surely?'

She shrugged. 'He must have been unbalanced.'

'Did you have any contact with the relatives?'

'No, they weren't from round here. Lived in Surrey, I believe.'

Clue number one.

'Could you tell me their name?'

She shook her head. 'I don't think I ever heard it.'

I tried another tack. 'Was any of the Sheridans' property left in the house or garden? Any old books or furniture, children's toys?'

'Actually, we'd come from abroad, so we bought it fully furnished. There were no books or toys, though, unless you count the swing and slide in the garden.' She paused. 'I did tell you I couldn't help, and I'm sorry, but I really—'

Might as well cut my losses, I thought resignedly. 'All right, Mrs Harrison, I won't keep you any longer. Thank you for seeing me.'

She walked quickly ahead of me out of the house, locked the door behind us, and hurried to her car. I glanced to my left, to the lawn leading down to the shrubbery in the corner.

'Would you mind if I had a quick look at the garden?' I asked on impulse, and, as she turned in surprise, added, 'I used to play here as a boy.'

'I really have to go,' she said.

'I could look by myself, if that's OK? Just a quick one, for old times' sake?'

If she'd not been in a rush, I doubt if she'd have left a strange man in her grounds, but she'd clearly no time to argue. With a vague wave of her hand, she started the ignition and drove quickly down the drive.

I stood looking after her, letting the flood of memories engulf me. The sun on my back as I helped Dad polish the car; the kids, down there in the shrubbery. The kids.

I started to walk slowly down the grass, accompanied by the ghost of my younger self, but almost immediately came to a halt. On my right, freshly creosoted but otherwise as I remembered it, stood the fatal shed. I reached out and tried the door. Locked. Still. Probably, now, to protect garden implements from theft, rather than dangerous substances from the reach of children. I wondered if there was still a sack on the floor, full of the particular kind of shale that, according to the *Post*, had been required for the rockery, and later been positively identified in the wrecked car.

I peered through the small window, but it was too dark to make anything out. For that matter, it was growing darker outside as clouds banked, threatening rain. I examined the fastening of the window, but there'd been no report of its being forced, and I doubted anyway if anyone could have fitted through the small aperture. I walked round it until the thickness of the bushes blocked my way, then inspected the other side. There was no other means of access, that was clear. Whoever had taken the shale must have used the door. But how, when it was locked, and Dad had the key?

I resumed my walk, seeming to see him everywhere – pruning the roses, planting dahlias, tilling the rich soil – happy to be out in the open. Oh, Dad, how could they do that to you?

As I approached the shrubbery in the bottom corner, memories came thicker and faster. It enclosed the old playground, containing the swing and slide Mrs Harrison had mentioned. The kids, all older than I was, had abandoned it long since, and I used to play there for hours, constructing space ships, dens and forts. Then, unaccountably, that last week or two, they'd reclaimed it, chasing me off with a flea in my ear.

I'd reached the entrance, now overgrown with brambles, but the way in was still passable, and I pushed my way through. With a catch in my throat, I saw that the slide and swing were still there. Perhaps the Harrison boys, in their youth, had also made use of them.

I stared at the slide – Health and Safety would do their nut if they could see it! – and remembered my alarm when I'd been caught underneath it. Remembered, too, complaining bitterly to Pete in the playground. *Why not spy on them?* he'd suggested. *Get your own back.*

And I had, I remembered, suddenly uncomfortably hot. I'd hidden among the bushes, and though I couldn't see them from my hide, I could hear their voices quite clearly. Pete had suggested they might be terrorists, then laughed at me when I believed him. So I'd listened, hoping to justify myself.

Twenty-three years on, I stood in the clearing with fists clenched and eyes squeezed tight, forcing myself to remember, convinced I might have heard something vital, and gradually, piecemeal, scraps of their conversation floated up to my consciousness.

Sack of gravel, so I took a handful. That had been the boy. Gravel? My heart was almost choking me. *The car's never locked when it's in the garage.* And at that crucial moment, a twig had snapped under my foot, and as I froze with fear, they'd all stopped talking. But it was all right – I hadn't been rumbled, and I breathed again.

The blood thundering in my ears, I opened my eyes, expecting, almost, to see the three guilty children facing me. *Guilty children*! It *had* to be them! Yes, the shed was kept locked, and yes, Dad had the key; *but it wasn't locked when he was actually in the garden*. And that's when the boy had seized his chance.

Alternating waves of heat and cold broke over me as the first, heavy drops of rain began to fall. My immediate thought was to go to the police station, tell them what I'd remembered, and insist they reopen the case. But what proof did I have? A childhood memory, totally unsubstantiated.

No, I thought, forcing myself to take slow, deep breaths, this was up to me. It was my task to hunt down the Sheridans' murderers – who'd also killed my father – and force them to confess the truth. And nothing, I swore there in the darkening playground, absolutely nothing would be allowed to stand in my way.

Nineteen

Looking back, that was the day that changed everything, when a cold, implacable hatred began to build inside me.

I remember nothing of my drive back to town, parking the car, or making my way to a pub. The first thing I registered was sitting at a small, round table with a double whisky in front of me. I promptly downed it in one, and went back for another. The barman eyed me askance, suspecting I'd already had enough, but he refilled the glass and I returned to my table, resolving to take this one more slowly.

Was it really possible I'd stumbled on the solution to the crime, the solution that the police, following Dad's death, hadn't even bothered looking for? In that stuffy pub, with the rain beating against the window above me, I tried to marshal my thoughts into some semblance of order, examining the shreds of memory in closer detail.

I'd heard those words, yes, but they hadn't meant anything. I'd assumed they were part of some game the kids were playing, and, having been hiding for a while, had begun to lose interest. And though the words had lodged in my unconscious, I never heard details of the crash, still less of the accusations levelled at Dad, so there'd been no trigger to bring them to mind.

But those kids had *known* Dad! That's what stuck in my craw. They'd spoken to him, asked his help, sometimes, when their bikes had punctures. How could they not have come forward when he was arrested? It was likely they hadn't intended serious injury, and they'd probably have got off fairly lightly. Whereas Dad had forfeited his life, dying because three spoilt and stuck-up children resented their stepfather, who'd dared to discipline them.

The banality of it was stupefying, but the upshot was that in addition to mourning Dad, our own lives had been torn apart. And while we existed cramped together in that poky room, and Mum worked double shifts to support us all, they were being pampered and cosseted over the death of their parents – *which they had engineered* – no doubt living a life of luxury, holidays abroad and God knows what. *It wasn't fair!*

Light-headed after the combination of my discovery and two double whiskies, I was in need of ballast, and, though not remotely hungry, ordered a steak pie and chips, eating mechanically while my thoughts spun in eddies and my anger built up. And when the meal was finished, I went out into the wet, prematurely dark evening and made my way to the B and B.

I didn't sleep that night. I lay listening to the rain and watching shadows on the ceiling, my mind and stomach churning; and as the room lightened with dawn, realized I couldn't spend another day in Scarthorpe, where even his friends thought Dad was guilty.

In my diary was the address of Liza Jenkins, who'd escaped the trauma by moving to France. And France no longer seemed a step too far to go for her story. It was now Tuesday, and school didn't restart till the following week. I'd pack my bag, drive home to collect my passport, and, if possible, fly out that evening.

It wasn't enough, now, to hunt down the three of them as I'd intended, and force them to confess. They merited a death sentence, not only for killing their parents, but, by default, for letting Dad die when they could have saved him. And since the state could no longer impose such punishment, it was up to me to do so.

Lying on the rumpled bed, I resolved to find each of them in turn, record their confessions, kill them, and, after death, string them up, in revenge for Dad. And when I'd dispatched all three, I'd submit the recordings anonymously, either to the press or the police, and demand a posthumous pardon.

Making the excuse of a family emergency – true enough – I was on my way before ten.

The overnight rain had given way to a morning bright with sunshine, the lake glinting like sapphire under a cloudless sky. It still tugged at my heart – it always would – but Scarthorpe had given up its secrets, and I'd never come back.

The flat, shut up for days, was warm and stuffy, and I threw open the windows, regretting the open spaces of the Lake District as the sound of traffic drifted up from the street. Then, sitting down at the computer, I went online to check the nearest airport to Liza's village – Fontaine-les-deux-églises. I'd established it was a few miles from Caen, and was gratified to find Caen itself had an airport, with, moreover, direct flights from Manchester. Minutes later, I'd not only booked myself on an evening flight, but secured a room for the night at a nearby hotel.

I tipped the contents of the grip on to the bed and repacked it with a fresh set of clothes; after which, since I'd emptied the fridge before going up north, I heated a tin of baked beans.

There was no more I could do for the moment, and the afternoon stretched emptily ahead. Knowing that my sleepless night was catching up with me, I set the alarm and retired to bed, sleeping dreamlessly for four hours, and waking much the better for it. A shower and shave completed the recovery, and I set off for nearby Manchester Airport in good time for the flight, the recorder in my pocket. I was hoping for great things from Liza Jenkins.

The brief flight was uneventful and landed on time, the hotel room was modest and clean, and despite my earlier nap, I managed several hours' sound sleep. After a breakfast of coffee and croissants – very different from Mrs Bunting's full English – I acquired some euros, hired a car, and, with a Michelin map on the seat beside me, set off on the next stage of my hunt for the Sheridans.

Patty and I had spent a motoring holiday in France a couple of years earlier, so I was prepared for the roundabouts, which cars approached rapidly from all directions, and able to recognize the various road signs along the way. Once clear of the town, lush countryside spread on either side, interspersed with apple orchards and fields of contented-looking cows, but I was in no mood to appreciate it, my mind concentrated on the meeting ahead.

While anxious to hear the story from her own lips, I was somewhat ambivalent about Miss Jenkins; she had, after all, reported the exchange between Dad and Mr Sheridan which helped to nail him. But perhaps, since she'd been employed by the victim, she could have done little else. I'd reserve judgment until I saw her. I remembered her as a comfortable woman with her hair in a bun, seeming old as the hills, though she was probably in her late forties, making her about seventy now.

She was also the one person from the past who might recognize me, and my interest in the case could nudge her memory. I hoped fervently I'd be able to deflect it. There was certainly no danger of that from the Sheridans when I caught up with them; they'd never given a thought to the small, sandy-haired boy who sometimes accompanied the gardener – except, when they found him in their playground, to send him packing.

I came upon the village sooner than I'd expected, and, seeing a large square in the centre with several cars parked on it, drove in beside them, switched off the engine, and got out of the car, breathing in the unmistakably French air.

To my right was a plane tree with a bench running round it, on which sat three rather large ladies, chatting volubly, shopping baskets at their feet. Along one side of the square, a parade of shops lined the cobbled street, the signs above them advertising their wares – Boulangerie, Bureau de

Tabac, Charcuterie – which their windows helped me to translate. Farther along, a group of women were clustered round some stalls piled high with fruit and vegetables, pinching and prodding at the produce. It'd be frowned on at Tesco's, I thought.

Turning, I surveyed the far side of the square, where a café, French fashion, had spilled on to the street. I walked across and sat down, hoping someone spoke English.

They didn't, but a request for coffee was understood and complied with, and when I'd finished it and was paying the bill, I showed the waitress the note I'd made of Liza's address. A flood of French followed, with much gesticulating, from which I gathered that the restaurant was just around the corner.

It was approaching noon, and some of the shops were already pulling down their blinds, reminding me of the obligatory two-hour lunch break we'd experienced on my last visit. But lunch was as good a time as any to brave Le Bon Gout.

My heart now beating uncomfortably fast, I rounded the corner and at once saw the cheerfully striped awning of the restaurant. It was smaller than I'd expected, not more than a dozen tables, but it was attractively furnished, and pictures of local views hung on the walls.

I seemed to be just in time; several tables were already occupied and others were filling up. I was surprised to hear English voices, and assumed there must be *pensions*, as Patty called them, round about, or even that some of the customers owned houses in or near the village.

Ignoring the comprehensive menu handed me, I ordered a modest *omelette aux fines herbes* and a glass of *vin ordinaire* to validate my presence. Suppose Liza Jenkins wasn't in? Suppose she was on holiday herself, and this was a wasted journey? I closed my mind to such doubts while I enjoyed the excellent omelette, served with a crusty baguette and pats of golden butter.

Incredible to think that less than three days ago I'd been in the rain-darkened garden of The Lodge. I finished my lunch with a cup of bitter black coffee, then, my heart in my mouth, asked the waitress if it were possible to speak to Miss Jenkins.

She looked surprised, as well she might, but nodded, said, '*Un moment, s'il vous plaît,*' and disappeared round the back of the premises. Had she understood? Or would someone completely different come to enquire my business?

But no; the woman approaching was unmistakably an older version of the Liza Jenkins I remembered, and I released my held breath. The first hurdle was over, but by no means the last.

I stood up and held out my hand, which, after a slight hesitation, she took. 'Miss Jenkins, I'm sorry to intrude on you, but I'm hoping you can help me.' I launched into my well-rehearsed speech. 'My name is Gary Payne, and I'm engaged in writing a book about the effects of crime on those left behind.'

Her brows drew together. 'Then I'm afraid there's been some mistake. I—'

'I believe you were housekeeper to the Sheridan family in Scarthorpe twenty-odd years ago?'

She drew in her breath sharply. 'How do you know that?'

'Your name was given to me by Mrs Eileen Morgan, of the Willow Pattern café.'

Liza put out a hand and gently lowered herself on to the chair opposite.

'You've been there? To the Willow Pattern?'

'Yes, earlier this week, actually. The Sheridan case is of particular interest, because three children were orphaned as a result. I'm hoping to find out how their lives were affected by what happened.'

'I'm not in touch with them,' she said.

That was a blow. 'Then I wonder if you'd mind filling in the background for me? I believe Mr Sheridan wasn't their natural father?'

She stared at me for a long minute, and I steeled myself to hold her gaze, praying I wouldn't see recognition dawn.

'I've come quite a way to speak to you, Miss Jenkins,' I went on carefully. 'I'd be very grateful for your help.'

She lifted her shoulders. 'I can't tell you anything new; it was all in the papers at the time.'

'But you were almost part of the family, weren't you? Since before the second marriage?'

She frowned. 'You seem to know a lot about me, Mr Payne.'

'Mrs Morgan was very helpful. You see, the case interests me for two reasons; firstly, as I said, because of the children, and secondly, because no one was ever charged.'

'Only because the murderer killed himself.'

'The police didn't look for anyone else?'

'What was the point? That more or less proved it, though I have to say I was knocked sideways at the time – couldn't get it to sink in at all. I'd known Jack Spencer for years, and would have sworn he was a decent man.'

'Tell me about him,' I said from a dry mouth.

She glanced around her. A couple at the next table were speaking English, and she seemed to think discretion was called for.

'You'd best come with me,' she said, and I followed her to the back of the restaurant and out on to a small patio behind the building, where she motioned me towards an iron chair.

I took out my recorder and, with a questioning eyebrow, put it on the table between us. She nodded permission, and I said again, 'Tell me about Jack Spencer.'

She sighed, thinking back. 'As I say, I'd known him for years – not well, mind you, but we'd have a chat sometimes over a cup of tea in winter or a glass of lemonade when it was hot. He got on very well with Mr Poole—'

'Poole?' I interrupted sharply. That was a name I'd forgotten, if I'd ever known it; Dad had spoken only of Mr Simon and Mrs Beth.

'That's right; Mrs Sheridan's first husband. He was drowned in the lake – a terrible tragedy. It doesn't seem right, somehow, that one family should suffer so much.'

'But she found happiness again, with Mr Sheridan?' I asked, hating the platitude but hoping it would press the right buttons.

Liza hesitated, then nodded.

'You're not sure?' I pounced.

'Only the two people involved know what goes on in a marriage, Mr Payne.'

So she wasn't to be drawn on that. 'How about the children, then? Did they resent their stepfather?'

She bit her lip, and after a few seconds, nodded. 'He was very strict with them,' she said. 'Came down on them like a ton of bricks. They weren't used to that. And they were at a difficult age, the two older ones, and Abby just followed their lead.'

Abby, the youngest. I wasn't sure I'd ever heard their names.

'Had there been bad feeling between – Spencer, was it? – and Mr Sheridan before?'

'Oh, yes.' She was relaxing now, as memories long buried resurfaced. 'There'd been rows ever since he came. See, Mr Poole liked working alongside Jack, digging and that, and as often as not gave him free rein on choosing what plants to buy. Mr Sheridan was a different kettle of fish.'

'So the Sheridan children—'

'*Poole* children,' she interrupted. 'They kept their father's name. Leastways—' She stopped, looking slightly embarrassed. 'Would you like a glass of calvados, Mr Payne? I sometimes have one after lunch, and it might ease the telling of the story.'

'Then thank you, yes.'

She stood up and called to someone inside, and minutes later a waitress appeared with two small glasses on a tray.

'*Merci, Clothilde.*' Liza raised her glass to me in silence, and I returned the salute. She drank, savoured the after-taste, and then continued. 'I wasn't entirely honest with you, Mr Payne; it's true I've not been in touch with the children, as I still think of them, for years, but I hear fairly regularly from their aunt, and she gives me their news.'

Bingo! 'You were saying they kept their father's name?' That's where she'd broken off.

'Yes; well, so they did, during the second marriage. But after the murders, their aunt and uncle adopted them, and they took their name.'

So I'd have been doubly on the wrong track. 'And that was?'

'Firbank. Mrs Firbank was Mrs Sheridan's sister. They had a lovely home down in Surrey, and the children grew up there. I went to stay with them a couple of times.' She paused, thinking back. 'But two years ago her husband died, and after a lot of deliberating, she went out to New Zealand to live with his widowed sister in Christchurch. She was lonely, and there was nothing to keep her, really; the children had grown up and moved away and she didn't often see them, though the girls used to phone quite regularly. I think they still do. Young people these days seem to think nothing of phoning all over the world.'

'So what are they doing nowadays?' Loaded question!

'Well, Jilly was always the flighty one, and when I last heard, she'd just got married for the *third* time, if you please, and was helping to run a hotel down in Sandbourne. God help the visitors, is all I can say!'

'Did her aunt fly back for the wedding?'

'No; she has high blood pressure and was advised not to. In any case, I think she's a bit disillusioned about Jilly's weddings. As she said in her letter, who knows how long this one will last?'

'So what's Jilly's latest surname?'

'Let's see now. Irving, that's it.' Liza gave a brief laugh. 'She'd have plenty to say on the subject of her stepfather.'

Though plenty she'd leave unsaid, I thought. 'And the others?'

'Well, Cal's married and living in Cambridge. He's got quite a high-powered job, but I couldn't tell you what it is. And Abby's running her own interior design business in London.'

'Is she married?'

Liza shook her head. 'And doesn't intend being, according to her aunt.' Caution belatedly returned. 'I hope you won't upset them, bringing all this up again. They never came to terms with their mother's death.'

'Don't worry, Miss Jenkins, I'll tread very softly.'

'It was bad enough when their father drowned – inconsolable they were, for a while. But they still had her and their home, and me, come to that, to keep things ticking over. After her death, everything fell apart, and the Firbanks had a very difficult time with them. She told me later that at first they were inseparable, spending all their time together and resisting all her efforts to come close.'

She took another sip of calvados. 'It got better after a while, but then, oh, years later, something happened – Mrs F never discovered what. It was just before Jilly's first wedding; they were all down in Surrey one weekend, and a terrific row broke out between the three of them. The Firbanks heard shouting and crying and slamming doors, then all three left, one after the other, with no explanation. The other two never went to the wedding, and as far as she knows, they've had nothing to do with each other since, though she keeps trying to bring them together.'

'But they're still in touch with her?' I had to have up-to-date information.

Liza Jenkins nodded. 'Leastways, the girls are. You know what men are like; it's Cal's wife who sends the Christmas card.'

Having digested that for a minute, thankful for the steadily revolving tape on the table, I cleared my throat.

'Now, to get back to that last day. It said in the papers that you overheard the row between Spencer and Mr Sheridan?'

Her face, softer when she spoke of the children, clouded again. 'Bits of it, yes, though I wish I'd held my tongue about it.'

'Why is that?'

'Well, it was rightly none of my business, but they questioned me because of the boy.'

I felt my face flush and took a hasty sip of Calvados, praying she wouldn't notice. 'What boy is that?'

'Jack's son. Quiet little thing, he was, always thanked me nicely for the biscuits I gave him. Well, it was the change in routine, you see, that made it seem significant. Jack always finished his work by washing Mrs Sheridan's car, and when he'd done, he'd lock up the garage and drop both sets of keys through the letterbox. But that day, he sent the boy to the back door with them, and the message that her battery was flat. I gave him a biscuit and chatted to him for a minute or two. He seemed upset, no doubt because he'd been there during all the shouting.

'Well, I thought nothing of it at the time, but the police reckoned Jack had sent him to the door to give himself time to put gravel in the car.

And the gravel itself was important, being a special kind, which was how they were able to identify it. You see, it was kept in a locked shed, and Jack had the key.'

There was a long silence, and when I felt I could trust my voice, I said, 'You actually heard the row? What was said?'

'Not really; raised voices was all, but I could tell they were very heated, and Jack had never made a secret of his opinion of the master. The family were talking about it over dinner. I heard Mr Sheridan say, "Too big for his boots, that's his trouble. Well, he won't be bothering us again, thank God. I'll put an ad in the paper tomorrow." So I realized Jack had been sacked, and I felt quite upset. He'd been coming to The Lodge for years.'

We were silent for several minutes, while the tape whirred on. I stared out at the little garden beyond the patio, where some birds were pecking at the grass, and started when Liza made a sudden movement.

'Look at the time!' she exclaimed. 'I must start preparing for this evening.'

'Sorry if I've held you up, but you've been a great help. Thank you very much.' I switched off the tape and slipped it into my pocket. Then I walked with her back through the restaurant as, days before, I'd walked with Eileen Morgan.

At the door, she held out her hand. 'Goodbye, Mr Payne. I'm not sure whether I've enjoyed talking with you or not.'

'I hope the memories weren't too painful.'

'Go easy on the children, if you see them.'

I smiled noncommittally, and was turning away when her eyes narrowed slightly. 'You know, I've been trying to think who you remind me of,' she said.

Alarm bells sounded. 'People often say that; I must have a run-of-the-mill face.' And with a quick 'Goodbye, and thanks', I set off back towards the square, not daring to check if she was staring after me.

Liza Jenkins had proved a gold mine. I now had names and rough addresses for all three of my prey, whereas without her, I wouldn't have had a chance in hell of finding them, not even knowing their right names. London, Cambridge and Dorset: they were widely spaced – even further from the Lake District where they were all born. Was that deliberate, a distancing of themselves from the past and from each other? And what was the cause of the break-up that had caused that distancing? I might never know, but it was immaterial anyway. It might even be to my advantage that they weren't in touch with each other.

* * *

It was only as I left the village that I realized I'd seen neither the fountain nor the two churches after which it was named, but as my brief visit had been confined to a few hundred yards, it was hardly surprising.

The hire car was hot and stuffy and there was no air-conditioning. I drove back to Caen with all the windows down and my mind in overdrive. I had hours to spare before my flight home, and since I was too wired up to sit around reading, I decided to take in some of the sights.

There were two abbeys, I discovered, quite a distance apart, one dedicated to men, the other to women. And never the twain shall meet, eh? Sounded like the Firbanks. I couldn't manage both, so out of solidarity opted for 'aux Hommes', and though I tagged on to a group following an English guide and wandered round for more than an hour, I couldn't afterwards remember a thing about it.

It served its purpose, though, and by the time I'd driven back to the airport and returned the car, there was barely an hour till take-off.

On the plane, I attached earphones to the recorder and replayed my interview with Miss Jenkins, gloating over the amount of information I'd obtained. And to think I'd almost not bothered coming. The half-term holiday, awaited with such impatience, had achieved more than I could have dreamed. It was now time to plan my campaign.

Twenty

I woke in my own bed on Thursday morning, and the outlines of the room melded with those at White Gables and the French hotel, before resolving themselves into the familiar shapes of home.

I stretched, put my hands behind my head, and stared up at the ceiling. Time for more detailed planning. So far, I'd not thought beyond killing the Firbanks and leaving them hanging, in revenge for Dad. But killing them how? A knife was the obvious weapon, and the kitchen drawer was full of them; I could select a small one with a thin blade, and hone it to lethal sharpness.

But the more I thought about it, the more difficulties I could see, particularly with the quick stab to the chest that had been my first thought. I was more likely to face them in their outdoor clothes – a coat or jacket – than in convenient nightwear or swimsuit, and a 'quick stab' through clothing mightn't be fatal. Even if the knife went in, it could be deflected by bone or gristle, and I certainly didn't fancy struggling with a wounded victim. No, on reflection it would be better to aim for the throat. That should be a lot easier; I could even practise in front of a mirror.

The stark reality of it, considered seriously for the first time, brought a faint queasiness, and I hastily switched my thoughts to the previous day. Would Miss Jenkins connect the Firbank killings with the man who'd come enquiring after them? Even if she did, there'd be no way to trace him; I'd travelled on my own passport, and there'd be no record of Gary Payne. Nothing to worry about there.

Meanwhile, since I wasn't expected home till Saturday, I had two days in hand in which to clear my head and plan my campaign, and my first task would be to transcribe the tapes from both Scarthorpe and France.

It was at that point that the idea came not just to copy down a series of disjointed notes, but to make it a coherent, ongoing report, illustrating how I unearthed the facts, planned my revenge, and achieved the end results – as I didn't doubt I would. I'd say nothing to Hayley in the meantime, but at that point she'd deserve a full account, and this would be a comprehensive way of dealing with it.

It was a daunting prospect, though; school reports were the only things

I'd written for years, but essays had been my strong point at both school and college, and I'd soon get back in the swing. I'd already used the recorder as a diary of sorts; this was just a step further. It mightn't be great literature, but it would serve its purpose.

I swung out of bed, eager to get started. The lack of food in the flat necessitated a quick trip to the supermarket, but by ten thirty I was seated at the computer, the recorder beside me. I'd begin, I decided, with that last visit to Mum, when I first learned the truth and embarked on this course.

For the rest of Thursday and all Friday I tapped away, attempting, with much deleting, to make a narrative out of the facts, and by lunchtime on Saturday had completed the account of my visit to France. From now on, a nightly update would be a much less onerous task.

It was with a sense of achievement that I clicked 'Save' and pushed back my chair, easing my aching back. I was now free to start planning ahead, but first I'd earned myself a break, and since I was due back from my 'trip' today, I phoned Hayley.

'Bry! Good to hear from you! Thanks for all the postcards!'

'Sorry,' I lied easily. 'I was off the beaten track most of the time.'

'Where did you get to?'

'The wilds of Cornwall. I – needed a bit of space.'

'So you said. And do you feel the better for it?'

'Much better, thanks.' That was true enough.

'Lunch tomorrow?'

'That'd be lovely, sis.'

'See you about twelve, then.'

I clicked off the phone, hesitated a minute, then pressed Patty's number.

'Hello, stranger!' she greeted me.

'Hi. I'm back from my travels, and wondered if you're free this evening?'

'I'm not sure I've forgiven you yet, for going without me.'

'Then let me make it up to you.'

I heard her low laugh. 'Now, there's an offer I can't refuse!'

'I'll pick you up about six. Bring your toothbrush.'

Throughout that weekend, at the cinema with Patty and later when we made love, even over lunch with the family, only part of my attention was engaged. The other, wandering, half was still dwelling on the events of the past week, brought clearly into focus by the recent retelling of them. Three child murderers in one family – quite a turn-up for the book – and all of them seeming happy and successful in their adult lives. Well, I'd soon put a stop to that.

Monday morning; back to school, and sessions in the gym and at the cricket nets. I joined in the staffroom banter, fielded questions about my week off, and counted the minutes till I could get back to my computer.

Deflecting various invitations, I hurried home after school and immediately went online. Liza said Abby was an interior designer in London, and since she had her own business, she shouldn't be hard to find. I typed in *London Interior Designers*, and Google came up with a directory, which obligingly gave a list of names, addresses and contacts, one of which, to my enormous satisfaction, was Abigail Interiors. It was almost too easy.

I checked my watch. Only four thirty; their offices should still be open, and since it was essential to check I had the right Abigail, I tapped out the phone number, my heart in my mouth.

'Abigail Interiors,' said a bright young voice.

I moistened dry lips. 'Could I speak to Abigail Firbank, please?'

'Who's calling?'

'Gary Payne.'

'One moment, please.'

A click, and then a different voice. 'Hello? Abigail Firbank speaking.'

I swallowed, my prepared speech vanishing without trace to leave my mind completely blank.

'Hello?' she said again. A low, plummy voice. 'Mr Payne? Can I help you?'

I opened my mouth, but still no words came. My hand had started to shake, and I made an effort to steady it.

'Mr Payne?' she repeated, impatience creeping in. 'Are you there?' Then, when I remained silent, there was a muttered expletive and the connection was broken.

Slowly, I put the phone back on its rest. Well, that went well, I thought. Yet after all, there'd been no need to speak; I'd learned all I needed to know. I had Abby's number, in more ways than one, and would hunt her down in my own good time.

I sat staring at the computer for a full minute before deciding that, while I was on a roll, I might as well try my luck with Jilly. Returning to Google, I typed in *Sandbourne Hotels*, and a list of about ten showed up. However, though I clicked on each in turn, none gave the names of the proprietors.

Still, I thought philosophically, I couldn't track them all down at once.

I'd concentrate on Abby – or Abigail, as she now called herself. My first task would be to find out what she looked like and where she lived, and the only way to achieve that was to watch for her coming out of the office and follow her home. But since my free time was limited to weekends, when her office would be closed, I couldn't even make a start on that. Hard though it was, I'd have to resign myself to waiting till school broke up at the end of July.

It was easier said than done, and the next six weeks passed agonizingly slowly. After the success of half-term, it was frustrating to have to sit on my hands and do nothing.

Patty and I continued our lacklustre relationship, I went to Hayley and Gary's for the occasional Sunday lunch, and for the rest, tried to concentrate on my duties at school. It was odd to think this had been the sum total of my life before I'd heard Mum's story; I'd been contented enough then, but with murder in mind, my life had notched up a gear and it no longer satisfied me.

At last term ended, and as I sat in Hall that final day, I was wondering what would have happened before I was next there. Seven weeks was a long time; would Abigail be dead? Would Cal? Would Jilly? How would I be feeling? A series of question marks hung over my life, and I was impatient to find answers to them.

Not for the first time, I blessed my decision not to allow Patty to move in with me. I'd have had to think up excuses for the absences, long or short, that were bound to occur as I put my plans into effect. And since I'd seen the family only the previous Sunday, there was no need to mention to Hayley that I'd be making a short trip to London.

The first Monday of the holidays, therefore, found me on the train, my A to Z in my pocket and my mind buzzing with anticipation. At last, things were beginning to move. I'd already located the address of Abigail Interiors, and noted that the nearest Underground station was Gloucester Road.

I booked into a cheap hotel near Euston, again borrowing Gary's name, left my grip, and had a bar lunch. I was presuming that, as I'd missed her lunch hour, Abigail wouldn't leave the office again before five, and since I was by no means sure how conspicuous I'd be if I had to hang about, it seemed wiser to delay going to Drayton Gardens until nearer the time.

In the event, I only just caught her. I'd no sooner taken up position on the opposite pavement when a taxi drew up, and minutes later a tall, slim woman with a cloud of dark hair came down the steps, climbed into it, and was driven away.

I cursed under my breath. So much for my plan to follow her home. I wondered if the taxi was a regular occurrence, and if so, whether I'd have to wait in one myself, and utter the immortal words *Follow that cab!*

I was turning away when it occurred to me that the woman I'd seen might not even have been Abigail; in my fixation on her, I'd overlooked the fact that there'd be plenty of others working in the building. I took out my mobile and rang her number, and the same bright voice answered.

'Could I speak to Abigail Firbank, please?' To my own ears, I sounded breathless, but hoped she wouldn't notice.

'Oh, I'm sorry, sir,' the girl was saying, 'you've just missed her. She left the office a couple of minutes ago.'

Confirmation, at least. 'Never mind,' I said, 'I'll try again tomorrow.'

'I'm afraid she's on leave now for the next three weeks; she only popped in to collect some colour charts.'

She waited for my response, but I was incapable of making one.

'Is there anyone else who could help you?' she asked.

'No – no, thank you,' I murmured, and rang off. Why, oh why had I not thought to check she'd be around, before paying out for a train ticket and hotel room? It was the holiday season, after all. No doubt the wealthy Miss Firbank was off to the Bahamas or somewhere equally exotic. Well, I thought sourly, she might as well enjoy her holiday – it would be her last. And at least I'd caught a glimpse of her and would recognize her when I needed to. In the meantime, all I could do was while away the rest of the day, and return to Manchester in the morning.

It was as well I didn't know then how long it would be before I caught up with Abigail. The following week, changing a light bulb in the flat, I stepped off the wrong side of the ladder, fell heavily, and succeeded in breaking my ankle. Apart from the excruciating pain, what irked me most was my enforced inactivity for the remainder of the summer. There was no possibility of returning to London – it took me all my time to hobble round the flat – and regrettably Patty and Hayley received short shrift when they tried to help. Yet again I was forced to bide my time – till half-term, for God's sake, at the end of October.

For some reason, probably born of frustration, this setback to my plans increased my hostility towards Abigail. I kept picturing her, slim, attractive and self-assured, stepping into that taxi, her mind, no doubt, full of the holiday ahead. Did she ever have sleepless nights, remembering what she, her brother and sister had done, all those years ago? I doubted it; it would have been safely buried long since, not allowed to intrude on the comfortable, successful life she now led.

It was this mounting hatred that convinced me a few minutes' fear prior to death was insufficient punishment; she should be made to suffer longer – have time to become really frightened that the past was, after all, catching up with her, and I passed long hours, my foot propped up in front of me, planning how best to achieve this.

One thing I *was* able to do in my invalid state was to print out all the pages I'd written so far, ready for the eventual handover to Hayley, and it was as I was sifting through the material the week before school went back that I came across the postcards I'd bought in Scarthorpe.

I stood looking at them – four different views but each featuring the lake – and realized I'd found my answer. I would send one to Abigail – no message, just her name and address. The picture alone should put the fear of God into her, but first I needed that address, which would entail another visit to London. This time, though, I'd phone before I went, to make sure she wasn't off on another of her jaunts.

So I went back to school, and, at opening assembly, reflected bitterly that I was no further forward than at the end of last term. But I would get them, I vowed to myself, all three of them, no matter what obstacles lay in my way, or how long it took. Because there'd be no peace of mind for me now until all three of them were dead.

My ankle, still fragile, curtailed my activities both in the gym and on the football pitch, but it was strengthening all the time, and by October would be fully operational – no worries about that.

I delayed phoning till half-term had started, to make certain she'd be there before I set out. But when, having identified myself as Gary Payne, I asked for Abigail, I was stunned to hear she no longer worked there. Panic washed over me. Would I have to start looking all over again?

'She's sold the business?' I asked incredulously.

'Oh no, nothing like that, but now she's married, she'll be working from home.'

'*Married*?' I echoed blankly.

'Yes, ten days ago. She's on her honeymoon at the moment, but they'll be home on Saturday.'

I said the first thing that came into my head, though it turned out to be my Open Sesame.

'But – she said she'd never marry!' That's what Liza had told me.

The receptionist laughed. 'You obviously know her well! That's what she always said, yes, but then James came along and swept her off her feet. They met and married in the space of six weeks.'

'James . . . ?'

'Markham. He works in IT, I believe.'

'Well, this is a surprise. Could you let me have her number?'

'Oh, I'm sorry, Mr Payne, we don't give out personal information.'

'But surely to friends . . . ?'

'Sorry. Company policy.'

'So how will her clients contact her?'

'Through this office. She'll be coming over once a month, but we'll be in daily contact, with emails and phone calls. You won't notice any difference in service.'

I thought furiously. How could I improve my credentials sufficiently to get the number out of her? Again I struck lucky, by repeating the question I'd asked Liza.

'Did her aunt fly over for the wedding?'

The girl's voice sobered. 'Mrs Firbank? No, that was very sad; she died during the summer, before Abigail and James met, so she never even knew about him. She'd have been so happy to see her married.'

'I'm sorry,' I said. Then, wheedlingly, 'And there's no way you can give me her number?'

'We can't make exceptions, sir, really.'

'At least tell me what town she'll be living in.'

She hesitated. 'Well, since you're a friend of the family, I suppose there's no harm. It's Inchampton, in Gloucestershire.'

'Thanks very much. And if you speak to her before I do, please give her and her husband my very best wishes.'

I sat back in my chair, glancing at the ready-packed grip by the door. So it wouldn't be needed after all. Once again my plans were put on hold and Abigail had gained a further reprieve – this time till Christmas.

And with the aunt's death, Liza Jenkins would be receiving no more news of the family; she wouldn't know Abigail was married – and nor, for that matter, would Jilly or Cal. Which meant, I reflected, that when Abigail Markham was murdered in a place called Inchampton, it would ring no alarm bells, believing as they did that their sister's name was still Firbank, and she lived in London.

It crossed my mind to start looking for one of them, rather than let half-term go to waste; but I'd been concentrating on Abigail for the past five months, and there was no way I could move on until I'd dealt with her. And once I'd found out her address, I could at least dispatch the postcard.

James Markham . . . I switched on Google, typed in *Telephone Directory*, and scrolled down till I came to *Residential Numbers — the BT Phone Book*. Then, in the box marked Surname, I wrote *Markham*, and in the space for location, *Inchampton*. And, lo and behold, I was looking at the entry I wanted: *J A Markham*, his phone number and his address: *4a The Square, Inchampton*. I was even able to click on a map showing the exact location.

Giving fervent thanks to the inventor of the Internet, I logged off and went for a much-needed drink.

It was unbelievable how long it was taking to track down Abigail, but at least it had taught me patience. To Patty's delight, I took her, on the spur of the moment, to North Wales, and even enjoyed walking along the cold, wind-blown beaches, watching the clouds rushing across the sky, and trying out my ankle on the less-steep slopes. The surrounding hills and water brought Scarthorpe to mind, but this was a different landscape and held no memories for me.

At Patty's instigation, we did some Christmas shopping in Llandudno, went to the cinema a couple of times, and explored the surrounding countryside. It was not how I'd planned to spend half-term, but it was a pleasant enough break. And, I promised myself grimly, Christmas was coming.

We broke up on the nineteenth of December, and the next day I set off in the car for the Cotswolds. It was a tight schedule; there'd be hell to pay if I wasn't back to spend Christmas with the family, but that was in the lap of the gods. I was determined not to return until I'd despatched Abigail Markham.

The journey down was horrendous — heavy traffic, and lashing rain all the way. By the time I reached Cheltenham, daylight had almost gone and I was in any case too tired and dispirited to drive on to Inchampton. I'd booked into a boarding house, and after lying on my bed for an hour, exhilarated by the closeness of my prey, I went down for 'supper' — home-made steak and kidney pie, followed by tinned peaches and cream — and then, in the grandiosely named television lounge, settled into a comfortable chair and let the moving wallpaper wash over me.

The next day, Sunday, it was still raining. James would be home, of course, but I could at least scout out the land, so I duly set off for Inchampton, thankful for the plastic raincoat I'd bought with quite another purpose in mind.

I managed, after some difficulty, to find a meter near the town centre, and set off on foot for the square, where I found, to my surprise, that

Number 4a appeared to be a flat above a café. Not what I'd expected of Miss High and Mighty.

Furthermore, as I saw at once, it was bad news; I'd been imagining a house and garden, set back from the road, where I could have forced my way inside when she answered the door. But this door opened directly on to the pavement, and the square itself was thronged with people; any pushing could hardly go unnoticed. Also, with the café directly below, someone might hear if she screamed.

I'd have to rethink my plan. In the meantime, to get out of the rain, I went into the café, ordered coffee and a mince pie, and sat down at a window table. But it was a wasted ploy; no one emerged from the next doorway, and my lengthy presence began to attract notice. I moved instead to a pub across the square, from where I had a view of the flat's windows. A light was on; no doubt they were having a cosy weekend at home. I couldn't blame them, and halfway through the afternoon, cut my losses and drove back to Cheltenham.

The next two days were a miserable repetition, and I was getting desperate. The heavy rain continued, and Abigail did not emerge from the flat. And then it was Christmas Eve. I *couldn't* go home with nothing accomplished, watch Jade open her stocking and eat turkey as though all was right with my world.

A watery sun had finally come through, and I hoped fervently that it would tempt her outdoors. But yet again, there was no sign. My parking meter had expired, and I resignedly got into the car to search – no doubt in vain – for another space. Then a thought struck me: where did the vans park to unload supplies to the café and other shops along that side of the square? There had to be an access road behind. I investigated, and, sure enough, came across it. Furthermore, I could see a space halfway along. I swerved into the alleyway and parked, realizing I must be directly behind the Markham flat.

And as I switched off the engine, unbelievably, Abigail herself came hurrying round the corner, and stopped at a car a few feet from mine. One of the men unloading a van called across to her, and she called back. Then she got into the car and drove slowly out of the alley. Heart in mouth, I followed her, wondering where she was going. If it was to someone's house, I'd have to find a way of intercepting her before she arrived.

She turned right towards the crowded square and negotiated her way slowly through it, turning left at the T-junction. This wasn't the Cheltenham road, and I couldn't see a signpost. All I could do was follow her, and await my chance.

Within minutes we were in open country, a narrow lane with no room to manoeuvre. Beyond the hedgerows a wet mist hovered, screening the grass. A couple of cars overtook first me and then Abigail, danger-ously near a bend. I stayed a fair distance behind, heart clattering, mouth dry.

A pub was coming up on the right, and she began to slow down. Was she going in? If so, I'd have to ambush her in the car park. But she continued past it, and I was taken by surprise when she suddenly signalled left and swerved into a narrow lane. I drew up just short of the turning and waited. It would be too obvious to follow her straight away – she might take fright.

After a couple of minutes, I nosed gently forward, and, to my amaze-ment, saw her car barely a hundred yards away, alongside a stone wall. As far as I could tell there was no one in it, but as I cautiously drew nearer, I saw a gap in the wall where a gate had once been. It was filled with nettles and weeds, but they'd been trampled down to give access. God alone knew what Abigail was doing here, but there was no prize for guessing where she'd gone.

I drew a deep breath. My tools were to hand, as they'd been since leaving home: recorder, knife, clothes line, confession. At very long last, her Nemesis had caught up with her.

I slid into place behind her car, and, having pushed my way through the brambles, was faced by row after row of wizened old apple trees. A derelict orchard, by the look of it. What the hell . . . ?

The rain had started again, and I pulled up my collar. Then I saw her, just ahead of me, reaching up into a tree, and realized what she was after. Mistletoe! Absorbed in her task, she was completely unaware of my pres-ence until, moving cautiously forward, I stepped on a twig that snapped beneath my weight – the echo of a long-ago snap that had startled three children.

She'd frozen at the sound, her hands motionless on the branch.

'Hello, Abby,' I said softly.

Slowly, fearfully, she turned to face me, her grip tightening on the secateurs – a weapon of sorts.

'You don't recognize me, do you?'

Wordlessly, she shook her head.

'Bryan Spencer, the gardener's boy.'

Her eyes widened and she made a choking sound, one hand going to her throat. Not so self-assured now, my lady!

'The gardener,' I went on deliberately, 'who killed himself because of what you did.'

Her skin had paled to the colour of old linen. 'It was you?' she whispered. 'Who sent the postcard?'

I nodded, pleased she'd made the connection. 'I heard you all that day,' I continued, 'you and Cal and Jilly. Plotting to sabotage the car.'

Her knees began to buckle and she slid an inch or two down the tree trunk, hands flattening against the bark behind her as the secateurs slipped from her grasp.

'No!' she said.

'Yes. But what's even worse in my eyes, you let my father die—'

She stretched out a hand pleadingly. 'No, not that, really! We'd already left—'

'You should have owned up when he was arrested. He was claustrophobic, and he killed himself rather than be shut up in prison.'

The horror in her eyes seemed genuine. 'We didn't know that,' she whispered. 'I'm so, so sorry.'

'But unfortunately sorry won't bring him back. The least he deserves is a posthumous pardon.'

'Yes,' she gabbled. 'Of course! Anything we can—'

She stopped, her eyes on the recorder I'd suddenly produced. I passed it to her, and she automatically took it.

'And here's how we go about it.' I took the prepared sheet from an inside pocket, opened it out, and handed it over. 'I'd like you to read this into the recorder.'

She nodded, moistening her lips, then flinched as I stepped forward. But all I did was switch on the machine, containing a brand new tape specially for the occasion.

'Right,' I said, and, her voice shaking, she began.

'I, Abigail Markham, née Poole, formerly Firbank' (that left no room for doubt, I reckoned) – 'wish to make the following statement in the presence of a witness: that, on the twenty-fifth of June, 1985, I conspired, together with my brother and sister, to put gravel taken from the garden shed into the brake-fluid of my stepfather, Harold Sheridan's car, causing the crash that killed both him and our mother. And I further state that by not admitting our guilt, we are also responsible for the death of Jack Spencer, who was claustrophobic and who, having been wrongly arrested for their murder, committed suicide rather than be locked up in prison. I swear the above to be the truth, the whole truth, and nothing but the truth, so help me God.'

She came to the end, and there was silence, except for the whirring of the tape and the pattering of the rain on the leaves above us. I'd taken a lot of time perfecting that statement, and I was pleased with it. It covered everything, and while she'd been reading it, I'd pulled on a pair of skin-tight surgical gloves and was now ready with the knife.

For a moment longer her eyes remained on the paper, and in that moment, I pounced. She'd barely time to gasp before my left hand seized her hood, jerking her head back as my right drove the knife into her exposed throat. Immediately, hot, red blood spurted out, covering my gloved hand, the confession – appropriately enough – and the plastic raincoat.

In the same instant I withdrew the knife and leaped back, watching, mesmerized, as, her head lolling forward and the blood continuing to stream, she slid the remainder of the way down the tree trunk.

Breathing heavily, I wiped the blade and my bloodied hands on the ground. The recorder had fallen clear, and I retrieved it before taking the clothes line, with its ready-prepared noose, from my pocket, and flinging it over the branch she'd been plundering.

Slipping the noose round her neck was a messier business than I'd anticipated, as it kept slipping on the wet blood that continued to gush everywhere. Eventually, though, I managed to tighten it and, choking down growing nausea, hoisted her up, supporting her body between my own and the tree and pulling on the rope until her feet were just above the ground.

I only just made it before I had to stumble aside and vomit violently into the bushes.

And now, I thought, wiping my mouth with the back of my hand, for the finishing touch. It had occurred to me before leaving home that Abigail's death mustn't be considered just another everyday murder. It had to be significant from day one, branded with my signature.

So I took from my pocket the last of the 'tools' I'd brought with me; one of the Scarthorpe postcards. Her husband was sure to remember the first, and it would give them all something to think about. Steeling myself, I reached up and tucked it into the pocket of her anorak.

Then I stepped back, looking at her hanging there, and shaken by a hundred different emotions.

'For you, Dad,' I said aloud. 'One down, two to go.'

Twenty-one

God knows how I managed to drive back to Manchester. Though the heater was going full blast, I was icily cold, and every now and then violent shudders shook me, rattling my teeth so that I repeatedly bit my tongue. My mind was totally disengaged, but thankfully my body performed all that was required of it on auto-pilot. I kept reliving the moment the knife went in, and wondering when she'd be found, if anyone had known she was there, who would find her. A nice Christmas present for someone. Not that I'd intended it as such; if all had gone according to plan, she'd have died during the summer, before she was even married.

Mentally, I went through a checklist: the knife, wiped clean, was in my jacket pocket, together with the recorder. The plastic mac, though the rain had sluiced off most of the blood, was in a carrier bag in the boot, together with the surgical gloves and the sodden confession, ready to be disposed of separately at the earliest opportunity. All that remained in the orchard was the limp body hanging from the tree, and the blood already soaking away into the ground. All was well.

The motorways were black and shining in the rain, and occasional accidents, lit by the flashing lights of emergency vehicles, reduced the holiday traffic to a crawl. All in all, it was a wonder I completed the journey in just over three hours.

The answer machine was flashing as I let myself, still shivering, into the flat. A message from Patty, rather wistfully wishing me Happy Christmas, and three from Hayley, enquiring, with increasing impatience, when she could expect me, and where the hell was I?

I poured myself a tumblerful of whisky, and drank it standing in the middle of the room. It looked strangely unchanged from the last time I'd seen it, before I became a murderer.

This, I told myself, would not do; it was essential that I pulled myself together. At long last, all had gone according to plan, and there was absolutely no way I could be linked with Abigail. Until, that is, I wanted to be, and I hadn't thought that through yet. Yes, I had her confession on tape, but I didn't intend handing it over till I had the full set.

After a very hot bath and some sleeping pills, I fell into bed and a deep, blessedly dream-free sleep, waking to the sound of church bells.

Thankfully, my self-control was back in place, and I was able to go through the routines of the day without giving any hint of the turmoil inside me.

By Boxing Day, however, reaction had set in, in the shape of flu-like symptoms – more shivering, a headache, sore throat. I took to my bed and stayed there, refusing all offers of help from my sister, and emerging only to heat up some soup. Though anxious to see the papers, I hadn't the strength to go downstairs, let alone along the street.

The murder did, however, make the television news: the body of a woman identified as Abigail Markham had been found in an abandoned orchard outside Inchampton; she'd been stabbed and left hanging from a tree. A post-mortem revealed the hanging had taken place after death, and police were puzzled by this apparent double execution. Another curious factor was that a blank picture postcard had been tucked into her pocket. According to James Markham, the dead woman's husband, his wife had received a similar card through the post some weeks previously, which had upset her at the time. Abigail Markham, a well-known interior designer . . .

The rest of it washed over me. They'd fastened on to the postcard; that was good. Don't worry, mates, you'll have two more before we're done.

I went back to bed.

Back to school again, and a new year. What a time this was all taking. Nevertheless, anxious to avoid falling ill again, I waited a week or two before turning my attention to Cal.

My first act was to repeat my Internet search of the phone book, and it didn't let me down: Callum S Firbank, The Poplars, Richmond Close. I copied out the address and phone number, and sat back to consider.

I was pleased with the postcard trademark and intended to repeat it, but since I'd only two left, I couldn't spare one to post as an advance warning. Some other method would be needed. Silent phone calls, perhaps? Trouble was, there was nothing sufficiently unusual about them to suggest a personal threat.

Although Cambridge, like Inchampton, was only three hours' drive away, a weekend wouldn't be long enough for my reconnaissance. No use trying to rush things, I told myself, reining in my impatience; once again I'd wait until half-term, in mid-February. My profession was certainly proving an asset; no other job would have given me so much leeway in which to scout out the ground. And it wasn't long till February.

* * *

Ignoring Patty's hint of a Valentine meal out, and hoping Interflora would let me off the hook, I drove to Cambridge on the Saturday morning, locating the relevant suburb with no difficulty. Very plush. Large houses, large gardens. No doors opening on the pavement here. All the same, a different approach would be needed.

As luck would have it, there was a small park almost opposite the house, which provided a first-class vantage point. The only drawback was that as it wasn't warm enough to sit there, I'd have to keep strolling about, and hope I wouldn't attract too much attention. Too bad I hadn't a dog.

Aware that I'd need to spend a fair bit of time in the area to monitor Cal's movements, I'd taken the precaution of bringing a variety of coats and jackets with me, even a baseball cap which might help my disguise. Also, though it was more expensive, I'd booked into an hotel rather than a B and B, feeling it would be more anonymous.

I hadn't brought any tools, since there was no chance of killing him on this visit; I'd need to know more about the layout and his lifestyle, and also I wanted to give the fear factor time to kick in. My aim this week was to learn as much as I could about him – where he worked, how he spent his spare time – and sow some seeds of disquiet. Then, during the second half of term, I'd settle on my plans for the Easter holidays.

It was obvious from the word go that the Firbanks and their next-door neighbours were best buddies. There was a continual toing and froing between the houses; in fact, the kids were running back and forth so much, I couldn't make out who belonged where. Then Mrs Firbank went round, returning minutes later with Mrs Next Door, and finally, when Callum himself appeared and began to wash his car, he was joined by her husband, who stood chatting.

While pretending to admire some blossom by the park gate, I studied Cal carefully. He was of medium height, slightly built, with mid-brown hair. Mr Average in person, he wouldn't be easy to pick out in a crowd. The other man was taller, fairer, more confident-seeming, and at first I thought this closeness between the families might be a handicap. But then I began to see it could be useful. I'd follow the neighbour as well, and, with luck, make use of him to put the wind up.

Sunday was, as usual, a wasted day, the two families not venturing outside their own front gates. But by eight thirty on Monday, I was in my car at the end of Richmond Close, waiting for Callum to emerge. When, at eight forty-five, he did so, in the newly cleaned Bentley, I slid in behind him and followed him to town. There, however, he eluded me by turning into a private car park, while I had to seek out a multi-storey.

Having left my car, I walked back to the building behind which he'd driven, and studied the brass plaques beside the door. Bingo! On the third floor were Hamilton and Firbank, Chartered Accountants. I dialled directory enquiries on my mobile, asked for the firm's number, and noted it in my diary. That would come in useful later.

I filled in the rest of the day as best I could, appreciating for the first time how dull a private eye's job must be, but by five o'clock I was back at the entrance to the car park, needing to know what time Cal left work. He was almost too predictable, emerging just on five thirty.

I signed myself off, and spent the evening at a cinema.

The next morning, I decided to try my luck following his neighbour. He didn't leave home till almost ten, by which time I was thinking I must have missed him. And, to my surprise, he led me not to the business sector of town, but the local hospital, where he parked in the doctors' bay.

Well, well! I hastily drove to visitors' parking, but by the time I reached the building, he'd disappeared inside. I went in after him, and approached the receptionist.

'Excuse me, could you tell me if that was Dr Davies who just came in?'

She looked up with a frown. 'We haven't a Dr Davies working here, sir. That was Dr Nelson.'

'Oh, I'm sorry. My mistake.' And I made my escape.

Dr Nelson. It didn't take me long to confirm that R J L Nelson lived at Tree Tops, Richmond Close. Once again, Bingo!

Having decided on my method of approach, I waited outside the hospital that evening, praying he wouldn't be on call or otherwise unable to leave at a normal time. I'd begun to think I'd miscalculated when he suddenly appeared, hurrying towards his car.

I caught at his arm. 'Excuse me – Dr Nelson?'

He stopped, frowning. 'Yes?'

'I'm trying to trace someone called Callum, and was told you were a neighbour of his.'

His frown deepened. 'Callum Firbank, you mean?'

'Ah, so that's his name now. Thank you!'

His brows drew together, and I went on quickly, 'Do you happen to know if he ever lived up north?'

Nelson gave a short laugh. 'That's a lot of questions, Mr –?'

I dodged that one, and, cutting off my next question, he said brusquely, 'I've no idea where he's lived. Now you really must excuse me.' And he walked quickly away.

As I'd intended, I'd aroused his suspicions by my odd questions, and I didn't doubt he'd relay them to Callum.

Sleep well, my friend!

Nothing much happened over the next couple of days. Each lunchtime, I followed Callum to a restaurant where he met friends or colleagues, but nothing in his daily routine gave me any clue as to where I could eventually approach him. My only consolation was that at least I now knew something of his lifestyle; I could make use of that in my planning once I got home. Meanwhile, the week was running out, and before I left, I wanted to insert one more seed of anxiety.

I hadn't been back to the Close, but on the Thursday evening I took up my post in the park, and waited for his car. Time moved on, and I was about to give up when I saw the doctor's car approaching, and moved quickly to the gate. I was wearing a conspicuous red anorak, and when I was pretty sure he'd seen me, I dodged back behind the gate post.

He turned into his driveway, got out of the car, and stood for a minute looking across the road. I held my breath. Would he come after me? That wasn't part of the plan. Fortunately, he decided against it and went into the house.

I was debating whether or not to wait any longer, when Callum's wife came out of her house, got into her car, and drove off. They must be meeting in town. I'd have to hope Dr Nelson would pass on the sighting.

That was the end of my preparations, really. Except that one morning about three weeks later, thinking a reminder mightn't go amiss, I phoned Hamilton and Firbank and asked to speak to him. To my surprise, he'd not yet come in, and his secretary offered to take a message. I told her it was a personal call, and when she suggested he phone me back, said it didn't matter and rang off, my heart racing.

Though actually, I thought, as I made my way to the gym, it didn't make much difference; I'd have hung up as soon as he answered. This way, he'd get the message, and with luck it would give him some more sleepless nights.

Then, a week or two later, something totally unexpected happened. I was having supper in front of the telly, only half listening to the news, when the name Richmond Close leaped out at me, and I straightened so fast I spilt my beer. A boy had been murdered during some kind of fête, and he was the son of Dr and Mrs Nelson! Must be one of the kids I'd seen on my visit. He'd been with 'a friend of the family' – Callum, I wondered? – when he'd disappeared.

Well, well, so my quarry would be having some extra sleepless nights, without me having to lift a finger.

Easter was later this year, so Mum's anniversary fell the first week of the holidays; and since Hayley wanted me to spend the day with her, it meant delaying my return to Cambridge.

What would Mum think, if she knew what I was doing? What would Dad? It was for them, really, that I'd embarked on this, but I knew I was now doing it for myself. And to be honest, I was enjoying the hunt. There was something exciting about playing detective, the initial tracing and tracking down, the secret spying, the injections of fear. It had become a deadly game, revenge not only for Dad's death and Mum's hard life, but for the slights and snubs the Pooles, as they'd then been, inflicted on me as a kid. They were getting their comeuppance, and before they died, they understood *why*. There was tremendous satisfaction in that.

'It doesn't seem a year ago, does it?' Hayley said tearfully, as we stood by the grave in the windswept cemetery. She bent and inserted the flowers we'd brought, one by one, into the holder.

I thought of all that had happened since, the change in me, the hardness, the cold calculation.

'In some ways it does,' I said.

'And that stuff she told us before she died. I just can't get it out of my head. How could she *bear* it, Bry, knowing all those years that whoever killed them had got away with it, and let Dad take the blame?'

I said carefully, 'What would you do, Hayl, if you found out who'd done it?'

She turned her tear-stained face, meeting my eyes. 'Stick a knife in them!' she said.

Shock went through me, prickling my skin. 'Really?'

She gave a choked laugh. 'Don't be daft, Bry.'

'Well, what *would* you do?' I persisted.

'Get the police on to them, of course. What else?'

I let it rest there.

It was Good Friday when I finally returned to the park, nearly two months since I'd been there. In the meantime, spring had arrived, and leaves on the trees obscured part of my view across the road.

I'd expected, since it was the holidays, that the kids would be running back and forth, but there was no sign of them – no sign of anyone, in fact.

Both front doors remained resolutely closed. The Nelsons would be grieving for their son, but the Firbanks should be around. Then, like a lead weight, a possible explanation struck me. *They'd gone away for Easter!* Why had that never occurred to me?

I swore fluently. Little point in hanging around, then.

I turned to go, stopping in my tracks as the front door of Tree Tops swung open and Dr Nelson, his wife and the little girl emerged. They all looked sombre and somehow deflated, very different from the carefree family they'd been. The doctor opened the garage doors and drove the car out, while his wife and daughter stood in silence. Then, still without exchanging a word, they got into the car and drove off.

I didn't bother to show myself, not wanting to intrude. In any case, with all that had happened since, he'd have forgotten me, even if Callum hadn't.

Well, I'd been wrong about the Nelsons being away; perhaps the Firbanks weren't, either. I considered ringing their doorbell, but decided against it. If they *were* home, I didn't want a confrontation. Not at this stage.

I walked back to my car, parked, as usual, in the next street. They might just be out for the day; I'd come back tomorrow, and try again.

But there was still no luck, which meant that, infuriating though it was, I'd have to kick my heels till the weekend was over. At least I'd the advantage that Callum had to be back at work on Tuesday, whereas I'd another week of holiday. And though as yet I'd no definite plan, I wasn't worried. It was best to remain flexible, and I'd no doubt whatever that my mission would be accomplished.

I spent the weekend wandering round the town, drinking coffee at the quayside and walking alongside the river watching the punts go by. But all the time, inside me, excitement was building, drying my mouth and bathing my body in sweat. Soon, very soon, I would cross Number Two off my list. Mingling with the other tourists in the spring sunshine, I wondered how they'd react if they knew I had murder in mind.

After dinner in the hotel on Easter Monday, I went to my room. The Firbanks should be home by now; time, perhaps, for a phone call. I took out my diary, checked the number, and punched it out, hearing the phone ringing in distant Richmond Close.

I almost jumped when a voice in my ear said, 'Callum Firbank.'

I held my breath for several seconds before breaking the connection. He was back. We were on track at last.

There was no point driving out to the Close in the morning, since he was sure to be coming into work. Instead, I waited on foot at the corner of his building, and sure enough, at five to nine, he drove into the car park.

I decided I'd waited long enough, and today would be D (for death) Day; I'd just have to trust the opportunity would arise.

And at lunchtime, I hit the jackpot. Callum emerged with two other men, and they made their way not to the usual restaurant, but to a pub down one of the side streets, where they joined another man at a table. Shoulder-high partitions divided the tables, making a series of little booths, and by a stroke of luck, the one next to theirs was free. I slipped into it.

'Good weekend, Callum?' That was the man who'd been waiting.

'OK, thanks. We were with the mother-in-law.'

'Contradiction in terms!' said someone else.

'No, she's good value, is Daphne. The family's staying on till the weekend.'

So he'd be alone in the house! I'd started to amend my plans, when a third voice said, 'Got your speech ready for this evening?'

'Just about,' Callum replied. 'I'll be glad when it's over.'

'Oh, you'll be great. And at least the food's always good at the Alhambra.'

So. Callum would be attending an official dinner at the Alhambra Hotel. Better and better. I'd be waiting for him afterwards in the car park.

As before, I'd prepared the confession before leaving home, with much the same wording as Abigail's; and the same tape was back in the recorder, so that his admission would directly follow hers. I'd also invested in another plastic mac and disposable gloves. There'd been plenty of chances to memorize Callum's number plate, so all I had to do was find it in the hotel car park. I'd also been practising opening locked cars – one of a range of skills I'd acquired in case of need – and though I'd only tried it (many times) on my own car, and once on Gary's when he wasn't around, I'd more or less perfected the art. So, as fully prepared as possible, I waited for the evening.

Since the hotel where I was staying was within walking distance, I left my car in its slot and, at ten o'clock, set off for the Alhambra, making my way to the car park round the back.

It was as well I'd left plenty of time, because I had to keep breaking off my search while a constant trickle of guests came to collect their cars. In all, it took over twenty minutes to locate Callum's, not helped by the fact that it was at the far end. He must have been late getting here, and while it was good it was so far from the building, a major disadvantage was the lamp directly overhead. When the coast was clear, I'd have to immobilize it, and I anxiously checked for security cameras. There was one a few yards to my left, and another further down on the right, but fortunately the car itself was in a blind spot. My luck was holding.

Seizing my chance, I smashed the lamp, then did my trick with the door, breathing a sigh of relief when it swung open. Climbing into the comfortable back seat, I settled down to wait.

No need for a blow-by-blow account; it was almost a carbon copy of Abigail's, except that I grabbed him from behind, so had easier access to his throat. It was lucky most of the other cars had gone, because I'd quite a struggle heaving him up, and another plus was that the lamp's crossbar was quite low. Finally, breathing hard after my exertions, I slipped the blank postcard into his pocket, removed my gloves and raincoat, and, an innocent-looking carrier bag in my hand, sauntered back to my hotel.

I didn't suffer the reaction I'd had after Abigail – must be getting hardened to it. Just as well, too, because it created considerably more interest. The fact that his murder so closely replicated hers – the stabbing, the hanging and the postcard – but had taken place at the opposite side of the country, caught the public's interest, and, it was to be supposed, that of the police. Theories about long-distance lorry drivers and commercial reps were being bandied about.

Blood inside the car proved it to be the scene of crime, and mud on the floor in the back, together with the smashed lamp, suggested the killer had lain in wait. Brilliant! But again what puzzled them was, why the double cause of death? Why the bother of heaving a fairly heavy body out of the car and stringing it up on the lamp-post, when he was already dead? Was the killer making a specific point? I could have enlightened them on that one.

Though the police admitted both postcards bore a Manchester postmark – making, as one imaginative reporter suggested, a Bermuda Triangle – the view depicted had so far not been disclosed, perhaps to deter copycat crimes.

Well, it hadn't worked, had it, and, perhaps acknowledging this, news broke soon after that in both cases it had been of Scarthorpe, in Cumbria. It also emerged that the police had made undercover enquiries there following the first murder and were now intensifying them, but reports that someone had been enquiring about local murders the previous summer had led to nothing, and the mystery continued.

Watch this space! I thought, and turned my attention to Jilly.

I'd already accepted that since their aunt, who used to pass on family news, had died before Abigail's wedding, neither Cal nor Jilly would have associated the murder with their sister. But Callum *Firbank*'s death was sure to ring alarm bells, especially once the postcards had been identified.

With luck, Jilly would already be extremely agitated – and serve her right. But it might also have put her on her guard.

As she lived by the seaside, I decided to take advantage of the fact, and at the same time enjoy what would be a well-earned holiday. And when both she and it were past tense, I'd pass this manuscript to Hayley and the confession tape to the police.

The trouble, of course, was that once they had it, the wronged man's son would become the obvious suspect, and a little digging might reveal that Jack Spencer's boy was now Bryan Reid. To avoid a triple murder charge myself, I reckoned I had two options: a) to dispose of the tape and content myself with having rid the world of three murderers. (Much the safest course, but it would be letting Dad down, since he'd never be vindicated.)

Or b) leave the tape in a deposit box, with instructions for it to be handed to the police in the event of my death. It was, after all, immaterial to Dad whether exoneration came in twenty, forty or sixty years – he was already dead and it wouldn't bring him back – but the drawback to that option was that the people who'd known him would never realize he'd been innocent.

A possible 'c' was that prison mightn't be so bad. I wasn't claustro-phobic, thank God, and liked my own company. I could write a fuller version of this document, and in time-honoured fashion sell it to the papers. Even branch into fiction. John Bunyan and Jeffrey Archer had written books in gaol, and possibly Oscar Wilde, as well. He'd certainly written *about* it. And I might be able to plead extenuating circumstances.

But I'd have time to decide on all this once Jilly was dead. I might even discuss it with Hayley and Gar; they'd want what was best for me. In the meantime, I had a third murder to plan.

A basic consideration was that a prolonged stay in Sandbourne would require adequate funding, and if I was calling myself Gary Payne – as I would be – there was no way I could use a cheque or credit card in the name of Bryan Reid. So I began to withdraw regular but differing sums of cash each week, with the aim of acquiring five hundred before I set out for Dorset. (Was there such a thing as a Bermuda Quadrangle?)

Since I'd had no luck on hotel proprietors, I approached the problem by way of my now routine trick of typing in the name Irving, helpfully given to me by Miss Jenkins. And sure enough, up came D B Irving, Bay View Hotel. Fair enough. I'd book in somewhere cheaper close by, and visit the Bay View for drinks in order to clap eyes on Mrs I. After that, it was in the lap of the gods.

Twenty-two

Since it would be the height of the holiday season, I wasted no time in picking a boarding house from the Internet, and, using my anonymous email address, booked myself in for four weeks. The deposit was a problem I'd not anticipated, but since one was needed, I posted off the specified amount in the form of a money order. God knows what they made of it, but they raised no objections.

Since guests were taken from Saturday to Saturday, I drove down the day after school broke up. Yet again, I'd had to dodge prospective holiday plans from Patty, though this time they'd been half-hearted at best. Not surprisingly, she was getting fed up with me and my absences, and just recently I'd noticed significant glances passing between her and Steve Blakely, head of history. He was recently divorced and no doubt lonely, so good luck to them. I'd been tiring of Patty for some time; it was obvious that now she was thirty she wanted to settle down, and I'd never intended it to be with me.

I was in no hurry to begin my search. For one thing, I was tired at the end of a long term, and the preparations for sports day had been exhausting; for another, the sunshine and blue seas filled me with a pleasant sense of lethargy. After the toing and froing with both Abigail and Callum, I intended this last strike to be a more leisurely affair. And it was my holiday, for God's sake!

So I spent the first few days reading paperback thrillers on the beach, plastered in a high-factor sunscreen to protect my fair skin. I slept long and deeply, breakfasted in fine style, and enjoyed the 'high teas' offered by the establishment – kippers, or smoked haddock, or pork pie and salad, served with pots of tea. The only drawback – that it was unlicensed – wasn't a drawback at all, since in due course it would serve as an excuse for trying the hotel bar. In the meantime, I contented myself with a local hostelry.

On the Wednesday, I started work. The first necessity was to identify Jilly, and to this end, protected by my sunglasses and a floppy sunhat, I braved the foyer of the Bay View. Once inside, the darkness seemed absolute and I had to wait for my eyes, still behind their shades, to grow accustomed to it. As my vision slowly cleared, it focused on an attractive woman behind the reception desk, and something about her – an air of authority, the way she held herself – indicated that she wasn't the receptionist; could this possibly—?

In quick confirmation, a voice from inside the office called, 'Phone for you, Jill!'

'Coming!' she called back, and disappeared through the doorway.

So *that* was Jilly – or Jill – Irving! I drew a deep breath. As far as I was aware, I hadn't any preformed mental picture of her – if I had, it would have dated from childhood – but she wasn't what I expected. Abigail had been lovely, even in the cold and rain and scared out of her wits. She'd also been dark, as, if memory served me right, were they all; but Jill was now stridently blonde. From a bottle, perhaps. Her hair was short and somehow spiky, and her face, though not pretty, was arresting. It startled me to realize that, if I'd not been determined to kill her, I might have fancied her.

Reminding myself forcibly that she was what Shakespeare alluded to as 'Third Murderer', I blundered back through the swing doors and, once outside, broke into a sweat, pulses racing.

For God's sake, I thought impatiently, get a grip, man! But a different approach, infinitely tempting, was beginning to suggest itself. It would be a novelty to meet my victim socially, perhaps even get to know her. Thrice-married Jill might have a wandering eye that I could use to my advantage, though any attraction between us would be purely physical, in no way lessening my implacable hatred. In some curious way, it might even add to it.

Even so, there was no denying my first sight of her had shaken me, and though I'd originally planned on going to the Bay View that evening, I postponed my visit. Tomorrow would be soon enough.

That night, I dreamed we were in bed together, though our activity couldn't be described as 'making love'; one of the uglier terms would be more appropriate. I was conscious, throughout the dream, of an intense desire to dominate, to inflict pain, and the feeling was still with me when I woke in the dark, shaking and drenched in sweat. I'd have to get myself under control before seeing her again.

In the event, I was unprepared. The next morning I stopped at the newsagent's-cum-post office to buy a paper, and was reaching for the door when it was pushed open from the inside, and I found myself face to face with Jill Irving.

God knows what my expression was as I muttered an apology, but there was a pleased little smirk on her face as she went on her way. Used to male admiration, perhaps; little did she know it was not admiration I was feeling.

That settled it; I'd go to the hotel that evening.

Seated at the bar nursing a beer, I was wondering how I could 'accidentally' meet her, when she obliged me by coming in and starting to hand out menus for that evening's dinner. And on reaching me, asked, with no hint of recognition, if I'd be dining with them.

Yet again, I was caught on the hop. I shook my head, mumbling something incoherent; but then, annoyed with myself and determined to make her admit she remembered me, added that I hoped I'd not startled her that morning. To which she coolly replied she wasn't easily startled. We'd see about that.

My eyes followed her round the room, filing away details of her appearance. She was fairly tall, though in high heels it was hard to judge, and on the thin side – certainly not as well endowed as Patty. It was, though, just the right figure for the designer dress she was wearing, and the effect was stunning.

For the rest, though her hair was honey-gold, her eyes were brown – reinforcing my theory – her cheekbones high and prominent, her mouth too wide for beauty and her nostrils too flared. Nonetheless they amounted to a lethal combination positively exuding sexuality, as was evidenced by the glances, admiring, assessing, or lustful, that, like my own, were following her progress.

Suddenly irritated that she hadn't looked back, I deposited my half-finished drink on the bar, and left the room.

The next evening I returned, and Jill, remembering, no doubt, that I'd not wanted a menu, made to pass me by. It gave me enormous satisfaction to call her back and request one. She apologized, obviously disconcerted, and I ignored her embarrassed smile.

God, the prices! That would be the only meal I'd eat there, or the five hundred would disappear like the Cheshire Cat. However, since I *was* there, I deliberately avoided the less expensive dishes and chose what I fancied. If she was interested enough to check, which I wouldn't put past her, at least she'd see I wasn't penny-pinching.

Before leaving the hotel that evening, I strolled casually to the reception desk and helped myself to one of the glossy brochures. As I'd expected, it gave both the hotel's web site and email address.

I didn't return to the Bay View, hoping my absence would arouse her interest, but I continued to track her movements, wearing an assortment of leisurewear to follow her at a distance about the town.

Most afternoons, she set off along the promenade with a beach bag, and although I realized this could be the ideal opportunity to confront her, two things held me back. The first was that it would be harder to remain unobserved, since there were fewer people about in that direction, and the second was that I was enjoying playing cat and mouse, and in no hurry to end it. However, curiosity finally got the better of me; halfway through the following week, I decided to try my luck and, clad only in shirt and swimming trunks, my book and sun-cream rolled into a towel, I set off after her.

A hundred yards or so along the prom, she turned off the road on to a grass track that led along the cliff top, and I fell farther behind, conscious there was nowhere to hide if she turned round. But she didn't turn, and we proceeded in single file for several hundred yards, the sea far below us on the left, the road to the right now out of sight.

Then I stumbled and tripped over a rabbit hole, nearly losing my footing, and when I straightened again, she'd disappeared.

I swore under my breath, scanning the flat grassland ahead. No one was in sight, and the only movement was the lazy, droning flight of a bee. Reasoning that she couldn't disappear into thin air, I went on more cautiously, fearing she might after all have seen me and be lying in wait, even though there was no bush large enough to conceal her.

I was concentrating so much on the way ahead that I almost missed it, but some sixth sense made me glance to my left and there, leading downwards at a precipitous angle, was a winding path.

I paused only a moment before starting down it. The sandy surface was slippery and interspersed now and again by worn steps, presumably in the interests of safety. Because of the vegetation on either side, I couldn't see where I was headed, and must have been more than halfway down before I caught sight first of the sea, and then of a silvery white beach surrounded by cliffs.

I paused, and as I did so, a figure ran out from beyond my field of vision, straight into the sea. It had to be Jill Irving, and she was completely naked.

For several minutes I stood motionless, breathing deeply, while all manner of plans came and went in my head. I hadn't, of course, got any tools with me; my intention today had been simply to increase the pressure before moving on to frighten her. In any case, it was too soon to move in for the kill; having had to rush both Abigail and Callum's murders, I intended to savour this one.

Slowly, I lowered myself to the ground alongside the path, the dry grass prickling my bare legs. I was now screened from below by a gorse bush, but still able to see the gold head bobbing among the waves. The sun beat down on the back of my neck, though I was scarcely aware of it.

Memories of my dream returned to torment me. I didn't doubt I could take her, either with or without her consent. But, again, it was too soon. I might be accused of rape, which would scotch all my plans at this late stage of the game. I couldn't afford the risk.

My mind was still fluctuating when she re-emerged, dripping, from the water and disappeared out of sight to my right – where, no doubt, she'd left her towel. It was the perfect opportunity to put her at a disadvantage, and if I could appear unmoved by her nakedness – *if!* – it would pique her still further. She might, of course, have dressed, but having swum in the nude, that struck me as unlikely.

Slowly, I eased myself to my feet, stooping to avoid being visible from below, and very carefully continued my descent. When I'd rounded another couple of bends, I at last saw her, stretched on a towel, still naked, her eyes protected by sunglasses.

As I reached the beach, I slipped off my sandals, wincing as the hot sand burned my feet. The small bay, I saw, was completely secluded, un-approachable from the seaside and invisible from above. I wondered how she'd come across it.

Very slowly I started to walk towards her until I stood within a few feet, looking down on her and steeling myself not be aroused. Small high breasts, flat stomach, long, lean thighs, and all of it a deep golden brown. A well-toned body, too, but on the whole I preferred Patty's more voluptuous curves, and I clung to that thought.

'Mrs Irving, I presume?' I said.

What followed was more or less as expected. She was in turn flustered, indignant, and furious, but, ignoring her demands for me to leave, I spread my towel, removed my shirt, and lay down, claiming it was a public beach and I'd as much right to be there as she had.

Also as expected, she lost no time in dressing and beating a hasty retreat. Lying alone in the sunshine, I permitted myself a satisfied smile. *I thought you'd gone home*, she'd said. My absence had had the desired effect.

But by no means all my time was spent shadowing Jill Irving. I swam, explored the coast, went on a boat trip. I tried a different pub each evening, and struck up amiable, if temporary, friendships in all of them. I saw a show on the pier and went to the cinema. I even chatted up a girl in one pub, and made love to her afterwards on the cold sand-hills. Damn it, it was my holiday, and I intended to enjoy it.

I no longer worried how I'd single out Jill when I needed to; I knew she'd come if I raised my finger. From time to time I watched out for her, and once she caught sight of me, which was no bad thing.

However, one morning I spotted her going into the library with someone I'd not seen before, a good-looking guy, and they seemed very much at ease with each other.

Disconcerted that someone was encroaching on my patch, I kept watch, and when they left the library, followed them to a café. It wasn't large enough for me to go in undetected, but they were at a window table, and I could see them from across the road.

The easiness had now given way to something more serious; the guy was leaning towards her, talking earnestly. What the hell was going on, and was the burly husband aware of it?

I was examining a shop window when they emerged, and although my back was to them, I could see them reflected in the glass. They exchanged a few words on the pavement, then went off in opposite directions. So what was I to make of that? If she had a new escort, she was unlikely to miss me. I'd have to step up my pursuit.

I held off for a day in case the guy was still around, but there was no sign of him, so the following morning I seated myself on a bench almost directly opposite the hotel. If Jill followed her usual pattern, she'd go down to town soon after ten. I could only hope the new man wasn't with her.

The ploy worked better than I could have hoped. She emerged alone and made a beeline for me, demanding to know if I lived in Sandbourne, and if not, why I was spending so long there. I really had got under her skin. I explained I was a schoolteacher with long holidays, which seemed to satisfy her. Then I pointedly returned to my paper, but for some reason she continued to stand there, until in the end I told her to sit down as she was blocking the sun. Whereupon she flounced off down the hill.

But time was running out. I'd dallied my way through three weeks of my holiday, and only one more remained. Though still loath to be hurried, I must make a move soon.

For another couple of days I maintained my policy of now-you-see-me, now-you-don't; but on the Monday I put my next plan into action.

As yet, Jill hadn't received the preliminary jolt of fear, but I'd made provision for it, bringing with me the photocopy of the *Cumberland and Westmorland Post*. I'd established there was an Internet Café in town, and I knew the hotel's email address.

I'd have given a lot to see her reaction, and was still trying to picture it when she took me completely by surprise.

I was in the café she'd visited with her friend, actually sitting at the same table, and the first I knew of her presence was when she plonked herself down opposite me. For an anxious moment, I wondered if she'd connected me with the email, though that didn't seem possible. What I definitely wasn't prepared for was for her to apologize for being 'unwelcoming' and then – I couldn't believe my ears! – invite me to dinner! And at a restaurant along the coast, at that! I'd spent some time planning how to inveigle her out of the hotel, and here she was, handing me the opportunity on a plate!

She suggested going that evening, but I quickly scotched that; I needed time to amend my plan, and pleaded engagements for the next two. Which brought us to Friday, my last night and the date I'd already earmarked for my task. We were to meet at the far end of the prom at seven thirty, after which the condemned woman would have her last meal.

Even better, she suggested taking her car; I certainly didn't want traces of her in mine, but nor could I afford to leave any of my own in hers. I already had a hand-held vacuum cleaner for the car; it would collect fibres, but I'd need other cleaning agents to remove fingerprints. Mentally, I added them to my shopping list.

The following day, I hired a bike from a shop in town and put it in the boot of my car, together with a carrier bag containing a length of clothes-line and a change of clothes. These last were necessary because, since a plastic mac would be out of the question here, I'd have to strip afterwards.

I then set off along the coast road, keeping an eye open for places to stop on the way back. It was all very open, and not promising.

Fortunately, the local map I'd bought showed an alternative, inland, road, that proved much more to my liking, running as it did through a couple of copses. I parked at each in turn to examine them thoroughly before deciding which to settle on. Having made my choice and checked that no one seemed to have been there recently, I drove the car fairly deep into the wood, where I removed the bike from the boot and cycled back to Sandbourne.

So far, so good. All that worried me now was that we might see some-body Jill knew at the restaurant. I'd no wish to be introduced to anyone who could describe me later, but it was a chance I'd have to take.

Seven thirty found me waiting at the side of the road, watching for her car. Unused to being sociable with my victims immediately prior to killing them, my nerves were stretched to the limit. How I'd be able to force any food down, I couldn't imagine.

She was spot on time, and we made inconsequential chat during the fifteen-minute drive. At least, she did; my tongue seemed glued to the roof of my mouth. This continued once we were seated in the restaurant, and though I knew I should make some positive contribution, my brain seemed to have atrophied, and it was left to her to broach every topic. When I did speak, though, I was exaggerating my accent, in the hope it might ring unwelcome bells, but she gave no sign of it.

She asked if I was married, if I had a girlfriend, where I lived, and I answered monosyllabically. But then she gave me an opening I couldn't resist, enquiring what kind of books and films I enjoyed.

'Murder,' I said promptly, 'every time.'

I was surprised by her reaction, though perhaps I shouldn't have been. Her face paled beneath her tan, and she gave a quick shake of her head, declaring that she hated all forms of violence; she'd never seen a film or read a book dealing with it, nor did she follow real-life cases in the press.

Twenty-four years too late, but it explained how she'd missed reports of Callum's death.

At last it was time to leave, and on the way to the car, I made the speech I'd rehearsed, suggesting we return home by the inland route. Though she warned me we'd not see much in the dark, she seemed happy with the idea, as I'd expected, and minutes later we were approaching the designated copse.

I cleared my throat, tried to sound seductive as I suggested stopping for a while. She was quick to agree, even taking the rug from the boot.

And that, really, was that. Except that she tried to kiss me, and despite all my lusting after her, I almost vomited. I sat her down on the rug and took out the recorder.

It went like clockwork. I located my car, collected the clothesline, and went back to string her up. Then I stripped, putting the bloodied clothes in the bag and changing into fresh ones. The cleaned knife, recorder and confession I left in the boot, and removed a fresh pair of gloves and the cleaning materials. Then I went back to her car, praying no one would drive past.

They didn't, and twenty minutes later, I was pretty sure not a trace of me remained.

Well, Dad, I thought, fait accompli, at long last. My mission was complete.

By the time the news broke I was back home, and learned the details, along with the rest of the country, from the papers and television. Jill's husband had reported her missing, a friend who'd provided an alibi was uneasy and came forward, and the restaurant confirmed she'd booked a table. After that, it wasn't long before search parties found her car.

Despite the fact that they'd had a recent row in public, her husband was never considered a serious suspect. More interesting, later in the week, was the report that another man was 'helping the police with their enquiries' – at a guess, Jill's mysterious companion. It amused me that they were considering him in the role of postcard killer.

Over the next week or so I watched or listened to every bulletin, in a very mixed frame of mind. I no longer had a goal, and combining with my sense of achievement was one of anti-climax. I almost regretted having no one left to kill.

So, having just finished writing the above, my journal, as I've come to think of it, is complete. Three weeks have passed since my return from Sandbourne, and the papers are still full of the case. I'm back at school, where I learned that Patty has moved in with Steve Blakely, though we're not supposed to know. They certainly didn't let the grass grow.

I'm due for lunch at Hayley and Gary's on Sunday, and I'll hand this over to them then. I wonder what they'll make of it.

Epilogue

In the last ten days, there have been two dramatic developments concerning the so-called postcard murders, which have also thrown new light on a double murder nearly a quarter of a century ago.

Firstly, on Sunday 14th September, Bryan Reid, aged thirty-three, was killed in a head-on car crash near his home in Stockford, Greater Manchester. The police, who were quickly on the scene, discovered a bulky buff envelope on the back seat, addressed simply to 'Hayley', and containing a document purporting to be a blow-by-blow account of the postcard killings.

In addition, a tape of three different voices was found in the deceased's pocket, giving their names as those of the victims, and apparently confessing to a murder that took place in Cumbria in 1985, in which Harold and Elizabeth Sheridan died in a car crash after their vehicle had been tampered with. Even more startlingly, the three identified themselves as the son and daughters of Mrs Sheridan.

At the time, a local man, Jack Spencer, had been arrested in connection with the crime, but hanged himself before the case came to court. Bryan Reid claimed to be Spencer's son, and had determined to find the real killer in order to avenge his father.

There seemed no reason to doubt the veracity of either the document or the tape, since in both cases details known only to the respective murderers were accurately described. Media interest has, of course, been intense, not least because of the hitherto unknown link between the postcard victims.

It is understood that discussions are taking place to consider whether these two items, taken together, constitute a sound enough reason to reopen the earlier case, and, pre-empting any conclusion, a pressure group has already been set up with the aim of obtaining a pardon for the allegedly wronged man.

However, following all this publicity, the case has taken a second, equally unexpected, turn: Sidney Lester, aged seventy-seven, of Crosthwaite, Cumbria, has made a death-bed declaration to the effect that he was also involved in the deaths of the Sheridans.

Appalled to learn the true identity of the postcard victims and the reason for their murders, Mr Lester claimed that in 1985 Harold Sheridan had been his accountant and, in his opinion, had failed to carry out adequate checks on a company in which he was considering investing a substantial sum of money; with the result that when the company subsequently crashed, he was left virtually bankrupt.

Following Reid's example, he requested a tape recorder and dictated the following, a few minutes at a time, over a period of three days, the last section being recorded the day prior to his death. Since the original recording was hesitant, repetitive and occasionally out of sequence, the published version has been edited, at his request, by his daughter.

Having set the scene as outlined above, Mr Lester continued: 'I was almost out of my mind; my wife had left me, taking the children with her, and I'd also lost my home, my business, and most of my capital. And, rightly or wrongly, I laid the blame for it all on Mr Sheridan and his failure to advise me of the risks involved. The more I brooded, the more enraged I became. I'd been told I'd no chance of winning a court case, but I'd worked myself into such a state that I had to do *something*, and spent weeks thinking up and then discarding a number of wild schemes.

'Finally, I decided simply to give him the fright of his life, and at the same time, ensure that he'd never forget me and what he'd done to me. I knew he drove down the lake road each morning on the way to work, so I took my shotgun and concealed myself in the bushes alongside the road. Though I'd have been more than happy to shoot him, I intended merely to fire a shot in front of his windscreen as he passed.

'He was later than usual, which suited me as there was less traffic about, but eventually I saw his car approaching. I took up my position, and was aiming the gun when I saw to my consternation that his wife was with him, and retreated hastily to the bushes – but not before he'd seen both me and the gun. He swerved violently to avoid me, then, to my horror, the car went into a spin, crashed at speed into a stone wall, and shot back towards me, rolling over on to its roof as it reached the verge.

'I like to think I'd have gone to their assistance, but I was still frozen with shock when a car came round the corner and, on seeing the accident, screeched to a halt. So, knowing help was at hand, I made my unsteady way home, where I was violently sick. The next week or two passed in a drunken stupor, while I blamed myself continuously for causing Mrs Sheridan's death. Then the news broke about the gravel in the brake fluid, and it seemed like a reprieve. I told myself I hadn't after all been responsible, and the suicide of the man we all assumed had put it there seemed to confirm that.

'This last week, however, I, together with the rest of the country, have learned not only that Spencer did not tamper with the car, but that his son had discovered the Sheridan offspring were the culprits, and murdered them to avenge his father's death. Therefore, by keeping quiet about my own part in the tragedy, I am at least partly responsible for the deaths not only of Mr and Mrs Sheridan, but of their three children, and possibly Jack Spencer as well. It is quite simply beyond bearing, and I'm truly thankful my life is now at an end and I shan't be called on to endure it for long.

'To sum up, it is my opinion that while the gravel would have seized up the pipes, it was unlikely to have caused death had Mr Sheridan not been panicked by my sudden appearance with the gun. By the same token, nor would the sight of the gun have had a fatal outcome had he been able to control the car. It was the combination that proved lethal.

'I, Sidney Lester, being in my right mind, swear that the above is a true and voluntary account of events that took place twenty-four years ago, and may God have mercy on my soul.'

It is sobering to reflect on the far-reaching consequences of two fatal car crashes, separated by a quarter of a century, and the crucial light that the second threw on the first.

Since none of the participants remain alive, it is to be hoped that the tragedies and misunderstandings the crashes revealed can now be buried with them, and both cases be finally closed.

DATE DUE